Songs of Life

Short Stories for Men and Women

by

Phillip R. Rossignol

Illustrations by

Kumiko Ono

author HOUSE

1663 Liberty Drive, Suite 200
Bloomington, Indiana 47403
(800) 839-8640
www.authorhouse.com

First published by AuthorHouse 08/11/04

ISBN: 1-4184-0620-1 (e)
ISBN: 1-4184-0621-X (sc)

Library of Congress Control Number: 2004094958

Printed in the United States of America
Bloomington, Indiana

This book is printed on acid-free paper.

Introduction

Songs of Life is a montage of short stories for men and women with an eclectic set of subjects having the common thread of the many types of love, inspiration, and compassion we encounter in life. Some of the stories *(The Wooden Chain, Jerry and Mike, Santa's Motorcycle, The Grandmother,* and *The Cognitive Farm)* are based on true events and have been slightly modified to maintain a level of anonymity for the real people and places. *The Compassionate War* is a short essay based on historic events. It illustrates how and why the World may be on the doorstep of global peace.

Broken Eagle Feathers, They Finally Meet, and *The Great Date* are classic love stories between men and woman with humor, tragedy, and happy endings.

The Eagle and the Rooster take up the inspirational themes along with *William's B-17, Close to God, The Gift of Giving,* and *The Courage to Change.*

Both *Mama Cheetah* and *The Grandmother* focus on the strength of women when faced with the challenges of life while *A Civil Affair* and *Nails to Rails* are based on historical events during the Civil War period with artistic liberties taken to enhance the stories.

Finally, the "non-shoot-em-up laser" science fiction stories revolve around the faster-than-light travels of Tom Crowley, who finds adventure and love among the many alien cultures throughout the Milky Way Galaxy. *Exotic Alien, The Veluxean Hunt, Progressive Creation, Odyssey III,* and *The Green Belt* are a continuing series with themes ranging from sensual love to deep family love and then to the "realistic" explanation of breaking the light speed barrier.

Extensive previews have shown *Songs of Life* has something for everyone—young and old, male and female. This is an unusual book that can be read in short spurts or in a few sittings. Take a casual browse through the abstracted Table of Contents to start your journey through the *Songs of Life.*

Songs of Life:
Short Stories for Men and Women©

Table of Contents

Broken Eagle Feathers

A long time ago in the Pacific Northwest, there was a prominent Indian tribe of the Great River. The people of the village worked hard to fish the abundant waters and hunt the majestic forests, and they were a happy lot, having all that a generous life could provide them. The abundance of the earth blessed them every season, and the days were bright, the nights clear, and the river spirits covered them with health and love. Tall Trees, the first son of the chief and a strong and fine hunter, provided much food for the people of the village, and he loved his people, and they loved him. He was tall, broad, and had smooth, tan skin shaped by the power of his arms and shoulders. His high cheekbones and thick, black hair reinforced the vision of his strength and confident stride.

A three-day walk easterly along the banks of the same Great River took one to another village where a second river blended into the Great River. Here lived another strong man named Big Rock. He was much like Tall Trees in many ways, and they could have been brothers by birth of the same mother. He, too, was a great hunter and gave much to the people of his village; he, too, was the oldest son and of tribe royalty.

Big Rock and Tall Trees had never met until one day at the end of the first season after the hard winter of rain, when they were both hunting along the Great River, midway between the two villages. They came upon each other with great surprise and curiosity, and their eyes met with intense astonishment and suspicion as they circled each other for moments with untrusting caution and stoned expressions. They moved closer and closer, with their suspicions growing, and they came together in a physical conflict for the rights to hunt at the midway point between the two villages. They struggled with each other's great strength, and Big Rock came upon Tall Trees. Then Tall Trees came upon Big Rock. They

1

struggled for what seemed to be an hour, and the battle of strength flowed to the banks of the Great River with manly grunts of struggle. It was a great and even battle that finally ended and the river's edge, soaking both warriors.

Finally, they both relented to their exhaustion and fell side by side on their backs on the river bank, breathing frantically from the extreme exercise of heavy conflict. Both of their bloody faces, contrasted scarlet from their chins to their foreheads, mixed with the river's wetness, and this wetness fell upon their chests. They breathed deeply and fast, lying on their backs, trying to relieve their tiredness. Then, in a moment of curiosity, they turned to each other, and their penetrating eyes made a deep contact of understanding and respect. They turned away and continued to recover their strength. Moments later, they both sat up, still breathing heavily. Their eyes met again, and Big Rock stood and extended his powerful arm to Tall Trees to get up in a gesture of peace. And they touched one another, this time in great friendship, understanding, and peace.

They spent the remainder of the day resting and sharing stories of their lives. Then a Great Spirit came over them, and they became bonded friends for what was to be a lifetime. They hunted and fished together and shared the twilight hours under the stars. And when they parted, they embraced as only strong men could do for their hearts and minds were together in this loving friendship, knowing that they would see each other again.

In the coming years, every first season after the season of cold rain, Tall Trees and Big Rock would meet in the forest to hunt and spend time with each other. Many times they meditated together where the two rivers bonded into the Great River, giver of life to all the tribes and village, and their friendship grew into a tight bond unlike any other in time.

As their wisdom and strength grew, they both became chiefs of their respective villages, and this prevented them from meeting as often to hunt in the first season after a winter of rain. They would meet in the great forest, share their leadership experiences, and ask each other together with the River Spirits to give them the wisdom and love to help guide and lead their people. They hunted together spiritually in great harmony.

Tall Trees, chief of the village to the west, became a man of great stature. He was good to his people. He was fair. He was gentle. He was strong. And the people loved him. Tall Trees had a beautiful daughter. Little Stream had deep and beautiful brown eyes that contrasted her smooth, tan skin and her long, black hair that glistened in the sun as it danced in the wind. Little Stream was well proportioned, and this added to her attractiveness. She was a gentle and loving girl

2

who moved with the gentle flow of a light wind. She was responsible and worked hard to contribute to the tribe, loving each day as a new experience. When she had come of age, new feelings filled her heart, mind, and body, and she longed for the day when the comfort of a man would complete her gracious life.

Tall Trees loved Little Stream with all his heart, and she adored and respected him like no other person. Pleasing her father was most important for she was so grateful for the life, love, and protection he gave to her. She prayed to the spirits each day for her father's good health and mind. She loved him so.

As was the custom in this culture, fathers betrothed their daughters at birth to the sons of the village. Tall Trees had betrothed Little Stream to the son of the great medicine man. The boy was called Four Stars and was born 10 years before Little Stream. Four Stars had become a great hunter and would go for weeks into the forests. He was a lone man of great quietness, and he had no interest in following in his father's footsteps as medicine man; his heart and mind were not into the world of the spirits. He gained much wealth in the tribe by hunting and trapping with strong earnest. The months that he spent away from the village grew longer each time, and he always returned with many things from the great fort to the west, which he could trade within the tribe.

Then, at the coming of age, Little Stream was called to the bonding ceremony with Four Stars, and they were married next to the Great Tree.

After a week in the village with Little Stream and their bonding, Four Stars returned to the great forests to again hunt for furs and such. He did not return for a whole first season, and then, when he did return, he stayed with Little Stream with remote interest while he cured the furs that would bring him more wealth. A week passed, then Four Stars returned to his trek in the forests. Little Stream was now alone again, and her heart had a great emptiness of loneliness while her nights were long and sad. She was very devoted to her father and would not show him her unhappiness. She lived each day doing the things required of her and dreaming of other things that were in her heart. Sometimes her tears would drop to the grass from the height of her golden face with the feeling of great sadness.

Three days' walk to the east along the Great River in the village of the two rivers, Big Rock became the leader and chief of his people. He was kind and fair, and the people loved him. As time passed, his only son grew tall and strong with the features of his father. He was known as Eagle Feather and was popular with all the people in the village with his kind and strong ways. He loved and played with the children and brought laughter to the village. He always maintained his generosity and became a great provider of the village. He hunted often to provide food for the people of his village. He would only go into the forests for a week, and when he returned, would stay in the village for a full moon cycle. He loved his great father, Big Rock, and hungered for his wisdom, listening to his beloved father for hours. With the love and example set by his father, Eagle Feather grew in wisdom and strength as each day passed. He grew strong with the spirit of sky, and there was much love between father and son. Big Rock often talked of his good friend Tall Trees and the hunting and wisdom they had shared with much affection.

It was late of the great summer of good hunting in the forest and when there was plenty from the Great River that an illness came over Big Rock, the father of Eagle Feather. Before the next moon turned, this great, strong man became very weak. Eagle Feather spent all of his time caring for his father and prayed to the great spirits of Mother Earth to make his father well again, but Big Rock became weaker and weaker. Then, on the day of his passing, Big Rock held his young and strong Eagle Feather close to his breath. He whispered in Eagle Feather's ear, "You must go to my friend, Tall Trees, and tell him of the passing of my body and the journey of my heart to the spirits. You must tell him that he is in my heart. And you must tell him that I will wait for him to hunt again together."

Big Rock grew soft with the feel of death. A great pain came to Eagle Feather's heart as he looked toward the heavens and wished his father a good and safe journey. All the people of the village gathered around the lodge of Big Rock and chanted farewell and safe journey for their great leader and loving friend. They were very saddened by their loss.

It took many weeks for Eagle Feather to gain the strength, courage, and spirit to make the three-day journey westerly to the village of Tall Trees, his father's most beloved friend. He followed the Great River on his saddened journey, and his heart was stone-heavy and hard with the loss of his missed father. Along the way, he supplemented the dried deer meat he carried with fish from the Great River, fallen nuts, and bright berries from the abundant forest. His days were hard and filled with the memories and loneliness of his departed father, Big Rock.

Then, early on the morning of the fourth day of travel, Eagle Feather came upon the village of Tall Trees. The lodges were neatly kept as in his own village, and the voice of the children playing echoed through the forest above the sound of the river. He came to the edge of the village and met an old woman who was stooped over, washing some clothing in the river. He placed his hand gently on her shoulder and asked her for the place of Tall Trees. She looked up and smiled, as if knowing who he might be, and pointed to a dwelling near the edge of the river. As he moved closer toward the entrance of the lodge, he called loudly for Tall Trees.

Very unexpectedly, Little Stream, the beloved and beautiful daughter of Tall Trees, showed herself shyly in the doorway. The sun blessed her smooth face with more beauty than usual, and Eagle Feather was overtaken with a great surge in his heart. Her beauty beckoned his senses, and with her head slightly bowed in bashfulness, she smiled shyly at his presence. With the sun at his back shining on her face, she could only imagine who this great image could be. It was moments that passed before Eagle Feather gained the composure to speak his voice to Little Stream's ears. "I am Eagle Feather, son of Big Rock. I have journeyed far to see Tall Trees." His heart pounded as if he had run many miles. He was taken by her deep brown eyes contrasted against her golden skin and the strands of her hair that glistened with the energy of the morning sun.

Little Stream's heart was also strong with beat. His presence filled much of the emptiness in her heart, and her loneliness began to melt. She replied in a soft, shy, and loving voice, "I am Little Stream, daughter of Tall Trees. My father is by the Great Tree with the council. I will bring you to him." She could hardly make the words. She asked to be followed, and they proceeded to the Great Tree where the council was meeting. As they walked, Little Stream's lower body swayed slightly with the soft motion of gracefulness, and Eagle Feather was taken by the flowing motion of her body over the clean, rich river gravel that bedded the village. Some of her black hair took gentle flight as they walked through the morning breeze. He was so taken by her beauty that the thoughts of his passed father left his heart and mind for this moment.

As they closed to the council, Tall Trees looked up toward the approaching couple. When he saw Eagle Feather, the vision of his great and longtime friend filled his heart. He had never seen Eagle Feather but could feel the presence of Big Rock's spirit in this young man. Tall Trees extended his hand to quiet the council and called, "Who is this young man that approaches with Little Stream? I seem to know you but have no recollection of ever seeing you."

"I am Eagle Feather, son of Big Rock. I have come a distance to bring you news of my great father!" responded Eagle Feather standing strong with a confident and proud voice.

A great smile came upon the face of Tall Trees and he replied, "I knew of your spirit but not where. I am honored with your presence as I would honor your great father. I miss his company, and it has been too long since we have hunted together. What news do you bring?"

Eagle Feather gestured to Tall Trees to walk with him. As they walked toward the Great River, Little Stream watched as Eagle Feather talked. In a moment, Tall Trees stopped, and with his hand on Eagle Feather's shoulder, hung his head in sadness. And his strong heart cried.

Later that day, Tall Trees requested that Eagle Feather stay in the village for some time. They were seen often at the edge of the Great River where Tall Trees shared the many stories of his time with Big Rock and the spirit that they had shared. There was much comfort for each as they talked about their love of the same man. And the bond between them grew, and it was like before, a father and his son. All their spirits had come together, and they came to love each other and cherish the many moments of their togetherness.

While Eagle Feather stayed in the village, he watched Little Stream many times as she worked her daily chores. Her bashful looks toward him beckoned his heart to fill with her presence, and the love grew between them without words ever being passed. They seemed to avoid each other in a distant fashion for some time and then, one beautiful day, Eagle Feather was walking in the forest and came to a clearing. Little Stream was sitting on a fallen tree, crying tears of sadness. He moved toward her and touched her black, shining hair softly. She raised her head and looked lovingly into his deep eyes. Their hearts finally met with this simple touch, and her tears began to dry.

In the following days, they spent much time together in the forest, sharing what was in their hearts and their desires for life. The bond between them became very strong, but their values kept them from being together in other ways. Tall Trees had noticed this bonding and was fearful of what might come to be. He was in great conflict with his feelings toward Eagle Feather and what was with Little Stream and Four Stars. He prayed to the spirits that they may come to these moments and thoughts, and they would resolve the questions that have grown over the days.

Then, one day as Eagle Feather and Little Stream were sitting by the Great River, Four Stars emerged from the forest carrying the burden of spoils from his long hunt. He saw Eagle Feather with Little Stream and came to them with impatience and sternness on his face. He exclaimed, "Who is this stranger in my village?"

"I am Eagle Feather, son of Big Rock. I have come to Tall Trees to bring sad news of his long-time friend, Big Rock."

"And why do you sit here by the river with my Little Stream?" Four Stars exclaimed.

"He only shares what is in his heart for my father, the long-time friend of his father," Little Stream replied.

Four Stars motioned to her to go to their dwelling, and he walked strongly away from Eagle Feather without another word of greeting or of welcome. The return of Four Stars to the village brought much sadness and tension to Little Stream, and her heart contained much pain from the burden in her spirit. She knew that she could not bring dishonor to her father. She could not leave with Eagle Feather, no matter how she felt. She was in great pain as the days passed, and she looked upon Eagle Feather often with sadness of heart. Eagle Feather's heart cried to the spirits with a great voice of lonesome want and heavy pain. But he also knew that he could not dishonor his father, Big Rock, and his great friend, Tall Trees.

For Little Stream, her life during these days with Four Stars was killing her spirit, and her heart became heavy with pain. She could not love Four Stars. She could not leave the village with Eagle Feather. What was she to do? She had to be true to what was in her heart.

After four days, her pain was too much to bear, and on the morning of the fifth day of the return of Four Stars, she followed the Great River east to the Tall Falls. She sat for many hours at the top of the falls and tried to speak to the spirits, but they had no words for her. She felt so alone and lost, and she cried many times and asked the spirits for their wisdom. Again, they did not answer. She listened to the songs of the birds, and they did not comfort her. She looked intensely down at the rainbow far below created by the marriage of the sun to the mist of the falls.

Then, in a moment of high sadness, she stood and offered herself to the spirits of the Great River, never to be seen again. She was now at peace. She now was free of the pain.

The next day, Tall Trees asked Four Stars where Little Stream was. Tall Trees had not seen her and missed her soft voice. Four Stars replied in a non-caring tone as he focused on the curing of furs. Without turning to Tall Trees, he exclaimed, "I have not seen her, and my bed was empty of her last night."

Eagle Feather was greatly saddened by her absence, and in his loneliness for her, his heart cried at the emptiness it held. He searched the forest and river for days and could not find her.

After five days, Four Stars returned to the forest to continue his hunting. And Eagle Feather searched and waited for his beloved Little Stream, but she did not return, and his great heart swelled heavy with sadness.

Many weeks passed without the return of Little Stream. Eagle Feather sadly returned to his own village, and the thoughts of Little Stream haunted his mind and heart. He could not imagine his life without her, and he wanted to join her and be with her in the land of the spirits. But he must honor his father's memory and the needs of the village. He had to stay of this Earth and serve the people of the village.

Little Stream's vision lived in Eagle Feather's spirit for all time, and he lived a long life without her. He could never love again as he had with her. He never took a wife and never had the joy of his own children.

His feathers were surely broken.

Chief Seattle:
"When the earth is sick, the animals will begin
to disappear, when that happens, the Warriors
of the Rainbow will come to save them."

Chief Aupumut, Mohican
"When it comes time to die, be not like those whose
hearts are filled with fear of death, so when their
time comes they weep and pray for a little more
time to live their lives over again in a different way.
Sing your death song, and die like a hero going home."

Big Thunder, Algonquin
"The Great Spirit in all things, he is the air we
breathe. The Great Spirit is our Father, but the
Earth is our Mother. She nourishes us, that which
we put into the ground she returns to us."

They Finally Meet

Maureen was 58 years old and had maintained her youth-like image over the years. She was very beautiful with shoulder-length blond hair, and at 5' 6", she was a stunning woman. After a 25-year marriage, she had been divorced for five years. Her divorce took a heavy emotional toll on her, and she did not date afterward. Her friends tried to get her out with some of their male friends, but nothing seemed to please her, and she only wished to work in her family council business, do her weekly exercises, and spend time with the many female friends she had acquired through some very active community efforts. Maureen was very bright, had a great wit about her, and was fast to exchange quips with a few of her willing friends. She joked with much intelligence and loved to have people respond back to her humor.

Most of all, she loved to spend time with her daughter and new grandson, and she often would volunteer to take the baby for a day or two so that her daughter and son-in-law could go out by themselves. She had a good life, but she missed the emotional, social, and physical company of a man. Maureen had much love to give, and this part of her life left a big emptiness in her spirit.

Her daughter, Michelle, became very concerned with her mother's welfare and continually encouraged her to get out and meet men. Then one day while Michelle and the baby were visiting, she showed her mother the types of dating match services available on the World Wide Web. Maureen was appalled and indicated that there was no way she would expose herself to such a thing. Michelle insisted and sat down with one of the services and entered her mother's information, including a wonderful picture that showed much of Maureen's shape and beauty.

In her heart, Maureen liked this idea, but she told Michelle that this was nonsense and she was not about to go looking for strangers in such a way.

When Michelle left, Maureen went straight to her computer and logged on to this new place. She searched for local men in the 58- to 65-year-old age range, and to her surprise, up came over 50 males in this age category and locality. She panned through them into the late hours, not really finding anything she was attracted to. Going to bed, she was kind of discouraged but still dreamed of finding someone special.

The next day, she was surprised to find 13 unsolicited e-mails in her mailbox from men who liked her. She took the time to look at each suitor, his summaries, and pictures. There were all types and varieties, but none appealed to her except one by a small amount. So, as her goodness would dictate, she wrote back to the 12 men who she did not care for with a pleasant note that she was flattered by their inquiry but did not think that there was a match. The remaining one she replied with the words that she was flattered and would like to find out more. She also included some more about herself and used a little of her wit in her writing and was fairly open about things, feeling a little excitement inside and thinking that there might be some hope.

Two days later, she got a response from her note that, in essence, said that while she was very pretty, he was not interested in such an aggressive woman. He thanked her and indicated that she was not a match for him. She was devastated, not because of the rejection, but because she had it in her mind that there was actually some hope. So, in her disappointment, she stopped returning e-mails but, often just to pass the time in some of the late evenings, she searched the many prospects, feeling that none were her type.

One day Michelle asked her mother how it was going and if she had any "hot prospects." Maureen said that she was very active e-mailing, but did not find anybody yet that suited her.

Paul was a reasonably successful executive and, at 59, had retired the year before. He was very good-looking and at 6', 190 pounds, was trim and fit. His second marriage ended five years earlier after ten years and was a financial disaster for him. His first marriage had produced a son and daughter who now had their own families. Paul volunteered much of his time to the local church food program, but this was not enough activity for him because his past career was filled with much liveliness, travel, and complexity. This retired life was not what he had expected, and he was becoming lonely for the company of a beautiful and smart woman. Several of his friends introduced him to the many women they knew, and they were all very nice, but the beautiful ones were not smart, and the smart ones were not beautiful.

One day his daughter, Denise, was visiting. She loved her dad with all her heart and was concerned for his happiness. She reassured him that he was a man who had a lot to offer a woman and encouraged him to get out there and meet someone. He was smart with a great sense of humor and could be very romantic. She pressed him to join one of the new computer-dating services, but he brushed that off as nonsense. The next week, on his 60th birthday, she placed a note in his birthday card that indicated she had signed him up for three months on a Web matching service. Denise had written his profile and submitted some great-looking pictures of him. Included in the note was his match name and password. He looked at the note and pretended to be happy, not wanting to hurt her feelings.

That night at home, he picked up the note that Denise had given him and went to his computer, logged on to the service, and sorted by location and ages 55-62. To his surprise, up came 50 choices. He started to go through them all, looking for his perfect woman. Many were very beautiful, and he enjoyed reading their summaries, but none had appealed to him so far.

Then he came upon the summary and picture for Maureen, and his heart jumped; there was something here. He loved her eyes and read her words very carefully at least five times. He especially noted her humor between the lines of her profile and really related to her. He started to dream of the possibilities. He just knew that she had to be already taken, and with a click of the mouse button, he pressed the e-mail icon and immediately began to write a few words. In the e-mail title, he brazenly wrote, "Hi, its Mr. Wonderful." While uncomfortable doing this, he was responding to her reference of "Looking for Mr. Wonderful." Here is what he wrote in the body of the e-mail:

"I enjoyed your picture and loved what you said in your summary. I think that we may be a match on paper."

This was his first e-mail, and he sent it with great uneasiness, but he was confident that once she saw his summary, she would e-mail him right away. The next morning, the first thing he did after putting the coffee on was to go see his e-mail box for Maureen's reply. It was not there. That afternoon, the e-mail still was not there. And that night, it still was not there. Paul did not know that Maureen was just deleting all her romance e-mail, not wanting to be disappointed again. Paul waited for three days, and nothing appeared. Though he was quite disappointed, his extensive business contact experience and natural humor went into full gear. He decided to send a second e-mail with the title,

"SECOND NOTICE."

The body contained the following text: "I really think you should look at my summary. I have been looking at yours for some time now, and I have a good feeling here."

The next morning, Maureen checked her e-mail, and Paul's bright title caught her attention. Curious, she went to his summary and liked what she saw and read about him. She looked much, but was very careful to watch her expectations. What she liked most in his summary was that he claimed to be a "hopeless romantic" and had an "intelligent sense of humor." She pondered this for a moment and decided to wait a couple of days before answering. This was the only e-mail she ever saved up to this point.

Paul checked his e-mail the next morning and found still no response from Maureen. He was deeply disappointed and vowed not to give up. He wrote her another e-mail.

Subject: THIRD NOTICE

"Are you usually this willing to play hard to get? I am a very romantic man and would love to share that with you, possibly!!!!"

Maureen got the e-mail the next morning and noticed the title in big type right away. She immediately opened it and read his message. "MMMMM," she thought. "I think this guy might be OK. I'll test him out a little." So again, she did not respond to his e-mail.

The next morning, Paul immediately looked for her response, and, as usual, it was not there. He could not understand why she did not reply. So, in great fashion and with all confidence, Paul wrote yet another e-mail.

Subject: FOURTH NOTICE

"Are you playing hard to get?"

Maureen, laughing so hard, could not hold out anymore, and she returned his e-mail.

Subject: FINAL NOTICE

"Of course I am playing hard to get. How fast can you run?"

When Paul opened his e-mail, his heart leaped with excitement, knowing that he had reached her. While he did not like the sound of the subject at first, when he read the content, he could not contain himself from being a little—but cautiously—excited. After some moments of composure from her wit, he wrote the following:

Subject: CHASING RAINBOWS

"Sounds like you are the rainbow that we chase and can never catch. I don't know if you are worth the pursuit. I thought so at first, but now I have great reservations. By the way, how fast can you run, really?

"Seriously, I am 6' at 190 pounds and in great shape. Are your pictures recent? Tell me more about yourself. Let's keep e-mailing."

"Paul"

Paul thought that he was being cool and offering a peace to the humor with some "serious" talk.

When Maureen got the e-mail, she was a little concerned that she might go too far with this guy and did not want to chase him off. She did enjoy the humor and wanted to test his metal a little more. She could always apologize later if it got out of hand. She sensed that he really liked her—as she did him—and responded with the following:

Subject: HEY SKINNY

"Paul,

"Well, I really appreciate you giving me your name, but you are not going to get mine. I don't care how short and skinny you are, I am not impressed. By the way, my pictures were taken ten years ago, and I have gained a few pounds. Why do you ask, and does that make a difference?"

When Paul got this e-mail, his funny bone turned on with some reservation. Then he became excited because he was starting to understand her humor, and he liked that very much. Paul knew in his heart that she was not playing games; it was a humor duel, and he loved it. "Could this be a woman who could keep up with me, and I would have to do the same?" He searched for a response and wrote the following:

Subject: DISAPPOINTED AGAIN?

"Well, you sure are not making many points with me. I think that you really like me and would love to talk on the phone. Here's my number: 555-1234. My instincts are very good, but I think that you are afraid to call. Don't call if you are uncomfortable. If you have a mind to—at least a little—then feel free to call. Scary, yes!!!!!!!!

"So, I wrote this little skit about what I believe YOU are REALLY thinking.

"Well, he gave me his number, so he must want me to call. Maybe he won't like my voice. I really like him, and I think he likes me. Why would he spend all that time e-mailing me? Well, let me go to the phone. Oh no, I can't. This could be IT, and I am afraid. What if IT is? That would be cool, and I am excited inside, but I don't trust this. It is too soon. God, help me do Thy will. And God says, 'Go for it; he feels the same way.'

"Paul"

When she stops laughing, Maureen replies in great earnest with the following:

Subject: HE WRITES, SHE THINKS

"Paul, Here's my response to your last e-mail, point by point.

"He writes, 'Don't call if you are uncomfortable. If you have a mind to—at least a little—then feel free to call. Scary yes!!!!!!!!!'

"She thinks… 'Nahhhhhhh, not at all.'

"He writes, 'Well, he gave me his number, so he must want me to call. Maybe he won't like my voice.'

"She thinks… 'Why does he want me to call him at this time when he told me in yesterday's message he wanted to continue to e-mail for a while longer? Did I miss something here?'

"He writes, 'I really like him, and I think he likes me. Why would he spend all that time e-mailing me?'

"She thinks… 'Hmmmmm, yes, he sounds great on paper, and I do like him. I assume he would spend time e-mailing me because he is interested in getting to know me, as I am him.'

"He writes, 'Well, let me go to the phone. Oh no, I can't. This could be IT, and I am afraid.'

"She thinks... 'Boy, is this guy in for a surprise! He had better hope I'm more stable than that and don't allow fear to guide my life.'

"He writes, 'What if IT is? That would be cool, and I am excited inside, but I don't trust this. It is too soon.'

"She thinks... 'Yes, I am excited inside also, but I do trust myself totally. Although maybe he is right about it being a little too soon for a love relationship. Friendship minus expectations would be the better choice for me at this time.'

"He writes, 'God, help me do Thy will. And God says, "Go for it; he feels the same way."'

"She thinks... '*They* might be right! I am very pleased he has a solid connection with God.'

"She thinks... 'This guy seems quite special!'

"Warm Regards, Maureen

"PS—My number is 555–5678. Call if YOU are comfortable!"

The next day, Paul opens the e-mail, and his heart jumps and pounds, and his ears get flushed. He waits for a couple of hours to compose himself and to gather his thoughts so that he can write an appropriate response to her humor, her invitation to call, and her expression of how she felt about him. He could not come up with the words for the e-mail no matter how hard he tried. The words just did not come to him.

That night at about 8:00 p.m., Paul picked up the phone with great anticipation and dialed Maureen's number. It rang three times, which seemed like an eternity. The rings stopped, and Maureen said, "Hello" in her wonderful and soft voice.

"Maureen, this is your e-mail suitor, Paul. How are you tonight?"

She says, "I am fine, and I am very glad that you called. Your voice sounds very nice."

He remarks, "I am glad that you like it. Yours sounds wonderful to me, better that I had expected."

Then they went on with much conversation that flowed very easily. 10:30 p.m. came, and it seemed as though only minutes had passed. Neither was disappointed, and the interest was very mutual, so Paul invited Maureen to meet for coffee the next day at a neutral place close to each other. They agreed on 11:00 a.m. and reluctantly hung up. That night, both of their heads were filled with expectations, tempered by the possibility of the usual disappointments.

The next day, Paul was filled with anticipation and tried to quell his excitement with a careful expectation of disappointment. It took him an hour to decide what to wear, and he finally selected a soft, dark brown shirt, light brown pants, and a brown tweed sports jacket. He was a fine dresser from his years in executive sales and marketing. The thought of being overdressed passed through his mind, but he wanted to look his best for this first meeting. His humor was seriously packed away in the back of his mind, and his thoughts of the upcoming meeting made seriousness and anticipation fill his mind.

Maureen was also in great conflict of what to wear. She took great pleasure to usually dress in a fashion that always accented her very lovely shape. She did not want to seem too provocative, but she certainly wanted to pull out the stops of attraction. She tried to control her expectations, but her excitement overcame her good sense, and she selected a subtle light cream silk blouse that was not quite see-through. It had a moderately plunging neckline that only showed a very slight peek. She liked this top because the clinging nature of the material accented and revealed her shape very nicely with good taste. She also selected black pants cut to accent her hips and other parts of her lower body. She wore a string of pearls that flowed halfway down the opening of her blouse. She was really ready for the meeting.

It was 10:50 a.m. when Paul arrived at the coffee shop. He wanted to be early so that when she arrived, he would be there for her, and she would not have to wait for him. He bought his usual large cup of decaffeinated French Roast without sugar or milk, and, since it was a beautiful day, he selected a table and sat down outside. 11:00 a.m. came, and she had not shown up yet. Paul's mind began to wonder if he had the right place, or if she remembered, or if she was hurt, or if her car had broken down. At 11:10 a.m., he could not contain his anxious heart and decided to call her from his cell phone. He dialed the cell number she had given him "just in case." It rang twice, and the voice said, "Hello, this is Maureen." Paul replied in sort of a funny tone without revealing his name, "Well, where the hell are you?"

Her voice came back, "I am trying to be fashionably late and make you worry a little. I am right behind you, so turn your phone off and turn around."

Paul stood up and turned. She was more beautiful than he had imagined, and she was taken by his style of dress and handsome face. There was an immediate attraction, and, with the connection of chemistry, they looked at each other for what seemed to be a long time. They looked into each other's eyes and wondered. With a great smile on his face, he broke the silence.

"Can I get you a cup of coffee or something?"

"No, thank you, I'll just drink the water I brought here," she replied.

They sat and talked and looked at each other, excited that the usual disappointment did not rear its ugly head. They talked seriously for some time, exchanging some of their life experiences, sometimes touching each other's hand in an expression of light affection. He could not keep his eyes off her, and he was very pleased at what he saw. It seemed as though they had known each other for a long time.

Then Paul's funny bone started to turn on. As he leaned a little over the table, he softly said, "You look much lovelier than I had imagined. I love the way you have dressed. Are you trying to seduce me?"

"Of course!" she said with a big smile. "I always try to seduce the men that I am very attracted to."

She was playing back to him her feelings in a very open way.

Paul said with a big smile, "It is working very well. By the way, how many men have you seduced like this?"

"About 20, all last week," she smiled.

And they held each other's hands across the table. They sat for two hours, enjoying the very pleasant day while talking of all sorts of things. They were having a great time.

It came time to part, and Paul asked her for a dinner date, which she accepted immediately.

"Maureen, when are you available?"

"Oh, anytime for you."

That evening, they had a lovely dinner in a very nice restaurant.

Soon they had become very important in each other's lives. Their respective daughters, Michelle and Denise, were very happy for their parents and wished them a great future.

This future was to come, and they were together, for "They Finally Met."

19

Exotic Alien

Tom Crowley had become a resourceful and monetarily successful trader of Marlarium, a critical material for the generation of energy throughout the Milky Way Galaxy. The rarity and high demand for this critical energy material and Tom's ability to isolate Marlarium crystal supplies and refine them provided him with a very lucrative life.

Tom was a sturdy fellow born of a father of Earth descent and a mother of Argon descent. His blond hair and very light brown eyes with brown stone complexion gave him an attractive visage even among many of the alien cultures he visited and served. He had a large frame and at 6' 3", presented himself as a strong individual. His pleasant and generous ways made him very popular with his customers in the fourth upper quadrant of the Milky Way Galaxy, and that trust provided him with a strong competitive advantage.

His ship, *Odyssey IV*, used a unique linear precession drive technology that provided him with very high, beyond-light speeds and gave him efficient access to the many locations requiring his valued energy material. The ship's shape was that of a graceful oval, measuring 100 yards across the major axis and 75 yards across the minor axis from front to back. The hull was made of the latest titanium and aluminum alloy oxide. This gave *Odyssey IV* a flat silver gray look that artfully matched the smooth shape that was totally without any protrusions, enhancing the graceful shape. This was Tom's home for most of his time, and he relished visiting the many inhabited planets requiring his product and services.

Tom had just delivered 15 kilograms of Marlarium to the government of Argon, a beautiful Earthlike planet. As the place of his birth, this was one of his favorite stops in all of the galaxy for he had managed to make very good friends in high places, and his relationships flourished more each time he visited. The residents were very much like Earth humans. Tom took the time to relax and vacation at the invitation and expense of Gala, the father of his Argonian mother. Gala had become like a father to Tom after his paternal grandparents died in a radiation accident. These two men enjoyed many conversations of wisdom, friendship, and adventures over the finest Argon tea and Argon sweet bread. Tom stayed for three weeks and looked forward to his return visit in less than a year, as he was cleared to take off from Argon in *Odyssey IV*.

Tom had received an order for 20 kilograms of Marlarium from a new customer, and it would take him almost six months to get to this far off-the-path planet. He had heard rumors about the strange but wonderful ways of the people on the planet Velux and was anxious to get there for a change of scenery. He was always open and excited about learning, and he enjoyed meeting new cultures, which was one of the major advantages of his business and travels. Tom put *Odyssey IV* into automatic navigation toward Velux and entered the suspension chamber in order to "sleep" during the long trip. The chamber provided Tom with nourishment during his hibernation and kept his physical structure, especially his bones, from deteriorating. *Odyssey IV* then accelerated past the speed of light in a moment.

Six months later, the suspension chamber controls automatically awoke Tom, and it seemed as though he had just gone to sleep. As usual, his muscles were sore, but after 20 minutes in the vibration chamber, he was back to his normal self. It did not take long for the automatic controls to start slowing *Odyssey IV* toward the final destination of Velux. He entered the Velux orbital space and called in for permission and location to land. They were expecting him and sent the landing coordinates to *Odyssey IV*'s guidance system and it went straight to the landing place.

After *Odyssey IV* gracefully landed and shut down, four very pleasant and polite "officials" met Tom and greeted him with much warmth. Their physical proportions and shape were very much like humanoids, and his language translator portrayed very genteel expressions from these new acquaintances. Tom was at ease immediately and sensed that this would be a good visit. The apparent leader of the greeting party opened up the welcoming conversation in their language with,

"We wlmcoe u to r palent of Velux. We hpoe taht yuor saty wlil be cfmorobtale."

Tom was able to adjust his language translator to convert their language into what was familiar to him. Then they ushered Tom to an elaborate lounge where they exchanged some cultural stories and traditions while consuming some of the local refreshments. Tom especially liked the very sharp Veluxion cheese washed down with a dark sweet carbonated drink.

Tom began to describe the shipment of Marlarium and the payment conditions. The Veluxions agreed immediately and gave the credits to Tom's universal bank account without question. Tom delivered the Marlarium to the delight of his newly found friends, and because of the ease of business, Tom gave his customers a 10 percent discount on this shipment and a 20 percent credit toward the next purchase. The Veluxions were delighted and invited Tom to enjoy the pleasures of Velux. Tom agreed and was assigned a tour guide. This is what Tom liked best about his deliveries and was delighted at the prospects of gaining knowledge of this apparently gracious culture. This place almost seemed too good.

Over the next two weeks, he was treated like royalty, and he was able to attend the many different types of entertainment of high cultural quality from music to lavishly computed visual stories. He liked the variety of food and was entertained each night by many of what seemed to be upper class homes and families. Tom relished this opportunity, and Velux quickly became one of his favorite stops. He made very good friends and found that the intellectual compatibility between he and the Veluxions was very strong, common, and gentle.

But Tom became very curious about the inside culture of the lower class, which every planet he visited seemed to have. He wanted to spend some time in the Velux local area and asked his hosts if he could have that opportunity. Since Velux was totally crime-free, they felt it would be safe for Tom to do so. The Velux Minister of Transportation, now another close friend, made arrangements for Tom to stay with one of the trusted locals and set up the appropriate transportation.

Tom was transported to a very sleek station that would be his departure place. His escort stayed with him, and in a few moments, the swoosh sound of the vacuum train became louder until it stopped. It was long and round like a tube, and the skin reflected like stainless steel. When it stopped, openings in the shiny skin opened very flush, and some Veluxions made their way out. Tom's escort bid him goodbye and wished him good speed. The inside of the vacuum train was as sleek and polished as the outside, and the benches were very inviting. He sat down comfortably on a soft yet firm material he had never seen before. The openings of the train closed, and after a few seconds, it accelerated very quickly with the sound of rushing air. The resulting ride was exceptionally smooth and fast.

Tom arrived at the vacuum train stop in the local area and was met by a modestly dressed Veluxion who was quite pleasant. They made an immediate connection that was so predominant among the Veluxions. Tom followed his host along one of the main streets, taking in the many crowded sights with great curiosity and he became eager to enter the many trading stores and feeding places along the main walkway. Tom arrived with his host at a modest home that was very neat and clean. He stored his few belongings under a bed that was pointed out to him. He was eager to get out and explore this great new place.

After some polite discussions, Tom's new host described a couple of local places for food and then entertainment. In spite of his host's insistence that he join Tom as an escort, Tom wanted the adventure of exploring the area on his own and courteously left without his host.

Once down into the commercial area, Tom enjoyed the hustle-bustle and efficient closeness of the many inviting eating places, which had pictures or lifelike wax models of the foods they served. He stopped at one place where the pictures of the food looked very appetizing, and he slowly entered that place. Many of the guests looked up as Tom entered, for they never had seen a real human before. Whispers filled the air, and a host came to Tom and graciously offered him a seat by one of the street windows, pointing with his hand while bowing his head slightly. The same type of graciousness that he experienced in the upper class was prevalent in the local area among the lower class.

Sensing that Tom did not know what to order, the host made a recommendation, and Tom agreed with a big smile. Water, a universal fluid of life that had been slightly sweetened, arrived at the table almost immediately, and soon after a server brought to his table what appeared to be bread. It was served with the Veluxion sharp cheese that had been softened with some type of liquid spice to make it easier to spread on the very thin, soft bread. The host showed Tom how to spread the cheese on the bread with his fingers, and he rolled the bread into a tight roll. The roll was dipped into a thick sauce that had the taste of sweet salt. The unique taste was a delightful combination of sharp in the cheese, sweetness in the bread and the round taste of the dip.

Other than a very sharp knifelike utensil, there were no other eating utensils. As on many planets, Tom would eat with his fingers. After about ten minutes, the main course had come to Tom's delight. The plate contained what appeared to be meat that was very tender, a piece of plant that was shaped like a carrot and that tasted like a sweet potato, and a custard like jelly with a soft crust around the edge. A small crystal container with a red powder came with the meal, and the host showed Tom how to season his meal. The red powder was very hot,

24

and Tom used it sparingly. Everything was wonderful, and Tom left not a crumb on the shiny metal plate. As he had observed with the Veluxions, it was customary to lick the plate clean. In fact, this was a compliment to the host, so Tom picked up his plate and licked it clean. The host returned with a delighted expression that Tom had liked his selection, and Tom handed the host a card that was given to him to pay for the meal.

Tom left the eating place and continued down the street looking for an entertainment location. In less than a block, he started to hear some gentle and beautiful music with a complex melody, and when he came to the door, he looked in and entered. The lounge was half-filled with locals listening to the melodic music, and it was dimly lit and very inviting with a sweet smoky smell in the air. Tom picked out a chair and table close to an elevated area that was the source of the music, which was made by five Veluxions with very strange-looking instruments. Tom sat down and was immediately approached by a server. Tom looked around and pointed to some clear liquid in a bottle behind the bar on a shelf. The server smiled with a bow and returned to Tom's table with a glass full of the liquid. The rim of the glass was laced with the appearance of a fine salt. And it was. The drink was delightful with a combination slight sweetness and thickness that coated his palate and throat, and the taste stayed there. Tom was beginning to feel light-headed after two small sips, so he watched his intake, wanting to stay of sober mind.

Some time passed, and Tom was approached by one of the locals. He was a tall male who was soft–spoken, and he asked to join Tom. Tom, of course, was delighted and immediately offered him the chair across the small table. The stranger was very curious about Tom, as was Tom about him. They began talking quietly, and it was obvious that they were developing a likeness for each other that could turn into a friendship. Tom had finished his drink, ordered another, and bought his new friend a drink. This time the drinks came with a flat bowl of small, spiny nuggets coated with a light, sweet batter. They were delicious and very crunchy, and the taste stayed on the palate. The more he ate, the more fluid he craved.

They continued to discuss many things and share some of the customs and adventures of each other's cultures. Both were very interested in each other's stories, and they took turns without either dominating the conversation time.

An hour had passed, and while Tom was looking toward the door, a tall shapely female entered the lounge. She had long, shiny, black, straight hair with a very tan and smooth complexion. She appeared to be about 5' 8" tall, her features were sharp, and her body was quite shapely, even without the aid of support clothing. The one thing that distinguished her from the other Veluxions was her very long fingers. There were four plus an opposed thumb, which completed the almost humanlike hands. The fingers were about twice as long as Tom's, and they were attached to her slender hands in a very graceful manner. Tom was overcome with feelings of attraction, and his new friend leaned over and whispered to Tom, "She is a Gorg and not of this world. Veluxions do not associate with these types."

Tom, startled, looked at his new friend and asked, "Why not?"

"They are very different, and association with them only brings trouble. She is of a lower social status and not worthy of our attention. Be very aware of her attraction, and do not succumb."

Tom stole small stares at her between the pauses in their conversation. His new friend sensed the attraction, looked around, and excused himself, leaving the lounge. Tom was now alone to pursue this exotic beauty.

The female Gorg's sensuous looks settled on Tom with a slightly alluring smile. She knew Tom was not a Veluxion, and she was mutually attracted to Tom because of this difference. It had been a long time since Tom was with a female, and that added to his attraction to this very lovely lady. He relished the thoughts of having a physical affair with her, and he raised his glass to her as he nodded with a smile. She smiled back at Tom in a very inviting way, and, slowly rising from her chair, walked across the room and sat down at Tom's table without even a word. Her eyes never left Tom's image throughout the entire graceful and sensual motion. She smiled very sweetly with a sexual look and seemed to tell Tom with her eyes what may be in store. She was very forward and open.

Tom's spine tingled with the prospects of being with this beauty. He ordered her a drink, and she smiled and touched his forearm with her long graceful fingers. Now closer to her, he noticed that each of her fingers had five joints. Each finger was very smooth with long and narrow fingernails at the end of each finger. Her touch was electric as it danced along his forearm. She began to speak in a low, gentle voice, asking Tom where he was from. He went on with his story while she listened patiently with a loving smile. While he was talking, she stroked the top of his hand with her long gentle fingers, and this seemed to increase their bond to each other. It had been only fifteen minutes since she had sat down, and Tom's whole being was spinning with desire. He had never experienced a feeling of this level, and her attraction had Tom clearly under her spell. He had physical experiences on other planets with many aliens, but nothing was like this.

Beyond Tom's attraction was a sense of curiosity, and he asked about her story. She was pleased to share and told Tom the following:

"I am what is called a Gorg and from a planet two secpars from here. We are a very loving people and require the companionship of a male to be complete. We are trained in making pleasure for our male companions and have very special talents. I was sent here five years ago by my people and have been without a male since then. You are not a Veluxion?"

"No, I am not," replied Tom. "I am from far off and will be here for another two days, then I shall return to my duties around the galaxy."

She continued, "I would like very much to be with you those days. There is much that I can share with you." Her fingers began to run up Tom's wrist and forearm. The hair on the back of Tom's neck stood straight, and the base of his skull tingled with pins and needles. His mind began to transport to a good place in nature, and his whole body became very relaxed and pleasant. It was like hypnosis; he knew he was there, but chose not to move or break the moment. It was a wonderful and very relaxing feeling.

She continued in her soft and gentle voice, "My heart has told me that a stranger from far away would come into my life and mate with my soul. I have been very lonely for a male in this place. The Veluxion males do not seem to like me, and I have been so lonely. I would pay extra attention to someone who would stay with me." As she talked, her long, smooth fingers wrapped around Tom's wrist. She could touch the top of his upper wrist with her palm while caressing the sensitive arm underside with her fingertips, much like taking a pulse. She knew exactly how and where to touch him.

The hypnotic sense deepened over Tom, and while he knew where he was, he succumbed to his senses and just let go of any type of control. It was an exotic feeling that he had never experienced before, and he started to fantasize and have vivid visions of their physical togetherness. As she slowly and softly spoke of her desires, she raised her hand in front of Tom's face, and with her thumb, she lightly touched his eyebrow. Her fingers reached around to the back of his head, and she caressed the lower portion of the place where his neck connected with his skull. As she continued to softly run the tips of her fingers in a small circular motion, her thumb, still on his lower forehead, pulsed with a slight bulge. Tom was mentally encircled in her presence, and it seemed as though an electric current was running from her thumb through Tom's head to her fingers at the back of his head.

Tom was now almost in a deep coma, although his physical appearance seemed to be normal and did not draw any attention from the others in the lounge. Her electrifying touches continued to deepen Tom's now helpless condition. Then she leaned over close to his ear and sensually said, "Come to my place of sleep with me. I want to be with you in a very special way." Her breath that carried these words lightly touched Tom's ear sending charges of feelings up his spine to the place where her fingers were caressing. There seemed to be a connection between the breath coming from her lips and her fingers through Tom's head. Without a word, Tom rose from his chair and went with her. As they walked together out the door, she encircled his limp hand with hers, and with the other hand, she caressed his forearm as they walked. She never stopped touching him, and the electricity in Tom's body grew to the front of his legs as well as the top of his feet.

They walked slowly, very close to each other, and she seemed to connect with Tom at the hips, matching his stride in perfect rhythm. It was a soft connection that told of what the rest of the connection might be. They came to a small, dark alley off the main street, and they turned in without any break in the rhythm of their walk. They came to a large, heavy door; she opened it and guided Tom into a dimly lit room with an intoxicating smell that covered Tom entirely like a thin shell of clear but strong material. She turned to Tom and pressed her entire body against his. She unbuttoned his shirt, and with both hands, she began to run her thumbs up and down his chest while wrapping her fingers around to the sensitive parts of his back. Her body felt fully connected to him, and it seemed as though she reshaped her body to fully match Tom's contours. She was soft all over but firm enough to hold a good shape, and he could feel all of her parts against many places on his body.

Tom's temperature was slightly elevated, as was hers, and she kept kissing his face and neck with electrifying lightness. Her long fingers were now touching every part of his body, and, without missing a touch, she disrobed her soft, silken dress. Tom wanted to take control and make love to her, but he could not under her sensuous spell. She lightly pushed him back into a horizontal position on a deeply soft, satin bed. He offered no resistance. She kept her touching ways, and she continued kissing his neck and shoulders while her long, black hair caressed his face and chest lightly and sensually.

Tom was now under her complete control and had no sense of where he was. His biology was firm and hard. The strength in his arms was limp, and he could not lift his legs. Her eyes and smile seemed to come out of focus and reflect her desire for him.

Just as she was about to take her physical contact further and bond with him, the door of her place opened violently with two uniformed Veluxions rushing in to grab her from Tom. Tom could hardly see and understand what was going on. It was total chaos to his ears. Everything was brightly lit through his closed eyes, and the noises of voices echoed in his ears without him understanding the words. His mind was ringing, and his body seemed to be spinning wildly without any control on his part. He could not move. While the two uniformed Veluxions took her aside and clothed her, the friend from the lounge entered the room from the darkened alley and sat next to Tom on the soft bed. Tom's head was spinning.

Tom was still incoherent, and his lounge friend injected Tom with something that seemed to flow and clean his arteries and veins. It was about five minutes later when Tom started to come out of his condition and his senses started to return to normal.

He asked, "What happened? Where have I been? What is this place?"

Tom's friend lightly stroked his forehead with friendly compassion. "You have almost gone to a place that you could not return from. She is a Gorg and has very special talents for the unaware. We Veluxions are immune to her spells. She was sent here from her home planet to serve her sentence for the rest of her life. On her planet, she is a criminal, and her loneliness here on Velux is her prison. She has to live without male companionship, and that is her punishment. Because we have no crime, we have no need here for containment, and we certainly do not terminate lives. So we watch her very carefully as we do for the other five Gorg females that we are responsible for here on Velux."

Tom was now fully awake and was beginning to understand what had happened. The occurrence seemed to be a very vivid dream that would always stay in his memory. Tom still did not understand the real danger that he was in as he sat up in the bed with his hand on his head in a slight bow. His friend, while explaining, lifted the Gorg's dress as the two uniformed Veluxions held her arms firmly. Her long fingers were waving wildly in all directions and with great speed. Her eyes were wide with hate, and she took on a very different look that appeared to be of deep evil.

Tom's friend pointed to a small pocket above her groin area. He placed his finger inside and pulled forward what seemed to be a small claw. It was curved and hollow and was shaped like that of a snake's fang.

"She was about to sting you while bonding, and you would have been dead in a matter of minutes. This is how she gets her pleasure," explained Tom's friend. "We have been watching you since the time we met in the lounge. I tried to warn you, but she had already started casting her spell on you."

Tom was quiet for awhile with his hand on his forehead. He was wet with sweat and began to think of the intense feelings of his recent experience. His legs felt like rubber.

His friend continued, "You will be OK now. Let me help you with your clothes, and I will take you back to your place of sleep." The two guards kept a hold on her and planned to stay with her until Tom left the local area.

Back at the home of his host, Tom tried to get to sleep, but he could not in spite of his tiredness because he had strong thoughts of returning to her. But he was able to overcome his desires. He rose and asked his host if he may return to the place of the upper class now. He did and the harsh realization of his experience became clearer.

His original hosts of the upper class met Tom at the vacuum train station. They knew of his adventure and talked with him compassionately. They now loved Tom as their own and looked forward to the time when he would return.

"Time will heal your feelings. Come back to us, and we will make sure that you are safe in any of the other adventures that you may seek here."

The next day, Tom returned to the place where *Odyssey IV* was parked, and he turned to his new friends and warmly said his good-byes. He will miss his new friends and started to plan in his mind the next visit.

Tom set the automatic navigation system and *Odyssey IV* gently rose from the pad, turned, and sped off into the direction of the stars. Before entering the suspension chamber, he spent time reflecting on his experience and the strong memories held in his mind and heart for the Gorg experience.

Then the words of his hosts rang in his ears. "Time will heal your feelings. Come back to us, and we will make sure that you are safe in any of the other adventures that you may seek here." He turned the suspension machine on and slowly went to sleep with the dreams of his exotic alien experience. He would return later for another adventure.

The Eagle and the Rooster

John was a farmer of the old family type, and he worked his farm hard to produce the crops that would give him his means of life and his daily bread. He has been married to his wife, Carol, for over 30 years, and they worked in harmony together with their respective roles of the family, farm, and community. They were very traditional and active in the field of friends they came to like over the many years.

Their only son, William, was a B-17 pilot in World War II and was lost over Germany during one of the many allied raids. John and Carol missed their son each day that passed, and they saved William's room as a great memory of his life. The high school pictures, the bowling trophies, and the great blue ribbon William won at the county fair all adorned the emptiness of the room. And most of all, his military picture of him in uniform in front of his B-17 centered the display. Carol kept it neat and clean of dust. They would often visit his room and think of their lost son and the memories of him. His vision stayed in their hearts and they missed him terribly while sitting softly on the edge of his always made bed adorned by a colorful quilt.

At the start of every day, John would raise this great flag of red, white, and blue in the front yard in honor of William's memory and for the many others that lost their lives giving us the freedoms we have come to enjoy. He raised it also for the pain and sorrow of the many other families who lost their loved ones to the horrific reality of war. There were many other farm families who lost their sons to the pursuit of freedom. They all comforted each other's hearts over the years with memories of their lost loved ones and tried to heal the hurt in their hearts.

One beautiful day while walking in the fields, John came upon a great bald eagle lying between the rows of corn. This great American symbol of strength was injured and could not move. It was helpless, and sadness and fear prevailed in the creature's eyes. John saw that the eagle's wing was badly broken, probably by a hunter's bullet. John bent down and gently touched the eagle in a loving way, and the eagle seemed to trust John. Their eyes met, and there seemed to be an understanding of some past connection between the two, as different as they were and as distant as their thoughts and ways.

John gently picked up the great broken eagle and carefully brought it to the farmhouse. He called to Carol from the porch to come help him with the door. She came, and her eyes widened at this sight of the eagle in John's arms. They gently placed the eagle on their kitchen table that had been the place for sharing so many meals. Carol said, "We shall care for and nurture this great creature until it is well."

Then they went to work on the eagle's wing, and the eagle trusted them with its life. They were gentle and loving, taking care not to raise the eagle's fear. They did the best they could with their limited knowledge of how to accomplish the task. They worked gently for hours, cleaning the damaged wing. They used bandages torn from a pillowcase and thin strips of wood to straighten and secure the wing.

Then, in the late evening far beyond the time in which they turned in to their place of sleep, they were finished. They did not know where to place the eagle for the weeks of upcoming recovery, but then John remembered the wired pen where the rooster lived and thought that this may be a good place. John and Carol brought the eagle to the home of the rooster and placed him in the wired pen. This did not bother the rooster, and the eagle felt safe.

The night passed, and in the early time of light, the rooster beckoned for the day to start its warm journey. The eagle lay in the pen, still in pain from his injuries but he found great comfort in the company of the rooster. John came every day to check on the eagle. He gave it ground meat for strength and water for thirst. They cared for the eagle well, and the eagle became stronger as each day passed.

The rooster became a great friend with the eagle, and the eagle accepted the friendship of the rooster with great earnest. They seemed to have a great connection and understanding, and their affection grew stronger with the passing of each day. This was in contrast to the normal relationship of natural enemies and the nature of the eagle to carry the rooster off to its young; they had made peace and comfort with each other in spite of their great differences.

A week went by, and the eagle began to act as the rooster did, sometimes cackling and pecking in the dusty pen floor for corn. As each day passed, the eagle became more and more like the rooster, taking on the rooster's personality. One day as John was passing by the wired pen, he noticed how the eagle was changing, and he was greatly taken back and saddened by the thought of a great bald eagle living and acting as a mere rooster. He called to Carol to show her what was happening, and when she approached the rooster pen and saw the eagle acting that strange, she began to weep.

John and Carol held each other while they tried to understand what they had done. They did their best to save the eagle, but it appeared that it was not enough. Should they have done something different? Should they have let the great bird die as an eagle in the field? They had never helped a creature like this, but they did the best they knew how to do. They knew of cows and chickens but not of eagles, and they were saddened at their "failure" and returned to the house in great pain.

The next morning, John and Carol went to the rooster pen to see if it was only a dream that the eagle had become a rooster. As they approached the pen, the eagle began to crow, and the sound that came forward was a terrible squawk unlike an eagle or a rooster. It rang in the ears of the saddened farmers, and they returned to the farmhouse.

What were they to do? They could not leave the eagle in this condition. This great symbol of America's strength had been reduced to a mere rooster. A rooster did not represent the American spirit.

Several weeks went by, and it became apparent that the eagle was healed on the outside and had a strong body. But the eagle's soul had been transformed to an unacceptable place and was severely diminished.

John and Carol talked for many hours on what needed to be done to return the spirit of the eagle. They agreed to use tough love, as painful as it may be. They both thought that it was better to die as an eagle than to live as a rooster. So they went to the pen and carried the fully healed eagle to their pickup truck, and they drove to a high cliff that overlooked the valley of wheat. They took the eagle, still squawking, to the edge of the cliff and looked at each other somberly. The pain in their hearts was clear with what they had to do. Then in a fast thrust, John threw the eagle over the great cliff and watched as the eagle fell toward the valley floor. They watched for what they thought was a lifetime of minutes.

The eagle squawked as he fell through the air. The noise echoed against the cliff wall and was heard throughout the valley, and the noise was terrible; it was neither eagle nor rooster. John and Carol felt a great sadness contrasted with their belief that they were doing the right thing.

Then, just before the eagle crashed onto the rocks below, it spread out its great wings toward the sky and flew, as an eagle should. The hearts of John and Carol leaped with joy, and their arms tightened around each other. They had done the right thing! And they shared their tears of joy with heavy hearts.

As they watched the eagle fly higher and higher, they kept holding each other for they knew now that the eagle was free on the inside as well as the outside. The eagle's flight looked so beautiful against the blanket of golden wheat on the valley floor. Now the sounds of the great eagle echoed over the valley with the screeches so typical of this majestic flyer. The eagle rose above the height of the cliff where John and Carol were standing together. As he passed above, the eagle looked at them with a great expression of thanks, and flew away never to be seen again.

On the way back to the farm, John and Carol savored their memories of the freedom of the eagle. They touched each other and felt good without saying any words. When they arrived at the farm, they walked by the pen that now contained only the rooster, and they were lonely for the eagle. And it was very quiet. They had a great feeling of emptiness with the eagle now gone, but they relished the thoughts of its freedom.

Then, in the pen over by the water trough, they noticed a great eagle feather laying in the dusty dirt. John went into the pen and retrieved the feather. It was thin and strong and shined with a lovely but strong brilliance, and they brought it into the house and laid it upon the kitchen table where they mended the wing that long night. Their memories of the love they gave and received from the eagle lingered in their thoughts. While there was certain sadness of loneliness in their hearts, they sat to look at the feather and reminisced with great love for some time. They thought again and shared the day when John had found the eagle in the cornfield and the long night of repair. The eagle had left them with this simple gift of remembrance of their kindness. And it was the greatest of all gifts.

Then, in a moment, John picked up the feather, took Carol by the hand, and went to their son's so carefully kept old room. He laid the feather next to William's military picture with William standing in front of his B-17 in his sharp uniform. William had named his bomber "The Flying Eagle," and the brightly painted eagle bust painted on the bomber's nose showed the strength of their son's resolve and love. This was a memory to always remember, and they sat on the bed together with great thoughts to cherish. They leaned together with arms about as one staring for several moments at the picture of their beloved son who flew in the sky for our freedom and at the feather of flight that adorned his memory. They now believed in their hearts that Creation brought the eagle to them as a messenger of love and comfort from their son, William.

And so the story of the eagle and rooster has many lessons for each of us. Each time you read of the eagle and rooster, you will learn something new. May we embrace those lessons in our lives and be kind to ourselves and to our neighbors.

William's B-17

It is suggested that "The Eagle and The Rooster" be read prior to reading this story.

William was twenty-two and three semesters away from a Bachelors of Science degree in mechanical engineering. The date was December 8, 1941, and the entire nation was still reeling from the sneak attack on Pearl Harbor by the Japanese. William made the decision to leave school and join the Army, as so many did during the next few weeks.

William was born and brought up on a Midwest farm, and his parents, John and Carol, paid special attention to their only child's sense of education and patriotism. He was always encouraged to read, stay with the news, and be involved with the local community. William was popular in school, he played sports, and he competed in the yearly state fair where he had won many ribbons for his husbandry with cows and pigs. He especially enjoyed bowling on the school team during the weeks, and he won many trophies that he displayed so proudly in his room at home. While living at the school dorm, he often thought of his room on the farm that was in contrast to the stark and impersonal style of the college dorms.

When he went off to college, his mother, Carol, always kept his room dusted and cleaned as a reminder of their beloved son who they missed so. Both John and Carol would occasionally spend time sitting on his colorfully quilted bed and reminisce of their time with their son as he grew to be a young man. They were very proud of their son and loved him so, and now their vision of him becoming an educated man gave great comfort and satisfaction to their parenthood.

December 7th also had great emotional impact on John and Carol with their great sense of patriotism and love of country. It was the next day, December 8th, that William called his parents and told them he was coming home from school, but he did not tell them why. But they sensed why William was coming home, and three days later, he arrived at the farm.

After much hugging and such, William began some talk with, "Many of my friends have left school and joined the Army. I have decided to do the same and will go to town tomorrow to enlist."

Even though John and Carol had expected this, William's words hit their hearts with great concern and sadness. Carol, with two watering eyes, put her hand on her son's cheek and just said, "I love you and will pray for your safety. Our hearts will always be with you."

John, with concerned pride, queried, "Well, what do you want to do in the service? Have you any ideas? What are your friends going to do?"

"I want to fly, and I think with my education, I could fly fighters. They are looking for my type to do this, so I have a good chance. I have looked into flying a little bit, and that is what I am going to volunteer for. And I pray to get accepted," answered William with much enthusiasm.

Carol was very sad and left the kitchen table to go to another room so she could cry by herself, and the next day, John installed a very tall flagpole in the front yard. Five morning crows of the penned farm rooster passed, and William left to be formally inducted.

It was two weeks later when William, with thirty others, stepped off a white bus to start his basic training for twelve weeks, then to go off to fighter school, or so he thought. William's farm strength, education, and attitude got him through basic training with flying colors, and he was considered a natural born leader among his recruit peers and training officers. He was then recommended for officer's training school for the accelerated schedule of ninety days. Again, William passed every part of the training with lots of margin to spare.

He was sure that he would now qualify for fighter school and upon his exit interview with his commanding officer, the officer told William that, in his opinion, William was not suited for fighter school. The officer was making the recommendation that William be assigned to bomber school. It was William's leadership skills when working in a team that gave his commander this perspective. William had his heart set on something else, but he saluted smartly and accepted his fate toward this new assignment.

William had some time before reporting to flight and bomber school, so he left to visit his parents for a few days to spend some quality time with them. He did not call, and when he showed up in his new uniform on the front porch, Carol and John were surprised and happy beyond words. John was so proud of his manly son, and Carol's vision of William in his uniform overcame her life-long thoughts of her "little boy," as a mother would. She now knew he was a man, but still she worried much over his future safety.

That night they sat at the farm's center of activity, the kitchen table, and reminisced over all of the old days of fairs, competitions, and such. That night William slept in his colorful quilted bed and awoke the next morning to the call of the farm's rooster. William always loved to start his day with the trumpeting of the rooster with its joyful announcement that a new day was beginning, and life could start anew.

William arrived at flight school, but this time he was in uniform and had a better sense of belonging. He was with others like him, all hoping to make it through the very tough flight-training program. They all knew that four out of every five trainees would wash out of the flight portion and most likely qualify for copilot, navigator, or bombardier, but William had only the expectations of making it through. As usual, failing was not an option.

William continued his popular style and had made many friends during the grueling training program. First there was the basic flight training, then many of the associated subjects such as navigation, flight theory, and basic flight engineering. William took to all the subjects very easily, but he liked the flight training the best, and it was not long before he qualified to solo, which he did without event. After 200 hours of solo flight and cross-country missions in a trainer, he was now ready to begin training for bomber command and flight. There were only two bombers at the training field; a B-24 Liberator and a B-17 Flying Fortress, which gave minimal training time for each of the new potential pilots.

During this period, William had earned his wings and wore them proudly over his left shirt or jacket pocket, whichever was the outer garment, so everyone would know he had made it. He had made several friends during this training time, as William was so able to do thanks to his personality. He had made special friends with Frank, a business major who also left school early to join the action. Frank was from Chicago and was very cosmopolitan. This complemented William's country style, and they became very close without showing it outwardly. They usually ate and studied together, and when they were off duty, they socialized in town together. Frank, however, was having a very difficult time qualifying for flight command, and when he washed out of flight school, he was assigned to navigation school.

Pressure was increasing to finalize the training because of the burgeoning need over Europe. Reports of continuous bombings of London and its non-combat citizens by the Germans made the urgency even greater, but the lack of actual bombers for training limited the availability of qualified pilots.

It was a cool morning in October of 1942 when a certain excitement proliferated among the base personnel. They were just notified that 30 B-17s were being flown in from the Pacific Northwest and were expected later that day. It was not the planes that were of great interest; it was the pilots. The bombers were being flown in by WASPs (Women's Air Service Pilots), three in each plane for a total of 90 smart and lovely ladies that were rarer than the bombers themselves at the base. Delivering planes to the combat crews were left to these civilian women so that more men would be available for the more dangerous combat roles. As civilians, they were not part of the military structure and were much more socially available and flexible.

Later that day, William, Frank, and about twenty other officers were socializing in the officers' club, playing cards, pool, and assorted other games when the heavy drone of many large engines filled the entire base, announcing the long-anticipated critical delivery. And what a sight it was! The planes were in formations of three, and they did a fly-by before lining up in the long landing pattern. At 3,000 feet, the rumbling noise could be felt with a great air of excitement as the planes passed overhead to make the turn to line up with the runway. With wheels and flaps down, each plane presented a very graceful and gentle sight as they floated down to the runway, one by one. As each plane landed softly, colorfully painted jeeps directed them to their parking locations, and soon after the engines came to a quiet halt, the crews disembarked and headed for the cafeteria for eats. Then they were ushered over to the special barracks for rest and clean up. They were all women, and pilots to boot.

The men were nuts with anticipation and were hard-pressed to stay away as ordered by the base commander, at least until the ladies got settled. Then slowly in small groups, the ladies came to the officers' club to socialize and relax. This time they were washed and out of their flight suits and heavy leather jackets and in some very feminine attire of the time. It was hard to believe that these flowers of loveliness were the pilots that the men wished to be. William seemed to have a disinterested attitude about the whole event and sat with Frank fairly removed from all the commotion of so many females at the club and base at one time. There was immediate socialization, and William joined in some casual conversation with

Frank and a lady that Frank had attracted and had latched onto. As the three sat together at a small table, there was lots of flying conversation, especially about the subtleties of the Flying Fortress. This common ground quickly developed strong attractions with many of the men and ladies. It was like a big matching game that fell out of the sky courtesy of some Higher Power.

It was about 20:00 hours (8:00 p.m.) and two hours after the ladies started to arrive when a very attractive blond entered the officers' club, drawing the attention of most of the men. With a smile and knowing that she was making an impression, she walked directly and smartly over to the table where William, Frank, and Mary, Frank's new friend, were sitting. As she arrived and stopped, the two men stood as gentlemen of the time should, and Mary announced, "This is my best friend, Jackie, our fearless leader." William and Frank stood speechless with little boyish looks under the visual spell of Jackie's presence; and she certainly had presence.

"Well, boys, may I sit down and join you?" she said with a very bright smile, as though she was used to this type of reaction from men. William stumbled a little and grabbed a chair for Jackie to sit in and answered, "Sure thing, it's our pleasure."

It did not take long for the table to get comfortable with all kinds of flying talk, and it was obvious that Jackie was attracted to William's boyish and handsome style. And he liked her also. There was a very strong mutual attraction for each other.

It was about 22:00 hours when Jackie got up from the table and announced, "Well, I have to check out our deliveries before turning in. Want to join me, William?" As she extended her hand for William to follow, he did so with a smile, trying not to seem too eager.

It was a beautiful evening with the stars brightly speckled on the velvet moonless night as they walked slowly hand in hand along the lined up B-17s. While William was familiar with and had flown the large plane with only about 20 total hours, Jackie had over 600 hours on the 17 and was well-versed in how the plane reacted in all types of situations. Jackie loved all the questions that came from William, and she was able to answer all of them and then some. Then, as they kept walking, a certain quiet came upon both of them. It was like all was said and nothing else was important to say. William had little experience with the ladies, and he was struggling a little with this apron-less woman, something he was not very used to.

They stopped by one of the 17's large wheels, and she looked up into the landing gear bay. William had his hand on the back of her neck, and when

43

she turned and faced him, they embarked on a really sensual and close body kiss that just seemed to work. This kept on for a while, then Jackie, breathing heavily, offered a tour of the inside of the plane. It was very dark, and as they climbed up into the belly hatch, William clumsily banged his head a couple of times. When inside, Jackie pulled several parachutes together for a makeshift couch, and they got comfortable and continued their long, close kisses. Well, as nature would have it, they ended up spending two hours in the 17 on the parachutes, and there was lots of deep lovemaking. This was William's first time.

Two days later, it was time for the ladies to head back, and five C-47 transports were warming up on the tarmac. Jackie and William hugged and shared a small kiss. As she climbed the transport's ladder, she stopped before entering and looked back at William. She waved a goodbye with an expression not obvious to William that said, "I hope he makes it."

Over the next eight weeks, all of the newly delivered B-17s were kept very busy with more training, which included bombing runs, emergency procedures, and flying tight formations, which was the most difficult. They went on long "missions" in formation, and they would "bomb" an American or Canadian city and sometimes a barn in a cornfield.

Then the orders came for their departure for overseas to Europe. All thirty planes were assigned to the Eighth Air Force stationed in Bassingbourn, England. The trip would take them across the northeastern part of the United States, over Nova Scotia, and into Greenland for refueling. The next stop was England. Flying at 32,000 feet, the crew got their first real taste of the intense cold in the open airplanes on long trips. Each had to be careful not to touch metal with bare skin, and taking a pee had to be a very fast event because the urine froze immediately when hitting the floor of the plane. They had to be on constant alert for frostbite.

Only the pilots, co-pilots, and navigators made the trip with the planes. The rest of the crew would be assigned on base at England. Including refueling, the whole trip would take eleven hours. The trip also gave the crews practice flying in close formation, a critical and required talent that required constant concentration and lots of strength and stamina to move the controls, which required about a hundred pounds of effort. William still had the softness of Jackie in his mind and heart, and he wondered how such a soft and lovely person could possibly fly one of these monsters.

The coastlines of Scotland and then England were a very welcome sight. The crews were tired and cold, and they were looking forward to a hot meal and a hot stove to sit near like the nonsense poem of "The Cremation of Sam McGee" by Robert Service. This was a high school favorite of William's, and he shared it over the radio with his colleagues. It was the story of a man from Tennessee who traveled to the Arctic in search of gold and became so cold that he chose to sit inside a wood-burning stove to stay warm. That is how desperately cold the crews felt.

All thirty 17s arrived at Bassingbourn, England without major mechanical incident, giving tribute to the quality and serious skill of the American workers, mostly women, who were building these magnificent birds of prey. They all landed and were directed to the appropriate staging area. It was cold and damp in the usual British manner, but it was very welcomed by the crews. They were treated to some good, hot food and shown to their quarters that were basic canvas tents deeply moist from the constant drizzle. Everything had a damp feel, including the bedding, and mud was everywhere. This was not the romance and comfort that William had expected as he thought of his warm and cozy room and the quilt at home on the farm.

The next day there was talk among the vets of the base that it was traditional that each of the pilots name his 17 along with the appropriate nose artwork. Most opted for artwork done by a wartime woman artist named Zoe, who was famous for her depiction of scantily clothed women in provocative positions with names such as *The Big Bottom, The Memphis Belle*, etc. William was not of that favor, and decided to call his 17 *The Flying Eagle* with the bust of an American bald eagle on the plane, highlighting an eagle's white feathered neck, curved beak, and penetrating eyes. Frank, his navigator and good friend, did not approve, but it was William's choice. The eagle had special meaning to William from his days on the farm where the eagles were plentiful and soared the farmland skies. William had a picture taken of him in uniform in front of *The Flying Eagle* with the newly painted image and had it sent to his parents.

Songs of Life

A slight reality of the war's discomfort was beginning to rear its head in William's mind. He was assigned the rest of his crew, which included a bombardier, a radioman, and five gunners. They all took a liking to William at once, but two of the veteran gunners of other missions were concerned for William's inexperience. While not talked about openly, the casualty rate over enemy territory was very high. In fact, not one B-17 and crew had made it to the required twenty-five missions yet. The British bombers were flying the night missions, and the Americans opted for day missions, which were much more accurate during the daylight hours, but left the bombers open to enemy flak and fighters in the daylight.

It was after three days when William and his crew were assigned to their first mission, and in the ready room crowded with pilots and copilots, the mission instructions were given. It was very early in the morning, and William took careful notes, and the complexity of the mission with all the details replaced any thoughts of the real danger and the possibility of not returning. When the briefing was complete, all the pilots left the large sheet metal-roofed hut and walked to their respective planes where their crews were waiting impatiently.

William arrived at *The Flying Eagle*, and his crew was waiting, some smoking cigarettes and some just standing around. William did some walk-arounds the Eagle, checking for loose parts, etc. but really trying to look unconcerned and in charge. He smiled and asked everybody to get aboard because they would be leaving in about twenty minutes. This was the first time this crew would go on a mission together, and it was the first for *The Flying Eagle*. She was very clean without any of the battle scars that adorned so many of the veteran 17s. Everybody got settled into his respective position while William was going through the preflight check. His good friend Frank was checking his maps and the course that they would be taking.

Instructions came from the small tower to start their engines, and the rumbling roar of the turbo-charged cylinders with open exhausts filled the base with a certain announcement that the seriousness of a mission was about to start. There were fifty planes that began to rev up their engines and slowly began to taxi in a line to the end of the runway. *The Flying Eagle* was positioned toward the end of the parade and would be one of the last to take off. A bright red flair from the tower signaled the 17s to begin their take-off, and they started to roar down the runway about twenty seconds apart. It was about fifteen minutes later, and William lined up the Eagle at the end of the runway, pushed the throttles forward, and began down the runway as he had done so often in his training flights.

It took some time for the fifty 17s to come together at 15,000 feet and close up in tight formation. The Eagle was to the rear of the formation and the crew had

46

a dramatic view of the formation up front. It was about another forty-five minutes into the flight when the sky seemed to fill with 17s from other bases and took their positions in the tight formation. There were over 400 17s in all, and the Eagle was well back. The entire formation then proceeded to the altitude of 32,000 feet where the cold became the crew's biggest enemy. Each of the 17s engine exhausts emitted a white contrail filling the sky with an almost solid curtain of white against the blue sky. It was a dramatic sight as they headed for their turn position to set them up in the direction of the target.

The target was a German industrial area near the French border. Civilians made up a great portion of the target area, and as with many others, William's thoughts of killing innocent civilians was tempered by the relentless German bombing of London itself, killing tens of thousands of innocent British residents. This was war at its worst, and William had to accept this fate. This is not what he had in mind when his dreams of flying romantically occupied his boyhood imagination. But this was war and a time to test men's souls.

The entire formation of 400 17s reached the turn point and proceeded to maneuver in this tight and complex effort. The turn was made without incident, which was unusual, and the target was now two hours away directly in front of them. They were now coming into the German fighter danger zone of the Luftwaffe. The British and American fighter escorts did not have the range to escort the formation to the target, leaving the 17s without fighter cover and at the mercy of the very experienced German pilots. The dead quiet on the Eagle seemed to be louder than the engines as they proceeded on.

Then the loud silence was broken by voices on the radio, "Bandits at ten o'clock high!" William looked up to his left and saw about a dozen German fighters coming out of the sun and diving toward the formation. They made a pass over the lead 17s with guns blazing, and then they swung back around into the middle of the formation to shoot some more, and then to the rear in an up-and-down pattern. Heavy bullets were flying in all directions from the fighters, and the 17s that were in tight formation concentrated over 3,000 50-caliber guns on the German attackers. The conflict lasted about fifteen minutes, which seemed like a lifetime, and it ended as quickly as it started with the remaining fighters retreating back into the sun. When it was over, four German ME-109s were shot down, and twelve 17s were either totally destroyed or damaged enough to force them to turn back and crash land somewhere in Germany.

German soldiers or citizens captured the American flyers who managed to bail out. The officers were taken to one of the many Stalag prison camps, and the enlisted non-officers were usually taken away and shot. Whenever a 17 was damaged to the point of spinning out of control and sure to crash, the crews of the other 17s would count the parachutes of those that managed to escape the falling hulks. "There's one, two and three. Four and five are out and there goes six!" as the count went on.

Being in the rear of the formation, William had a front row seat to the unexpected terror while he struggled to keep the Eagle in formation and listened to the noisy action of the guns down in his own fuselage. After a large noise and shaking of the fortress, the top turret gunner hollered that the top three feet of the vertical tail had been shot off. William had to use all his strength on the controls to stay in level flight and in the formation. The violence of the attack took its shock toll on the men, but William was able to keep the rookies together.

It was only ten minutes later when the sky was filled with a wall of black explosions and the flythrough of the heavy flack began. Flack was everywhere, and a 17 would explode violently when hit directly. William saw eight direct hits where the crews had little chance of surviving. The Eagle had made it through the flak with only minor damage. Many times there was no counting of parachutes.

Very soon the target became visible though a light and scattered cloud cover, and at the right time, the bomb bay doors opened, and the bomb release toggle switch was thrown. Eight 500-pound bombs clicked off the rack and headed for their targets. With the 380 17s left, over 3,000 bombs blanketed the area, including the residential areas.

After the bomb run, the formation made a wide turn to home and went through the flak wall and fighter attacks again with more 17 crews being lost. It was a long and quiet return trip over the channel to the base. William was still in emotional disbelief of what happened in the last four hours, and other than some frostbite, no one was seriously injured on the Eagle.

It was in the officers' club that William started to really reflect on his first mission. He was sitting with his good friend Frank when two other pilots, Jerry and Peter, joined them at the small round table. The conversation went as follows:

Peter: "So, William, it looks like you made it through your first mission!"

William: "It was like nothing I had imagined or dreamed. If I thought it would be like this, I would have chosen some other branch. We killed thousands of innocent people today and lost many of our own. The flak was really bad, but we were very lucky."

Jerry: "And you'll get much better at getting in and out. Today we lost 38 17s and crews with this daylight bombing strategy. But we could not have hit the targets in the dark of night."

William: "There must be another way than this killing and violence. I just can't imagine that this is the only way."

Jerry: "Well, if you have a better way, write President Roosevelt and Churchill. I am sure that they would be very interested. We did not ask for this war. There are many more dying at the hands of this tyrant Hitler and unfortunately, this is the only way to stop him. You can bet that if he's not stopped, England would be devastated, and the next step would be on the shores of New York. Someday we will be able to drop one bomb on one target without killing any civilians."

Peter: "William, you need to remove yourself from the personality and think of what we are doing as eliminating a target making weapons being manufactured designed to kill us as well as innocent citizens themselves. If not, you will not survive."

That night, while trying to get to sleep, "This is the only way" rolled in William's mind over and over, and he did not get to sleep at all.

The next morning, there was another briefing for that day's mission. Instructions were given, planes took off, fighters encountered, and the deadly wall of flack took its toll. And thousands more died on the ground. This was the Eagle's second mission, and knowing what they were going to encounter was giving the crew little comfort.

The Eagle participated in three more missions over the next week, and the morning thought each day was, "Is this the day I am going to die?" All of the crews lived with this thought, minute by minute.

It was the morning of the Eagle's sixth mission that the heavy rain threatened to cancel that day's raid. After the usual briefing, the crews were ordered to their planes and instructed to wait for word that the weather was clearing over today's target. The word came within thirty minutes, and the parade of fortresses rumbled off the runway toward the formation point. This raid was going deeper into Germany, and William, by now, had learned to cover his concerns with his natural confident personality for the well-being of his crew. He was now learning a very important aspect of combat leadership: keeping the crew on the mission track.

Again, the large formation went through the fighter attack and lost four planes and crews, and the formation was now headed for the wall of flack. William's crew had managed to shoot a German ME-109 down, and the gunners were competitively shouting and arguing over who made the vital kill. Soon after, they reached the fatal concentration of flack. The Eagle experienced some light hits, and the sharp metal fragments could be heard echoing throughout the fuselage.

They were almost out of the wall when the Eagle took a very direct hit on the left wing, which tore the entire wing and two engines completely off the fuselage. There was no time to react because the dramatic event took less than two seconds, and the Eagle was put into a fast and violent spin. The centrifugal force of the spin created massive "G" forces, and William was thrust against the control wheel, breaking his ribs and pinning him to the wheel so that he could not move. His head felt like it was going to come off his shoulders, and his arms were pinned against the front instrument panel.

The wing was shot off at an altitude of 32,000 feet, and at the current rate of fall, it would take almost three minutes to reach the ground. There was no hope to bail out, and William could hear the cries of his crew as they were also pinned by the spinning force. He was able to see out of the side of his right eye that his co-pilot seemed to be close to death with blood rushing from his neck and painting the inside of the windshield red. William could do nothing except take the ride down and accept the fate of what he knew was to come in the last minutes. He had accepted his death in those first moments.

His first thoughts were of the thousands of civilians that he would not have to kill anymore. The visions of his youth on the farm became very vivid with the smell of the barn and the crow of the penned rooster that signaled the start of each day. He thought of the many meals at the kitchen table with his mom and dad, Carol and John. He especially longed to see his carefully kept room again with the brightly colored quilt crowning the soft white bed that provided him with his childhood security. And the trophies he won in his earlier youth along with the picture of him in uniform standing in front of *The Flying Eagle*. His parents were so proud of their son and the commitment that he had made as so many others of his age.

A minute of falling in the twisting spin had passed, which seemed like an hour, and William, with his broken ribs, was beginning to feel faint, and blood was trickling down his chin. There was no pain, just the knowledge that he was going to perish. He thought of his two-night encounter with Jackie, a woman that he had great affection for and the night on the parachutes, in her arms making love. He thought of his high school history teacher who had such an impact on his attitude, and of the bowling alley that was the stage for so many of his trophies and fun with friends.

Two minutes had passed, and William felt weaker, and he could still hear the chaotic cries of his crew members, but he was powerless to help. It now seemed like a lifetime and not minutes. He could see the ground getting closer as it spun before him in a blur. *The Flying Eagle* was spinning to its death, taking ten souls with it. William was able to move his arm and put it on his wings over his heart. He clutched them, as this was the only physical thing that he could do. He was now feeling fainter, and he had a hard time seeing, and the crying sounds had turned to distant echoes.

Then, in a moment of brightness, calmness, and serenity, a great American bald eagle appeared to William in the spinning cockpit. The eagle seemed to float in front of William, and its large black eyes with large pupils stared into William's eyes with great strength and understanding. William looked back, and they seemed to make a very deep spiritual connection with each other. The eagle's strong look and presence touched William as a miracle of life. This was to be William's last vision of life.

It was then that William broke the silence between the two, and with a very broken voice with hard breath, said to the eagle, "Go to my parents and comfort them with what you know of my life and death. Give them a lesson and a gift for life, and a memory of me that they can cherish." The eagle seemed to understand and responded with an expression of strength and compassion. Then the vision of the eagle faded.

The other crews still flying in the formation watched as *The Flying Eagle* spun to its fiery death in the German countryside. They had counted no parachutes and knew that the report would indicate that all was lost.

Now the spirit of the eagle was free to carry its message to the farm where William had grown to be a man and who now was missed by his loved ones, John and Carol.

The Compassionate War

War is a horrible event and must be avoided, but at all costs? And worldwide peace may be finally at hand, but at the great cost of scores of millions of lives in the 20th century. All too often, the innocents are forced to defend themselves from the many tyrants of war. They can be enslaved, or worse, killed through extreme violence. The invasion of Europe by Hitler and the transcending invasion and occupation of China by Japan were the results of tyranny of the worst kind and resulted in the violent massacre of MILLIONS of those who had no warring intent but were just in the way.

This bloodshed of the world's history is dramatic and well illustrates civilization's pursuit of power throughout the centuries by societies that never learned the lessons of the complete insanity of destruction and death of our citizens and cities. The most dramatic period of the complete horror of war can be seen vividly in the world history of the 20th century. In "just" 100 years, scores of millions of non-combat men, women, and children had their lives taken in terrible bloody and fiery methods. It is not a period of time that we can be proud of as a race in this universe of which we are such a little part. Only a few men, who had absolute control of their societies and used that control for their own self-centered gain of insanity, drove these horrific events. And it was the *apathy of the people* that enabled these tyrants.

History of the centuries has shown that members of the human race cannot live without warring among themselves. The greed of territories, the quest for power, and the need for resources are the transparent spoils that victories are supposed to bring those who wage war. And in some cases, tyrants will exercise their power just for a cultural difference. They are the aggressors, and the defenders

53

like those in a chess game, are the unfortunates of man's indignant thinking. We must always defend against these tyrants of hate and destruction no matter where they live, hide, or kill.

When we analyze the history of the 20th century and the numbers of dead, we are surprised to find there was a dramatic reduction in lost lives from the first half of the 20th century to the second half by scores of millions. This is no small matter and should be taken very seriously and well understood for it is here that we might find the road map to a great reduction in deaths by war. And just maybe, after the many centuries of senseless killing, we may be getting closer to the elimination of war, the killing of millions and millions, and a true and lasting peace. The facts of the numbers clearly show that we are, in a dramatic fashion, reducing the numbers killed, even in spite of our view that horrible killing still exists in the early 21st century.

In the first half of the 20th century, it is estimated that the total number of deaths was well over 100 million. For example, in WWII, the Russians lost over 25 million, mostly civilians (Stalingrad and Leningrad), the Chinese over 25 million, Northern European, 10 million plus, etc. The United States lost over 500,000 but was very fortunate not to have war waged on American soil, which would have probably killed tens of millions. This does not include "the war to end all wars," World War I, where one-third of the Parisian males lost their lives in the trenches bordering "no man's land." And the count goes on.

In the second half of the century, an estimate of less than 15 million were killed; mostly in Southeast Asia and some in the Falklands, and some other pockets of violence. The reduction in deaths in the last half of the 20th century was almost ten times less than in the first half of the century, a very dramatic reduction not to be ignored. So are we making progress toward a true and lasting peace over time?

To find what is at the root of this progress, we need to go back to 500 BC and examine the works of Sun Tzu, an ancient Chinese warrior. Sun Tzu, an expert at warfare, created many essays on how to organize and wage war. His works were found in the late 18th century and translated by the French into Western languages. Today you may find many different translations of "Sun Tzu, The Art of War" by various authors with their own interpretations of the translations in your local library or bookstore.

There are many premises to the various chapters of the translations that outline the basic aspects of waging war including terrain, leadership, spying, tactical and strategic positioning, weather, organization, supplying the troops, and many others. The most important premise that the essays make is the *ultimate Art of War*, and that is to

"Win the battle without engaging the troops."

Yes, there are no casualties or citizens killed in *A Compassionate War!* This is a dramatic concept that is 2,500 years old and ill understood by most civilians but understood by many of our military leaders.

While the common visions of war mostly include bloody encounters on the battlefield and the rape and pillaging of the cities, it is hard to imagine that a war can be won without the fighting, the bloodshed, and the killing of innocent citizens. This is not well understood by the general public and is the most critical premise on the road to a lasting peace. The very basic import of Sun Tzu's principle is to make the consequences of war so terrible that the troops would not be engaged and a peaceful solution will ensue. A good example of this was "The Cuban Missile Crisis" in the early 1960s between the United States and the USSR. Neither side, in the final analysis, followed through with the threats of complete annihilation through total nuclear engagement. The battle was settled without engaging the troops.

A further example of "The Art of War" is the almost five-decade cold war between the United States, China, and Russia with "Mutually Assured Destruction" (MAD for short) using the nuclear threat as the foundation. All sides understood that a war between each would result in a total nuclear disaster, so the violent war never took place. Imagine if the Third World War had taken place and hundreds of millions of innocents would have been incinerated in a matter of days. And even worse, many would have died a slow death from burns, diseases, and hunger.

It was commonly thought in the 1950s that the Third World War was imminent between a combination of any two of these nations and the United States, and the American society lived with the prospects of a fiery nuclear death or worse, starvation and sickness. But in the late 20th century, peace came to the world, and the doomsday scenario never enfolded. Instead, the Soviet Union reorganized into a more free society, and Mainland China continued to grow economically through manufacturing and world trade.

At the start of the 21st century, only small remnants of war violence remained in the form of isolated, but still dangerous, terrorist groups. While they pose a great threat, as with the World Trade Center disaster, the overall danger of massive innocent deaths is all but a memory. More importantly, MAD is nothing but a memory today replaced by social and economic trade between those nations that were once bitter enemies. Strength in the Sun Tzu tradition led to a working peace, and *it is that strength that will keep us safe.*

In the Middle Eastern wars in Afghanistan and Iraq, the blanket bombing that was so prevalent in World War II, killing millions of citizens, did not happen. Instead, surgical strikes using high technology were directed at military targets only, all but eliminating collateral damage. While today we are faced with the insanity of war, we must keep in mind the perspective of our terrible world history. If only the tyrants of conflicts were to suddenly not exist, today there would be no war.

As the visions of the terrible atomic attacks on the Japanese cities of Hiroshima and Nagasaki stay in the forefront of our history as the greatest lesson of war, we must also think in terms of the hundreds of millions that were incinerated by conventional means. It just took more time and more airplanes. The firebombing of Tokyo took two weeks and killed over 200,000 citizens, and this was a much greater damage than that of Fat Man and Little Boy, the names of the two atomic bombs that killed more than 140,000 men, women, and children. So while the nuclear attacks stay in our history, in perspective they were only a very small part of the overall devastation to human life, but they did dramatize the horror that could ensue.

The justification of the decision for those nuclear attacks is complex and is a subject for another story, but one thing is for sure, and that is the lesson and vision it gave to the tyrants of war as the greatest warning of all time. That dramatic vision and the use of technology gave the world the doomsday scenario that keeps the big peace and protects the innocents. Those innocents of Hiroshima and Nagasaki gave their lives for the future peace of the world, and the ultimate sin would be to disgrace their memory by not remembering what they really died for—*a true and lasting peace.* Like millions of others, they paid the ultimate sacrifice, only theirs was more dramatic and horrible.

There is peace in strength, and just maybe the ultimate Sun Tzu principle has taken hold upon the world's leaders who won't risk total annihilation of the masses for some vacant selfish principle by a very few. We are now enjoying worldwide commerce, and the average wealth of the common is becoming higher. While we are not perfect and killing still takes place, great progress has been made, and we should be thankful for we are getting very close to the ultimate war, which is total peace. We MUST support the strength that keeps us safe.

This has been clearly proven and undeniable, and the result has become "A Compassionate War."

The Courage to Change

All good fantasy stories start with…

Once upon a time, there was a small, frail seed that fell to the ground from what was once a great and beautiful flower. She looked around at all the other seeds that sprinkled to the ground around her, but they did not move or talk, and they were all very solemn and provided no comfort to her. She was so tiny, alone, afraid, and her life had become very tough, trying to hide from the many birds who wanted to carry her off as they did with so many other seeds around her. Many times she was stepped on by all sorts of animals, and often the very large creatures of the garden would also step on her and force her deeper into the very dry and dusty dirt. She spent much time as a seed, just lying there on the ground for many days. And it was very lonely. She did not know what was to become of her, and she thought often that there must be more to life than just sitting motionless in her loneliness.

Many weeks went by, and one day it began to rain, making the soil around her very wet. She began to swell with the moisture from the heavens. She got softer and larger and could not understand this new feeling, and she became more afraid of change, not knowing what all this meant. The next day, the warm sun made her feel so good, and now she thought that something was going to finally happen, but she knew not what. Her whole life was spent as a seed, and the prospects of change from the only life she knew amplified her fear, but she accepted the fate that might come. She swelled more, and the shell that was her clothing for so long began to split and shed from her moist body. She began to see things in a different light but did not understand her new thoughts of life that raised new fears and questions.

57

Then one day something great from deep within her began to grow and penetrate the soft soil beneath her. Deeper and deeper she penetrated.

"What is this?" she exclaimed with surprise. "What is happening to me? It feels good, like nothing before but I do not understand." The excitement of these new feelings began to overcome her fear, and she let go of the painful security of the known past. She turned herself over to the wonderful creation around her and began to have faith that a new life existed beyond these changes. She just let her instincts and the thoughts deep in her heart overcome the fears that threatened her very soul.

Then, as though growing arms, she began to reach upward, and she grew and grew, reaching for the warm sun and cotton puffs of clouds, growing stronger each day. She grew taller, and the lower part of her body penetrated deeper into the soil, giving her a great strength to stand tall in the light breeze. This enabled her to bend with the breeze and not break. She was now free of the lonely dirt, and she looked around and saw that there were many others like her growing as she was. She was not alone now, and she embraced their quiet company. They became her friends, and she cherished their companionship.

Far from the soil that was home for so long, she was now able to see beyond what was her life of dirt. Many new thoughts came to her that were very different, and she began to dream of what might be. The unknown of the future was now not so fearful since she now had some pleasant experiences. She began to look at the clouds of cotton against the bright blue sky and still wondered what was to become of her for she just knew that the changes were not complete and that there were more to come. Now she looked forward to the future, and the fear left her because of the faith that came to her with each day of growth. She trusted in the process, and it was good to just let go and let a Higher Power take her to new places, even though she knew not where.

Then one day she had another great feeling of growth and change like nothing before. The great bud that became her soul over the short time of her existence began to swell and stretch. This feeling again was new, and she was afraid. Her deeper penetration into the soil gave her the strength to dance in the light breeze as these mysterious feelings of growth continued. The bulge grew larger as each day passed, and she saw that all her growing friends were also bulging with this new and mysterious life.

Finally, after several cycles of the warm sun, her bud swelled so much that she began to split and explode into a beautiful delicate lightness that was a pastel blue flower. Her petals stretched as arms from a long sleep as she slowly rocked in the gentle breeze, and the sun turned her delicate blue petals into the shade of the sky. She could now see the rest of the world. All of her friends were bursting open with great color and fragrance. There were yellows and reds and all sorts of other colors, and they were all different yet holding a common home. She was no longer alone, and the excitement of this new life filled her heart. Yet she did not know what was to come.

She no longer had to fear being carried away by the birds and being stepped on, and she felt part of a greater meaning and community. She was a full and beautiful flower with a fragrance of great goodness.

She lived on the edge of the great garden, and her fragrance and color beckoned to the bees. Their busy attention visited her as well as her colorful friends. She gave to them the great gift of nectar, the sweet honey of life. She loved her role of giving, but as time passed, she grew very lonely for something else and did not know what. She still felt even stronger now that more came to her life. Her petals felt the pain of loneliness as they curled and closed at the start of each night of sleep and dreams. She could not understand this feeling of not being even with her busy days of giving life to the bees. And the nights grew long. She was still saddened by the aloneness that filled her being. Her petals would open to the morning sun with more aloneness, and it grew as each day passed.

Again, once upon the same time…

In a far-off land, a small egg fell upon a leaf and rolled into the grassy ground. After some moments in the sun, the egg began to change shape and seemed to struggle in a bulging motion. Then, as an escape from a lonely place, a tiny caterpillar popped out of the egg. He was wet with birth, and his blue fur began to dry in the warm summer day. He began to eat the grass and the leaves where he was born. He ate and ate and ate, and over the next days, he grew large and strong.

Over the next days, he explored this new world in great wonder, experiencing many new things and adventures. He loved to crawl to new places in the grass and lay in the warm sun. He became very adept at the challenges of life and was able to hide from the birds that would carry him away to their young. His blue fur shined in the sun like the sky that reflected his happy life, but something was missing. There just had to be more to life than nibbling leaves and rolling in the grass. There were few places that he had not been, and a new feeling grew in his heart with feelings of loneliness. The loneliness grew stronger each day, and he just knew that there was something else meant for him in this life beyond the life that he had come to know. But he did not know what.

Then one day he came across a bright yellow caterpillar eating and roaming in the grass. They looked at each other for some time and became friends. This softened the loneliness that each held since their births. They explored the many places around, they ate together, and their friendship deepened. The yellow caterpillar was older than the blue one and knew a little more about life.

Then on one bright day the yellow caterpillar seemed to be very distant and was not his usual eating and crawling self. There was a blank stare on his furry face and a glaze in his eyes as he crawled to a nearby bush. He climbed up to a lower limb and began to spin some silky stuff around his furry body. He continued until he was just a dull bag of silk with little to no color. And he was gone.

Many hours went by, and our little blue caterpillar became lonelier than before. He now had the experience of friendship, but that friendship was now gone, and he was even more alone again. The emptiness was unbearable, and he did not understand why his friend had left him. There was no reason that he could find or understand.

Then one day while crawling among the bushes, he began to feel a very strange motion deep within his body. He looked up and noticed two other caterpillars clinging to a branch while making some of the same stuff that his old yellow friend had. They saw him and beckoned him to join them in this great new adventure. He did not know what they were doing, but it looked like something he needed to do. But he was afraid to let go of the wonderful life he had come to love—the exploring and finding of new things of his great desires.

Somehow he knew deep inside that beyond the fear of making change, there may be a good life greater than the one he had now, but he had to let go of everything and turn his future over to his instincts. His old thinking of crawling had to go so that other thoughts could become part of his dreams. So he climbed upon one of the barren branches with great faith next to his new friends and saw them begin to disappear into their little hanging caves of silk. He did not know why, but a voice inside directed him, and he began to spin his own threads for himself. And it grew dark as time passed.

Slowly, in the darkness of his new place, he felt great changes but could not see what was happening. He could only trust his feelings and the example of his new friends, and something inside told him that this was good while he maintained the courage to change. And his place grew tighter and tighter with his change of shape, and he became more afraid.

Then one day his darkness began to break open, and while the light of the warm sun was shed upon him, he fell to a leaf as before. This time he felt very different, and began to look at what had happened to him. Now he no longer had the fur that he was so accustomed to, but instead he had a slender body and long graceful legs. He was still wet with the new birth of change, and when the sun warmed his body, great wings of blue and black began to unfold. They were beginning to take shape, and the beautiful blue was trimmed with black that shined as the wings dried. His wings had been tightly folded, and as they dried in the sun, they began to open and flatten. He stretched and stretched with a great new strength, and he was now a beautiful butterfly. He felt so different but good, and he did not question the life of his past crawling, which was a fast fading memory. He just accepted this new world, and it was exciting to him.

A short time passed, and he began to wave his lovely new wings as they continued to dry. The sky blue color of his wings sometimes glistened in the sun with the color of deep florescent purple. He was not sure of their function, but when he offered his newfound wings to the wind, he was carried into the air with an excitement and freedom he never experienced before. He did not have to crawl anymore; now he could fly. At first he was very frightened, but he soon learned to control his flight. He flew and flew and visited many places he could not visit before. His life had now become a daily adventure, but even after these great changes, he still felt in his heart that there must be more to life and that he was destined for greater things.

Then one day he came upon this great garden with hundreds of beautiful flowers, and their fragrance beckoned him to visit. He flew over the many colors and scents, moving in the soft wind, and he was pleased at this great place. The many colors filled his eyes with nature's beauty, and he flew and explored over the garden. He had many places he wanted to visit, for in all his time, he had never seen a more beautiful place. His heart raced with a new excitement, and he could not make a decision on where to visit.

Then, he saw a great sky blue vision at the edge of the garden. His heart jumped when he saw her petals and captured her wonderful fragrance. She beckoned to him with her beauty and softness as she waved in the gentle breeze. He had never seen such a beauty, and he flew to her.

He hovered over her, casting his shadow upon her soft petals, looking deep into her being. She looked up at him and sensually invited him to visit, and her petals became firm with anticipation. She knew of only the bees. She had never seen a sight as mysteriously beautiful as this new vision.

Taking her invitation, he hovered for some time, looking closer to her soul. Then, in a moment of trust and excitement, he landed gently on her delicate petals.

61

He looked deeply into her heart as he stayed with her and took of her nectar. She looked up at him so softly as she felt his gentle being upon her soul. He touched her inner being as she gave him the gift of life—pollen from her very soul to bring to others in the garden. Together they would start a new cycle of life.

With the courage to change, they were together at last and learned to give to others.

There is more to life.

Mama Cheetah

Few things are as strong in nature as the love of a mother for her offspring, and she will defend the safety of her children to the death, and do so many times. It is the great bond of love and sacrifice that provides the many societies with new life in the continuous cycle and challenges of nature. There is a multitude of examples in nature, but few will compare with the great sacrifice and hard work of the lone cheetah mother for her cub children. Their vulnerability to life's dangers bridges the very delicate balance between life and death. She is very alone and not part of any society.

Grace, as called by the naturalists and photographers, is a fine young female cheetah that was in her fifth season and starting the prime of her life. Last season, her first litter of two did not survive the birth process.

Of all the cheetahs on the plains, Grace was one of the finest hunters, and she had perfected her hunting technique to a graceful art. Her golden coat and crisp black spotting, combined with her sleek shape, made her a lovely vision while having the solid strength to survive the harsh rules of nature on the vast plains. She had a strong but gentle face, accented by very large crystal-like orange eyes. Her long, curved tail gave her balance when making sharp turns in speedy pursuits of fast running and turning prey. Her elegant paws had no retractable claws for stripping prey and defense as the other large felines did. Her paws were like those of the dogs of the plains, built for intense running speed. She was very vulnerable to many of the predators on the plains, and alertness combined with flashing speed was her only defense, which was held in a delicate balance.

Many evenings, she would sit on some of the plain's mounds, her sleek and tall shape majestically silhouetted against the large, red setting sun, keeping the sky from becoming lonely-looking. She would watch as the plain's residents bedded down for the night after the daytime, and, except for the giraffes, Grace's proportions seemed to make her the tallest on the flat plains. Most all of the creatures survived one more day, but a few would come up missing. The nightly chaos of the hyena's and lion's shouts and moans keep her on continuous guard. And the constant pulsating songs of the crickets and tree frogs gave a subtle peace to the long evenings. Grace had a good and prosperous life, but she was very lonely.

She had a great sense of how to avoid the relentless pursuit of the hyenas and strong lions that would often steal the spoils of her hunts. She would lie for hours during the afternoon heat under the great rain tree where the grass was thick and soft with nature's comfort. The rain tree was special. It was shaped like a large umbrella because of the elephants eating at the lower branches. The top was round, and the branches looked like lace against a blue sky or fire-colored sunset. The tree shaded the grass under to make it soft and long and not parched by the hot sun. It was a great and special place.

When the feeling of hunger came, she would leave the place of her daily comfort and go on the hunt as nature had meant her to do. One day when her stomach growled with emptiness, she slowly walked to the edge of the plains where the tall grass edged the flat dining table of lower grass, giving life to the many varieties of grazing residents. A large group of gazelles were lunching carefully in the short grass. The season had been unusually plentiful with the falling of new gazelle life. In just a few hours, dropped gazelle fawns would start walking and then jumping. Nature had protected them in this way so they could stay within the safety of the herd. While the gazelles grazed, their heads and large black eyes were always high on alert as their mouths chewed the grass quickly. They were the fastest runners on the prairie and were always able to keep out of the reach of the many predators on the plains such as the lions, leopards, and hyenas. They lived in constant caution while living their daily lives and each morning brought new challenges during their day of grazing and working to survive the harsh environment.

From her tall grass hideout, Grace saw the herd in the short grazing grass 100 yards away. There were males, females, and fawns. She studied with an intensity of concentration. She watched, and she was patient. Then she noticed a small male that she was attracted to for some mysterious reason, and her head moved forward, away from the rest of her body, with a concentrated look of intensity. Her eyes stared, shiny as crystal, clear with the background of bright orange. Her long curved tail was twitching in anticipation, with the bright white spot at the end of her tail blurring the top of the grass. She slowly moved in the tall grass toward her intended target. Slowly, watchfully, she slithered as a snake, and closer and closer she came. The young male gazelle did not notice her and continued to nibble quickly on the rich grazing grass.

She continued slowly until she was only thirty yards from her life-saving target. Her look and concentration intensified to an almost hypnotic stare. The great muscles in her legs and hips seemed to fill with a shaking, explosive power. She steadied and then thrust as a bullet, and in less than a second, was within fifteen yards of her prey. The male gazelle exploded with a bolt and had become a flash of motion. Grace knew that she had only a few seconds before she would heat with exhaustion and fail. Her very long strides were blinding and enhanced by the arching of her back that hinged for the extreme speeds. The chase went on with blinding speed, and the gazelle, expert at turning, directed the chase into flashing zigzags, raising clouds of dust to fill the prairie air. Grace kept on turning, bolting, using her long, large tail as the counterbalance in the extreme turns. Then, very close to the gazelle, she bolted one more time and tripped the hind legs from under her pursued. The gazelle fell and rolled over, trying to maintain balance, but he had to surrender to Grace's powerful inertia. Grace pinned the gazelle and put her classic choke on his neck.

The whole chase and downing took less than six seconds, but it seemed like an eternity of a lifetime in slow motion. Grace, while holding her prize in her strong jaws, panted and began to cool her overheated body. Her eyes seemed to pray thanks to the gazelle for giving his life so that she could live. This is the true great gift that nature has blessed the creatures of the world with; to give of one's life for the other is the greatest of all gifts.

Her panting slowed as she cooled, and now she began to think of her hunger. There were many black shadows of great buzzards circling high in the white cotton castles against the blue sky. They were signaling to the prairie residents that a kill had been made. She knew that she had to act quickly. Grace dragged her prize nearer to the tall grass, but before she could begin her feast, the chaotic sounds of a pack of hyenas filled the air. It was too late as they entered the scene without breaking a stride. Grace could not protect her life-giving prize and turned to reluctantly leave. She could not risk injury by one of the powerful hyena's jaws for she would die from any injury that compromised her powerful but delicate skill of speed. She surrendered to the gang and left, looking back woefully as she moved away from the scene. They savagely devoured the gazelle, tearing at it feverishly with selfish abandon.

She returned to her grassy place under the rain tree and rested from her run. The day's sun was beginning to blister the plains and those who lived there. She rested in the shade and slept cautiously, and as the sun passed midday, it became cooler. Her hunger woke her, and she began to think of the hunt again. She returned to the tall grass, and the gazelles were grazing cautiously as they do. Again she bolted, and her efforts again yielded success. She quickly had her fill and returned to her dwelling under the rain tree, full with new life-giving energy. Her midsection sagged with the spoils of the hunt.

Grace was in season for mating. Many males came by, and she promptly rejected their advances, as to be very selective.

Then "he" came. A strong and hearty male of eight years was he. He came to her, and she seemed to welcome him almost immediately. With nature's wonderful chemistry, they began to sensually bond in moments of togetherness. Closer they came, head to tail, slowly and gently gracing each other as they turned and turned. Her barks of approval chirped as he began to softly caress her with the side of his head. He cleaned the front of her rear legs with gentle strokes of his masculine tongue. He seemed to clean her everywhere, getting intimate with all of her being. She also cleaned him as to thank him for the feelings of good, and she softly relented to his loving closeness and caresses. They became as close as beings could be with a rhythm of nature's great gift of love. She softly barked with approval as they became close inside. He held her by the back of the neck, firmly but gently, as he made love to her.

After some moments, he rolled to his side with great feelings of pleasure. She rolled with him, and they rested together in the soft grass under the rain tree. Their front paws gently touched each other as they rolled, creating a playful atmosphere between the two. They enjoyed the company of each other after each being alone for so long.

It was two hours later when they came together again, first with the foreplay of their togetherness, then with the inside closeness of nature. They finished and rolled again with the satisfaction of an afterglow. It seemed as though they were deeply in love as he cleaned her. They were so close and loving, and it seemed as if this would go on forever after.

The sun lowered into the western edge of the plains with stark redness coloring the cloud wisps, and they curled softly together under the rain tree and slept together. This was surely of nature's loving peace.

The morning came, and they woke before the sun had vertically escaped the eastern horizon. They caressed each other again and came to be close inside again. And they rolled and rested together with a greater closeness than before.

Hunger came upon them before the midday heat, and they just seemed to know what needed to be done. Together they went to the edge of the tall grass to view and study the herd of gazelle. They seemed to melt their stalking concentration as one with perfect timing. Grace picked a target, and he was with her thoughts. Without looking at each other, they slithered closer to the unwary. Slowly, they crawled with intense stares. Their heads stayed stationary on a horizontal plane while silently advancing their position.

Grace bolted first, and he bolted slightly behind her on her left side. The gazelle exploded with motion, trying to stay ahead of Grace, then turned sharply left where "he" was waiting in full stride. And he extended his front paw with the classic cheetah trip, and Grace pounced, trapping the gazelle to the ground. She held on, praying thanks for the great gift of life. He sat patiently next to her and seemed to join in on the prayer. They quickly had their fill and returned to the soft comfort of the rain tree sanctuary.

Grace and her male partner rested and enjoyed the weight of their meal bulging from their streamlined bodies. The sun went down again with its usual fiery display through the wisp of high, thin clouds painted pastel with red. The sun returned after nighttime, and they began their dance of love again. And he cleaned her lovingly, and so did she to him. They were together many times during the lighted hours, and night came again with the serenade of the tree frogs and the crickets lulling them to sleep in their nested home.

In the early morning, Grace woke with a sense of great aloneness; he had left quietly in the night. She sat tall for what seemed to be hours, looking out over the prairie for her lost one, chirping her barks for him to return. She will no longer have the company of his caresses. She will no longer hunt and feed with him. She will no longer roll in the grass with him. Now she was alone again in quiet solitude.

Months passed, and Grace started to show the growth of her family. Her days were good, and she felt the strong presence of life within her. The sleek shape of her midsection was now growing and making her midsection sag slightly. She would roll in the grass with her paws pointed to the sky, enjoying the sometimes motion of her loved ones inside her and the warm sun on her chest and abdomen. She could feel the life move within her, which generated soft expressions of tenderness on her lovely face. Her eyes were large, clear and untouched by the thick brush thorns of the plains that have taken their painful toll on so many of the residents. The feelings of motion inside her seemed to make her love grow.

It was becoming difficult for her to hunt successfully now because of the added weight of her soon-to-be family. She had to work much harder to survive. She became so hungry at times that she would seem to despair in thoughts of not being able to make it. Days would slowly go by without any sacrifices of life from the gazelles. One day she had a great hunt and was able to take down a fine specimen. She filled herself to the point of pain for she knew that she would not be able to hunt for some time. She returned to her soft place under the rain tree.

That night the movement inside her became more active. As nature talked to her, she knew what to do. She moved to a secluded place in the brush and lay on her side in her anticipation of the coming event. The motion got stronger, and her motherly pain increased. She pushed and pushed for just a few moments, and then one little head appeared and came forth, then a second. They were brothers encased with birth, and she loved them so. She cleaned the wetness of birth lovingly as a mother would. They were so helpless as little balls of wet fur, and their eyes were closed while they shook clumsily with their new life, not knowing where they were. She cared for them and protected their vulnerability.

The brothers moved carelessly in no single direction and seemed to roll against each other in helpless confusion. As they slowly dried, Grace cared for them. After some time, their fur began to fluff into a delicate softness. Lying on her side, Grace watched as she cuddled them in a safe place near her. She began to direct their motion to her life-giving body, and they seemed to know what to do. She tightened her forelegs lovingly, and they found her tits swelled with life's great promise and need. The brothers connected to their newly found mother. She loved them as the feeling came all over her body from the giving soft release of her nature into her new children. And it was very good.

A week went by, and Grace was now painful with hunger. The new demands on her body strained her reserves, and the hunger pain grew to overcome her protection of the brothers. She curled and covered them, and, with their eyes still closed, they seemed to know that staying quiet and still was crucial. Grace left and went to the tall grass where she was so familiar. There were no gazelles grazing on the plain near the tall grass. She waited patiently for hours, but nothing showed. On her way back, she was able to catch a long-eared rabbit, and after taking the fur off, devoured it. That gift was not enough as she returned to the brothers who were still quiet and safe.

As the sun raised the next morning in the east to start the day, Grace felt a new hunger and now a weakness—a weakness that could tip the scales to her not providing for even herself. Her speed and cunning were of the utmost importance to her life and now to the life of the brothers. Again she left the hidden place with the brothers still, and she returned to the tall grass, then peered through a small opening.

The plain was full of gazelle in what seemed to be a new herd, and she watched carefully, slowly moving closer. Her intense concentration was above all as she moved closer and closer with careful stealth, but her body was weak. She slowly moved even closer, and at thirty yards, she darted toward her target, which was slow to bolt, and Grace made an almost immediate capture. She was not overheated this time for the very short run, and she gave thanks for the life that is given to the survival of her family. She acted quickly and devoured much before the sounds of the approaching hyenas penetrated the high grass. As the sound of their advance became louder, she abandoned what was left. She had her life-giving fill.

Weeks passed, and the eyes of the brothers were opened wide and contrasted the outline of their cute round ears. They were very alert, and sights of their surroundings delighted their keen curiosity. Over the next weeks, they began to tumble with each other and delight in the constant arrival of new adventures. A small tree frog unknowingly came by the front of the den and became an object of great wonder. They did not know how to proceed with this strange creature while it jumped to their amazement and delight. They carefully pawed it and jumped back with great anticipation of fear of their first encounter with another life.

The brothers were older now, and they came out of the den to explore their whole new world before them, complete with insects, plants, and rocks, all new to them. They explored intensely much of the morning and collapsed with exhaustion together in a ball. Grace looked on protectively. They slept, awoke, and began to satisfy their new hunger with Grace's giving love. They relaxed and explored again.

The days, weeks, and months went on, and the brothers grew to about one-half the size of Grace. She had taught them much of the lessons of life. Now it was time to teach them the greatest cheetah lessons—the lesson of the run and trip. Grace would capture a very young gazelle and gently bring it to the place under the rain tree. She would release the baby gazelle, and the brothers would chase and trip it many times. The baby gazelle was playing nature's great role of teacher, and Grace looked on with approval, making sure that the classroom stayed intact, and the teacher did not get away from the student hunters.

Grace began to take the brothers on hunting trips with her. In the tall grass, she would crouch in her famous stance, and they would mimic her, oh so clumsy and shaky. They were so cute with their baby hair still adorning the backs of their necks like a Mohawk Indian hairstyle. One day, on a hunt while Grace was close to her bolt, one of the brothers jumped prematurely, sending the entire herd scattering. He sat and looked dumbfounded and dejected, sitting alone on the short grass. Grace gently scolded him with quiet reserve, and another new lesson was learned.

More months passed, and now the brothers were almost to the shoulder height on their beloved mother and life giver. It was now a constant challenge to keep up with the growing appetites of her boys. When Grace bolted for the run, they would follow at great speed, honing their running skills. Each time they learned something new, and the mistakes they made were of the greatest of lessons and the basis for survival in their later years. They did not help; they were just nature's students of life. Grace had to work beyond her apparent abilities to keep up, and it would take her four or five runs to catch and keep a meal. It was hard work, but she managed with her courage and the talents that nature gave her.

More time passed, and the crowning baby hair on the backs of their necks became thinner and thinner, and now it was almost gone. They were now the size of Grace, and they joined actively in the stalk hunt and flashing runs. They had not been able to trip yet, but they soon learned the neck clutch and the prayer of thanks. Life for the family of three was good and plentiful. They were active in hunt and play, preparing for their lives to be.

It was eighteen months since their birth, and on a scarlet morning, the twins woke to the absence of their mother. She was not there. The emptiness under the rain tree grew with time, and the day passed without her return. They slept that night in quiet anticipation for the next day, and a deep loneliness they had never experienced before overcame them. The sun rose, and Grace still did not return. That night, as the scarlet sun lowered into the western horizon, they watched for their beloved mother and giver of life and its lessons. They called with their high-pitched cheetah barks over and over. The brothers sat on the mound that Grace so often adorned, silhouetted as one against its soft scarlet tenderness of the early evening. The next day Grace did not return, and the next, and the next.

Two weeks passed, and the pains of hunger overwhelmed their loneliness, and they left the familiar rain tree and went to the tall grass together as one. They peered and stalked as Grace had showed them so often, and their intensity grew the closer they came to the edge of the tall grass. Well before they arrived at the optimum bolting location, the herd sensed their presence and scattered in all directions. The brothers lunged onto the plain of emptiness. It had now been twenty days since they last ate, and the pains of hunger were, at best, overwhelming.

The next day, they returned to the tall grass and stalked the herd. This time they were about thirty yards apart. They both focused on their selected target, and they seemed to know which it was, as far apart as they were. They were within thirty yards, the optimal distance. They concentrated intensely, and in a sudden explosion, one of the brothers bolted toward the target, and the other followed in a split second. The gazelle twisted and turned, and in one sudden error, turned into the path of the second brother and was tripped. Both brothers held on with great pride and with the solemn look of thanksgiving. They cooled a few moments and began to feed.

Over the next two years, the brothers became great hunters of the plains and led a prosperous life. The memories of their giver of life, Grace, slowly faded as each day passed. They stayed close to the rain tree, and that became part of their territory, which they defended with earnest from other cheetah intruders. One cloud-filled day, they had traveled to the far side of the grazing plain in search of new territory and exploration. They were wary of the territories of other cheetah males who were also protecting their own sacred ground.

It was about 200 yards away when their keen eyes spotted a lone cheetah silhouette. They approached warily and closed the distance to a mere twenty yards. They looked and stared and looked. It was a beautiful female, and she seemed to be not afraid. They had encountered other cheetahs before with great difficulty and caution, but this was different. As they closed the distance between, their hearts raced with anticipation, and they began to realize that this was their beloved mother, Grace, of two years ago. Memories of the past and her lessons to them arose with great feelings of closeness. They met and chirped their cheetah barks in loving tones of excitement, and they moved with great tenderness, touching each other's heads and rubbing their bodies in a twisting circle of love.

Grace stayed with the brothers for two days, and they hunted together in great harmony. They slept under the great rain tree as they had done so often before. Their maturity of nature came together in peaceful moments of the days, and on the third morning, the brothers woke to find their mother once again gone as long before. And they were alone again. This time, their aloneness was not of fear, it was of the memories so cherished in their hearts. They now belonged to the world of nature.

It was of Grace's love, sacrifice, and example that gave the brothers their lives to survive on their own.

Close to God

A young woman was walking along a path in an ancient redwood forest where the lofty giant's origins went back over 2,000 years to when they were just the tiniest of all the tree seeds. The sun spread its rays through the tops of their majesty over the entire forest, and the air had a cool way about itself. As she walked, she saw a young man walking on the same path from the opposite direction. When he was closer, she could see his gentle and peaceful expression and felt no danger at his closing presence on the lonely path. Closer he came, and she saw that his eyes were of a pastel turquoise. Sometimes the sun's rays would shine on his face, and his smile was subtle with a comforting expression.

They walked toward each other and stopped in front of each other just a few feet apart without a word. She broke the silence by asking, "How do I get close to God?"

He replied, "That is easy. All you have to do are these three things.

"First, you follow the wonders of nature from the expanse of the universe to the crawling ants; the birds making nests and the animals of the plains following the instincts that Creation gave them to live. Enjoy the streams, fish, and rocks. Stop for the flowers and trees, and cherish them. These are surely the works of Creation of which we are just a small part.

"Second, you look for the good in other people.

"And third, you look for the good in yourself.

"Do these simple things, and you will become close to God."

Then they each continued on their walk, and when He was just a few steps behind her, He declared, "Enjoy My old trees for they love you, too."

She stopped, turned around, and He was gone, and so was the shuffle of His steps on the rocky path.

The Wooden Chain

A story based on true events, and the names have been changed.

Reno was a fine and good man of French Canadian descent. His parents and three brothers immigrated from a little town in Quebec Providence to a mill town thirty miles north of Boston in the mid 1930s. All of the boys were very handsome and popular in the local schools, and their parents encouraged them to study well and learn this new language. Reno was the youngest of the four boys, and he looked up to his brothers with great admiration. They all took good care of him. They were a modest and happy family, and they all worked hard to pay their way in life.

At 22, Reno grew to be a fine-looking man, and even at 5' 9", had broad shoulders and a slightly barreled chest. His face was sculpted slightly with the blood of Native American heritage so deep in the early history of the French Canadians. He was thin and trim and very popular with the girls. He was becoming a very good man who worked hard, prayed softly, and, with a playful spirit, was very social. His three brothers were either married or with a steady woman, and he longed to have that special woman in his life. Dating and being popular with the many local women did not fill his heart with the satisfaction that the close comfort of a soft woman could. He was very lonely and longed for a mutual commitment.

One Friday night, with a group of his friends, he went to the usual church dance, as he had often done. There was the usual bevy of people, and the band was playing some lively jitterbug music. Reno decided to get a soft drink before mixing in, and he went over to the drink counter where he immediately noticed a pale peach dress standing in line. Her shape was very beautiful, and he was very

75

attracted to her without even seeing her face. He slowly walked up to her from behind and said, "Hello there." She turned to face him, and his heart jumped with strong beats, flushing his face with surprise. Her lovely face and soft-looking body overcame his ability to talk. She had the most beautiful auburn hair, which flowed to her shoulders, and very bright hazel eyes. Her name was Yvonne, and she was from a little town on the Canadian border at the most northern part of Maine. She, too, was French Canadian.

Seven months later, they were married, and they spent their honeymoon days on Cape Cod. The beaches were warm and the water lovely, and they played in the glistening sand and loved each other. Within a year, they had a child and called him Peter. They were very much in love, and their time together flowed as a soft breeze. In the first moments of each day, they would bring Peter to bed with them and love him and touch his sweet little face, and Peter would smile and giggle with the love they gave him.

When Peter was only three, a great tragedy came to the togetherness in this household. Yvonne had developed a sickness, and her passing was very devastating to Reno. Peter did not understand where his mother had gone. When Reno went to work in the morning, he would take little Peter to Yvonne's sister's house. Claire was married and had two children herself, and she loved Peter. The look of her sister, Yvonne, on his little face gave her comfort for the beloved sister she had lost and missed.

Time had passed, and the bond between Reno and Peter grew. Reno spent many hours in the little shop at the back of the house. Reno was always working on all these projects that spawned in his creative mind, and Peter loved to watch and help. Reno was very careful to do projects that inspired his son's curiosity and imagination. He showed Peter how to make an electrical coil. They would wrap some wire around a heavy nail and apply an electrical current to the coil, and the nail magically became a magnet. The most special project was the carving of a great wooden chain from a single piece of wood. The chain links were about three inches long, and there were fourteen links, all connected without break and made of beautiful red mahogany. Reno carved an anchor to complete the chain, and it was very special when finished.

When Peter was 13, Reno started to date a very fine Irish woman by the name of Mary. They were married two years later, and, within a year, they started to build a new family together. There were four children, two boys and two girls. Peter loved his new family, and he played with the children for hours. And they loved Peter and looked up to him.

At 24, Peter met a wonderful Italian woman and, within a year, married her. They moved to California to build their own life together, and as the years passed, Peter was able, through business trips, to visit at least twice a year his family in New England. He was very successful as a sales executive for a large high-technology company.

Reno had always loved to drink beer, and he always had a can nearby. He never appeared to be drunk or nasty as so many do when drinking. In fact, he seemed even funnier and more loving when drinking in this way. He especially loved to play little tricks on the kids, and they would scream in delight and love him even more. He was always doing things for people, such as mowing the lawn for the elderly lady across the street. One Christmas, all the family got together and bought him a beautiful riding mower with all the bells and whistles. He even had a little place to keep his can of beer. When not riding through the neighborhood, he would work in wood, making things for other people. The carved wooden chain now became a symbol of his goodness as it hung in the family kitchen.

There were many gatherings of the family, especially during the holidays. Lots of food and drink garnished the togetherness. Many conversations were had over beer, wine, and whiskey. In spite of the drinking, there was never a harsh word that was ever noticed. The cunning mystery of alcohol had set its hooks in this new generation and was hidden deeply in their hearts, waiting for the next generations to receive its deadly grip and the ultimate fatal conclusion.

More time passed, and Peter's two children were off to college and starting their own lives. Peter maintained his contact with his dad, Reno, and they both looked forward to the times they would visit together. Peter treated Mary and Reno with trips to California, and they loved to sightsee along the coast and go into San Francisco. While the girls explored the local shops, Peter and his dad would find a comfortable bar or lounge to pass the time in conversation and refreshment. Reno always collected tourist magnets wherever they went, and they probably had the largest collection of magnets in the world on their refrigerator door at home, sparking daily memories of their many trips.

It was on a cool California Saturday afternoon in January when Peter answered the phone, and it was the youngest brother, Bob. Bob always had a spirited voice, but this time he was very monotone and solemn.

"Dad has become very ill, and we had to take him to the hospital." There was a dead moment of silence that seemed to last an eternity. Then Bob continued, "There may not be much time left." Peter immediately told Bob that he was coming right home and would probably be there tomorrow, Sunday morning.

The night flight across the country was very long with sadness. Peter could not sleep; his heart was very heavy with the times he had spent in his youth with his beloved father. He could not imagine his life without his dad and never imagined that this day would ever come.

He arrived in Boston in the daylight morning, rented a car, and drove north to the house of the family. Mary answered the door, and they exchanged looks without saying anything. And they hugged with great emotion.

"How bad is he?" asked Peter. Walking into the kitchen and sitting at the table, Mary told Peter of the failing condition of Reno. There was a long silence, and they began to tearfully share the great moments of the past with feelings of joy. Peter took the carved wooden chain that was hanging on the kitchen wall and shared the time that he watched his dad slowly and cleverly cut away the wood that was not needed, leaving this great piece of visible memory.

That evening, Mary, Peter, and the others all went to visit Reno. They were all crowded in the small hospital room with only two chairs and the smell of antiseptic. Reno, heavily medicated, was on dialysis. He would, from time to time, seem to mumble something that the family strained to hear but could not understand.

Then the doctor arrived to look in, and he checked the chart, then listened to Reno's heart. He walked toward the family. They all gathered around, and Mary asked what the prognosis was. The doctor softly and carefully replied, "Well, his kidneys are not functioning, nor is his liver. His heart is running at about 10-20 percent of its strength." Mary asked him if there was any chance, and the doctor said that there was little hope. Peter asked how much time Reno had, and the doctor replied, "A day, a week, maybe a month. But he will not know anything of this life during that time. He is fully unconscious and has no awareness. It is all those years of drinking that have caught up with him. You may want to consider disconnecting the treatments. He would go peacefully." And the doctor left.

There was a great silence in the room for many minutes. All the family members looked at each other with disbelief that this was really happening. Then the dreaded discussion reared its ugly head. The boys were in favor of disconnecting, the girls were not, and there was much sadness in the room. The subject was not discussed again.

An hour went by, and everybody left except Peter. He sat in one of the two chairs and visited with his beloved father. Then in a stroke of love, Peter pulled his chair close to his dad's bed and rested his head next to Reno with his mouth very close to his dad's ear. He took the limp hand of the man who gave him life and knowledge and began to softly whisper in his ear.

"Dad, I have always loved you, and you will always be in my heart. I thank you for my very life and for all the things that you taught me." Then Peter began to bring all the memories to his voice in great detail. "I remember the time you taught me about electricity with the coil magnet and all the plaster molds that we made." Peter continued on for a long time and sometimes with a weeping, shaking voice and a heavy heart. "I especially remember the time when you carved the great wooden chain. It is a symbol of your giving life." There were moments when Peter thought he felt his father's hand tighten gently in Peter's clutch. Peter felt that his dad could hear him. An hour passed, and Peter said goodbye to his father and left the hospital with a great feeling of closure.

Reno held on for many days, and Peter decided to return to California with the knowledge that he would be called if there were a change. On the flight back, there was much peaceful sadness in Peter's heart, but he still could not sleep. Six days later, on January 29 at 10:30 p.m., Peter's phone rang, and he just knew it was his brother Bob. He picked up the phone, and it was Bob. "Dad has just passed away." There was a moment of silence, and Peter said, "I'll come right home tonight. See you in the morning."

On the plane trip back to Boston, Peter had been suddenly hit with an amazing thought of fate. Peter was born January 30 at 1:30 a.m. in Massachusetts, East Coast time. The call from Bob had come in on January 29 at 10:30 p.m. Pacific Time; that was 1:30 a.m. East Coast time on January 30. Reno had passed away on the exact hour and day that Peter was born, 55 years prior. This was stunning to Peter, and he took comfort that a Great Spirit was looking over the love they had shared and that this was a clear message from a Higher Power of their love. With the comfort of this great message from his God, Peter fell asleep for the rest of the flight.

The funeral services were filled with over 400 people, most of whom were touched in some way by Reno's kindness over the years. All the children eulogized their father's life, sometimes with humor. All mentioned the great wooden chain that became the symbol of their father's life and that hung on the kitchen wall in the house of the family. While there was much sadness, there was also a great feeling of love. "We will miss him so. We will remember him so. We will always love him so," came from the children, and Mary hugged the moments with her heart.

Peter arrived in California three days later with the thoughts of his dad occupying much of his time. For two weeks, Peter could not relieve the pain of the loss, so he took some time off from work. He went to his wood shop and selected a fine piece of California redwood. He planned his thoughts and began to carve the wood away that would leave a great chain complete with anchor. It took eight days of careful work, and when it was finished, Peter hung it in his kitchen. It was beautiful and quite a conversation piece. "My dad taught me how to do this. It is carved out of a single piece of wood," Peter would always proudly exclaim to those who asked.

Today, Peter always remembers to thank his dad for his life and success. Many times, when Peter would be sitting down to eat, he would feel the presence of his dad inside him and felt that he was looking through the eyes of Reno. The love continued for many years. The great wooden chains kept in the kitchens of Reno and Peter keeps them together in peace and love.

Over the next years, all the children reflected on their own drinking habits and what drinking had done to their beloved father. They remembered the words from the doctor "in all those years of drinking," and they each moderated in their own time.

Breaking the "chain" of excessive drinking was the final gift that Reno gave to his children that future generations of their children would come to enjoy.

The Veluxion Hunt

Tom Crowley had just delivered 15 kilograms of Malarium to one of his best customers on the planet of Argon, the place of his birth, as he has done from the very start of his galaxy-wide enterprise. As always, he spent some good time on this planet, and again spent much of that time with his father-like friend, Gala. He always enjoyed the total hospitality he received and the many friends and families he had met over the years. Tom really knew how to give of himself, and this is what the Argonians liked so much about Tom's presence.

Tom was on Argon for a little more than three weeks when he received a message from Velux. The message received, as translated on his sub-space linguist, went as follows:

"Tom, we certainly miss your company as we really enjoyed your last stay. We would like you to return with an order for 60 kilograms of Malarium. We have a new project that requires much Malarium and are eager to start, and we are especially looking forward to seeing you."

Tom was delighted because he looked forward to returning to Velux. Their parting words at Tom's last visit were, "Time will heal your feelings. Come back to us, and we will make sure that you are safe in any of the other adventures that you may seek here." This and the exotic experience he had with the female Gorg rang in his memory and fueled his eagerness.

Tom decided to stay one more day on Argon before departing for Velux, a six-month's journey at the full power of *Odyssey IV*'s linear precession drive. The next day he bid farewell to his many friends and set *Odyssey IV*'s navigation system on the path to the planet of his fond and exciting memories. *Odyssey IV* took off slowly and went into full drive when clear of the Argonian atmosphere, speeding off in a flash, and instantly disappearing. As Tom moved toward the suspension chamber, his thoughts were of the feelings he remembered with the female Gorg. He was very curious as to what type of new experience he might encounter on this very gentle planet. He certainly hoped for another intense physical experience. As he went into full suspension, all thoughts of Velux were quickly lost.

Six months later, the suspension chamber woke Tom up, and he spent time recovering in the vibration chamber. Afterward, he went to the holographic navigation monitor to see that he was very close to Velux, and *Odyssey IV* was about to slow out of multiple light speed. As it did, he received landing coordinates from Velux with a very warm welcoming message. This gave him a good feeling and sparked eager excitement in his thoughts.

Tom was met by many of the friends that he made on the last trip including his best friend, the Minister of Energy. Again, they quickly disposed of the business that brought Tom to this place. In consideration for such a large order, Tom gave them an additional 20 percent discount as previously promised. Then it was off to the home of his host for a meal and some great company with a party that was planned prior to Tom's arrival. Tom was treated to his favorite, Veluxion sharp cheese and a glass of the clear drink laced with salt that he so loved and had enjoyed that fateful night with the Gorg. This time he felt safe, but he still anticipated a new adventure as suggested in the Veluxion's departing comments in his last visit.

Tom spent several days with his friends, having dinners and going to social events. He especially liked to dress in the very luxurious Velux clothing that felt so special on his skin. Tom was very reluctant to be so forward as to ask of what new adventure he could take part in, but he broke this ice by asking about the people he had met in the lower class part of the planet. This was where he had the last great adventure, and his host sensed this. At a social gathering, he introduced Tom to a very lovely Veluxion woman by the name of Esti.

She was very shapely and flowed when she walked with a gentle sway that directed her clothing to stay in harmony with the motion of walk and dance. She had very bright turquoise eyes that melted into her dark facial skin, and her short, very black hair complemented her exotic and sensual look. Her body seemed very athletic and toned, while very shapely. She reminded him of the many female athletes he had encountered over the years, but she was also very feminine with a softness that covered her athletic being. Her clothing draped over her body revealed much of her true shape. On occasion, during their many discussions, she would touch Tom's forearm sensually when making a conversational point. While Tom loved this, he was reluctant to take the liberty to do the same.

Esti felt that Tom was very attracted to her and wondered why he was not returning the affection she was showing him. Then she verbally opened up with some of the Veluxion romantic culture. "You know that here on Velux, woman love men who show their affection, especially soon after just meeting. We believe that it is a sign of feeling and intention. We believe that physical expression between two can lead to deep friendship that will last over time."

Tom was taken because he always had the opposite view of friends first with a flowing physical expression later. She continued, "A man who expresses himself physically to a woman is very desirable and will receive very special attention from a female. Veluxion women are well versed in the art of physical togetherness."

Tom started to open up and return physical affection to Esti. He became very excited and began to hope that they could end up as close friends after a physical sexual encounter. He was beginning to learn more about the Veluxion ways. Esti invited Tom to her place after the social event, and they spent a wonderful night of lovemaking.

The next morning, Esti treated Tom to a Veluxion breakfast, and they spent most of the morning talking about a montage of subjects, especially the social differences between Veluxions and Earth humans. After some time, Esti expressed that she was beginning to feel a great sense of friendship with Tom and expressed that she wanted to spend more time with him. Tom called his host and told him that he was going to spend some time with Esti and not to worry.

His host's reply was, "You are in very good hands. Esti is a very special woman, and I knew that you would get along just fine. I am very happy that you are experiencing a Veluxion woman such as Esti."

Late that afternoon, Esti and Tom decided to go out for a special dinner in what was known as a very romantic Veluxion eating place. When they arrived and Tom walked through the front door, he immediately noticed the very special atmosphere and the wonderful smooth Veluxion music echoing softly to every small corner. They were shown to a remote table by the usual gracious host. It was obvious Esti spent much time here for she seemed to acquire special attention from the host. Esti ordered the meals for both, and while waiting, they continued their diverse conversation.

As they talked, both Esti and Tom touched each other very gently, deepening their friendship. Tom began to query what Esti did for a profession, if anything. She smiled and explained that she was of the upper class and, as such, all her needs were taken care of. For excitement and sport, she finally revealed that she was sort

85

of a hunter of wild animals and took great pride in taking upper class Veluxions on hunting trips. This did not make sense to Tom because he had come to believe that Veluxions were very non-violent. He asked Esti why this was allowed on the gentle planet of Velux.

Esti replied with the following: "Oh, we don't hunt for the kill. We hunt for the sport. We would never think of killing an animal for sport. We use a special tube that shoots a dart containing a serum that immobilizes our prey safely for a time. The major animal that is very special to hunt is the Rotpar. It is a very smart and dangerous creature, and we must be very careful. Rotpars have killed some Veluxions, and we must be very alert on such a hunt." Later, Tom found out that Esti was the leading hunter of Rotpars on Velux and that she was always requested to lead the hunts for the very noble upper class. She was sort of a hero and legend, explaining the special attention that she always seemed to receive.

After a fine dinner, they returned to Esti's place, and she shared her trophies with Tom while trying to maintain a level of humility. Esti suggested that a Rotpar hunt would be a very special thing for them to do together and that this type of intense adventure would bond them closer together. Tom immediately agreed without understanding the significance of such an event. Esti immediately made arrangements for the hunt with some of the people who served to support the hunts with supplies. The hunt was to start in two days and last for two days or until a Rotpar was stunned and documented with a holographic image.

Two days later, Esti and Tom arrived at a very simple but luxurious building that was standing at the edge of what appeared to be a very dense rain forest. Tom had not seen this part of Velux before and was impressed with the abundance of plant life. The lodge was built on several five-meter-high metal stilts with only one entrance at the top and what appeared to be bars on the windows. It was a very sturdy-looking structure that compromised beauty and style for strength and security. This was a mystery to Tom. He had not seen such a building on Velux, and this type of structure certainly did not match the open architecture and gentle nature of the planet.

Tom and Esti climbed up a ladder to a small porch, entered the building, and were met by two short men of light color, almost pale green. Esti explained to Tom that they were from a land far off and were especially adept at providing support for Rotpar hunting expeditions. Esti learned much from them about the ways of the Rotpars, and she had become an adept Rotpar tracker. Tom was getting little pieces of information about the Rotpars that increased his curiosity with a twist, and he was becoming a little concerned. Tom asked Esti of the origin of the green men, and she told him that they were of another species on Velux. They lived on the other side of Velux and stayed in their geography by choice and culture. They were a very tough species.

That evening, the little green men, as Tom called them, made what turned out to be an exceptionally unusual and delicious meal. Tom had never tasted such treats and variety. There was a root of some type that was very tender and sweet, which was cooked on a hot flame and basted with a sharp-tasting dark brown paste like seasoning. They also mixed a combination of leafy kinds of plants with nuts and a very sour liquid that complemented the roots. What Tom liked the best was a meat similar to filet mignon that was very tender and juicy and seemed to dissolve as soon as it touched the saliva in his mouth. It was covered by a light white sauce that lasted slightly longer than the meat in the mouth. Then there was a small bowl of some very crunchy tidbits that were coated and cooked in sweet oil. The taste of these was a little pungent and the tidbits stayed with the palette for the entire meal. Tom was used to exotic foods, but in this case, he was afraid to ask what these were in an effort not to spoil his dinner.

After dinner, the green men completely disappeared, leaving Esti and Tom alone. They sat together on a very soft freeform couch covered in a scaly but extremely soft and flexible material. Esti began to touch Tom in all the sensitive places that she had learned to make him feel good. He returned the favor, and they continued for what seemed to be a very long time. During this time, they experienced all of their favorite physical connections and softly fell to sleep. When light broke through the barred open windows, Esti caressed Tom to awareness. After this special night together, she hugged Tom softly and expressed her growing friendship for him by cuddling softly.

Later the green men returned and made some wonderful food to start the day. Today was going to be the first day of the hunt. Tom was given a variety of appropriate clothing and a waist pack with food and water. On the belt of the pack was a series of slender cartridges that contained the serum to be used for the hunt. Tom was then given a long metal tubular item that was assembled with some very exotic wood that was beautifully carved. The workmanship and artistry was like nothing else Tom had seen, and Esti also pulled a like instrument from a heavily secured cabinet. She sat with Tom and instructed him on the operation of these beautiful devices. Tom had been on hunts before on other planets and was a good marksman. After some practice, it was evident that Tom was an expert marksman, and Esti loved this about Tom. She was a crack marksman herself, probably a little better than Tom. There arose a little competitive spirit between them that deepened their growing friendship further. Tom had never experienced this particular type of closeness and he was taken aback by these new feelings of a deep friendship connection.

87

Tom's curiosity about the Rotpars finally overcame his reluctance to ask, and he did. Esti was willing to tell all. She began, "Rotpars are a very ancient animal that predates the Veluxion race, and they once ruled Velux with their intelligence and cunning. When Veluxions evolved over the many years, they were the primary prey of the Rotpars. In many cases, Rotpars would and could capture Veluxions and use them as slaves." This reminded Tom of many of the ant species found throughout the galaxy. She continued, "However, the Veluxions were able to overcome the cunning nature of these ferocious predators and finally became superior as the dominant species. In the early days, Veluxions hunted and killed Rotpars almost to extinction, and were then able to advance in culture to today's level. Then, about 500 years ago, Rotpars mysteriously began to show up only in this rain forest. From afar, we keep very close watch on the Rotpars and make sure that they do not reproduce to any degree."

Esti then showed Tom a holograph of a Rotpar. It was about two meters tall (six feet) standing upright, and had a long, broad mouth full of small, sharp teeth in what appeared to be a double row both top and bottom. The forward-looking eyes suggested a higher intelligence. Its upper arms were smaller than expected with three fingers on each "hand." Its long but powerful legs suggested a fast running ability. Each foot had three strong, padded toes and a large, sharp, hooked claw that was used for killing and tearing apart prey. Its skin appeared to be scaly, but Esti said it was of a soft nature. Esti pointed out that they were very expert trackers and hunters in their own right.

Tom became very anxious about being in the vicinity of such a creature, but Esti assured Tom that she and the green men had encountered this creature several times, and the stun guns were very effective against the Rotpars. This was the excitement of the adventure, but Tom had a deep sense that this was not right and that he should back off and return home. He had a very bad feeling about this. Of all the adventures he encountered in the galaxy, this was the most questionable.

It was early midday when the four set out on their quest and challenge of the hunt. They would spend that night in the forest. Walking single file through the dense forest, one of the green men was in the lead, then there was Esti, then Tom and last, the second green man followed up the small procession. Both green men were expert in maneuvering through the dense forest, and they were very careful to be observant and cautious. The one taking the rear was careful to be especially observant of those who might follow.

They were out for just three hours when they came upon a newly created small clearing. The first green man gestured to those in the rear to stay back while

he explored the site for potential dangers. The second green man kept a sharp lookout around the other areas. Esti was brightly aware and watched the first green man as he carefully examined the site. He gestured to Esti with a few hand and face signals, and she responded with a bow of her head. She turned to Tom and exclaimed, "We are in luck. This is a Rotpar kill site. Apparently a large animal was killed and eaten here. Look at the many small pieces of broken bone on the ground. This is a sure sign that Rotpars have been feeding. Their jaws are very strong and crush bones to extract the nourishment inside."

The troop continued on very quietly, seeing other subtle signs of the Rotpars along the way. It was getting late, and the early evening was about to start making settling down a priority. While the green men began clearing for a small camp, Esti positioned three motion detectors around the periphery of the camp so as to ward off any intruders that may attempt to breach the camp. The sky began to darken slightly, and the group settled down to some food and drink. The climate was perfect, and the predictable weather required no shelter. The sky became totally dark, and the first green man took the initial watch.

It was about four hours into the evening when the second green man awoke to take his turn at the watch. There was a subtle quiet, and the first green man could not be found. The second green man then woke Esti and Tom immediately but quietly. Their most pungent fear was realized. A member of their team had been taken. They stood sharp, watching and listening carefully. Esti could not imagine how the Rotpars got past the motion sticks and why they had not come after the rest of the group. This just did not make sense, and she feared the Rotpars had figured out how to bypass the motion sticks and had some other objective in mind, such as slavery.

It was decided to carefully wait the night out with their serum guns readied, and each one of the three sat back-to-back together in a different direction so as to have a full 360 view. The light came slowly back, and revealed a small amount of blood where the green man had stood watch. This was a chilling reminder of the impending danger, and the second green man spent some time in what looked like a solemn spiritual ceremony near the capture site.

It was decided to return to the lodge because of this new impending and ill-understood danger. It would take at least four hours through the dense forest, and the three had to be on top alert along the entire path. The green man had indicated with a very worried look that something had changed with the Rotpars; something he or Esti did not understand. This was the first time someone had been taken from a Rotpar hunt. They carefully began their trek back to the lodge. The way was a little easier because the previous day's journey of cutting through the forest left a clear and easy path. All three were very alert and had their respective serum tubes fully loaded and ready to use.

It was about an hour into the forest when rustling noises of subtle motion came from the surrounding path, and it became evident as the three walked astutely. They knew that they were being watched and possibly stalked. The green man took special attention, and when the moment was right, he shot a serum dart into the forest on their left side. It hit its mark without the green man seeing his target. The Rotpar fell over a shrub and became limp very quickly. Now they were sure but did not know if there were more. They continued on very cautiously.

About an hour later, they heard the same type of rustling as before, but this time it was from both sides of their path. They were still about two hours from the safety of the lodge. Tom, walking second in the line, watched carefully in order to try to get a look. Esti and the green man's attention tightened as they walked, looking for an opportunity to take another shot. Tom caught a slight glimpse through the foliage and quickly took his shot to the right, and another Rotpar collapsed. Esti nodded with approval that Tom made the shot, and he felt that he had contributed to the group as they continued.

Soon after, a large noise in the foliage caught the attention of the three. They concentrated on trying to catch a glimpse for a shot, and in a flash, another Rotpar came from the other side, grabbed the green man, and made off with him into the foliage. The event happened so fast that a shot was not possible. Tom and Esti were stunned that the Rotpars could employ such a strategy. Esti had never seen this before, and this heightened her concern. They continued and were just 30 minutes away from the safety of the lodge when they heard the familiar rustling in the foliage. They stopped, readied their serum tubes, and stood back-to-back. The rustling stopped, and they continued. About five minutes from the lodge and without any warning, a Rotpar struck Esti and carried her off. Tom could not react fast enough. He then started to quickly continue on the path and kept thinking that this was too much to handle. This stopped being a sport when the first green man was taken, and Tom was now in a total panic.

Tom finally reached the edge of the rain forest that circled the lodge. He stopped and carefully scanned the area. He spotted a Rotpar to his right, made his shot, and, in the confusion, was able to make it to and up the lodge ladder. His heart was pounding as he pulled up the ladder. He now was safe but paralyzed by his fear, and he was very alone.

In the lodge there was a communicator used to call the home front, and it took Tom about an hour to figure out how to use this device. He was able to contact an official voice. He stated his predicament and was assured that help would be there in less than twenty minutes. Tom's thoughts now turned to Esti and the green men who were taken by the Rotpars. He kept a very careful eye on the edge of the rain forest in the direction from which he had come.

Ten minutes passed when the vegetation started to come alive, and to Tom's surprise, out popped Esti and the two green men. They were running hard. About 50 yards behind them a Rotpar emerged from the forest, chasing the three. They would not make the ladder. Tom raised his serum stick, carefully aimed, and took his shot. The dart hit squarely in the middle of the running creature's chest, and it slowed almost immediately, then fell to the ground. Another Rotpar emerged from the forest, but by this time, the three had made it to the ladder.

As Esti and the green men entered the lodge, Tom was stunned and delighted by their sudden appearance. The remaining Rotpar stopped below the lodge floor but could not get to his prey. Esti explained that they were lucky that the Rotpars were more interested with enslaving their prey than using them for food. The Rotpars had taken the serum sticks but did not understand that it was the darts on their belts that did the actual damage. One by one, Esti and the green men were able to stun most of the Rotpars by stabbing them, allowing the three to escape. They had expended all their darts when they had reached the edge of the forest. It was Tom's precise shooting that saved them, and the green men, usually without emotion, smiled as they patted and thanked Tom.

Esti gave Tom a long, sensual full body hug. She whispered in his ear, "Well, I guess this makes us best friends." Tom smiled with approval as the sound of the rescue vehicle called a Remmuh started to permeate the forest greenery. As the vehicle appeared, the sound frightened off the last Rotpar that had reached the retracted ladder.

As they were returning, the sound of quiet relief rose above the hum of the Remmuh. No one ventured a comment. As they arrived at their destination, the Minister of Energy Affairs met them. His grave expression as he met them expressed his concern for the welfare of his friends and servants.

That night, Tom and Esti spent the evening with good food and friendly exchanges. The respect for each other was evident, and it became a positive part of their relationship. As the night passed on, they hugged each other for some time, and the feelings of friendship between them were intense.

It was time for Tom to leave Velux. Esti and Tom's other friends were there to see him off. Esti put her hand on Tom's shoulder and remarked, "I hope that this experience did not spoil your view of Velux. We certainly wish to see you again, and you are always welcome as one of our own. You have become my best friend."

Before Tom entered *Odyssey IV* he turned and replied, "I look forward to coming back to see my special friends again. I especially cherish my friendship with you, Esti."

Tom entered *Odyssey IV* and took off to the upper atmosphere for the jump to multiple light speed. He set the guidance system for Eliet, a new planet that he had never been to. It is known that the Elietians, a very intelligent race, were of reptilian origin and not of primate origin. Tom had never experienced this culture, and he was very eager to get there.

After the jump to light speed and as he was entering the suspension chamber, he thought of the whole Rotpar experience and the relationship he had with Esti. The physical relationship that led to their deep friendship with her was very special; but most of all, he missed her company. She had become his very special friend. He went into a suspension sleep with the thoughts of Esti in his mind and heart, and thought about plans to return to Velux.

The Gift of Giving

Joseph was a successful merchant who was well respected in the city of Assisi in Northeast Italy and had many close friends who he socialized with much of his valuable free time. His social nature and giving personality contributed to his successful import and export business, and he spent many of his days discussing mid-19th century world and local events with his friends. He was a short man with dark black, curly hair with a few gray strands starting to show his age of 55. He had a spirited smile that made people who associated with him very comfortable. He was a very gentle and gracious man.

Joseph, being a generous man, contributed much to the community and was known to make loans to people in need. Those who could would pay him back. Those who could not, the loans were somehow forgotten. His closeness to the friar of the local Franciscan Church was his closest and most generous relationship. The friar spent much time with Joseph in the years past, comforting him on the death of Joseph's beloved wife who died eighteen years ago during the birth of Anthony, the youngest of three boys. The two oldest were eight and ten years old when Anthony was born, and they had the benefit of a mother in their early years.

Over the years, Joseph's sadness for the loss of his wife turned to guilt, and he compensated for this guilt by being overly generous and spoiling his youngest son, Anthony. He tried to make Anthony feel better by allowing him his way most of the time, and, unlike the two older boys, giving in to Anthony's constant demands from the very beginning of his youth. Anthony was always forcing negotiations on his father and usually getting his way since a very early age. By the time Anthony was eighteen, the two older brothers had started their families and were making a good living as merchants. Anthony now lived alone at home with his father, and the two were in constant conflict. This was the only bleak time of Joseph's daily life.

Joseph was always protecting and making excuses for his son's behavior in the community, and the good friar made a special effort to counsel his good friend on the art of being a good father. Anthony would come home late many of the evenings, drunk and stained with wine, and he would not acknowledge the soft questions from his dad; he just went to bed. In the mornings after such a night, Anthony would accuse his father of not taking proper care of him and continually reminded his father that he was different because he did not have a mother. This always went to the core of Joseph's guilt, and he did not know how to handle or respond to these accusations. Anthony knew how to use his father's emotions to accomplish what he wanted. Anthony also felt that he was required to live up to the successful ways of his brothers, and this caused much friction between the brothers and deepened Anthony's insecurity, fueling his misbehavior.

As Anthony became older and his indiscretions in the community became more serious, local officials began to express concern to Joseph about his wayward son. Everybody went out of their way to understand and give Anthony a wide berth for his actions, and as they did, his behavior became worse.

It was two hours after sunset one starlit evening, and Anthony had much to drink in his usual way and was particularly in a negative mood, feeling sorry for himself for some made-up indiscretion by others. In the local drinking place, he was sitting at a table with a new lady friend when he began to raise his voice and abuse her verbally. He then grabbed her and began to shake her violently until she slipped out of his hands and fell to the floor. On the way to the floor, she hit her head on the arm of her chair and severely cut her forehead. As she laid on the floor unconscious, the owner of the drinking place sent for the officials and the town doctor. Anthony sat solemnly in his chair with his head in his hands, not saying a word.

In a few moments, the officials arrived and shortly after, the doctor. He immediately started to examine the young lady as she started to awaken with blood running from her forehead. Ultimately, she would recover, but she would have the scar on her face for the rest of her life. The officials, after talking to the owner, took Anthony into custody and brought him to the local jail of only one modest dirty cell; then they sent for Joseph, who arrived in a matter of minutes. Joseph was able to talk the officials into letting Anthony come home in his custody after promising to be responsible for the actions of his son.

It was four weeks later and the district magistrate, who was an old friend of Joseph's, came to Assisi to preside over the trial of the young and now humiliated Anthony. The night before the trial, Joseph stayed with his long-time legal friend, and he pleaded for his son to get the mercy of the court. After some long and compassionate discussions, it was decided that Anthony would be sent to a small island off the coast of Greece to live with Joseph's younger sister and her Greek husband. It was a small island of 2,000 people, and it was self-sufficient with its own agriculture. This remote island would isolate Anthony in a place that would provide little opportunity to get into trouble. He would have no way to come home and cause more trouble, and this just might make Anthony a little more humane.

The sailing ship taking Anthony to his new home was a fast two-mast schooner that carried tea and spices to the traders around the Mediterranean. The captain was a long-time friend and business partner to Joseph, and he promised to make sure that Anthony was delivered intact. The accommodations on the schooner were modest with none of the comforts that Anthony had become used to at home. He became very angry about his new situation and vowed never to speak of his father again. His only thoughts were of how everybody had treated him over the years and how much it was their fault for his unhappiness. He spent most of his travel time looking over the rail of the schooner, blaming other people for his own self-centered ways.

It was after score of days on the Mediterranean waters when the schooner arrived at the small Greek island and carefully docked at the only pier setting out into the peaceful harbor spotted with many white and red fishing boats. A local merchant and the many others who were expecting the long-awaited spices, teas, and assorted communications from distant places met the schooner with great anticipation. Anthony grabbed his only bag off the boat deck and left from his seaward "prison," looking for those he expected to meet him. He wandered among the small crowd and no one came forward for him, and he started to become very apprehensive in this unknown place. He waited for what seemed an hour and walked slowly down a cobblestone street into the small town that seemed to be the center of activities. He was now alone for the first time in his life and left to his own resources. He stopped and asked where the people who were to meet him lived and where they might be. He was directed by an abrupt old man to a small, rough, rock-strewn road and was told that their residence and farm was about five miles up that road, almost to the northern tip of the island.

The road was very rough for walking, and the weight of his bag did not help his balance and strength. It was very close to dusk, and he began to hurry his walk so that he would not get caught on the road without light. After about ninety minutes he came to a hill on the road where he could see a small house and what appeared to be a farm profiling the now very dim horizon. He hurried, anxious to get to his destination before complete darkness. Darkness did come, and the only guide he had was a dim light coming from the small house in the distance. Many times he tripped, and one time he tore his pants badly, scraping his knee on some of the road rocks.

Anthony had become very tired, lonely, and hungry, which added to his frustration and desperation. He had never been this alone or on his own before, and thoughts of an uncertain future rambled in his scattered mind. He arrived at the house of his destination and, stepping up the stairs, knocked on the door.

Mary, a soft-spoken woman, answered the door. She was Joseph's sister and had his giving and gentle ways. She smiled wildly, hugged Anthony, and called loudly to her Greek husband of twenty-five years to come and see. John welcomed Anthony with a sharp, "Where have you been, boy? We have been expecting you hours ago." John took Anthony's bag to an almost ladder-like staircase. "You can put your things up there, and you will find a place to sleep," John offered.

Mary had never seen her brother's son, and she continued to rub his hair and squeeze his cheeks as you would with a small boy. "You look so much like your father did when he was your age. I am so pleased that you have come to stay with us."

Mary and John had been childless after the death of their first son at birth. Mary welcomed the opportunity to be a mother of sorts to Anthony for a period of time. She offered Anthony some wonderful ground lamb that had been seasoned and pressed, some seasoned baked eggplant, and a large piece of flat bread with some homemade country wine.

After Anthony had finished his meal with delight, John began to question him regarding his home life. "So what did you do at home to earn your keep? I heard that your brothers are business people and are doing well as hard-working merchants."

Anthony replied in an offhand manner that he was his father's assistant and was going to take over the merchant business. He then asked to be excused to go to bed.

The next morning before the crow of the rooster, Anthony was awakened by the noise of breakfast and the getting ready for the usual day's work. He stayed asleep until an hour after the rising of the warm sun. Then, when he was sure that John was well outside and not likely to return for some time, he climbed down the awkward stairs to the kitchen where there were fine smells of cookery waiting to be consumed. Mary hugged Anthony, reiterated how nice it was that he was here, and graciously invited him to sit for breakfast. He did and had a fine fill of the best home-cooked food he could remember. Mary sat with him at the modest table, and she told Anthony that John wanted to see him in the large garden after breakfast.

Anthony walked slowly out the front door and was now able to see the entire farm. It was artistically and cleanly cared for. From the porch, to his left was a large neatly rowed garden of a multitude of vegetables. To his right was a rolling field spotted with sheep. To the far left was a small barn fronted with a large bookshelf of roosting nests for the chickens to lay. As Anthony moved to the left side of the porch and house, the northern coast began to unfold in his sight. From the advantage of the house perched on the top of the hill, he was able to pan 360 degrees of the horizon in which he could almost see the curvature of the Earth. It was a beautiful and peaceful place with only the sounds of the farm animals breaking the eerie silence of the countryside.

John was working in the garden and hollered to Anthony to join him. "So, you are here. Tomorrow we will start your chores to earn your way with us. Take today to explore the fields and farm." Anthony did explore the area and vowed that he was not going to stoop so low as to do chores, especially cleaning the chicken roosts. He never had and was not about to do so now. He found a large rock on the north side of the farm and sat looking over the ocean, dreaming of the great world adventures that better deserved his talents and attentions. Later he fell asleep in the warm early afternoon.

The next morning just before the early light, Anthony was starkly awaken by John with a hearty kick to Anthony's feet. "Time to start the day with breakfast and a prayer before we go to work. You get up now!" Anthony was startled, rubbed his sandy eyes, and rolled out of bed. He dressed, gingerly climbed down the stairs, and joined John at the table. John did not say a word while eating, and the silence during the feeding was ominous to both. It was a very uncomfortable feeling for Anthony because John was not catering to his emotional needs.

John broke the silence with, "Today I'll show you what chores you will have to earn your keep with us. Come with me now, and I'll show you." John got up from the table and walked out the door. Anthony was slow to follow.

John took Anthony over to the neatly aligned book shelf chicken roosts and showed him how to collect the eggs and afterward how to clean the chicken roosts of smelly droppings. Other chores included filling the food and water troughs, pulling weeds in the garden, tying the tomato plants, cleaning the small barn floor, and many other small items of effort. There was much wood to split and fences to repair. The list seemed to be endless.

Anthony poked at a few of the chores, thinking that this was very beneath his stature in life. John worked in the sheep field, and when he disappeared over the hill, Anthony took the opportunity to head over to his resting rock, north of the farmhouse. In a few minutes he was asleep in the warm sun. An hour later, John returned from the fields. He could not find Anthony and saw that the assigned work was not done. He looked and found Anthony in his sleeping place, and placing the bottom of his foot on Anthony's leg, gave a hearty push. "Wake up, you lazy boy. You won't get supper this way."

This went on for three days and finally John, at wits end, told Anthony that if he did not shape up, he would have to leave. The two argued for a time, and a frustrated Anthony went to his sleeping place, packed his bag, and exclaimed, "I am leaving and won't come back." Mary was broken-hearted at the prospects of losing her new son.

John shouted to Anthony while shaking his fist that if he left now, he never could come back. Anthony started walking down the road expecting a "Please come back," but he never got one. He walked down to the small town, wondering what he was to do. He was sure that he could find someone that would take him in for at least a few days. As he approached the town, he saw a small church with a neatly placed cottage-like building in the back. He went to the door and knocked, and a short, dark, curly-haired priest answered and offered Anthony to come in. Anthony told the priest his version of the story. The priest was gracious, and told Anthony that he could stay just for tonight. Anthony was relieved for he just knew that he would fine someone to help him.

The next morning, the priest served Anthony some gruel-like cereal that had a very musty smell and taste. It was not what Anthony was accustomed to, and while Anthony was eating his fill slowly, the priest explained to him that he could not stay here because the bishop would not allow it. Anthony left with his bag over his shoulder and headed to the center of town. It was fully awakened with the activity of the day, and the locals started to emerge for their daily doings. Anthony was a stranger, and the locals noticed and wished him a "good morning." He felt a little better and went down to the pier that was his first welcome to this place of serenity. He sat on the same rock wall as he had done on the day of his arrival and began to think of what he might do and where he could stay during the night.

Leaning against his bag, he fell asleep with his thoughts, and when the sun was at its highest point, his growling stomach woke him in a start. He began to walk back into the town and took a closer look at some of the shops and house fronts. He passed by what appeared to be a shop that sold metal goods such as cooking pans, metal containers, hammers, hoes, and such. There was a fabric and candle shop next to what appeared to be a food shop. He stopped and went into the food shop and saw a short, smiling woman behind a small, thin counter. There were cheeses, hams, sausages, bacon, salt pork, etc.—some displayed in the cases and some hanging from the ceiling. There was a large bin of fresh bread by the counter. All the smells came to Anthony's nose and amplified his hunger.

"May I help you, young man?" the woman queried. "Do you see something of your favor?"

After looking for some time as if trying to decide, Anthony replied, "I would like some ham and bread." He did not have any money to pay for what he asked for, and his merchant host sensed his poor condition of the moment.

"How will you pay for this?" the lady said with a doubtful tone. "Do you have money?"

"Not yet, but I am expecting much money from my father who is in Assisi," replied Anthony in a confidant and knowing voice.

"Well, if you have no money, you can do what others here in the village do and exchange for something you have of value like a chicken, or eggs, or vegetables. Everybody who lives here contributes to the welfare of others in the village as exchange for what they need. What do you have of value?"

Anthony thought for a moment and, removing a silver frame from his bag, replied, "I have this fancy picture frame."

"I have no need for an item of such. I do have some work that needs to be done behind my shop. If you work for two hours, I will give you some bread, ham, cheese, olives, and tomatoes for your lunch."

Anthony's hunger drove him to agree, and he went to work. He was able to complete his tasks in less than two hours, and he reported back for his lunch that was waiting for him on the counter. After having his fill, he thanked his benefactor and left the food shop. He walked for about twenty minutes, exploring the entire town, and there was not much else to see or do, so he went back to the church where he first stayed, just to seek the company of the priest who befriended him that morning.

Anthony knocked on the door of the small cottage, and when the door opened, he immediately exclaimed, "I am not here to stay or eat. I am here to talk of my loneliness." The priest immediately pointed to a neatly trimmed garden on the side of the church for a place to walk and talk. Anthony told the priest of his fear of the situation and did not know what to do and how he would survive. They walked and talked for about an hour, and when they returned to the front of the small cottage, the priest passionately advised Anthony that he should start learning to give instead of taking and that he should think in terms of serving and not being served. Most of all, give openly of his self.

Anthony did not really understand these thoughts that were so alien to his basic nature and past behavior. He picked up his bag and walked back to the stone wall near the pier of his first coming. There were only a few fishermen cleaning the bottoms of their white and red boats and mending nets. It was late afternoon and Anthony, feeling a slight yawn, set his bag down by the wall and settled down to a comfortable position and was soon asleep. He awoke at the time of dusk to a sore back and an empty stomach. He jumped up and went directly to the food store, hoping to get some food for work. It was closed as were all the other shops. There was no one in the streets, and in the darkness, he realized that he was very alone again. His mind had nothing to do but feel a deep feeling of loneliness and self sorrow. He returned to the wall, dropped his bag, and tried to fall asleep, but the continual rotation of the fears in his mind and his hungry stomach kept him from falling off for some time. And he was desolate.

It was late morning when he awoke to the sounds of the fishermen getting ready for their day of gathering fish from the sea. He grabbed his bag as he had so often and returned to the food store, offering to work for food. There was no need for work, but the soft shopkeeper pointed to the metal shop, advising him that there might be some work there.

Anthony went directly to the metal shop decorated with hanging pots, pans, and tools of all types neatly arranged on some of the shelves.

"Hello, I will work for food if you have need," Anthony remarked sheepishly. The metal merchant indicated that he had many iron pans and pots that needed curing and that he would be pleased to share his robust lunch with him in exchange for the work. It took Anthony three full hours of hard work with the hot oil used to cure the cast metal. It was heavy and hot work over a smoky outside stove fire. When finished, the metal merchant offered Anthony the chance to clean up the soot mixed with oil that painted his body over by the water pump and trough. Anthony did so and reported eagerly to this benefactor for his long-awaited lunch longed for since his awakening.

He sat with the metal merchant and was treated with a vast assortment of tasty morsels. The merchant, interested in Anthony's roots, queried about his home of origin and how he came to this small island. Anthony told him that his mother had died at birth and that his father was a great merchant homed in Assisi. He added that he, tired of the merchant life, came to this island to begin a new way of life. While this did not make sense to the merchant, he accepted Anthony's strange reasoning. Anthony liked the nature of this man and was comfortable with his gentle nature and wise ways.

After two hours of open conversation and food, Anthony left to return to his wall by the pier. His mind began to think of the reality that he had made for himself and thought of the blame he had for his father sending him here. The fishermen were returning from their day of gathering in the clear waters past the inside harbor. Curious, Anthony slowly walked to them as they unloaded their catch with manly actions and quiet song. They were smiling and singing for their success of the day.

Anthony announced himself with, "Hello. That sure is a lot of fish. Where do you bring it?"

"These are for the people of the village," was the proud reply. "And who might you be?"

"My name is Anthony, and I am from Assisi. I have been working here for some of the merchants in exchange for food."

"Well, we might have some work for you tomorrow. Come to us and we'll see," replied the fishermen. "We have lots of work for a young, strong man like you. In the meantime, here is some bread and dried fish for your dinner."

Anthony was delighted, and he started to see how he might manage with his life. He eagerly ate the fish and bread and settled down against the wall to sleep. The noise of the ocean waves splashing onto the shore was in perfect rhythm of a lullaby that soothed him to sleep, something he had not noticed before.

Over the next four days, Anthony was able to acquire the "contracts" of several of the merchants and quickly developed the reputation of being a quality and efficient worker. They were always pleased to provide Anthony with much-needed food as consideration of his efforts. Each night he returned to the now familiar stone wall that had become his home at night.

On the fifth day, the metal merchant, knowing of Anthony's plight, brought Anthony to a small shack in the back of his shop. It was about twelve by fourteen feet, had a dirt floor, and only a knee-high large shelf furnished the sparse domain.

"You can stay here at night instead of at the stone wall," offered the shopkeeper. Anthony was stunned as well as grateful and promised to work hard for the favor. Later, one of the other shopkeepers gave Anthony an old quilt that was heavy enough to use as a mattress and blanket for the now cooler evenings. An old bent pan served as a wash place with water from the hand pump, and Anthony could now wash regularly, making him a little more pleasant to be around.

That night Anthony fell asleep in his new home with great comfort as compared to the wall. He used the shelf as a bed and placed his bag under the shelf. Morning came and he awoke without the usual pains of sleeping in the open by the stone wall. He hurried to his normal chores that the shopkeepers had become used to, and they were grateful for the pleasant nature of Anthony, who was now growing graciousness. His humiliating situation and the need to survive made him a more agreeable person. He now had a means that occupied much of his thinking, and he thought of ways to make his chores more efficient and how to please the merchants he served. He did this on occasion and was rewarded with extra items of use.

It was two months past when a large, three-mast schooner docked at the pier. Anthony followed many of the merchants to the pier, and they were eager to receive things that were ordered months ago. Anthony stood by the commotion, feeling part of the activity. He offered to help two of the merchants carry goods back to their shops. This was outside his usual chores, and he did not ask for anything in return. He just joined in with the joy of the arrival and the break in the usual monotony of the village.

Upon returning to the pier from his first trip to the metal shop, he could not help but notice a dark-haired woman departing the ship. She was of about thirty years, some seven years older than Anthony. She was dressed in soft beige lace, which provided a contrast to her long, curly, beautiful hair. He could not remove his eyes from the surprise of her presence.

Later he found out that her name was Alonna and that she was the sister of the candle and fabric merchant. Her husband of twelve years died of a sickness, and she was returning here to her home from Italy. She was childless. That night her image danced in his head as he fell asleep with the thoughts of her beauty and his anticipation of meeting her some day.

Anthony woke up at dawn and began to take extra care cleaning and shaving. He had some better pants and shirt other than his normal work clothes.

and he tried to comb his hair with his fingers the best he could. He had some salt to gargle for his morning breath, and he took all the care he could to make himself presentable. Leaving his modest shack, he casually hurried to the candle and fabric shop.

His friend, the candle merchant, was dusting some shelves while in conversation with her sister Alonna when Anthony casually opened the door of the shop. He pretended not to notice Alonna when asking, "Do you have anything for me today?"

"No, not today," she replied. "Try tomorrow. By the way, have you met my younger sister, Alonna? She has come back from Italy to live here with us."

Raising his eyebrows in surprise, he exclaimed, "No, I have not. I am Anthony and very pleased to meet you."

With a great smile and extending her hand, "I am Alonna, and it's very nice to meet you."

The tension in the air was like a romantic play with all the blushing and uncertain questions between the two. Anthony finally left after much small talk with Alonna and went on with his duties of the day. That day he worked for the fishermen cleaning boat bottoms, and he was given a large quantity of fish, bread, and some clams that just had been steamed in seaweed and garlic. He returned to his stone wall and sat down to eat his cache, and his thoughts turned to his time in the morning with Alonna.

In a start, a soft voice behind him gently found his ears, "Hello there, again." Anthony turned, and it was Alonna who had come to the pier area to enjoy some of the sea breeze and the soon-to-be-setting sun. "May I join you?"

"Of course, I would like that," replied Anthony with a great smile.

They talked of things until well after dusk, and the coolness reminded them that it had become late. Their mutual interest in each other flourished in this short time, and what initially appeared to be a potential romantic relationship turned instead to a strong friendship. They spent many more times together in friendship, and Anthony developed deep feelings with the metal merchant and gracious priest as well. Over the next few months, the relationships flourished to Anthony's great pleasure and comfort, for this was a new experience for him.

Occasionally, his Uncle John and Aunt Mary would come to town to bring eggs, chickens, and goats in trade for items such as cloth, candles, wheat, spices, and such. Anthony had made his amends to his Uncle John a few weeks past and a fondness was now beginning to develop between them; Mary was delighted.

Five years had passed, and Anthony had developed quite a life in the small town. His friendships grew deeper and with many more people. His conversations with others turned from small talk to thoughts of comfort and wisdom that came to him naturally. He would often do unseen favors for people he cared for without any expectations of being recognized for his efforts, and he tried to do at least one small thing for someone each day—like the time he split a cord of wood for Alonna and her sister. He had also fixed up his little room to be quite comfortable, clean, and neat.

He had come to love the wisdom of the metal merchant, the spirituality of the priest, and the soft comfort of Alonna. More years rolled by and Anthony's graciousness, generosity, and gentleness grew. Many of the townspeople would come to Anthony for advice, and his place in the town became that of a leader, friend, and comforter. His ability to give of himself made him very popular, and his priest friend would often seek conversations with him. His mutual love for Alonna grew very deep without being physically romantic.

It was one day on the fifteenth year of Anthony's arrival to the island that a small schooner arrived with the usual treasures of long-awaited items. Many of the townspeople went to meet the boat as usual. The boat docked, and as packages were unloaded, the captain approached Anthony. He had an envelope in his hand that had Anthony's name on it in large letters. It was a carefully written note from his father that read,

"I have heard of the life that you have built for yourself over these years, and I am certainly very proud of you. I have always been able to see the goodness in you. I have been ill and not been able to work as much as in the past, but my many friends have been able to help me along. I do love you as my son and would hope that you understand why I sent you away. It may be time for you to return home, if you have a mind to.

"Your Loving Father."

The words brought tears to Anthony's eyes as he put the note into his pocket. Alonna came to his side to comfort his troubled expression and body language. She sensed his feelings as she usually could and touched his shoulder and the back of his neck softly without saying a word. In a bolt, Anthony ran to get a pen and paper to write a note back to his beloved father.

"Father, I am well and have become very happy. I felt the love in your words to me, and I now realize that you have always loved me. I will return on the next boat to Assisi. It is time for me to come home.

"Anthony"

He handed the sealed note to the captain for delivery to Assisi.

It would be two months for the next ship scheduled for Assisi, and Anthony had much time to prepare for the departure from his beloved friends. He worked as usual, helping whom he could with all his earnest and without claim of reward. His modest ways grew deeper as time for his leaving became closer.

The day before the expected arrival of his ship home, he traveled the five-mile road to John and Mary's farm. He stayed that night and enjoyed their company, exchanging the many of the last fifteen year's memories over some delightful food. At the break of dawn, he slowly finished his breakfast in the company of the two who first welcomed him in and who he had treated so selfishly. The time to leave had come, and he did not want to miss his place on the boat to his distant home. Leaving the farm porch, he turned to the rock where he had spent so much of his time. It was a great place in nature that overlooked the harbor. In the distance he could see the white sails of his transportation entering the harbor, and with great reluctance, he left down the rocky road to the town.

He went directly to the familiar pier in time to see the schooner tie up. He waited patiently for the business of the ship to clear before he boarded to check on his reservations. His berth was reserved and paid for in advance, probably by his father. The ship was to leave on the morning tide, which would give Anthony some time to bid his farewells to those people he had learned to love and serve over the years.

When he turned to leave the boat and prepare for his departure tomorrow, he saw a large crowd gathering by the stone wall led by Alonna, the metal merchant, and the priest. It seemed as though the entire town was there. As he walked down the pier toward the crowd, they approached and started to encircle him with soft talk and compassion. Anthony in a slow, quiet voice asked, "Why are you here? Why do you come to this place?"

Alonna replied with a soft smile and loving voice, "We have all come here to honor your stay with us and to tell you of the love we have for you. You have given us much over the years, and we wish to tell you of what is in our hearts for your goodness."

Anthony was stunned. He had never realized in all these years how people felt in spite of their actions to show him.

"But I have given you nothing of this world. I have no money or possessions beyond what is in my modest home. What have I given that takes such a place in your hearts?"

Alonna began, "You have given us of yourself. You have been honest with your feelings, and you have comforted us in our times of pain. You always tried to understand us rather than be understood of yourself."

The metal merchant added, "You have kept me company and talked with me of the many worldly matters. I have come to expect seeing you during the day, and now I will not have that privilege. I will miss your company."

The priest continued, "And you have shown us the way to true humility and a love for the small things in life."

Many of the others gathered around and expressed those things that he had given them. Anthony was astonished at all this attention and was greatly moved by their words. These were the greatest of all gifts.

The next morning Anthony came to the pier with his bag on his shoulder, much in the way he had arrived fifteen years ago only now he was older and wiser. The hardened and stressed expression that adorned his face when he first arrived fifteen years ago was replaced now by a gentle and loving look. His friends Alonna, the priest, and the metal merchant were at the pier, wanting to see him off.

There were some great hugs and some tears with the thoughts of departure and the prospects of not seeing one another ever again. Upon stepping onto the deck of the schooner, Anthony turned and with a choking voice gently exclaimed, "No matter what the future brings to me, you will always be in my heart and thoughts. You have taught me much and for that I am very grateful."

The schooner slowly glided away from the pier with the outgoing tide, and Anthony, leaning against the port railing, waved slowly with a heavy heart and a small tear on his cheek. At the entrance to the small harbor, the remaining sails were raised to catch the westerly wind northward to Assisi. The sails filled full, and the schooner leaned slightly and began its long journey. The sea was reasonably flat for the season, and the wind, while strong, was steady and gentle.

The schooner arrived at the port east of Assisi fourteen days later, and Anthony's two brothers were there to meet him. The passing time aged the boys, but they still recognized each other as brothers. They hugged tightly as if the time away had healed the pain of the past. Anthony was surprised not to see his father, and on the long carriage ride to the family home, the brothers explained that father's illness had gotten worse.

They arrived at the gated home an hour before dusk, and Anthony was surprised at the elegance of the entry. The large wooden doors, the stained glass windows, and the marble steps leading to the doors were memories that Anthony did not have. He had never noticed the plush nature of his upbringing. Walking in, Anthony could not imagine this new sight of his home, and while it was the same, it seemed to him as completely rebuilt with a gracious elegance.

The brothers brought Anthony to their father's bedroom, and the setting sun cast shadows of colored light through the stained glass bedroom window. Joseph's good friend, the Franciscan friar, was visiting and sitting by the fluffy and well-groomed bed that supported Joseph. He turned to his newly arrived son and stretched his arms out to welcome him. Anthony hesitated slightly and went to the side of the bed and embraced his father lovingly for what seemed to be many minutes without any words but with many tears.

The friar and brothers left the room without suggestion and closed the front door, departing for their respective homes, leaving Joseph and his long-away son alone to catch up.

"Stand up, my boy, and let me see what kind of man you have become. My, you have really matured into this fine-looking man I knew you could become," Joseph said with a proud and joyous voice.

With great emotion, Anthony replied, "I have learned much of the ways of the world and soul. It was you who gave me this great gift of self, and my heart is full of those things that you always spoke of but I never understood. Through these things, I am a great part of you."

The two men talked of many things during the night.

Over the next two months, Anthony began to do much of the merchant things that his father had come to know so well. It was the sense of his past on the Greek island that stayed in his heart as he dealt with the many business people in the widespread merchant business. Anthony very quickly gained the reputation of being a fair and generous man, much like that of his father.

A year went by, and Joseph's illness progressed to keep him in bed for most of the time. Each night, Anthony would sit with his father and discuss the business of the day, then listen to the wisdom of his father, but this time he accepted the words and asked many questions. One morning after rising from his sleep, Anthony went to visit his beloved father as usual, and after a few moments realized that the life of this world had left Joseph during the night. Joseph had a peaceful expression on his face. Anthony sent a messenger to get the good friar and also his two brothers, who were in anticipation of this event.

The friar came quickly, and gave Joseph the last rites of the Church. He spoke to Anthony: "Your great father has given you the most important gift of giving. You will live your life with love as he did and become as beloved as he was from his great example. Anthony, you have become a good man of the world and will continue as he has done for so long. I will pray for your happiness and will be your friend as he was to me."

Anthony took the friar's hand and told him what an honor it was to be here with the love of so many good people.

The friar then responded with a quote from Francis of Assisi,

"Remember that when you leave this Earth, you take with you nothing that you have received—fading symbols of honor, trappings of power—but only what you have given: a full heart enriched with honest service, love, sacrifice, and courage."

Anthony bowed his head in great comfort that he had truly learned "*The Gift of Giving.*"

Over the years to come, Anthony became a beloved member of the community and left this Earth with peace and honor as his father had done.

The Heart and Mind

I have often wondered why some very smart people continue to do some apparently stupid things and get themselves in trouble. This has always been a little paradox for me, sometimes including my own behavior as compared to how smart I thought I was. While in a large bookstore, I was thumbing serendipitously through a book that had some interest for me and came upon this little couplet by Edna St. Vincent Millay.

"Pity me the heart that is slow to learn,
What the quick mind sees at every turn."

It struck me that the mind (our thinking) and the heart (our emotions) were separate but with a very strong connection to each. If I believe that this makes any sense, I can now realize that some of us can have a grown-up brain and our emotional maturity could be less mature and behind the thoughts of our mind. I believe that explains the disparity in many of our thinking and feeling and why smart people may do things that are not quite appropriate as driven by their feelings. Now, I am not a trained physiologist nor do I have the slightest bit of training in that area, but this does make sense to me. And when the maturity of the mind far exceeds the immaturity of the heart, the difference typically causes much pain that we try to relieve with all kinds of unnatural behavior and addictions.

This premise is supported by the science of cognitive thinking that says that the way we think can, and most often, directs our emotions. I had never thought of this in a manner of such. Techniques in cognitive thinking will affect our emotions, and we are encouraged to think in terms of positive thoughts so that our emotions stay close or on the positive side and may have a chance to mature. For some, the greatest challenge is to *remove* the negative thought visions and fears to make room for the positive; this will be transmitted to the emotions.

So what does this mean to me in actual daily practice, and what do I do to maintain some reasonable level of serenity that brings me peace much of the time? There are lots of philosophical and psychological theories, and many books have been written on this subject; so much so that I have difficulty keeping track and deciding which is the correct one for me. The words and theories just keep going on and on, so I try to keep the concepts in my mind very simple. For many of us, simplicity of thought is an unnatural effort, and we are continually reminded to "keep it simple stupid" (commonly referred to as KISS). That way, I have some part of a chance to apply a technique that has a chance to specifically help in the quest for emotional balance and happiness.

I like to think that the basis for positive thinking is *constructive imagination*, and as long as I think in this way, negative thoughts have trouble invading my mind and causing my emotions to go off into the many fields of dangerous territory. So, how do I put these concepts into a simple action that I can understand, remember, and practice?

I try to reduce the complex concepts to a simple statement that I can use on a daily basis. By taking the lessons and examples throughout our history, very complex actions have been articulated and directed with a simple statement of vision.

One that illustrates this in a dramatic way is the famous "Go to the Moon" speech of John F. Kennedy in the early 1960s. At that time, the morale of the American citizens was very low, and the economy was suffering greatly. In a stroke of genius, President Kennedy created the vision of "Going to the moon and returning safely by the end of the decade." This single sentence gave America hope and put thousands to work in constructive projects that spanned the imagination of many and built a technology base that has affected our society to great ends (semiconductor and computer technology as well as medical, etc).

So, what is my vision for constructive thought? I remember the years in the 1960s and '70s when many were in search of "the purpose of life." Trips to India and guru philosophies seasoned the society at that time.

For me, "The road to happiness is to create, and this will keep positive thoughts in my mind."

Sound too simple? It might be, but I have observed that when I am creating or building something, I am very happy. Planning and cooking a meal, building a model airplane, painting or taking a picture, decorating a room, and planting a garden are all creative processes that require our *creative imagination*. I believe that is why crossword and picture puzzles are so popular—that is sheer creation in a very simple way. When we have achieved the result, with some exceptions, the destination reached is not quite as satisfying as the journey we have taken to complete the project.

I try to remind myself that "The road to serenity is to create, and the result is happiness." I find that when I am busy doing something creative, I am most often protected from the dangers of negative thinking that will ultimately make me unhappy. When I am nervous or sad about something, that is the time to get that project going, and it may not always work, but most of the time it does. Some may say that this is "Sweeping our feelings under the rug." But I believe that we can at least try to have constructive thoughts about even the most devastating occurrence.

This may be a definition of courage.

So for me, the prescription of creative dreams in my head is the greatest happy pill I can take. I do try to dream all of my dreams in my thoughts and embrace the pulse of contentment in those journeys of creativity.

And so now, I write them down.

The Great Date

Gary was a very fine man and a hopeless romantic. He was 45 years old, trim, slightly athletic, and very handsome in an innocent way. His career was serving him well financially as he worked hard and smart. He has been divorced for six years after a twelve-year marriage that produced a daughter who was now 13 and so beautiful. His wife has primary custody, but Gary was able to see and have his daughter as much as he wanted. Gary and his daughter's mother kept a sound relationship for the little one's welfare, and the girl loved her daddy, having many special times together. Gary worked hard and had many male friends for play activities, but it had been a long time since he loved a woman and he was now longing for that kind of love. There was a great emptiness in his heart.

Kathy was 42 years old and such a beautiful woman. She was slim and had a very shapely body. She liked to dress in clothes that flowed over her shapely curves, and she had long, curly, light brown hair. And her eyes were of light turquoise. She was without children, and her husband of fifteen years had died two years ago in a severe and tragic automobile accident. She did not date for eighteen months and with the encouragement of some of her good friends, she started to reach out, but she became very disappointed in what was available. Nothing seemed to attract her, and thoughts and comparisons stayed with her husband of the past.

It was completely by accident that Gary and Kathy came together. It was at the local supermarket, and Kathy was leaving the store with a basket full of carefully selected items. Gary, who went through a different check-out counter, was walking directly behind her. He noticed her flowing walk with great attraction. The thought of meeting her flashed through his head and excited his anticipation, but he felt in his heart that she must be attached to someone very nice. She was so beautiful, he thought as she walked through the automatic doors. He followed close behind, watching her carefully and hoping for a chance to say hello.

Before he could even think of approaching her, a speeding car in the lot suddenly crashed into Kathy's carriage scaring the daylights out of her and spilling the contents of her carriage over a twenty-foot area. While she was not hurt, she was very shaken and became overcome with fear and started to cry. Gary, being directly behind her, came to her side and tried to comfort her. She did not look at Gary but she knew that someone was there for her while her face was buried in her hands. He spoke to her gently and asked if she was hurt while he had his hand gently on her shoulder. He was concerned for her, and as the moments passed and it became obvious that she was not physically hurt, he began again to think of the attraction he had for her, noticing that she did not have a wedding ring.

Some of the store clerks, seeing the commotion, ran to the outside of the store, and they began to pick up all the groceries that had been dumped. Many were damaged beyond use. One of the managers came to join them and offered to "re-shop" her order as a service. Kathy was now gaining her composure, and in a couple of minutes indicated to the manager that she would like that very much and expressed her appreciation. She now had her wet with tears face out of her hands, and the little bit of makeup she wore was quite smudged.

She finally turned and looked at Gary, the hand that touched her shoulder, and the comforting voice that had come to her aid in her moment of distress. The store manager indicated that it would take about thirty minutes to refill her order. She did not hear the manager, but Gary did and replied, "That would be nice." Then looking straight at Kathy, he offered, "Why don't you let me buy you a cup of coffee while we wait for your groceries. That way, you would have the chance to relax and get yourself together." She immediately agreed with a huge smile that went from ear to ear, and they entered the coffee shop next to the store, and sat for what became two hours. Her ice cream had melted, and so did Gary's heart.

Gary and Kathy dated for three months and had some great fun. They went dancing and hiking and had many lively conversations. They enjoyed each other's company, and when they went home apart from each other, the thoughts of the other prevailed in their minds and hearts. When they were apart, they missed each other. They took the time to grow together, and both wanted very much to be intimate, but they liked each other so much that they were both afraid to take the physical intimacy step and spoil the friendship connection they had developed.

Then, five days before Kathy's forty-third birthday, Gary called her to invite her on a date doing most of the things that they liked to do together. He wanted to build her a day for her birthday that she would always remember, and it was going to be next Saturday. On that Saturday morning at 10:00 a.m., Gary showed up at Kathy's door. They gave each other a hug that was tighter and closer than normal. It was very long without a word, and there seemed to be a new communication between them in this new day. It was softer, closer, and quieter, and something wonderful had changed, yet neither was acknowledging that. It was different for some reason, and it felt strange but very good.

They sat for a moment at Kathy's kitchen counter and made some small talk for a little while. Then they went to the front door and onto the walk, and Gary opened the car door for Kathy, handing her the seatbelt. He got into his side of the car, put the top down, and Kathy put a white scarf on her head. Her pretty face peeked out of the scarf at Gary, and he looked at her, smiled, and off they went.

It took about two hours going to the coast through the mountains and redwood country. Halfway along, they stopped at an overlook to view the bay and valley. Kathy stood close to the edge near the railing, and Gary stood behind her, closer than usual, and his arms were around her stomach as he held her firmly and gently. Their bodies were closer now that any time before, and they were comfortable, and it felt natural to both of them. Kathy laid her head back on Gary's shoulder, and her soft hair gently touched the side of Gary's face. He kissed her lightly where her neck and shoulder came together, and their already strong feelings became much stronger.

They returned to the car and continued the drive to the coast, enjoying the passing redwood forest and the sun that filtered through the tops of the trees. As the forest thinned, they became closer to the beach area, and when they got there, the air was clear and the sun strong. They parked the car and walked to the great pier. Some of the pier flooring was worn and loose with age, and their footsteps as they walked together echoed in perfect timing and harmony on the wobbly deck.

The fresh air gave them thoughts of hunger, and they proceeded to one of the many restaurants on the pier. They got a window seat and sat together on the same side of the table so that they could be close and enjoy the same view. They both ordered cracked crab and Caesar salad with shaved Parmesan and some whole anchovies that they both loved and fought over lovingly; and warm bread, of course. The crabs were in season and very full, and they made conversation together as they slowly extracted crabmeat from the shells. Their arms would bump often as they wrestled with their crabs.

They enjoyed the view of the bay with the white puffy clouds contrasting against the blue ocean. There were many boats with sails full of the summer sea breeze gently moving along in a graceful fashion. Some surfers were enjoying the energy of the ocean as it came to the shore.

After lunch they walked slowly arm and arm to the end of the pier where there were no fishermen. Kathy leaned up against the rail, and Gary was once again behind her so very close with his arms around her. They felt so good together, and this time his arms were a little higher so that they touched the lower part of her breasts so lightly. She was so soft, and she loved that sense of closeness. She again laid her head back on his shoulder with her soft hair against his face. She was so happy with Gary, and he felt so good. They did not say a word and just enjoyed their closeness in the sun and fresh sea breeze. They stayed motionless for awhile, enjoying the silent togetherness, and the feelings passed along without any spoken words.

They slowly walked back to the car arm in arm, and again, Gary opened the door for Kathy and handed her the seatbelt. They drove north along the coast and came to the lonely lighthouse balanced on the rocky cliff. The lighthouse was painted very white and reflected the sun in a blinding fashion. Their eyes became constricted with the brightness, and when they held each other face to face, they had the sensation that this was a dream. It was a wonderful feeling and was not a dream; it was very real.

They returned again to the car and traveled home by way of the freeway, and they were eager to get home for they were a little tired. Their faces were flush from the day of sun and wind. When they got home, Kathy put some water on for tea, and Gary pulled out a movie he had rented. It was a great love story called *Somewhere in Time* with Chris Reeves, and the haunting music was by John Barry. Kathy placed the finished tea on the living room table while Gary started the movie. The sofa was deep, and they fit together very closely and softly. His head was shoulder high on her so that the side of his face touched the side of her breast. Kathy's arm was above, and she stroked and fiddled with his hair. The movie was gentle and sweet, and the music kept a mellow tempo with the story having the usual highs at the romantic parts. They slowly melted into the story and became closer, touching places on each other that they had not touched before.

They hardly noticed what was happening because it was so comfortable and natural, and they grew closer without any effort. The romance of the movie captured their attention, and when the story ended, there was a great feeling of quiet and closeness. Nothing was said, and Gary turned his face to her soft breast, and his other hand touched the other. He wanted to do this from the very first day they met at the supermarket, and now the excitement flowed through his body. Kathy smiled lovingly, accepted his touches and stroked his hair, neck, and ears.

Her lovely touch sent chills up his back and to his head and finally settled in the base of his spine. She placed her head back and closed her eyes and enjoyed Gary's touches that were now in a soft full swing. He loved to touch her, and she loved to be touched by him, and his caresses were gentle and full. He now was beginning to feel the body he had so longed for, and they became even closer.

Kathy breathed heavily, enjoying Gary's closeness, and he enjoyed the sounds of her loving sighs that created a melody of pleasure. Her arms wrapped around his neck as she held him close to her breasts. Kathy pushed Gary back as if to reject him and started to unbutton his shirt. She pulled the shirt off his arms. His chest had the right amount of hair that she loved so, and she ran her fingers lightly over his chest, letting his hair tickle her fingers.

Before he could move forward to be close again, Kathy pulled her sweater over her head, revealing her full and soft beauty, and he put his hand up and touched her lovingly. Then she leaned forward and unsnapped her bra and dropped it to the floor. She was so beautiful, and Gary kissed her with delicate touches from his lips; and he touched more. Then they slowly came together again with his bare chest against her firm softness. She felt the hair on his chest against her, and he felt her nipples against him, and they were just close enough to feel each other lightly. They kissed very passionately for a long time and it was like they had never kissed before. Their hearts pounded as if finishing a long run.

Then, in a quite moment, Kathy pushed Gary back and looked lovingly into his eyes. She pushed him gently back some more and took his hand in hers and stood up while gesturing him to follow. She walked in front of him, still holding his hand, and headed to her bedroom where she had lit a candle earlier. Then in the bedroom, next to the bed, she turned to him and put her arms around his neck, and she kissed him softly and lovingly. His hands were on the top of her hips. She then looked down and unbuckled his belt and pants top, and he returned the gesture for her and undid her slacks. They stood in the faint light, touching each other as they had imagined in their dreams for a long time now. The shadow of their togetherness from the dim candlelight was projected on the wall as one image.

Then they came together again in a firm embrace, but now their bodies were freed of all clothing. They stood together closely and touched every part of each other that they could reach. It felt so good to feel each other this way. Some tears of joy came to Kathy, and Gary touched them with his finger and gently kissed them dry.

Slowly she turned and gestured an invitation to join her on the bed. She lay back, and Gary, resting on his elbows, started to kiss her beginning at the neck and shoulders. He kissed her arms and breasts, and he slowly moved down one of her sides, softly kissing her and touching with all his gentle love. And it was natural. Kathy kept her hand on the back of his head, playing with his ears and closing her eyes and breathing deeply and slowly.

Gary kissed her more and more and continued on his kissing journey to his loved one. His soft lips caressed her, and she grew excited and pressed the top of her back against the bed. Gary continued for some time with her hands on the back of his head as to direct him to her pleasure places. She lovingly touched the bottom of his ears as to beckon him back to her lips. With this soft invitation, he began his loving trek to her lips again. Their eyes met again, and they loved so much. There could not be any higher feeling. They continued through the lovemaking and when they finished, they held and kissed each other and rested in each other's arms for some time. He loved to touch her hair, and she ran her fingers lightly up and down his back.

Soon after, they were married and spent their time with each other in great joy and comfort. Gary kept his romancing of Kathy, and she kept the passion in their togetherness. They started each morning together in some talk in order to start each day with each other. During the course of each day, they did something for the other without the need for recognition. This went on for many years.

And so, it was "A Great Date"!

The Grandmother

A true story

Margaret, at the age of 67, had been retired as a high school English teacher for two years but still volunteered her days as a part-time teacher for special children requiring language skills. Her husband of 38 years had died of a stroke the year before, and she missed him terribly. Frank was a successful doctor, and together they had a wonderful life that produced a fine daughter. Margaret was the product of a strict Baptist family and spent her early life in Georgia. She was educated in literature and continued her college education until she received a master's degree and a teaching certificate.

In her very early days, Margaret was sort of a liberal rebel in her family in the small Southern community, and for the times was highly sensitive to the ecology and environmental issues of the day. In fact, she was very active in the then-new and unknown movement of "Save the Whales." After two years of teaching in a very conservative environment, she became very frustrated with the local educators and her inability to successfully introduce innovative teaching principles brought forth by national programs. The social and professional environment was just too conservative to accept her ways, and she finally realized that a change of geography might be more appropriate. So she joined the newly founded Peace Corps.

Her two years in South America with the Corps was exactly what she needed to satisfy the innovative and social thoughts that danced as "sugar plums" in her head. It was there that she met Frank, a recently graduated medical doctor who was giving his early career time as a volunteer for the needy in South America. Frank was from the Pacific Northwest but was educated in a prestigious Massachusetts medical college. Working in the same community, they became very good friends, and after a year, their friendship turned to a passionate romance. Their love had grown very quickly, and similar thoughts and ways melted them together into one emotional and intellectual motion.

Margaret's volunteer time had come to a conclusion, and she was required to return home, which she reluctantly did. The home of her upbringing and family seemed totally strange compared to her past two years of giving and satisfaction to the needy. She longed for the comfort as a volunteer, and she missed the company of Frank and the life connection they had made.

As the weeks went by, she became totally listless without the social excitement and gifts that she had been accustomed to in her rewarding volunteer experience. After two anxious months, Frank's time was also up with the Corps and, returning to the United States, he went straight to Georgia as he and Margaret had planned earlier. With the few possessions she had and her bags packed, she returned to the Pacific Northwest with Frank, and they were duly married. Frank had grown up as an orphan and had no family as such. Margaret's family was over 2,000 miles away and became alienated when she decided to leave for her own life. They were now together alone to build a happy and productive life together. And they did.

Carol, their only child, had the advantage and influence of a well-educated and loving household. As an only child, she received much work and attention from her parents and later graduated with honors from a prestigious school with a master's degree in education. She became a teacher like her mother, and during that time, she met John, an electrical engineer for a local aircraft company. They were married and settled near her small but close family. Through their love, they produced an only son, Dennis.

Carol and John were very active in the community and felt the obligation to return to the community some of their time. They had a good life, and the closeness to Margaret and Frank grew very deeply as they enjoyed all the joys of a well-rounded family, especially during the holidays.

The only point of friction was the difference in upbringing values that Carol and John employed with their son, Dennis. Margaret and Frank felt that Dennis was allowed too much latitude and that they were spoiling Dennis to a point of unpleasantness. Carol allowed Dennis to do and act any way he wished, and what especially bothered Margaret was the way Carol let Dennis manipulate his parents to his end. Dennis was always negotiating his way, and at eight years old, he was able to maneuver to his way at any time. This hurt Margaret and Frank very much, and they spent much time discussing the issue when not in the presence of their children. They were careful not to nag on this subject, as they were afraid to alienate their loved ones by interfering. This tended to spoil the once joyous visits with an undisclosed tension that strained the emotional well-being of the relationships.

Dennis was nine when tragedy struck the family. One evening and without warning, Frank suddenly had a massive stroke. The rescue team arrived in a short time, and, after stabilizing Frank's condition, rushed him to the hospital of his own medical service. Margaret went in the ambulance, caring and praying for her longtime partner and loved one. Arriving at the hospital, Frank was rushed to the emergency room and was given immediate and careful care; then Margaret called the children, and they arrived in short order.

Above the silence of fears and memories of their beloved Frank, the waiting room was filled with Dennis' constant and seemingly unimportant inquires and whining. Carol tried to quiet him with some entertainment, but he did not seem to grasp the danger of his grandfather. John had to take Dennis to the cafeteria and other places that might be interesting to the disconnected mind of his son.

It was two hours since Frank's hectic arrival when the doctor in charge came to the waiting room. His expression shown a solemn smile that Frank had so often used, and Margaret was familiar with it as a doctor's wife.

"He has had a major brain stem stroke and will probably lose much of his left side and speech. We will know more in 24 hours, and we will put him in ICU where you can visit in awhile," the doctor passionately explained about his own colleague.

Margaret was stunned and could not believe that her loved one's life had taken such a turn in just a split moment. She thought and finally began to realize the import of this event and started to visualize the uncertain future and the possible loneliness to come with the loss of her lifetime partner. Carol and John decided it was best to leave their mother alone and take the now very unruly Dennis home. It was now late in the evening.

Margaret went to stay with Frank in the ICU; he was conscious and recognized that Margaret was there. She slowly approached his bedside with a compassionate look, took his right hand, and, without any words being passed between them, they looked at each other with loving hopes. Frank broke the silence with a very slurred, "I really did it this time." Margaret held on to his hand with both of hers and told him how much she loved him and that everything would work out. The next evening while Margaret and Carol were at his bedside, Frank had a respiratory arrest and in spite of much effort by the hospital staff, passed on.

Margaret was devastated. and in the next months she found it very hard to do even the simplest things. Carol came by to look in on her mother, and when together, they reminisced on the many pleasant memories of their passed loved one. Margaret found great comfort in talking, and this seemed to partially relieve her depression.

It was just about a year later when Margaret was asked to baby-sit Dennis for an overnight weekend. It was Carol and John's wedding anniversary, and they wanted to take some romantic time away over the weekend. Margaret welcomed the company in spite of the young one's behavior, and it was only going to be for one night, so Margaret looked forward to the visit and the chance to help out her daughter and son-in-law. Dennis arrived with his parents and was seemingly quiet, which was not the usual case. Carol and John went on their way, instructing Dennis to be a good boy for his grandmother and kissed him goodbye.

Margaret was uncomfortable with how to entertain a ten-year-old. She suggested that they go see the latest Disney movie, and Dennis yelled with delight. So off they went to the local cinema. "One child and one senior!" was Margaret's ticket request, and upon entering the cinema lobby, Dennis ran directly to the candy counter without even stopping at the ticket taker's position.

Margaret followed him and took him out of the line that he just cut into, then she asked Dennis what he wanted and he answered, "Some popcorn and soda." The server handed to Margaret over the counter a medium-sized buttered popcorn, and they moved further down to the candy section of the counter for the soda. When they were in front of the candy section, Dennis exclaimed that he did not want the popcorn and pointed to a very large chocolate bar. Margaret became very frustrated and told Dennis that he had to finish the popcorn first and that she would get the candy bar later. Not being agreeable to this request, he started to whine loudly, making an embarrassing scene. Margaret firmly indicated that she was not going to give in to his request and told him to be quiet. Dennis did not and continued with his loud and embarrassing whine. Margaret then threatened to leave the movie house if he did not settle down; he did not stop, so she took him by the hand, left the lobby, went outside, and continued on to the car.

Dennis was quiet in the front seat of the car, still in disbelief that someone would do this to him. His strategy always worked with his parents. Margaret headed home, and after a few minutes of driving, Dennis declared that she did not love him and that he hated her. Margaret was very hurt and worried whether she had done the right thing. Tension was high for the rest of the journey, and when they arrived at home, they both entered the house without a sound. Dennis stomped into the family room, put the TV on, and sat on the couch with a pouting look and his arms folded.

Later, Margaret asked Dennis what he wanted for dinner, and he replied that he was not hungry and to leave him alone. His attitude was wearing on Margaret, and she was tempted to give in but did not.

It was 9:00 p.m. when Margaret announced that it was time to go to bed. Dennis started to whine again and exclaim that he was now very hungry. Margaret relented this time and made Dennis his favorite peanut butter and jelly on white bread and a glass of juice. Dennis poked at the sandwich, trying to extend the time he would stay up. He succeeded in extending his pre-bedtime a half hour then went to bed without much discussion. He turned his face when Margaret went to kiss him goodnight as if to punish her for her behavior and "lack of love" for him.

Margaret returned to the playroom sofa to try to get some reading done, but her emotional tiredness had exhausted her to the point of only being able to lie down. She wanted to cry. She had never felt so much unhappiness and discouragement, and her long life of giving and leading a gentle life did not prepare her for this challenge. She looked very forward to her daughter taking Dennis away, and she finally went to sleep on the couch.

Soon after falling asleep, she started to dream about a bell ringing far off in the distance and awoke to the sound of the telephone on the third ring. It was almost twelve midnight, and she slowly moved toward the ringing phone. She began to wake up as she picked up the phone. She did not recognize the voice at the other end and thought that it may be a wrong number or crank call. Who else would be calling at this time?

The voice at the other end asked, "Are you Margaret Williams?"

"Yes," she replied, and her curiosity began to rise.

The voice that she did not recognize continued, "There has been a terrible accident, and we are afraid that your daughter and her husband have been hurt very badly."

Margaret's heart sank, but she still believed that this was just a dream, a terrible dream. As the moments passed and she became more awake, the voice continued, "We have brought them to Community General Hospital, and we need you there."

Margaret, now fully awake, asked how they were. The voice explained that the car accident was very severe and that their condition was not known yet and that they were still in surgery.

Margaret, wanting to get to the hospital as fast as possible, hung up the phone and hurried to the room where Dennis was sleeping. It took many long moments for her to get Dennis out of his deep sleep. Dennis, rubbing his eyes and whining under his breath, began to wake up. Margaret dressed him hurriedly, and each second seemed like a minute. She was very firm with Dennis, and he seemed to know that this was a time not to misbehave and helped with the dressing. It was quite exciting for him to be getting up at this time.

Margaret drove hurriedly to the same hospital she had a year ago for her beloved husband, Frank. The drive brought back many painful memories, and she began to now worry and fear for her only children. Prayers came to her head and heart as she quietly cried. Arriving at the hospital, she parked the car, grabbed Dennis, and dragged him hurriedly to the waiting room. She was met immediately by a very good doctor friend of her's and Frank's. He pulled Margaret aside into the waiting room, sat her down, and holding her hand as a friend would, solemnly explained, "Margaret, I am so sorry. The accident was very bad."

A fearful look entered Margaret's eyes that her friend could compassionately understand. He went on, "We are doing everything we can for Carol, but it is too late for John. We could not save him. He had passed on the moment he arrived."

Dennis overheard some parts of the conversation but did not realize the import of the content. He was more interested in some of the toys in the waiting room. Margaret was now crying in shock and began to fully realize that life was beginning to dramatically change before her eyes and heart. She asked, "And what of my daughter, Carol?"

He began to reveal that Carol was in very bad shape but did not let on of the hopelessness of the condition. He slowly got up from his chair, trying to comfort Margaret, and he compassionately noted, "I'll stay in touch and let you know as soon as something changes. We have some of the best people working on her." And he left through the traditional double hospital doors.

Dennis' play voice could be heard above the lonely quiet of the room, and Margaret began her sorrowful thoughts. She prayed to her God and tried to make all kinds of deals if only He would save her beloved daughter.

It was three eternal hours, and Dennis had fallen asleep in the comfort of his grandmother's lap. She was anxious to hear of her daughter's condition, and just then, through the glass of the double doors, saw her doctor friend returning. As he approached, he did not take his eyes off her face. Somehow she knew what the message was that he was bringing to her, and she began to fearfully cry as she looked at his eyes for each step that he took. He sat down next to her and, putting his hand on her shoulder, softly exclaimed, "Carol has passed away. We did everything we could, but there was just too much internal damage."

Unbelievable shock and pain came to Margaret, the same pain she had felt a year before. Except for Dennis, she was totally alone with only her intelligent strength to keep her together. Her doctor friend offered his wife to spend the night with her and help with any of the things that needed to be done. She declined for the moment and just wanted to be alone with her intense grief.

She woke Dennis again, but he did not understand that Margaret was his only family now. After the short but quiet drive, they arrived home at 4:00 a.m. and again, Dennis went to sleep, leaving Margaret very alone with the realization of what was happening. She could not sleep, and what was to happen in the future danced in her head, giving her no peace from the agony. The many memories that she had come to cherish rolled across her mind and brought great pain to her heart.

It was 8:00 a.m. when Dennis awoke and, scratching his eyes, came downstairs to where Margaret had been sitting quietly for the last four hours. Her face was pale and flushed at the same time. Dennis started to murmur for his breakfast, and Margaret quickly complied with a bowl of cereal and his favorite juice, then sat him in front of the TV to be entertained with morning cartoons. This was something she had always discouraged before, but now she could not manage a verbal battle with Dennis. She started to make herself some coffee when the phone rang. It was the first of many calls that day from friends giving her their sympathy and offering her their help and support.

Later that day, Margaret decided to sit Dennis down and explain what had happened and that his parents would not be coming back. He was quiet throughout the whole story and did not budge. He started to cry, and Margaret held him close to her and assured him that she loved him and would take care of him from now on. For once, Dennis was serious in his sadness.

Five days later, services were held for John and Carol. There were over 400 people attending the event, mostly colleagues and friends. Later, after the service was over and people had left, Margaret sat by herself with the thoughts that this was final and that closure was a reality. Except for ten-year-old Dennis, Margaret was now alone for the first time in her life, and she had no family and was now the leader of the two-person family. At 67, she now had to deal with a very active and difficult boy. She was able to acquire the services of a social worker through her connections at the hospital to help her with some of the many childhood details such as registering for school, dental records, medical records, etc. Margaret had much to learn and was facing the next eight to ten years trying to accommodate the needs of a young Dennis.

Margaret had considered putting Dennis in state foster care but those thoughts quickly dissolved. There was too much of Carol in him, and she, with the help of a few friends, was able to acquire legal custody and become executor of the rather large estate left to him. With all these details coming into place, Margaret was now faced with the actual interaction and guidance of a young boy two generations away and the product of an upbringing that she had never endorsed.

It did not take long for Dennis to get over the loss of his parents and return to his self-centered and manipulative behavior. This was also showing up at school, and his teachers would often call Margaret for a conference or two. Margaret was really struggling, and she sought the help of some child-rearing counseling but that seemed to be too liberal and modern for her instincts. The advice seemed to be too complex for her to really be able to implement, and Margaret was at her wit's end.

Dennis was now eleven years old, and one Friday, Margaret received a notice from school that there was a serious problem with Dennis and that she was required to come into the school for a conference right away. Margaret arrived at the school and went straight to the principal's office. She opened the office door, and there sat Dennis to the side with a scared look on his face. Margaret announced herself to the administrator and was immediately directed to the principal's office and told, "Go right in. We've been expecting you."

The principal greeted Margaret with a wide but concerned smile and graciously offered her to sit down. Margaret immediately queried, "What was the problem with Dennis?"

"Well, Margaret, you know that we have been having a continual problem with Dennis' behavior but I am afraid that he has gone too far this time. This morning one of the teachers on hall duty caught Dennis trying to light a locker on fire. He now has gone beyond misbehavior and has become dangerous to the school as a whole. This cannot go on, and I felt that it was important to call children's services. They would like to have a meeting with you without Dennis."

Margaret was devastated to the point of feeling a little faint, and she began to fear that she might lose her only family to the administration of the state. Dennis was temporarily expelled until a resolution was outlined. Later that day, she called the social worker to make an appointment, and a time two days later was agreed upon and that the social worker would come to Margaret's home for the meeting.

It was 10:00 a.m. when the doorbell rang. Opening the door, Margaret greeted the social worker. There was an immediate positive chemistry between the two, and the hope of having a fair meeting was evident. They sat down, and Margaret offered some coffee that was previously made.

The social worker started out, "Well, I have read the school report on Dennis, and it looks like we have a serious problem here. I just want you to know that we have Dennis' best interests in mind, and I can assure you that I will do everything I can to help you keep him in your household. But it does not look good with your age and all that. He certainly appears to be a handful and may need a stronger influence."

Margaret replied in a careful solemn tone, "I have tried my best over the last year with the boy, and he seems to be improving."

"Well, not according to the school report. He has definitely become more disruptive and now, dangerous," she retorted.

The conversation went on for another half hour, and it was agreed that Dennis could stay with Margaret for the next 90 days on a trial basis. At the end of that time, his progress would be evaluated and a decision made regarding his future. Margaret was shaking slightly through the conversational ordeal but was greatly appreciative and relieved for the second chance. The social worker left and Margaret sat quietly for awhile, trying to envision what she was to do and how to get through this great challenge. She decided to tell Dennis the truth and point out the impact of his actions with the possibility of being relegated to a state foster home; there was no negotiating here.

Margaret waited for the next day to sit down with Dennis and try to make it clear what needed to be done and the import of such action. After breakfast, she brought the still-expelled Dennis into the family room and sat down with him. He looked at her with a look that gave away that this was going to be a serious subject, and he was unusually attentive.

Margaret started the conversation with, "Dennis, you know that I love you very much, and it has been hard for you with your parents gone. You are my only family now, and I am yours. We are both in serious trouble now, and the state has threatened to put you in a foster home because they think that I am too old to care for you. You are a fine and smart young man, and I love you, but I do not like some of the things that you do. The teachers in the school feel the same way."

Dennis looked at her expressionless as if he did not care. Margaret continued, "The woman I met with yesterday was from the state child services, and she feels very strongly that you would be better off in a foster home. You and I would not like that. I did convince her that she should give us another chance, and she agreed to give us 90 days. At the end of that time, she will evaluate our behavior." Margaret was careful to include herself in and as part of the problem in every sentence. Dennis still did not say a word.

She continued, "I have a plan that just might work if we both try. I have marked out the 90 days on this calendar with some things that we probably should do." Margaret put her hand on Dennis' shoulder and looked him in the eyes that were looking down at the floor. With a strong and loving voice, she said, "I do love you and would hate to lose you to some strangers." Dennis' face was scarlet with emotion, and his eyes were becoming glassy.

Then, without a word, she put her arms around him and with a hug, "We can do this together."

Dennis with an inhaled gasp started to cry, and with a sobbing voice he said, "Grandma, I don't want to leave you and go live with someone else. I am scared." And his crying deepened while he hugged her back with a clutch that said, "Help me."

The time that followed without a word being passed seemed like an eternity. They just held each other. Margaret broke the silence with, "Well, I certainly don't want to give you up, and I think that we should fight this with all our might." And she looked at him with a big smile. "Are you up to it?"

"But Grandma, I don't know what to do," replied Dennis with a more lively tone. His wet checks were starting to dry as curiosity overcame his fear with some hope.

"Well, let's start out by using the calendar each day and make a plan, just you and me," she proposed. "We can start each morning after breakfast and write down on a piece of paper what we need to do for that day." Dennis, with a little smile of hope, agreed.

Margaret then invited Dennis to go to a movie that afternoon to celebrate their new plan, and this time he behaved. The next day they started with a list of things that they were to do that day. Each contributed to their own actions. The list looked like this:

Grandma to make lunch
Grandma to wash clothes
Dennis will watch TV
Dennis will pick up room
Grandma will read a chapter in her new book
Dennis and Grandma will go food shopping for dinner
Grandma will cook dinner
Dennis will help Grandma clean up

At this point, Dennis did not want to put any more for him to do. Margaret sensed this and told him that it was ok and very good for the first day. That night she reminded him how much he did and what a great help he was, even though he did not really clean up his room. Dennis smiled with a small feeling of accomplishment.

The days went on, and the lists became easier and even included bedtimes that Dennis determined by himself and stuck to most of the time. It was not perfect but progress was being made, a little each day. After four weeks, Margaret called the school principal and suggested that they should try with Dennis again. She told him what she and Dennis were doing and the progress that was being made, and he agreed. The next morning, Margaret suggested to Dennis that he should pick a day to return to school and put it on the calendar. She also suggested that he make a list of the things he was to do and not do at school, just like they had done at home. They both had fun putting some humor into this, and it became a little game for both.

The weeks went on, and while not perfect, Dennis made good progress at home and at school. The teachers were reluctantly optimistic, but as time passed, Dennis showed marked improvement with only an occasional disruption. Margaret was careful to make sure that Dennis would mark each day off the calendar himself as a reminder that he was making good progress, and that the state decision was still going to be made.

After about eleven weeks, Margaret was contacted by the social worker to set up a meeting to discuss the Dennis disposition. In their meeting, the social worker told Margaret that she was impressed with the progress that Dennis had made and agreed to another 90-day probation period. That night Margaret and Dennis went out to celebrate their achievement at Dennis' favorite restaurant and arcade. The noise was deafening to Margaret, but she sat patiently trying to read her book in the turmoil of electronic noise and chaotic running children.

The months went by, and Dennis still improved. As the years went by, Dennis was becoming a young man and teenager. He had become quite popular in high school and was elected vice president of his class, and his marks were quite good.

Dennis was a senior now and on the honor role. Margaret was now 74 years old and still active and spry. Over the years, their morning list making and nightly inventory of the day had turned into moments of being together. They openly shared their feelings without reservation, and that trust grew into a very deep love and mutual respect.

Margaret was delighted when Dennis had announced that he was accepted into medical school. Over the years he did well and graduated at the top of his class. Margaret was now 83 and slowing down quite a bit. Dennis did his internship at the very hospital his grandfather served and had passed on, and the same place of his parents' deaths. His internship presented many challenges, and his busy schedule reminded Margaret of the many nights that her beloved Frank had left her in the late hours to come to the aid of someone in need. Her heart was filled on a daily basis with so much love and happiness. She would sit and embrace the many memories recalled.

It was on a Thursday afternoon and Dr. Dennis had duty in the emergency room when he was notified that the ambulance was arriving with an elderly woman that had a massive heart attack. The double doors exploded open, and the paramedics rolled the gurney frantically into the emergency room. Dennis and two nurses arrived at the same time, and the frantic pace to save this woman increased, as done so many times. The nurses began their usual, and as Dennis approached he looked down at the woman, and it was his beloved Margaret. His professional instincts over took his shock, and he immediately went into full doctor mode.

The team managed to save Margaret for the time being, and she was wheeled into ICU. Dennis sat by her for quite some time while she was still unconscious. She awoke and Dennis was there for her. He held her hand with one hand and stroked her forehead with the other. "Well, looks like after all the years of me giving you trouble, you are finally getting me back," he said with a soft smiling voice. She grinned and said nothing. They just spent some quiet time together.

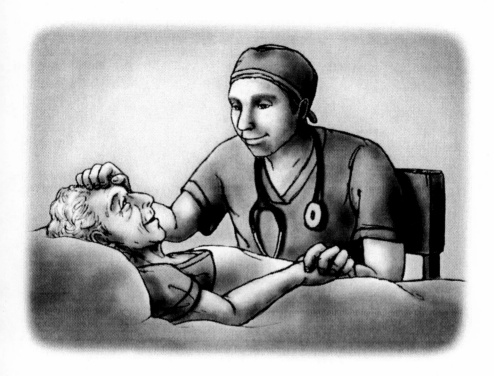

Dennis went on to continue his shift and later looked in on Margaret. She was slightly awake, and he sat down next to her and took her hand again. She smiled at him and told him how proud she was of him and what a fine man he had become. "Well, I had a good teacher," he replied.

Dennis then began to share with her the gratefulness in his heart toward her. "You gave me my life. You helped me to grow into a person, and by your example, you gave me many values that I cherish and follow. You truly saved my life, and I know that it was not easy for you. Your love for me persevered over my difficulties." Tears came to Margaret's eyes, knowing that she had given Dennis of herself and shared with him his challenges. They spent more quiet time together. They did not need to make a list. They did not even have to talk. They just knew.

That night, Margaret passed on. A year later, Dennis met a wonderful woman while he was in Puerto Rico in the Peace Corps. She was a language teacher, and they fell deeply in love.

Back in the States, they spent many years having a family and working in their respective fields. Their two children, Dennis Jr. and little Margaret, learned the many values that would serve them well in their later years.

So, the grace of "The Grandmother" passed on to live in the hearts of others to be cherished and enjoyed in their own lives for the next generations.

Progressive Creation

It was five months after leaving Velux and the excitement of the Rotpar hunt. *Odyssey IV* came out of multiple light speed and entered the surrounding space of Eliet. The suspension chamber automatically awakened Tom from his long sleep, and he spent the usual 20 minutes in the vibration chamber to recover from his long sleep. He was very hungry and prepared some very tasty molecular reproduced food from recipes acquired around the galaxy that he had been able to program into his molecular food constructor.

Tom was filled with much apprehension in meeting the Elietians from many of the stories he heard regarding their evolution from reptiles and not primates, as most of the galaxy was seeded throughout the millenniums. Tom had to manually enter the landing coordinates in his flight computer for landing because the Elietians did not have the computing technology to do so. He also had trouble programming his language translator and hoped that its translation algorithms did an accurate job. The last thing he needed was to risk insulting the Elietians with language that was improper or misleading.

Eliet was a very different planet than he had ever seen before. Eliet was in orbit around two stars and circled the two in a figure eight trajectory, first around one star, and then around the other. This combined with a slow axis spin produced a very long day with very pleasant warming temperatures. The nights were slightly cooler, and it seemed to Tom that there was very little difference in lighting, making the distinction between night and day that of temperature and not light and dark. This made the evolution from cold-blooded reptiles very possible and preferable. The climate was more suited to the DNA restructuring of the species from reptiles rather than primates, and Nature complied with the resulting culture.

Tom found the landing pad without incident and was met by five Elietians that seemed to be of high order and very official. Tom was instantly surprised by their attractive appearance in spite of their reptilian roots. They were slightly shorter than the humanoids around the galaxy and had a very strong-looking physique. Their light green skin had very slight ripples on their backs that blended into their cream colored chests and abdomens. Their faces were not pointed at the jaw, as Tom had expected, and their eyes faced forward as with humans. Their noses were slightly flattened and shaped in such a way as to be complementary to the overall look of their faces. They were very much like humans and had very pleasant and attractive appearances. Their clothing was very sheer and limited to only shoulder and waist shawls that were very stylish. Later Tom learned that this was to let heat into their cold-blooded bodies, and he was able to observe their entire bodies through the sheerness of their very limited clothing. They were not the usual humanoid features, and this made their exposed appearance very acceptable because their reproduction organs were not visible. They were very smooth and graceful to the eye and radiated a sense of goodness.

Tom had experienced many greetings throughout his visits, but the Elietians had one that was very special. One of the Elietians came forward to meet Tom and extended both arms in a welcome. He then took both of Tom's hands in a very warm gesture while a bright smile extended across his face. Tom felt the coolness of his cold-blooded nature in his hand, but it was not objectionable and actually quite pleasant combined with the softness of his skin.

The head Elietian remarked to Tom, "We are vrey peaseld taht you hvae cmoe to vsiit wtih us. We lokeod fworrad to metineg u and hpoe taht we wlil mkae yuor saty paelsnat and felild wtih hpipasnes." Tom now had enough data to adjust his universal language translator, and he replied with, "It is I who is honored with your reception, and I look forward to learning more about you."

The differences between male and female were very subtle, but in general, the males were slightly larger than the females, whose facial expressions were a little softer than the males. These were the only distinctions Tom could observe. Tom later discovered that the males and females were of equal stature in the entire community hierarchy that included government, industry, and business.

After the brief meeting and introductions at the landing site, the apparent leader of the group motioned to what appeared to be a very sleek transportation vehicle. They all got in and traveled to a more populated area and stopped in front of a large official-looking building, then got out. They entered the very plain but stylish building, and it was lit inside with very warm temperature lighting. The lighting was everywhere inside all the buildings, and Tom realized that this was to maintain a warm temperature for the Elietian's physiology when not in the direct sunlight. Their very sheer clothing allowed the generated heat to reach their soft skin and keep their cold-blooded bodies comfortable as well as keeping them awake.

Tom explained the nature of the Marlarium that he was delivering, and they had many questions for him so the meeting went on for two hours. At the end of the question and answer period, Tom was invited to stay on Eliet for an extended time so that he could enjoy the culture. Tom agreed with great enthusiasm, and the Elietians brought him to what was a general lodging place where he was given a very pleasant room. The entire facility was kept pleasantly warm with the very soft lighting.

Over the next days, Tom was kept very busy with gatherings and visits to many of the cultural and historical exhibits. Tom learned that at one time, the Eleitians were a violent race with many centuries of war. They were able to develop weapons that, if unleashed, would destroy the entire planet. Because of the fear of complete annihilation, this changed the entire planet's attitude toward war and, in spite of some isolated cases, peace was finally forced on this culture. The Elietians took a doomsday approach to war, developed a single army, and, over the years, developed mutual economic and technological efforts that benefited residents of the entire planet. War and killing had become ancient history. Everyone was enjoying the prosperity, and the remaining violent holdouts either joined the prosperity or died out over time.

Tom also learned that the Elietians were a very spiritual people with different areas of the planet having slightly different versions of the same beliefs, which gave them a common link. Their scientific culture was primarily directed toward the health and welfare of the people, medicine, astronomy, structural science as applied to their buildings, and environmental engineering. Since the Elietians were only carnivorous, they had no agriculture except for that used for medical and decorative purposes. They did have very large farms that produced a variety of staples as well as exotic meats. The staples consisted of a variety of insects and grubs that complemented their diet of meat, and Tom was not pleased with the food but found a few items that he could stomach.

The days were very long and well lit; the slightly cooler nights were just as long. Sleep was traditionally done during the cooler times. When the temperature dropped slightly, it took great effort for the Elietians to stay awake. Their sleep time was based on temperature and not on lighting, and most all slept at this time with the exception of a very small group of Protectors that wore warming suits. The

Protectors were assigned to keep peace and order among the Elietians, especially during the cool periods. And they had very little to do.

After Tom was on Eliet for a week, he became eager to get deeper into this culture and expressed to his hosts that he wanted to get closer to the real and daily life of the Elietians. They were very pleased with Tom's interest and suggested that he stay with a family that offered some different perspective. Tom was delighted, and his hosts took him to his new lodging.

It was a classic Elietian home with a mated male and female, a young female child, and one on the way. His original host introduced them and left Tom to his new family.

Her name was Alox, his was Unton, and their young female child was named Uta. The young female was of three years and stood almost as tall as her parents. The Eliet children grew up very fast as compared to humanoids and usually reached full adulthood capable of reproducing in six years.

Alox and Unton were very excited that they were picked to host Tom, and they were instructed by the elders to act as they would normally do. They invited Tom to sit in what appeared to be a resting or gathering room. It was simply furnished with very soft bench-like pieces to sit or lay on, and each was slightly heated. Alox worked in the local educational facility as a science and history instructor with two- and three-year-olds, and her mate, Unton, was an anthropologist who worked for the local museum. Tom was very surprised at their attractiveness, and their little female, Uta, was quite cute. By all standards they met the classic profile of a perfect family, and Tom was very curious about the new baby on the way. He asked Alox how she was feeling.

"I am feeling very well. Why do you ask?" replied Alox.

"Well, you are soon to have a baby, and you do not show any physical signs of the baby in progress within your body," Tom said with a curious tone.

Both Alox and Unton broke out in what appeared to be a compassionate laughter. "Come, let me show you," remarked Alox with a big smile, and she gracefully put out her hand in a gesture to follow her. She walked into another section of the dwelling revealing to Tom a small warmed basket that was covered by some very fluffy heated material. She lifted up the fluffy material and revealed a small egg being incubated by the warmth.

Tom slapped his forehead while exclaiming, "I should have known. It is going to take awhile to become more familiar with your biology. When will it come out?"

Alox smiled and, while covering the egg, explained to Tom, "Well, we have been seeing movement for the last two days and he should come out in the next day or two."

They returned to the gathering area and sat with a smiling Unton. Tom wanted to learn more about the history of their culture, and he began to see the wisdom in his host to use this family as an example of Elietian life.

Tom began his questions with, "What is the origin of your species?"

"That is under great discussion for these times," Unton replied. He went on, "Some believe we were created in a single moment by Lodi, creator of our universe. This is based on very old scripts recovered in ancient tombs and translated by many of our prehistory scholars. The scripts are the basis for all our traditions, laws, and morals. It was the scripts that gave us knowledge about creation, both in space and here on our gracious planet."

Unton went on, "Then there are those who are theorizing that we are descendants of the lower species, and they call that process Progression. There are very aggressive discussions among the spiritual leaders of our government and many of our scientists about how our species originated, whether as a single event taking only a few days by Lodi, or through Progression over a long time."

Just then Alox broke into the discussion. "Yes, and that pack of old male and female leaders have restricted my ability to teach Progression in my learner rooms, and they warned me that if I continue, they will incarnate me for many years. Roa, our Prime Leader, is behind all the restrictions. She is afraid that her position as Prime Leader will be threatened, so she keeps a tight hold on those who teach the young learners, such as I. She uses the old veteran Mesi to keep us in line for he is a very well respected believer of the Lodi scripts. We can't even bring a Progression script to our learning areas, and the major rule is that there will be no talk of such nonsense. Well, I did share the theories of Progression with some of my students, and the head leaders found out and restricted me from the learner place until they decide what to do with me."

Unton began again. "I am very concerned for Alox. Talk among various colleagues is that the head leaders are planning to punish her very harshly as an example to others who might break the rule."

They all talked some more, and far in the back of Tom's mind there seemed to be ancient Earth stories of a similar nature. It was starting to get cooler, and the family was beginning to slow down. Unton, Alox, and Uta suggested that they retire to their resting areas, and they had made a very comfortable Earthlike bed for Tom, and he retired also. Their resting areas were very plain and without blankets because the warmth came from outside their bodies. Their beds were very plain and covered with a soft material that was not heated so they could slow down and rest.

It was about eight hours later when Tom awoke after a very restful sleep. The cool, well-lit evening still had about sixteen Earth hours left, and all of the residents had settled down. Tom decided to explore the now very quiet city, and as he walked down one of the many paths, he was struck with the eerie feeling of total quiet, realizing that he would be alone for the remaining sixteen hours without any company.

Tom went to the local museum where Unton worked as an anthropologist in order to find out what he could about this very interesting culture. The museum was open, and Tom was free to roam to any of the areas of his interest. This seemed to be the perfect place to pass his time while all the residents slept in the cool air. He was unable to read any of the scripting, and it was difficult for him to put labels on the various exhibits. Then he came to a very large area with artwork painted around the entire room on the walls and what appeared to be a pictorial of the planet's history. The artwork was very bright and detailed with pictures depicting the historical events.

Tom was able to find the beginning of the history pictorial. The pictures told of the creation and that the sky and ground were created in a very short period of time, and that the sky was created from energy within the ground. It was pictured that all the various species of life were created in parallel by a mysterious power from Lodi. The Power was depicted as rays coming from the being of Lodi, and the pictures went on to show the creation of the first intelligent beings across the entire planet in one event. The pictorial then went on to show the advancement of the cultures from the early time to the more recent, and continued with the great violent wars that plagued the planet over the centuries, killing millions.

Also illustrated was the complete destruction of much of the species around the planet from extremely cold temperatures. The planet was covered almost entirely by ice, keeping large amounts of life from starting again, but some did survive. The Elietians only knew about the ice from legends and history. It was with Lodi's strength that a good number of each species survived to continue the growth for the future.

Tom spent many hours going through the large facility, trying to understand the various exhibits without being able to read the text descriptions. Just about all of the animal types were represented in the exhibits and were ordered by the species that Lodi created. It appeared that the Elietians believed strongly in the process that the species were created in parallel, as organized in the exhibits. This was the proof of Lodi's power and the process that he used to create all life on the planet. Then, after a time, Tom returned to the home of his hosts and went to sleep again.

Many hours later, Tom was awakened by some quiet activity in the household. The temperature had risen, and the entire city was coming alive again with the hustle of the normal activity. There seemed to be additional activity with Unton and Alox, and he went to see what the quiet commotion was about. When Tom entered the gathering room, Alox had their egg on her lap. Something was breaking though the shell, and Alox was helping slightly with the struggle. First a little head appeared, then an arm, and then part of the body. Alox continued to help lovingly by breaking some of the shell very carefully. It took about a half hour for the entire process. The little male was wet with birth, and Unton had some warm cloths ready to help with the cleaning. Alox held her newborn close to her chest and cleaned much of the birth fluid with her tongue. The young one was very bright-eyed and seemed to know where he was. He was very natural and considerably more mature and alert than humanoid babies, and he had great expression and bonded with Alox immediately while she lovingly cleaned him. Unton used a small heating light to keep the new baby active and alert.

Tom was a little overtaken with emotion and with the loveliness and difference of the event for he had come to feel very close to his new friends in a very short time. This was one of Tom's finest experiences in all of his travels. Alox gently held her new offspring in her arms very softly, bent her head down close to her young one, and began to feed him mouth-to-mouth with food she had stored in her gullet after partially digesting the meat. It was as though she was kissing the baby, and this added to the picture of love.

During the early part of that day, there was much celebrating in the house. Uta was especially excited at the prospects of having a new brother to play with, and Tom enjoyed holding the newcomer. It will take only thirty sun cycles for the baby to start walking upright, 120 to begin talking reasonably well, and 400 to begin instruction in the learning area. The family had many scripts of all types, and learning was a key activity in the household. The baby would have a great start before the formal learning started with the knowledge and intelligence of his parents.

It was a day later and Tom was sitting in the gathering room with the family discussing many of the significant historical events of the past centuries when a hard knock on the front entrance startled the quiet and echoed loudly to break the conversation. Unton stood from his place and opened the door. It was one of the head leaders with two protectors, and they walked in without an invitation. The head leader went straight to Alox and firmly, without emotion, explained, "Alox, the leaders have found that you have violated the basic rules of our society by continually exposing our young learners with the absurd tale of Progression. They have instructed me to have you taken to internment until we can schedule an investigation by our High Board. You will be able to present your defense at this hearing, and the High Board will decide what your internment should be."

There was silent shock in the gathering room, and Unton began to show a strong defensive posture in his body language. "How could our happy home turn so badly in such a short time?" thought Unton as he restrained himself from doing something that would make the situation worse. Alox stood and put her hand on Unton's arm while saying, "It is the way that we talked about before, and I must go with them to fight for our beliefs and truths."

Tom wisely sat motionless, holding the baby and staying quiet so as not to interfere in something that was not his business or to make matters worse. The two protectors went to Alox and took her by the arms out the door with the head leader following, leaving the rest stunned and very alone. There was total silence except for the gurgle of the baby.

"It will be a very short time before they have the hearing, and I have no idea how we can defend something that has been clearly restricted for us to publish or give learning to," Unton sadly said, bowing his head in despair. "And, I don't know where to begin. Leader rules are something I know very little about."

With the baby still in his arms, Tom stood up and put his free hand on Unton's shoulder and then tried to comfort Unton with, "You are very good people, and this will pass. Just have some faith that things will work out. Who knows of the leader rules that could defend Alox?"

"That will be very hard because the leaders will look badly at anybody that will try to help," Unton replied in a very somber voice. "I will ask my colleagues tomorrow, but now I need to go to the internment place and give comfort to Alox. Will you stay here with the young ones and keep them while I am gone? And of course, you will have to feed the baby later." With that, Unton quickly left without another word, leaving Tom with the young ones.

"Don't worry, I'll take good care of them!" Tom shouted as Unton rushed out the entry.

A very short time after Unton left, Tom realized that he had agreed to feed the baby. He had seen Alox feed her loved one a few times and knew what was required of him. After awhile the baby started to gurgle for food, and Tom had to proceed. He went to the food storage area and selected a piece of whitish meat and cut it into chewable pieces. He then put two pieces in his mouth and chewed

145

them while being careful not to swallow. The taste and smell were awful, but he had to comply and, holding the baby in his arms, Tom put his mouth down close and slowly fed the baby. It took several chews to satisfy the baby, and by that time, Tom had become used to the process and the closeness that he developed with the baby. He especially enjoyed the feelings of the aftermath. The food was the worst tasting he had ever had throughout the entire Galaxy Quadrant, but it seemed to be worth the effort.

Unton arrived at the internment place and was allowed to visit with his mate, Alox. The internment area was very plain and clean, and Unton was let into the area through a small waist-level gate. He sat with Alox, who had a very worried look on her face.

"What will happen to the young ones if I am interned?" she sadly asked. Her eyes were glazed over, and her whole expression showed of great sadness and worry. Unton stayed for awhile to comfort her, and then sadly left for his dwelling.

When Unton arrived to his place and entered, he found Tom still holding the baby. It was evident that the baby liked the feel of Tom's body heat, and he had a very satisfied expression on his face. Uta, who was reading some scripts, ran to her father, and with a tight hug asked what was going to happen to her mother. It was a sad moment in a normally happy place.

The next morning, a stranger showed up at the front opening. He was very sloppy and worn in his attire and, as an elder, was sort of wrinkly. Unton went to the front opening and asked who was this spectacle of a male.

"I am Lerrad, and I understand that you are in some really cold water," replied the old one with an all-knowing expression.

Unton was astounded for he knew this male as the best investigative defense expert. He had seen this legend only in graphic presentations, and his reputation was renowned among the leaders and the Rules Committees.

Unton replied, "Yes, we are, and we are very fearful of the consequences of our beliefs." He then offered Lerrad to come in and sit down.

Lerrad open up with, "Beliefs are useless and not considered by the High Board who will determine the fate of your Alox. What we need to do is create great questions among the High Board who will decide her fate. I am not sure that is possible, but we can give it a good try. The leaders are very closed to these ideas because they threaten their most sacred rules directed by the Lodi scripts; Alox could not have insulted them more."

Unton became very discouraged at this thought. Lerrad continued and, finally looking at Tom, with sarcasm asked, "What is this strange creature? Is this your proof of Progression? If so, you are surely in trouble."

"No, he a visitor from far away. The higher ups thought that he would find our family most interesting, and they sent him to us. He is very wise and has become a very good friend," replied Unton.

Lerrad shrugged and continued, "I will go to the museum and look through the old script translations to see if I can find something that we can use as a defense. You stay here, and don't talk to anyone. I'll see you this next early day. The investigation is scheduled for the day after, and we must work fast."

Tom queried, "What can I do to help?"

"Nothing, just stay quiet and do not interfere. The leaders will not like interference from the outside. Especially from those they do not understand," Lerrad exclaimed in a very sharp tone. "We will have enough to think about without having to deal with an additional confusion." Then Lerrad left with a strong walk and his head down in careful thought.

When the cool came, they all retired for the evening. The next day, Lerrad showed up with bad news, for he was unable to find any rules in the scripts that could be used to affect the upcoming inspection hearing. He looked throughout the entire night, using a heating cover to keep him active. There was nothing, even in the very old rules. Then he left to spend the time with Alox to try to figure out a strategy. Lerrad was very aloof and in deep thought and walked with a preoccupied expression. While he was at the investigation hall, he found out that Exar was going to represent the leader's position in front of the High Board. This was very bad news because Exar was well known as the best leader representative, and she had a very high record of success. Plus, it is to the leader's advantage of image to have a female represent against a female.

The next day, the investigation hall was crowded to overflowing with interested parties in this very controversial subject, for it had become the talk and interest of the scholars, scientists, and leaders, near and far. This case would possibly set an official standard for future beliefs and learning givers. The stakes and divisions were high between older traditions and new thinking.

Tom was invited and was able to sit in the front row with Unton. He had the baby in his arms with Uta sitting close to her father. They represented the family of Alox, and many of her learning colleagues and friends were sitting in the next rows directly behind them. The area was filled with pro and con Progression thinkers, and it was to be a crucial event that would take a large place in the history scripts.

The time for the investigation to start was near, and Alox was brought in to sit in her place next to Lerrad. There were many murmurs coming from others in the area and opposite Exar, her accuser. The area became very quiet when it was announced that the five High Board leaders entered the area, and they sat down in front of the two sides of the issues.

The top leader, sitting in the middle of the five, started by warning those present that any outbreaks would result in expulsion from the investigation area. Her name was Boxar, and she was well respected among the leaders as being fair, impartial, and logical in these types of matters. The remaining leaders on the High Board of five were male, some young, and some older.

The following is the transcript of the proceedings:

Boxar: "Alox, you are charged with presenting to our young learners the unapproved scripts of the Progression theories that are unproven and have no merit as such. This is in direct opposition to our policies and rules. You have taken it upon yourself to disregard the direction of the high leaders. Is this your understanding of the charges?"

Alox: "Yes."

Boxar: "Are you ready to defend these charges."

Lerrad: "Yes, WE are!"

Boxar: "Then we shall proceed without further discussion. Exar, will you call your first witness."

Exar: "Will Goe please come forward."

Goe was a learning colleague and friend of Alox, and she was ordered to bear witness for the high leader's position with the High Board. She was very reluctant to do so but was threatened with internment if she did not give truthful witness.

Exar: "You are a colleague of Alox, and you have observed Alox presenting Progression to the young learners."

Goe: *Very reluctantly.* "Yes, on a few occasions, I have."

Exar: "Have you ever presented the theory of Progression to your learners?"

Goe: "No, it is forbidden."

Exar: "Do you yourself believe in Progression?"

Goe: "No, I don't."

There was a very low murmur among the observers.

Exar: "No further questions. Lerrad, you may ask your questions."

Lerrad: "Thank you. Goe, why is it that you do not believe in Progression?"

Goe: "I am much older and have the beliefs of previous generations. I learned that Lodi was the creator of all things and that there was no other way."

Lerrad: "Why is that?"

Goe: "I am required to think this way in order to stay with the young ones. I really love doing learning and don't want to endanger my position."

Lerrad: "Then you believe this way because you have to. Are you not able to think your own thoughts?"

Goe: "I do think my own thoughts, but I cannot share them with others."

Lerrad: "This is all I have to ask of Goe."

Boxar: "Thank you, Goe, and you may step back now. Exar, call your next witness."

Exar: "I now call Masi."

There was a larger murmur in the investigation area. Masi was at the top of all high leaders, and he was a very powerful and familiar figure, second to only Roa, the prime high leader. He was of the older high leaders and was the driving force behind having Alox investigated. He was a strong advocate of the

Lodi scripts and was considered an expert learner in the content and meaning of the Lodi scripts.

Exar: "We are honored today that you took the time to help us understand the nature of the beliefs and facts of the Lodi scripts."

Masi: "It is I who is honored to be among such a distinguished group on such an important issue, and I hope that I can clear up some of the confusion over these ridiculous Progression thoughts."

Exar: "For the record, could you tell us of your status, knowledge, and position among the high leaders?"

Lerrad: "We will stipulate that Masi is one of our culture's great authorities on our lifestyles, rules, and, of course, the Lodi scripts. I have known Masi for many years and have come to respect his thoughts and words as one of the most knowledgeable. I, too, am honored that he is here today."

Boxar: "Fine, let us move on with the investigation."

Exar: "Masi, tell us, are you a believer in the theory of Progression?"

Masi: "No, I am not. It would be impossible for the Progression theory to have any truth. It has no basis, and the scripts of Lodi have more logic than a mere idea that might be only possible. For centuries the teachings of Lodi have directed our ways, and they have stood the test of time. These teachings took us from our violent past, survived the great ice, and have given us a good and peaceful life with the moral direction that keeps us safe from violence. The teachings of Lodi are the only way we must live. All life on this planet has adopted these ancient teachings, and they have worked very well."

Exar: "What makes you so certain that the Lodi scripts are true?"

Masi: "The scripts are very specific and follow the only kind of logic that makes sense and can be true. They are clear that, in the beginning, our ground was created in two days and the sky in the next three. When the sky was created, our two suns came into being to give our ground the basis for supporting life. Lodi then created all the lower species in five days. Some days later, Lodi, in his thoughts, created our species simultaneously around all of our entire ground. This is of the true teachings and facts of the Lodi scripts."

There was absolute quiet in the area. Masi had good presence, and his position in the leadership gave his arguments solid truth. And everyone was captivated with the exception of the pro Progressionists.

Exar: "Why did you come here today?"

Masi: "I, of course, am very concerned for the welfare of our culture and want to make sure that our best interests are maintained and that we are kept safe with our beliefs. I have always held our culture in the greatest esteem and devotion, and I would sacrifice my life to maintain the safety of our culture. I love so much what we have accomplished and how we have prospered because of the Lodi scripts."

Exar: "When did it come to your attention that Progression was being presented to our young ones in the learning areas?"

Masi: "Many colleagues of the learning leadership informed me. I was shocked to find that this was being presented, and the high leaders had many discussions concerning this very important subject. We could not answer how we, as a culture, could have originated from the crawling creatures that give us so much of our nourishment. We all agreed that this instruction must discontinue."

Exar: "What did you do then?"

Masi: "We drafted a special script asking that the presentation of Progression in our learning areas be stopped. We delivered it to the leaders of the learning area where Alox was present."

Exar: "Did it stop?"

Masi: "No! We found out some time later that the presentation was still in place, despite our very specific script of rules."

Exar: "Who is at the center of this refusal?"

Masi: "Alox, as she sits here in this investigation. I believe that she is very well meaning and is trying to do her best, but she has been misguided and refused to discontinue this practice. She is very young and lacks the wisdom that we do in all the leadership. It would have been much better if she allowed the young ones to decide later and subjected them less to these outrageous theories. I am not against people's beliefs; I am only against the misplaced efforts to displace our proven Lodi scripts among the early learners."

Exar: "Your explanation of this very complex issue is deeply appreciated by this investigation group. We thank you for your keen wisdom."

There was a great hush in the area, and most were very impressed with the impeccable logic of Masi. Exar had completed her investigation for the leadership

151

and turned the area over to Lerrad. It looked very bad for Alox. During Masi's testimony, Lerrad had been taking many notations in his investigation script and, for most of the testimony, did not make any eye contact with Masi.

Boxar: "Lerrad, you may begin your questions."

Lerrad: "Thank you so much. I have only a few questions of our distinguished authority. Masi, it is nice to see you again. We have been colleagues for many years, and I am happily reminded of the early days when we were together. I hope you have been well."

Masi: "I have been quite well, thank you. And it is good to see you, also. I have great memories of our past togetherness."

Lerrad: "Like you, I am also a believer of the ancient Lodi scripts, but I do have some minor questions I would like you to help clear up for me with your expert knowledge."

Masi: "That is my honor, and I will do my best to help you."

Lerrad: "So, the Lodi scripts are the accurate explanations of our birth, our ground, and all the species?"

Masi: "Without a doubt?"

Lerrad: "And there is no room for untruths?"

Masi: "Yes, none."

Lerrad: "Well, that really confuses me."

Masi: "You are not alone. There are many that need deeper knowledge of the scripts."

There was a low laughter among the spectators.

Lerrad: "Okay! There is a question that I have always had in my mind, and I hope you answer it."

Masi perked up, smiled, and pushed his chest out.

Lerrad: "You have said that the Lodi scripts are accurate without question. Is that correct?"

Masi: "Yes."

Lerrad: "And that our ground, sky, suns, and species were created in just a few days in that order."

Masi: "That is right."

Lerrad: "Well, tell me, how is it that our two suns were created after our ground? Doesn't that seem a little backward? I mean, our best science leaders have calculated that we are traveling around those two suns. How did our planet travel with our suns not in place? How is this possible?"

Masi: "That was the power of Lodi. Lodi is at the center of all life and can create any structure. So, being at the center, he created our ground first."

Lerrad: "Well, I agree, but that still doesn't make total sense to me, and I still have questions, but thank you for your explanation anyway."

Masi: "It is my pleasure, as always."

Lerrad: "Was it not long ago that our best minds discovered that the ground is round and not flat like we had always thought in the very early time? Our proof is indisputable, and we have come to accept the round ground as true. This clearly shows that our beliefs can change based on new information. Do you believe that facts can change over time based on new information from our science?"

Masi: "Of course I do, but in this case, the original thinking of flat ground was created by scholars and was not in the original scripts. The scripts are all-knowing and complete. The flat ground vision was culture-made and thus imperfect."

Lerrad: "Yes, I see. That is saying that we are imperfect and may interpret information to get different results. Is that true?"

Masi: "Well, of course, but the scripts are true and complete."

Lerrad: "Yes, I see that also. You are quite knowledgeable with the ways of Lodi, aren't you?"

Masi: "Yes, I have spent much of my time reading and studying the scripts."

Lerrad: "This is obvious with your great knowledge."

The investigation area was getting quite intense with curiosity. Members of the Investigation High Group were taking careful notes in their scripts.

153

Lerrad: "We are privileged. I have another question. If we are imperfect and can make mistakes of such large proportions, how can we know that the scripts have been translated accurately? Was it not our ancestors who translated the Lodi scripts?"

Masi's expression was starting to change from the confident to very uncomfortable, and he was beginning to squirm in his seat. Others in the area were noticing this and waiting for a response.

Masi: "Well, the translators were guided by the words of Lodi."

Lerrad: "And how do you know that for sure?"

Masi: "It is written that the translators were guided by Lodi."

Lerrad: "I am still confused, but let us move on to some other points. The Lodi scripts tell us that our many cultures around the ground were created at many locations simultaneously. How can that be? Wouldn't Lodi have to be in many places at the same time?"

Masi: "That is also what is written, so it must be true."

Lerrad: "But you said that the translators were imperfect. Could they have been wrong?"

Masi: "That is not possible."

Lerrad: "Ok, I don't want to embarrass you any more. I am finished for now."

Masi: "But I must explain more…"

Boxar: "Please step away, Masi."

There was considerable murmuring in the area. Alox put her face in her hands and started to cry. Unton reached over to her and touched her shoulder for a moment. The baby was gurgling again for something to eat, and Tom volunteered to feed him. Tom took some of the white meat from a container and began to chew, getting it soft and ready for feeding.

Boxar: "PLEASE QUIET DOWN, OR I WILL REMOVE YOU ALL! Are we now ready to summarize for the investigation of the High Board?"

Lerrad and Exar: "Yes, we are."

Boxar: "Exar, you must start first."

Exar: "Thank you. I will be very brief. This investigation is not about history, what is truth, how the ground was created, nor any other subject that was discussed here. Our success is based on rules, and that is how we have survived the violent times and grown to a healthy, happy culture. We have been successful at passing our morals and rules on to our young ones in the learning areas. Critical to our continual safety and success, we must retain strong control over our rules in our culture, and especially in our learning areas. If we let this go without internment, we will risk the beginning of the end of our culture. What will be next? By the evidence and her own admission, Alox has broken the rules of our leaders, and as such, should be interned.

"I have great feelings of like for Alox and do not want to see her punished, but she did break our most important rule. There are no other facts that are important, and this is the only point that should be considered. At all costs, we must not deny what is so much a part of us.

"Thank you for my opportunity in this investigation."

Boxar: "Thank you, Exar. If you are ready to summarize, Lerrad, please do so."

Lerrad: "Thank you, I will also try to be brief, but this is a very important investigation, and I want to make sure that everything is covered.

"Yes, Alox did break one of our most important rules; that is not in question here. The issue here is, are we so rigid that new ideas cannot help us to progress? Just as the ground was once known to be flat, our technical colleagues have shown beyond all doubt that our ground is actually round.

"I am a faithful believer in the Lodi scripts, and often there were things that I could not understand. But in spite of this new knowledge, I did not lose my faith, nor did that change my mind about the things in which I believe and love. The early Lodi script translators had their own language in those ancient days and may have used different words than we use today. If we do not consider this, we will forever believe that our ground is really flat and not discover what is true. And our young ones will suffer with the lack of truth.

"There are many things that we do not understand or what still remain mysteries. As we move forward, we learn more things that answer those mysteries and, in fact, create more mysteries. This is the history of our culture, and we must continue."

155

Lerrad then turned to Tom, who was bent over feeding the baby and caring for him in a loving way. Lerrad raised his hand toward Tom while he turned.

"If you have thoughts that things and ideas we do not understand are not true, look at what we have here. This is a stranger from far away from our ground and suns, from grounds that circle their own suns. He has come to us in peace and feelings to share his points of view and to learn from us, and he has certainly learned some of our most precious values. There was a time when we would have laughed at such a sight and interned those who professed these ideas. Here it is, right before us and is beyond denial. Do our eyes trick us? I have touched him, and he is real, but, unlike us, he is also warm to the touch. Imagine that, warm to the touch!"

Everyone in the entire investigation area looked at Tom as he raised his head in great surprise. He had pieces of chewed meat on the side of his mouth. Unton compassionately placed his hand on Tom's leg, and Alox turned and looked at him with a loving smile.

"These things are far beyond our imagination and not of our ground. Who knows what else is beyond our current beliefs?

"Maybe Progression is the method that Lodi used to create our great culture.

"If we close our minds to these thoughts, our future will perish from the stagnation of ignorance. I cannot answer these questions for certain; I can only have my beliefs that are in myself, and each of us deserves that freedom as the scripts do say. We are free to think and express our thoughts. Why else would Lodi have given us our free spirit and mind as part of our own creation?

"So, today is important to our future, for it is here that we decide for faith and freedom, or stay prisoners of the past. Shall we deny our Lodi-given rights? The right for us to think.

"Thank you so much, and I know that this wise and fair investigative group will extend its wisdom to this issue. Your wisdom here today is our only hope for us as a species and culture."

Boxar: "Thank you, Exar and Lerrad. I believe that we are finished, and it is time for us to meet and come to a decision. We will make a decision by tomorrow. This investigation is closed."

End of transcript.

The High Board left the area, and so did the others. Alox was brought back to the internment area for the night, and Unton, Uta, Lerrad, and of course, Tom with the baby, left to go home. When they arrived at home, they all sat in the gathering room with a solemn quiet among all because it was now that the fate of their beloved Alox was being decided, and they were very afraid for their loved one.

Lerrad sharply broke the silence with a loud voice to Tom, "Well, my sky-man, you did a great job today. You became one of the important evidences during the investigation, and it was only your love and caring that made the point. You said nothing."

Tom only smiled with great love and satisfaction. His expression said it all.

Uta was very upset and cried, "When is my Alox coming back? I miss her so much."

Tom was still speechless as he held the baby, who was very active in Tom's warm arms, and Unton replied, "She will be home soon."

Lerrad bid his farewell with, "I'll see you in the morning, and we will go to the investigation area together."

The next morning, the investigation area was filled to capacity very early, and there was much verbal rumbling among the crowd. When Lerrad entered with the others, there was an ominous quiet that came over the crowd, then Alox was brought in and sat in her place. It was only moments later when the Investigative High Group entered the area and sat down in an authoritative way, and the silence of the hush was overwhelming. Everyone was anxious and careful to hear of the decision.

Boxar broke the silence with, "We have come to a decision. Will the accused please rise with her defender? We have unanimously found you in great violation of our rules and have decided for your internment period."

There were many groans from the attendance, and the sad look on the face of Alox turned to fear. This was the end. No more talking was to be had. Lerrad had a very stern look for Boxar as she continued.

Then Boxar began with the penalty. "We have considered very carefully what your internment should be, and we are in unanimous agreement that you should spend one day period in the internment area. Since you have already spent several day periods there, you are free to go back to your family and that very strange friend of yours."

The High Board left quickly from the stunned silence of the area. A simple moment passed and those in the area broke into great celebration with the realization of what just happened. Unton hugged Alox, and they both had great tears. Alox went to Tom with a big hug, almost crushing the baby between them. Uta was jumping up and down while Lerrad's hand was on her head.

"See! I told you she would come home," replied Lerrad. There was great joy in the area, and it took much time to clear with all those who wanted to give Alox their good wishes. Finally they were able to leave for home.

As they were all finally together in the gathering area at home, they began to look at each other with great happiness. They were especially grateful for Tom's quiet participation in the investigation.

"See, all you had to do was stay quiet," Lerrad commented. They all laughed.

The news of the investigation spread throughout Eliet, even to the far-off places.

Two days later, it was time for Tom to leave, and his beloved new family was part of the send-off group at the landing place of *Odyssey IV*. Many of them warmly extended their regards to Tom, especially Alox and Unton. Alox gave Tom a great soft hug that was cold but pleasant. He had not touched her in this way before and was very pleased with her soft coolness. She remarked about his pleasant warmness. Tom and Unton also hugged, which was very uncommon among the Elietian males, and it was strong, as men do, and quite pleasant for both.

Tom extended his affection to the baby in the arms of Alox and took him in for what became a big hug in Tom's warm arms. The baby gurgled with a smile, and Tom bent his head as if to feed the baby, but this time, kissed him lovingly. It was one of Tom's best experiences, for it moved his heart in a way he had never experienced. It was like having another family of blood, as different as they were in every way.

Tom's parting words with the translator turned off were of the little bit of Eliet language that he had learned. He turned at the foot of *Odyssey IV* with great emotion and gave these departing words, "We are vrey derfifnet in all our wyas but the lvoe of the uvniesre has tcuohed our mndis and cnetocned our hraets fvereor. I wlil aylwas lvoe you as my own."

Tom entered *Odyssey IV* and set the navigation system for his next adventure. He was still feeling deeply from the great experience he had with the Elietians. *Odyssey IV* gracefully lifted, and when it reached the outer atmosphere, it went into multiple light speed. Tom did not go to the suspension chamber right away; instead he went to his holographic display and inserted a small, shiny cube into a slot on his control console and gave some commands to the machine. It was the history album of his natural family and of the early years of his ancestor's time on the planet Earth. He sat for some time, watching the old holograms and reminiscing about his past while cherishing his stay with the beautiful Elietians.

His heart was heavy with thoughts of both his families, and he was on to his next adventure with a happy tear in his eye and another fulfillment in his heart. It was of these feelings that made his odysseys so worthwhile.

A Civil Affair

It was 1858 and before the start of a civil war that would split in two the still young nation of America for scores of years to come. There will be many untold tragedies, especially among the many sons, fathers, mothers and entire families of the nation. Few will escape the pain of this terrible nightmare, and many will not survive. This is the conflict that will show the horror and hell of war in its most real and tragic image. At stake was the issue of state's rights and the burgeoning confederate politics, considered America's second fight for independence. Ironically, it was a sense of freedom at stake for the southern states (state's rights) that still *favored* slavery, this country's tragic spot on history.

Michael was a strapping, good-looking man of forty-five that owned and worked one of the most successful farms in southeastern Pennsylvania. His wife, Carol, was a lovely woman of forty with a sturdy and shapely body and was the perfect match for Michael. They had been happily married for twenty-five years and worked hard to make their farm luxuriously simple with fine hand-made quality possessions. The farm had 100 acres of neatly plowed fields that produced corn and alfalfa, supplying a major portion the valley's feedstock, and it was also very productive with milk and hog products. Many of the German immigrants settling in the area and to the West worked Michael's farm during the seasons of planting and harvest. Unlike the southern states, there were no slaves. After years of work, many of the German immigrants settled their own farms with religious fervor in what was to become Lancaster County.

Michael and Carol had two children, a second-born daughter now of sixteen years and a first-born son now of twenty-one years. Charlotte took the image of her mother, and Shawn was an uncanny image of his father, Michael. Shawn was a handsome boy with blond hair and crystal blue eyes, and working the farm gave him strong arms, back, chest, and character. His open shirt and rolled-up sleeves revealed his manly characteristics with dramatic shape. Many of the nearby farm girls always eyed him with great attraction, and Shawn's polite and shy ways seldom responded to their flirtatious advances at the monthly social events. He was a fine catch who maintained an aloof attitude toward the many ladies, but he just did not favor any and kept to himself in this matter.

Michael was a major in the Pennsylvania Militia and was very active with the military and social aspects of his rank. He was prudent and influential in the local politics and attended the monthly council meetings on a faithful basis. While he refused to run for local office, his intelligence and clear articulation made him the favored speaker when an impasse stalled the monthly meetings. People respected his opinions and looked toward his thoughtful wisdom for guidance.

The meetings were held in a local church that served many of the God-fearing farmers and merchants of the area. It was a pristine wooden building that reflected white at the edge of the central merchant area, which was slowly becoming a small town. The craftsman talents of the many residents was evident on the inside with quality wood and workmanship, and it was the common place where people came together to worship as well as discuss the many issues of the time. It was the social glue of the widespread community and provided the atmosphere of a city hall and local government. Michael had become a leader during the meetings, and Shawn, his now maturing son, loved to attend the meetings and watch his father in very selective articulate action. The great debates always filled the agenda with speculation, opinion, and politics that filled the need for drama in the lives of the hardworking citizens. Feelings were high and opinions strong, but most favored the maintenance of the Union and the abolition of slavery.

Tensions between the northern and southern states had been building to a high fever, and the talk of state's rights and the possible separation of many of the southern states from the Union echoed throughout the land. News was slow to come, and it was most often inaccurate and exaggerated, adding complexity and confusion to the monthly debates of the community leaders. As time went by, it became apparent that a political solution was not at hand and the country began talking of military violence as a solution. The northern and southern states became very polarized with strong feelings that would lead ultimately to a great American tragedy.

Michael, as a major in the Pennsylvania Militia, was commissioned and charged with the organization and training of the many local volunteers. Shawn joined the Army and was relegated to a private, but because of his expert horsemanship and command of language, he was promoted to sergeant and began training for intelligence activities for the Army by Pinkerton in New York. Shawn spent much time in New York as a student of intelligence techniques and would dream of becoming a master spy for the Union.

The tragedy and violence of war broke out in the South.

Initially, Pennsylvania was spared the early violence and was isolated. Michael was assigned to the task of training troops while Shawn continued his knowledge growth in the art of intelligence gathering and analysis. The war and their mutual interest brought father and son even closer than before with talks of the various opinions, strategies, and politics. A higher level of mutual respect grew between the two in their many hours of political discussions, and they became more like friends than father and son. Working the farm became more distant and relegated to the German immigrants. The war interest became a passion for the two in spite of the potential dangers that had not reached into their location. Most of the violence was far off and removed from their daily reality, and the dirty red of spilled blood was not yet a vivid vision.

Shawn had gone to New York for three months to deepen his training and later received a commission as a second lieutenant in just seven months. The home education that Michael and Carol meticulously gave their son and daughter gave Shawn a college graduate and gentleman image. Returning to his home after this more advanced training, it was evident that Shawn was becoming a very mature man with great intelligence.

One day while riding together over the pastures on a wonderful sun-lit and breezy day, their loving man-to-man discussion turned very serious to the progression of the war. They both knew that it would not be long before they were drawn into the dangers of real battle, and the high risk of death would become a reality. They both cherished this time together but did not let on to each other for their concerns.

While riding together over a knoll, the sun started to lower toward the horizon while the cool breeze surrendered to the coming of a still nighttime. They had lost the perception of time while deep in conversation. Shawn, in a burst of energy, shouted, "Race ya back to the barn, Dad! Come on!"

Both their horses bolted, and they sped down the field with the setting sun at their backs. The horses were of fine quality, welcomed the freedom of the run, and coming to the edge of the field lined with a rail fence, both men and horses flew gracefully over the fence without missing a step and in perfect togetherness. The jump was flawless and their mutual expert horsemanship showed as they both mastered the terrain to the barn. They arrived at the same time, which meant that

Shawn was now becoming the horseman of his dad. Michael taught him well and was so proud of his fine son. They took care of the horses and reminisced of the day's events with a sometimes challenge from Shawn to his dad about "Next time, I'll..."

Two weeks later, Shawn was ordered back to New York for additional training. He and his dad talked for some time before Shawn was to leave, and they hugged a goodbye to acknowledge the harm's way they might come upon. This time, Shawn would not return to the farm of his youth and maturity for some time.

Two months later, the Union Army assigned Shawn to his first intelligence assignment. He was given a new identification as a young gentleman from Tennessee, and he was instructed to infiltrate the Confederate Army in Atlanta, Georgia. He also had introduction papers that positioned him potentially as a junior officer. His education and gentlemanly ways would reinforce this image and position, and it took Shawn twelve hard days to reach his destination in the heart of Dixie.

The main street of Atlanta, Georgia was bristling with finely dressed gentlemen and graciously decorated Southern women with flowing lace, broad-rimmed bonnets, and decorative umbrellas casting their cool shadows as they spun. There were many soldiers in cleanly pressed gray uniforms bustling along the sidewalks with seemingly important chores to accomplish. Shawn slowly rode down the main street lined with neatly painted stately homes and businesses. He was in enemy territory now, and the subtle beauty of the scene blinded his vision of the mission for only a moment. He approached the Central Hotel, dismounted, and entered the lobby through a great white double door embellished with artful stained glass. It was a stately image that Shawn had only seen in the upper parts of New York. The wooden craftsmanship reminded him of his home and the great care his dad put into the quality of the farm.

His charm with people made him very likeable, and the desk clerk gave Shawn a choice room overlooking the street. While very young, people viewed Shawn as a mature man. With the desk clerk, he reserved a hot bath in the local bathhouse just behind the hotel, and it was good to finally remove the twelve days of hard travel from his body. The black attendant at the bathhouse was also very gracious and went out of his way to make Shawn very comfortable.

Refreshed and feeling relaxed in this alien but welcoming town, Shawn's stomach beckoned for the first full hot meal in several days of travel. He walked across the busy street to a very appetizing-looking restaurant almost full with well-dressed customers. The smells were very appetizing, and he eagerly entered and was shown to a seat by a gracious host. The host handed Shawn a neatly hand-printed menu with only entrée items on it.

The entrée selections were southern-fried chicken, breaded soft-shell crawfish, open-fired beefsteak, and breaded baked catfish fillets. Side dishes included spiced rice and red beans, hush puppies, mashed potatoes, carrots, and fried onions. Before he could decide what to order, a server came by and placed a basket of hot cornbread on the table with soft fresh butter and an assortment of jellies. The server left and came back shortly when he felt that Shawn had decided. Shawn opted for the southern-fried chicken, mashed potatoes, and hush puppies. The food came in about twenty minutes while Shawn consumed all of the cornbread. The plate was very full, and Shawn was not disappointed in the taste of the chicken. It was as good as his mother's, and it reminded him of home, a place he felt lonely for.

Halfway through the meal, a richly dressed man of about forty years approached Shawn's table and in a friendly, very French accent announced, "Bonjour, mon ami." He bowed slightly.

"What?" replied Shawn with a surprised smile as he looked up from his half-completed dinner. Shawn knew that this was French but did not know what was said.

"Ah, my name is Jean Claude Pacquet," He said with a smile and a very romantic accent. "May I join you?"

Shawn pointed his hand out toward a chair and exclaimed, "Sure thing. My name is Shawn, and I am from Tennessee." And Shawn extended his hand for a shake.

Jean Claude took his hand firmly, sat down with a smile, and asked Shawn if he was new in town and was he in the service of the Confederacy. Shawn explained that he was here to join as a junior officer and was eager to get started. Shawn's excellent home schooling came through with proper English and table manners. Jean Claude saw that Shawn was a young man of intelligence and proper upbringing and was probable material for a commission. His manners and ways came across as a gentleman should, and they showed that he was of a quality family.

Shawn asked Jean Claude why he was here as he started to politely finish his meal with good table manners. Jean Claude explained that he was in Atlanta as a strategy consultant on loan from France to the Confederation, and he was to take active part as an officer in some of the special operations that might be needed. The pair talked on and made a good connection as time passed, and when Shawn was finished with dinner, Jean Claude invited him to join him in the smoking lounge just next to the dining hall. Shawn enthusiastically agreed. This was good company for his lonely heart.

The two men sat down in two lushly upholstered scarlet chairs matching the elegant décor of this fine room. Jean Claude ordered two French brandies of his knowledge and offered Shawn a cigar. Shawn had never smoked and only had a few tastes of homemade ale and applejack. Jean Claude cut the tip of his cigar off as Shawn watched, and he followed the ceremony with his own cigar. This was going to be a manly adult time for Shawn. Jean Claude lit his cigar and, leaning over with a long match, lit Shawn's. Shawn's throat exploded with choking immediately and expelled the thick air from his lungs. Jean Claude laughed with respectful joy, and Shawn soon followed in the humor. The server put the two brandies on the smartly finished table between the two men, and this time Shawn was careful to sip the brandy slowly as the two continued to talk.

They had talked for about an hour, and Jean Claude admitted to Shawn that he was very well connected to many of the high-ranking Confederate officers and he might give Shawn a proper introduction to the right military people. Shawn became excited inside and flattered at this prospect and thought that this was more than he had expected so soon. The two men separated, and Shawn returned to his room for what would be a very good night's sleep.

Early the next morning, Shawn returned to the restaurant for a breakfast of eggs, fried potatoes, and fresh hot biscuits with sweet honey. Again, halfway through his meal, Jean Claude joined him, wishing Shawn a good morning. "I have made arrangements for you to interview with Captain Pierce in about an hour. He is the main assistant to General Johnson and has much influence."

Shawn attended the interview and was offered a commission as a second lieutenant on the spot. Shawn was delighted with his fast progress infiltrating "The Enemy."

Over the next few weeks, Shawn became popular within the Atlanta military social circles and was invited to many of the social events that sprinkled the Atlanta area. He was invited to one of the most important parties and prepared to go with his finest uniform. Jean Claude came by and picked up Shawn so that they could go in each other's company. They looked as though they belonged together as they strolled down the wide street to the Heart's Mansion just at the edge of town. In the thirty minutes it took, Jean Claude briefed Shawn on who were the important people and their roles in the complicated war preparations.

Jean Claude and Shawn reached the large white mansion with pillars extending from the long porch to the stately slated roof beams. They walked up the wide front stairs, entered through the large open double doors, and were greeted by a very polite black man with a stiffly starched white shirt coat. He took their hats and respectfully pointed the two toward the main room where music was playing joyfully with a lively and happy beat.

There were many gray uniforms throughout the large room, some dancing with elegantly dressed ladies and some lined along the walls talking of political and military interests. Shawn immediately saw Captain Pierce and went to his side with a cheerful hello.

"Well, hello, Shawn. How are you doing? Have you settled in yet?" Before Shawn could answer, Pierce introduced Shawn to the circle of gray uniforms as a rising star in the new Confederate Army in spite of his rank as only a second lieutenant. Shawn was embarrassed and flushed with a slight red on his fair skin. Shawn was able to fit right into the discussions with a naive intelligence that the others enjoyed and respected. This was a great connection, and, it occurred in less than a month.

Shawn was involved with listening when he noticed out of the corner of his eye a beautiful vision of a young and fine lady. She captured his attention as she had noticed Shawn first in the early evening. Both had a strong but shy mutual attraction. Shawn waited for some moments and then excused himself politely from the discussion group. As he walked away, several of the senior members of the circle smiled with approval and understanding of Shawn's newly born social mission.

Shawn walked directly to her from across the room and with a big and confident smile, said, "Hello, my name is Shawn." She smiled brightly, extended her hand and bashfully replied, "My name is Janet, and I have not seen you before here in Atlanta."

"Yes, I arrived here for my new commission as an officer four weeks ago and since have been very busy with military affairs." Shawn was trying to impress Janet with his newly acquired importance.

While she was not very impressed with his credentials, she was very attracted to his presence as he was with her. They talked for a while, and Shawn's charm made Janet giggle shyly and with affection. They talked for about an hour, enjoying each other's company as naturally as old friends. Janet invited Shawn for a walk through the well-kept gardens that encircled the mansion. As they walked in the half moonlit gardens, Janet politely put her hand around Shawn's extended arm with a natural motion. They talked for some more time, and both their hearts became excited with attraction and the affection of new love. Shawn, usually aloof from females, felt very comfortable with Janet.

Two weeks passed, and Shawn continued his military duties during the day and at night spent most of his free time with Janet. This was Shawn's first experience with romantic love, and he was overcome with these new emotions, as was Janet. One Sunday, they had planned a picnic together in a special place that Janet used to play as a child. It was a knoll in a small valley near a slow moving stream. They arrived in a one-horse carriage that Shawn had rented in town, and Janet had brought a basket of food that she had prepared that morning. Shawn spread out the beautiful quilt that Janet brought, and she emptied much of the basket contents. Knowing that it was Shawn's favorite, she made southern-fried chicken as well as boiled eggs, fresh bread, and assorted other foods.

It was a beautiful, sunny day, and much of the discussion revolved around the plight of the state's rights of the Confederation. This subject was continually in the forefront of Shawn's mind because of his daily military duties and especially with his good friend Jean Claude. Shawn was building sympathy toward the cause of the South in his affection for Janet and others.

The warm sun and cool breeze whispering through the trees set a peaceful setting, and Shawn began to hug and hold Janet. He kissed her, and she responded with her arms around his neck returning the affection. Their hugs and kisses grew very passionate, and without any question they began to make love, each for the first time. It was wonderful and natural, and they held each other with great feeling. They were both now very much in love.

It was hard for Shawn and Janet to leave each other that night, but they did part. Shawn dropped Janet off at the home of her parents and returned the rented carriage to the stable master. Shawn's mind was still rambling with the thoughts of this new experience and his strong feelings for Janet. He was not ready to go to sleep, so he went to the restaurant lounge where he spent much time with his good friend Jean Claude.

He entered the room, and Jean Claude was sitting reading what looked like some very important papers and a map. Shawn sat down across a small table with a great and different smile on his face. Jean Claude noticed Shawn's flushed face and, with a knowing expression remarked, "Did you have a good picnic today?"

Shawn shyly replied, "It was OK." And they both smiled.

Jean Claude put down the papers that he was so intent on before. "Tomorrow you will start training and briefing on a new and important mission that will take place two months from now. It will deal with the railroad, and Captain Pierce will discuss the details tomorrow. I will also be on the mission, and this will be our first real military mission together."

They spent more time talking as close friends did with the thoughts of his intelligence mission far from Shawn's thinking. The next morning, Shawn dressed in his uniform and reported to the military conference room after a hurried breakfast. There were over twenty officers in the room buzzing with fervor and verbal commotion. Shawn found a seat next to Jean Claude and, with a southern-like greeting, sat down. During the conference, Captain Pierce detailed plans to secure the railroad lines heading northward. This was a critical mission for the transportation and the supplying of armies in upcoming battles in the North. The meeting lasted for about three hours, and assignments were handed out. Jean Claude was to lead an advance party along the train route and scope out any enemy activity, and Shawn was to join him.

The mission was not to take place for six weeks, and this gave Shawn the opportunity to take leave. He bid farewell to Jean Claude and spent much time saying goodbye to Janet as he left in civilian clothes for the long trip home. His friends assumed that he was going home to Tennessee and not his home in Pennsylvania.

Shawn arrived 13 days later to the farm of his family, and his thoughts were still of his beloved Janet and the many friendships that he had made in Atlanta. His mother was surprised by his arrival and greeted him with great joy that he was safe and healthy looking. He seemed to be different to her with a new expression of maturity. After many minutes of a mother's welcoming, she told Shawn that his return was quite timely because his father, Michael, was returning tonight, and then she offered Shawn some of her home cooking.

That night as Michael was close to the farm, he sensed a newness in his heart and, upon arriving, went straight to the house instead of going to the barn to take care of his horse. Shawn was sitting at the table where they so often shared meals together. He stood, and father and son came together with manly and sturdy hugs and hard pats on their backs. Michael rustled Shawn's light hair as he had done with him as a boy. Shawn was far from a boy now, and Michael smiled with approval. They had many discussions about the politics of the growing war, and Michael was impressed with the new knowledge Shawn was expressing. Shawn shared with his dad how deeply he had infiltrated the high levels of the Confederate

Army and as a trusted officer, he was getting closer. Michael was delighted and invited Shawn to a communication meeting the next day in the Central Church.

Upon arriving at the church the next morning, the front yard leading to the church was filled with horses and carriages, some of a military nature. Every one stood as Michael entered the building. He went straight to the pulpit to take his place as the leader of the meeting. Shawn took a seat in one of the pews, smiling and waving to the many friends of his neighborhood that he hadn't seen for some time. Michael took control of the meeting, and a quiet hush filled the large room.

"Many of you have now have reenlisted, and some are still of the Militia and have been training now for eight weeks for a special mission deep into the South. I can't tell you the exact nature of the mission, but it is critical to the Union." Michael went on to explain how the mission would start and what support supplies would be needed. The 100 handpicked members of the Pennsylvania Militia complemented the regulars and were to meet at the Wilson Crossroads three weeks from now in the early morning. From there, they would travel south to their destination, which was still kept a secret. Michael hosted many questions from the anxious audience, and the meeting broke up after two hours of discussion. Most of Michael's responses to the many questions were, "I can't tell you that at this time." This was going to be a covert mission.

On the way home, Michael felt comfortable revealing the nature of the mission to his beloved son since Shawn was a trusted member of the Union Army. Shawn grew quiet and expressionless as Michael explained that they were to penetrate almost to the Georgia border and along the way, destroy the railroad support structures such as water and fuel stops, stations, and repair terminals along the 200-mile routes. Michael explained that this would severely cripple the efforts of the Confederate Army to transport and supply any northern penetration. Shawn was very quiet and did not say anything, and he was tormented at the potential conflict that was unfolding inside him. His thoughts of his beloved Janet and his good friend Jean Claude ricocheted in his mind and heart, and he was in great pain and fear.

That night, Shawn could not sleep and restlessly walked around the center of the farm. Daylight came without Shawn getting any sleep, and his mother called him for breakfast. Michael became concerned with Shawn's quietness at the breakfast table and asked him what was wrong.

Shawn replied, "I am just worried about this war and all the killing that will destroy the many families from both sides." Michael was sensitive and proud of Shawn's mature feelings and concerns.

For the next three days, Shawn was listless, and his mother became very concerned, for her mother's instincts told her that her son was in great pain over some conflict in his heart. As Shawn prepared to leave for his long southerly route, Michael assured Shawn that all will be well and that God would protect them as he showed concerned for his son and bid him to be very careful.

Shawn arrived back in Atlanta twelve days later and went directly to the house of Janet to see his missed loved one. Janet ran out of the door before he got off his horse. He dismounted, and in spite of his twelve-day unclean nature, she threw her arms around him, and they kissed for quite awhile. Shawn held on to Janet in a very different way this time, and his heart was deep with sadness. She sensed this uneasiness that was so unlike Shawn's usual spirited manner.

After returning to town and cleaning up, Shawn went to the restaurant to heal his hungry stomach. He had lost some weight on the trip because he did not take the time to eat regularly, and Jean Claude just happened to be there. They hugged strongly and sat down together. Jean Claude was eager to hear of Shawn's time off, and the two men talked, but Jean Claude sensed Shawn's strong apprehension. He questioned Shawn about this, and Shawn untruthfully explained that a close friend of his had died early in battle.

A week passed, which was full of planning for the campaign to protect the critical rail lines. Shawn was full of conflict, knowing that Union soldiers led by his own father would meet his now friends in actual battle. His sympathy for the Confederate cause, his love for Janet, and the love he had for Jean Claude began to overcome his loyalty to his home and family. He was thinking in terms of rationalizing that it would be better for the covert Union mission to fail, and that path would result in the least number of casualties, with his naive thinking.

The next morning, he met Jean Claude early and asked to speak with him on a subject of great importance. They sat on a cast-iron bench on the wooden sidewalk in front of the hotel. Shawn slowly and quietly explained to Jean Claude his plight and of the Union plans to destroy the railroad beginning in the next week. Jean Claude listened intently and trusted Shawn that this was the truth, and he cautioned Shawn not to speak of this to anyone, no matter what, and that he would take care of the situation.

Later that day in one of the final planning meetings, Jean Claude proposed a second contingent of Confederate troops to lead the main force, led by Captain Pierce, by two days. This was to engage with any forward Union forces that may be planning an attack on the rail line. The officers agreed, and Jean Claude was assigned to lead this advanced group, and he, of course, assigned Shawn to his group.

As the contingent of over 400-mounted Confederate soldiers left on their mission, Shawn was filled with sadness fueled by the insecurity that he had not done the right thing. He justified in his mind that the result of this action would only produce a few deaths and mostly prisoners. Jean Claude did what he could to comfort Shawn as they followed the train line directly, with horses on both sides of the track. They were supplied daily with fresh provisions and maintained a fresh condition from trains on the railroad that followed back and forth from Atlanta.

Eight days into the campaign, forward scouts returned to the lead horseman and reported that about 200 Union soldiers were advancing southerly toward the Confederate line, mostly on foot. They were about five miles back. Jean Claude called his officers together and told them to hide their men in the woods on both sides of the track. The horses were brought back southerly along the track and far out of sight. They would wait until the Union soldiers were well along the trap before engaging. It was about 90 minutes when they heard the horses and footsteps of the oncoming troops, mostly dressed in blue.

As the leaders passed, the hidden gray uniforms waited patiently and Shawn was among them. He looked carefully at the faces from far off to see if he could recognize anyone in the line from his home. Shawn had never been in combat before and was not aware of the reality of the violence. He only knew of the sounds of gunshots and not of the blood to be shed. This was his naive view. He was waiting for the signal to be given to surround and capture the blues.

Then, the signal to fire was given, and a volley of 400 guns made their mark, downing about 50 Union soldiers in the first volley. There was no place for the blues to go because both sides of the tracks were covered with the fire of the grays. Twenty minutes had passed, and most of the blue Union uniforms were either gone or laying still on both sides of the tracks. The ambush was complete, successful, and most of the blues had died. Blood covered the tracks and gravel along the line. Many of the grays were picking up the few prisoners left and securing them.

Shawn could not believe his eyes because this is not what he had imagined, and he could not contain his shock. Jean Claude came to his side, "This is the reality of war. This is why we should always avoid this tragic venture."

Unknown to anyone, Michael, who was leading in the front of the line, made it to the woods and behind the victorious Confederate soldiers. He was alone, and blood was coming from his left forearm. As he crawled along the floor of the woods hidden by the thick brush, he was able to see some of the grays standing and talking. He was shocked to see his beloved son, Shawn, talking with what appeared to be the senior officer. His heart broke into a million pieces, and he could not believe that his only son had betrayed him in this way.

The feelings of anger and justice filled his heart as he crawled closer to get a better look at those who ambushed them, including Shawn. He wanted to make absolutely sure that this was Shawn and not a look-alike. It was Shawn.

When Michael was about 50 feet from Jean Claude and his Shawn, he stood up with pistol in hand, pointed at Shawn with careful aim and hesitated to pull the trigger. Jean Claude caught this out of the corner of his eye, and before he could react, Michael squeezed the trigger, hitting Shawn directly near the heart. Shawn saw his dad in shock and cried out "Father, I am sorry!" and fell to the ground dead. Jean Claude looked at Michael with compassion, raised his pistol, and shot Michael critically.

Many of the other soldiers came running to see what the shots were about and saw that their good friend Shawn had been killed and that a blue officer's uniform lay in the bushes farther into the woods. A sergeant asked Jean Claude what had happened.

Jean Claude began solemnly with his head down and his voice shaky in great sorrow, "Here lies the family fabric of good people, victims of a great tragedy. This will be a long, bloody war that will destroy the very heart and soul of this new nation. The families will suffer the most while our leaders argue over petty political principles. Man in all his smartness has come to this point of hell, and it will be many centuries before we might learn to solve our differences in peace. I hope that the sacrifices made today will be remembered by the generations to come.

"I pray that God will show us that way and that we will be shown the way to more peaceful solutions to our perceived differences."

The war continued for many bloody years, and one the bloodiest battles took place in southern Pennsylvania just west of Michael and Shawn's home farm.

This was Gettysburg.

Jerry and Mike

This story is based on actual events.

Good times and hard times bring some men together in a great friendship that spans their hearts and minds, most often beyond the ability to describe in mere words. It is a great deed when men learn to open themselves to love for one another and, unlike the stereotype of non-feeling men, some learn the true feeling of deep friendship and give to each other from their hearts without embarrassments.

Jerry, now 48, was originally trained as an electronics engineer and progressed through the years with his hard work and natural creativity into marketing positions and then finally into a lucrative sales position. With 25 years of high-tech experience, Jerry was very knowledgeable with the industry he served, and he had a deep knowledge of a street sense that served him and his customers well. His performance in his sales position was outstanding, and he achieved many awards and bonuses. Jerry was a senior member of the local sales team for a large technology company and was looked upon as a mentor by many of his colleagues.

Mike had been a customer engineer, and his people skills gave him the potential for a sales career. He was hired into the sales office as a junior sales executive and was assigned to Jerry as an apprentice. Mike was a very bright and warm person, which made him very popular with most people. He had a lovely wife and a wonderful four-year-old son. Mike and his wife were very excited with his new opportunity in the sales department, which promised to at least double his income.

Jerry and Mike were immediately attracted to each other as friends with common likes, and Jerry had a great respect for Mike's gentle and likeable people skills, a talent that had always eluded Jerry. Mike admired Jerry's experience and knowledge of the industry and was very appreciative of Jerry's willingness to share and explain his knowledge of this complex industry. They had many instructional meetings in which Jerry shared all he knew in a very open and instructive way.

In addition to their professional relationship, Jerry and Mike quickly developed a personal friendship based on their common interests, and the affection that started to grow between them. They would often play their guitars together, and many times Mike would bring his electronic keyboard to the home-style jam sessions. While Jerry's music skills were very immature, Mike's were very strong, and Mike helped the musical clumsy Jerry along. They would play together for hours while drinking wine, smoking cigarettes, and exchanging philosophies and solutions to the problems of the world that turned to vague memories in the morning.

Jerry was already a heavy drinker from his many years in the marketing side of the industry, and in spite of that, was able to maintain a high level of job performance. He never missed a day because of a hangover. He considered himself a happy drinker and never showed any of the nasty personality changes that so many people exhibit when drinking heavily. Mike was also a heavy drinker and was of the same good nature as Jerry. The drinking meetings of song and philosophy strengthened the already tight bond between them, and many of their music and talk sessions would extend into the wee hours of the morning.

They worked together for two years, and Mike was finally offered his own territory. Mike was very successful, and he exceeded the promise of higher income by a wide margin. Six months after Mike's promotion, Jerry left the company to take a sales management position at another company, and he and Mike slowly became less connected because they were not together on a daily basis. A year passed, and they came together only a few times socially. When they did, much of the talk was about the old days and rumors of who went belly-up or became successful in their very highly complex industry.

Jerry's drinking had become heavier as the pressure and responsibilities of his new management position increased. He had for a long time known in his heart that his drinking was not good, and he promised himself every morning that he would stop or cut down, but he always succumbed to the desire later in the day. Over the next two years, it got worse. Jerry was able to maintain a reasonable level of job performance and hid his problem very well. That little voice in the back of his head kept telling him that he needed to do something about the level of his drinking, but the illusion of business success kept him from following his instincts to stop.

One day in September, coming back from a business trip on a coast-to-coast flight, Jerry had used some of his mileage points as an upgrade to first class on the cross-country flight. His drink of choice was straight scotch, and he used his charm on the cabin attendant to have it served in a large glass without ice. Jerry was able to consume six large glasses of straight scotch during the five-hour flight. When the plane landed and approached the gate, the cabin attendant who served Jerry approached the still-seated Jerry, put her hand on his shoulder, and, with a concerned look and tone asked, "Do you need help getting off the plane, sir?" In spite of the unusual amount of drink consumed, Jerry was stone-cold sober. He looked up at her and replied, "No, thank you. I can manage."

Jerry got up, removed his carry-on from the overhead compartment, and walked steadily by the cabin attendant with solid footing. He smiled and thanked her for the service and kindness, and she again looked straight into his eyes with a compassionate look and replied, "Have a safe trip home." Going down the ramp, Jerry walked straight, carrying his large carry-on on his shoulder by the strap. He thought of the cabin attendant's expression over and over, and then, when he was about 100 yards into the terminal, he dropped his bag, started to cry, and asked his God to help him to stop drinking. He finally had enough and surrendered to that haunting little voice reminding him over the years.

For some unknown reason in that single moment, he had lost his desire and obsession to drink in the manner that had been so much of his daily life. He did not drink for the next few months, and during the Christmas season, he shared only a bottle of champagne, and it seemed as though a miracle had happened.

Soon after the holidays, Jerry joined a widely known twelve-step program. He immediately took to the program and developed many non-drinking friends with some of the same feelings he had shared with Mike in the previous years. He finally had found a solution and started to feel better emotionally almost immediately. He now had hope for his future without the need to drink alcohol, and he became alive again and was starting to perform much better at work. His professional efforts seemed to go smoother and more efficiently, and, most of all, he began to treat people with more respect and compassion in his management role. He was making good progress.

After about a year, Jerry's company was going to have a booth at a trade show—the same show at which Mike's company was going to have a booth. Jerry took the opportunity to call Mike and schedule a lunch at the show for old times' sake, and Mike welcomed and looked forward to this opportunity. They had not seen each other for at least fifteen months and looked forward to getting together.

It was lunchtime on the second day of the trade show, and Mike showed up at the local restaurant first. Jerry showed up a few minutes later, and they shook hands and gave each other a big hug, as only men do. They were very glad to see each other after the long time apart. As soon as they sat down, a young server came to their table and asked if they wanted to start with a drink. Mike ordered a glass of white wine while Jerry ordered a tall soda water with lime.

They immediately began to reminisce about the old days and the many events since their last togetherness. There was lots of gossip about many of the people in the industry and what companies were emerging as leaders. The food came that they ordered, and they continued their talk. The server came by and asked if they wanted another drink, and Mike ordered a second glass of wine, and Jerry got a refill on his soda.

Mike eyed his longtime friend across the table with great curiosity that got the better of him. He asked Jerry, "You are not drinking today?"

Jerry replied, "I have not had a drink now for eleven months. It just got to be too much, and now I feel a lot better than I did when I was drinking."

"Well, I am still going strong," was Mike's reply. "Well, you do look great. Did you lose some weight? How did you stop?"

Jerry went into a few of the details but not too much, and he told Mike that one day he just "had it" and asked God to help him. Then he joined a twelve-step program that helped him to maintain his sobriety and provide a sense of friendship and support by others who had the same problem and had made the same decision to stop.

They continued their lunch with all kinds of discussion, and Mike was taken back by Jerry's new soberness. Mike's body language became a little uneasy. Mike did admit to Jerry that he was worried about his own drinking and shared with him the many times he had emptied the mini-bars in his hotel rooms on business trips. Jerry sensed Mike's discomfort but did not push him or make any judgments. Jerry knew that Mike, over time, would either come around himself or would probably have great difficulty. They left the restaurant and parted with a warm hug.

It was six months later on a Monday morning, and Jerry had just arrived in his office. One of his sales people, who was also a friend of Mike's, came into Jerry's office, closed the door and sat down in front of Jerry's desk.

"Did you hear that Mike had a major brain stem stroke Saturday night?" exclaimed the salesman. "He almost died and is in ICU as we speak. It was very serious and he came very close to death."

Jerry was taken back with the news and asked for more details, but there were none to come. Jerry was devastated and very concerned for his longtime friend and once spiritual drinking buddy, and he felt sad for Mike's beautiful wife and son. He called a few people and found that it was worse than indicated and that Mike and his family were not taking visitors and not to send flowers. They needed to focus on their devastating new life-changing situation that took just a few seconds to precipitate and would dramatically last a lifetime.

Jerry respected the wishes of Mike's family, and for the next four weeks he did not seek to visit Mike. But he did hear of Mike's condition on a continuing basis and tried to stay in the information loop. Jerry also heard that Mike had lost 90 percent of the motor control on his left side from his face to his toes. This was very serious, and Jerry was filled with much emotion of sadness for his friend. Mike was having a hard time and had a near-death experience due to a respiratory arrest five days after the actual stroke.

Then, in a moment of compassion, Jerry stopped by the hospital and gave the attending nurse one of his business cards. Jerry had written on it "Call me when you are ready. Your friend, Jerry." He just knew in his heart that Mike would understand and would call when he was ready. Jerry had to make sure that he did not push or lecture; this is what he learned to do in his program. This was an effort of attraction and NOT promotion.

Mike spent the next two months in ICU and was then moved to a recovery ward. Jerry was concerned that Mike had not called him and felt that his friendship with Mike had somehow moved out of reach. Jerry also had a sense of guilt that he did not try to save his friend from the pain of the drinking merry-go-round earlier, but he knew that Mike had to come to his own realization. His heart was very heavy, but he continued to think of Mike on a daily basis.

Then, one Saturday morning, Jerry received a call from Mike's wife.

"Hi, Jerry, Mike is getting better and would like you to visit. Can you stop by the hospital today?"

Jerry immediately replied, "Of course. I have been worried about him and will be delighted come by this afternoon." Jerry asked her none of the details of Mike's condition. He just accepted the request without question or reservation. His heart jumped with joy with the knowledge that Mike was still in touch in his mind with Jerry.

Jerry hung up the phone, went into the backyard, and began to cry with his feelings for Mike and the connection that they had as distant as it might have seemed at times. This was the first time that he released his hurt for Mike's condition in this way, and because of his intellectual closeness with Mike, Jerry knew what Mike wanted and meditated for the strength and words to come. He knew that Mike had had enough also and was looking for some guidance from Jerry as he had in the past with business. Jerry had to show Mike that he was not alone and that only a fellow drinker could understand what was in Mike's heart and what needed to be done to maintain a level of sobriety. And that only a recovered drinker can have a credible position in the recovery process of another.

That afternoon, Jerry showed up at the hospital and asked for directions to Mike's room. As he walked down the classic shiny tiled floor of the hospital corridor, uncertainty filled his mind on what to say and how to help. He knew that he could not push or nag and he just had to be there for Mike and answer questions that Mike might have. He came to Mike's room and entered. Mike's head was turned away, and he was looking out the sunlit window. In many respects it was, and would be, a beautiful day.

Jerry walked slowly to Mike's bedside and said, "Hey, man, how are you doing?" Mike turned and they looked at each other without a word being exchanged. They knew without even talking what the other was saying. And they hugged. Mike could only use one arm for the hug and joked, "See, now I can only give you half a hug!"

Jerry responded with some humor by saying, "Well, half-ass, when do you think we can start playing music together again?"

The left side of Mike's face had been greatly paralyzed by the stroke and in a very slurred voice, Mike replied, "It will be a long time. I can't lift my arm to press the frets."

Jerry then got serious and asked, "Hey, man, how bad is it really?"

Mike told Jerry of his inability to use his entire left side from head to toe, and then he also shared with Jerry his extreme guilt over his drinking, which he thought had caused his stroke.

"I remember what you said to me at lunch that day at the trade show. Your words haunted me for the next six months. I guess that God had to hit me with a two-by-four off the side of my head to get my attention." Mike's shaky and slurred voice continued, "The worst thing about all this is that in a single short moment my life changed completely, forever. I continually lay here thinking how it could have been if I did not drink so much, and I wish that I could go back. I really don't know how to deal with this, and most of all, I am ashamed that I let my family down." This was Mike's truth.

Mike went on to tell Jerry of his near-death experience, and Jerry did not say a word while holding Mike's right hand. "One night I woke up in ICU with very bright lights everywhere. I heard all kinds of loud panic-sounding voices calling to me, trying to wake me up. I was in this very peaceful and pleasant place that was very bright and like a long corridor with many doors on each side waiting to be opened. I wanted to stay in the corridor and did not care for anything of this world and just wanted to let go and move on to where I was going. Then the voices stopped for a moment, it was very quiet, and the silence was broken by the sound of my son's voice."

Mike's son was not there at the time.

"Daddy, Daddy, don't go. Stay with me. I love you."

Mike went on, "Ahead of me, my son's face got bigger and bigger, and his voice got louder and louder, and I tried to reach out to him, calling his name.

Then all was quiet, and the next thing I knew, my wife was holding my hand. I was back."

Mike later learned that his respiratory arrest caused a three-minute pause in his life.

"Jerry, something happened in that place I went to. I am very different in my mind. I have not had a drink or cigarette now for three months and do not have the desire. But I am afraid that I will start again, and I feel so guilty and don't know how to handle this. Please tell me how you stayed sober. I really can't do this by myself."

A great feeling came over Jerry, and he tightened his hold on Mike's hand in a soft way, holding back a flood of tears.

"Well, one day, after one of my famous business trips, I also had enough. I finally listened to that little voice in the back of my head that told me that drinking was not good for me. I had promised myself many times that I would stop. I did not know how and just went on drinking to excess. Then on *that* day, I stopped in my tracks in an airport, having had enough, and asked God to help me stop. I was out of control and needed help, and I, too, had no idea how to stop. Three months later, I started going to twelve-step meetings and learned a whole new way of thinking. I met some wonderful people who had stopped, and they shared their experience, strength, and hope with me. Actually, it has been a new way of thinking that relieved my desires and thoughts. I could never have imagined going through a day without a drink. Now it is hard for me to imagine taking a drink. It just takes time and the courage to change."

Jerry paused and Mike chimed in saying, "That day we had lunch, you really caught my attention, and your words haunted me. You didn't try to make me stop and push your ideas on me. In my heart, I was jealous, but I knew that I was not ready. I just could not face the challenges of stopping. Then this happened as my wake-up call."

Jerry continued, "Sounds like you have taken the first step and are ready to go on."

"Jerry, I am not sure I can do it, but I must. I really don't know what to do from here on. I just don't want to sit around trying to drink my self-pity away," Mike returned with a very emotional voice.

Jerry then replied, "If I can, you certainly can. It is not that hard once you have made the decision."

Mike then looked squarely into Jerry's eyes and asked with a solemn and serious voice and a small tear, "Will you help me?"

And they continued to talk for another hour, sometimes laughing and sometimes crying.

Over the next four months, Jerry visited Mike two times a week. They shared with each other their experiences from deep within. Mike had many questions, and Jerry did his best to answer them, sometimes not too well but always just enough. Sometimes Jerry took another recovered friend with him as a re-enforcement for some of the basic principles.

Mike was released from the hospital after another four months and confined to a wheel chair. It would take Mike almost two years of physical therapy to begin to walk with the aid of crutches. Jerry still continued to see Mike, and they kept up their mutual sharing of feelings. Jerry had a little two-seat British sports car, and once a week, Jerry would come by and take Mike to a twelve-step meeting. Jerry would help Mike into the passenger side of the car, and, with the top down and wheelchair strapped to the trunk rack, off they went to a local meeting. Afterward they went to a popular ice cream shop and indulged together in the creamy treat always covered with chocolate. They were now together as they once were with alcohol.

Because of the complexity of getting Mike in and out of the car, the whole event would usually take three hours.

But it was good. Jerry and Mike were back together in their friendship, and now they played a different kind of music and talked about the more important things of the heart, and not of an elusive and meaningless God soon to be forgotten the next morning.

It took Mike two years of therapy to be able to walk gingerly with crutches and another four years to walk with just the aid of a cane. Jerry and Mike went to many meetings together and worked hard at not gaining weight from all the ice cream. They would laugh and joke and remember the old times, now without guilt and only the joy of moving forward.

When Mike's son was 15 years old, Mike had to sell the house and move about 100 miles south because the financial strain of not working was taking its material toll. With the help of parents, matured stock options, and house equity, Mike was able to retire to a small community where he and his family still live. Jerry stayed put and, with the distance, visited about twice a year. Most of their conversations started with, "Remember when…"

The joy of their memories deepened their friendship and love for each other as they traveled many roads together and shared many common experiences. They never played music with their guitars again, but their hearts were in complete tune and rhythm with each other's feelings and experiences. While it appeared that Jerry was helping Mike maintain his sobriety, Mike in return, just with his presence, strengthened Jerry's program. A thought of drink never passed Jerry's mind while he was helping Mike, and the real give-and-take took hold while their love deepened.

Their two beings passed each other in life as many do, and this time they stopped and gave each other the great gifts of life. In the passage of life, we often pass many people and don't even take the time to look into their eyes. It is when we stop and take the other's hand that we bring true happiness to our hearts and that of others.

These are the things that we get to take with us when we leave this life. It is not the things that we have been given or pretend to have achieved.

Odyssey III

Tom Crowley was thirty minutes into his next journey from the planet of Eliet and the incredible experience he had with his new family that became so close to his heart. The beauty of this gentlepeople that evolved from reptiles and the thought of his relationship experience with them sang a song in his heart. Tom was especially moved by his relationship with the baby. The warm to cold touching he had when feeding the baby was a harvest of good feelings, and especially for the baby's feeling for Tom.

Tom did not go directly to the body suspension chamber as usual for the long trip to his next destination. This time he went to his molecular food generator and coded in for some old-fashioned Earth food, and it did have a new taste meaning as compared to the Elietian food of the past two months. While enjoying his morsels, he inserted a small crystal cube into a slot in his control panel and entered a command. The panel came brightly alive with a three-dimensional holograph of Earth's chronology and the origin and history of his genetic family. Tom was very touched by the memories of his Earth family origins as the bright illustrative memories passed on by. The loneliness of not seeing his genetic family in many years slowly turned to melancholy by the dynamics of the realistic holograms combined with his recent Elietian experience.

Tom set the holographic directory to his paternal grandfather's early work in inertial physics that was Tom's favorite part of a very eclectic period. He was always fascinated with the role that his grandfather, Alex Crowley, played in the advancement and influence of physics and technology, which had major impact on the lives of the human race and the limited exploration of the solar system. The hologram started with the development of linear precession, the basic drive for

185

current space travel as a basis for this complete story and founded on fundamental principles going back to the 19th century on Earth.

The images began to cycle through the many periods of time and the technologies that were developed as the basis for the current technology that served him so well. The data pack crystal that stored the image data was converted to three-dimensional lifelike illustrations combined with the appropriate dialect-containing information in a very informative and concise manner. As the holograms progressed with a subliminal sense, Tom's mind began to imagine what those times were like and seemed to be so vivid as in a realistic ongoing dream.

Linear precession was to be the first technology that brought close to faster-than-light speeds out of the laboratory and into actual space applications. It was based on the large amounts of energy that could be vectored in a straight line by large masses spinning at very high speeds. The resulting forward thrust, independent of outside influences, propelled vehicles in a forward motion and the energy applied would accumulate from the higher speeds, making very high velocities possible. But limits approaching the speed of light would always prevent higher velocities from being reached.

Technology for faster than light velocities had roots in some of the very early physics of speed limits since the 19th century when the speed barriers of boat and ship hulls moving through water could not be broken. It was thought to be impossible to exceed the hull speed limits by the best scientists of the time. It was not until the early 20th century that it was discovered that shaping the hull of a boat a certain way and with enough power that the vehicles could overcome the pressure buildup at the nose (bow) of the boat. This would overcome the compressibility and cause the boat to rise above the water and plane, eliminating the friction on the hull, thus enabling the speed of the boat to travel many, many times faster than the waterline limits of non-planing hulls.

The same theory and principles were repeated in mid-20th century with another impossible limit: to break the sound barrier. This time the compressibility in the air at the nose was overcome by shaping and streamlining the airframe to allow overcoming the pressure buildup at the nose of the plane. The same principle that worked in water worked in the atmosphere, except the air speeds were orders of magnitude faster in the less dense air. The limit in both cases became the compression buildup at the nose of the hull or airframe by the water or air and the mass of the surrounding media that created friction against the hulls and airframes.

Friction of the media and nose buildup were, of course, removed from the equation when vehicles were built for the vacuum of space with no nose buildup and friction to be found. Speeds of far beyond the barrier of sound were reached without the friction of a media in the vacuum of space. But the chemical reaction engines called rockets in the second half of the 20th century just did not have the power and energy to propel space vehicles at high enough speeds to venture outside the solar system. The limit now was the development of a suitable energy source and drive that would bring speeds up to uncharted numbers. The speed-of-light limit was now the new far-off and "impossible" barrier to effective space travel.

Many of the most learned physicists of the 20th, 21st, and 22nd centuries did not pursue vigorously the drives and power systems that could provide the force that might possibly approach the new limit because it was agreed and accepted for three centuries that this limit could never be breached. But as with the previous limits of water and air, they did not consider what was beyond the speed of light. It was the general thinking by most that light was the ultimate speed and could not be passed, even though it was learned that the speed of light does change. So theorists and fiction writers turned to the now unlikely technology of wormholes and warped space to cover the extreme distances found in just the small Milky Way Galaxy.

It was only during the great Ice Age of the mid-22nd century that initial success began to make progress with advanced space drives and power sources.

As massive amounts of ice advanced over the Earth's surface early in the 22nd century, much of the food supply infrastructure collapsed with the exception of a small band at the equator about 1,000 miles wide around the entire circumference of the Earth. The cause of the global temperature change came as a direct result of a major sun cycle that raised the Earth's temperature enough to melt much of the northern and southern icecaps. In turn, the large amount of fresh water that was emptied into the North Atlantic and South Pacific mixed with the salt water and dramatically interfered with the circulation of the oceans thermal flow extending from the Northern Pacific, around South America, and up to the North Atlantic. This allowed the oceans to cool dramatically, and the advance of the new ice began with the largest impact to the growing of plant life in northern Europe, Russia, Asia, South and North America, and of course, Australia was completely covered with a two-mile-thick sheet of ice.

As the ice advanced and there was less food, only the useful people and their families were allowed to live in the equatorial Green Ring. The others were left to fend for themselves with the advancing ice, and while this was arbitrary and cruel, it was the only way for humanity to survive; billions perished in the process.

187

The Ring of Green border was carefully monitored, and those who intruded were zapped without question. The entire society was under the control of the Government of Green and a very large army of well-armed protectors. Defense of the Green Ring was crucial to the survival of the species, and even the once strong and most important industrial complexes collapsed, leaving hundreds of millions of people without purpose. CEOs, executives, high government officials, and factory workers lacked usefulness and were all reduced to the same level and struggled to survive outside the Ring of Green.

During this period, Earth's population had been reduced to 25 million from 9 billion, and most of the technology, along with the many original species of animals, had survived. It was predicted that those affected areas north and south of the Ring would begin to be habitable in another 200 years as the ice receded. Only those with a useful purpose were allowed the safety of the highly protected Green Ring.

Many of the useful scientists who survived were allowed to work primarily on survival issues such as agriculture, medicine, constructive genetics, energy, etc. Only a few were allowed to work on the extravagant sciences such as space travel.

The holograph continued on Tom's console, and he selected the directory that would project the life and work of his grandfather, Dr. Alex Crowley. Alex and his wife, Maria, were selected for survival in the Ring of Green because of his work with inertial drives, which were the mainstay of land, sea, and air transportation. He was allowed to work on those principles that suited him. While Alex worked primarily on maintenance and revision of current drive needs for Earth travel, he managed to do much of his work on space drives, his first love.

Alex met Maria during a project refining the integration of the Malarium power source to inertial drives. Maria was the foremost quantum physics authority on the refinement of this critical power source, and she was able to bring forth procedures that dramatically improved the power output of the valued crystals in order to drive the inertial precession engines with an incredible increase in power output. The aligned atoms of the crystal structure emitted large amounts of energy when the protons and neutrons of the atom's nucleus were stretched apart slightly. Unlike the chain reaction of a nuclear fission process resulting in the immediate release of energy in a large explosion, the stretching of the nucleus released its energy in a controlled and slow process. Very slow "fission" was the key and generated incredible amounts of electromagnetic energy.

Alex and Maria fell deeply in love within the first moments of their meeting, not only because of their attraction to each other, but also because of their strong complementary technology expertise. It was not long after, that the Government of Green approved their formal bonding. Many an evening over dinner they would have deep and inquisitive discussions around their mutual technologies, which would extend into the early mornings and usually ended with some very passionate lovemaking.

One evening after a long day, while they were at the dinner table, Maria announced to Alex, "I am pregnant, and the government has approved the full term of the child."

Alex was overcome and replied with a tear, "Maria, that is great! How did you get approval?"

"Well, it was relatively easy with our value reputation. I am so happy we are together, and now we will have a son," Maria whispered as she hugged and kissed Alex with loving softness. Later that night they went to sleep and cuddled in each other's arms.

With the integration of Marlarium and the latest inertial drive systems, the speed of light seemed, at best, approachable. With further work from Alex and Maria, the energy output from the Malarium crystals was enormous, and this energy was able to spin and drive the inertial masses to deliver the power required to just approach the speed of light. The first test ship was *Odyssey III*, and tests across a small portion of the solar system resulted in speeds of 75 percent of the speed of light. At this speed, *Odyssey III*'s hull began to shudder violently and was not able to overcome the force buildup at the bow of the ship.

At the speed of 75 percent of light, space began to warp and compress at the nose of the hull, much in the way air pressure built up when trying to break the sound barrier. The warp wave buildup prevented *Odyssey III* from achieving further speed, but it was so close.

Odyssey III's hull was a very sleek and shapely oval of 100 yards wide in the major diameter and 75 yards long in the minor diameter. It was made from a high temperature firing process of an alloy of titanium and aluminum, producing a very high-strength oxide ceramic hull. The result was of the highest hardness and strength with excellent thermal qualities, and the graceful smoothness gave the ship a very credible look. The ship, at its highest point, was over 15 yards high and sloped gracefully to the edges to provide an aerodynamic look. There was plenty of room inside to accommodate the large amount of equipment and the very comfortable quarters for the passengers.

It was a cool evening when Alex and Maria were sitting on their balcony that overlooked what is now the Great Amazon Bay. Maria was seven months into her pregnancy and was having strong thoughts of her son's future in the Ring of Green. Alex shared his concern with Maria. Two months later, John was born, and there was much happiness in the household, but their thoughts of John's future haunted their inner thoughts over the next years.

As John grew, his advanced schooling was complemented by the efforts and care of Alex and Maria to make sure that John was well educated, especially in the sciences. By the time John was ten, research on the light speed project had advanced very slowly until one day, Alex thought of trying to disrupt the space warp compression at the nose of the ship. He and Maria made many calculations and came up with a method that they thought might work. Alex had a heavy coil of platinum with a Malarium core integrated into the titanium oxide alloy hull at the nose by his engineers. When that was completed, a test was planned, and Alex was to man the controls this time under the premise of wanting to make direct observations. The course plotted was out past Neptune and back—that covered a little more than a billion miles. On the day of the test and after a final checklist, Alex entered *Odyssey III*, closed the hatch, and sat in the control chair. He shut off the flight recorder and turned on his own for an anonymous record of the flight.

After the hundreds of test flights, this one felt very different, and if success was achieved, he wanted to be the one to announce this or have the option to keep it quiet.

The linear precession engines were spun up to 500,000 rpms, which took about an hour, and this gave Alex some time to check the plan and to reflect on what he thought might happen. Once the spin up was completed, Alex pulled back on the three axis slide lever on the console, and *Odyssey III* began to gracefully lift and was soon out of the atmosphere. An orbit was not required, and it took about three minutes to take up a stationary position at the point where the Moon's and Earth's gravity were equalized. Alex entered the planned course into the computer and turned on his personal recorder, which would record the details of the flight for his ears only. Then he pushed forward on the console slide, and *Odyssey III* quickly reached 25 percent of light speed. The Mass Grid Matrix, also powered by the Malarium crystal, kept the incredible forces of acceleration from the internals of *Odyssey III*, and for Alex there was no sensation of motion. The Matrix also protected the masses contained in the ship from increasing, and this force was directed back into the power input and output. It was the perfect combination of energy converting to mass and visa versa, resulting in incredible amounts of additional power. The faster it went, the more energy and mass was available to drive toward the higher speeds.

Alex began voice recordings of the flight, and Tom's holograph had an accurate version of his grandfather's voice recording. The following was what was on the recording along with a pictorial that had been constructed to match the event:

"I am now at 25 percent light speed, and everything seems normal as in many of our previous tests. I will now push forward to 50 percent. Still everything is normal."

Alex had just passed the path of the Mars orbit and would soon pass the orbit path of Jupiter.

Alex continued to record, "I am now at 75 percent, and I can feel the normal vibration from the space warp compression."

Alex now turned on the Marlarium platinum coil a small amount, and the vibration lowered significantly. Alex was now excited with the anticipation that this theory may work.

Alex continued. "*Odyssey III* is still at 75 percent with *no vibration*. I am going to push forward a little. Reading, reading. *Odyssey III* is now at 85 percent with only a small amount of vibration."

Alex turned up the power on the coil, and, as before, the vibration smoothed out. Alex was elated with the new speed record and thought about pushing on more. This was the fastest velocity ever reached.

Breathing very heavily, Alex went on, "I am now increasing speed and increasing the coil power. I now have a reading of 92 percent and no vibration. I am now going to increase the coil power and speed."

Odyssey III was now running at 98 percent with no vibration, and only 30 minutes had passed since the initial start. Alex's excitement was beyond description, and he stayed at this speed for more moments before attempting higher speeds.

Alex now voiced more onto his recording with great excitement, "I am now running at 98 percent light speed, and there is still no vibration. The coil is now at 100 percent of power, and I will now push the speed forward. *Odyssey III* is beginning to shudder slightly, but I am at 99.5 percent and accelerating. The vibration is now increasing, and I am getting concerned for the structural integrity of *Odyssey III*."

Tom was watching history being made before his very eyes on the hologram, and he shared the excitement of his grandfather, Alex. The recording went on, "I will now try to push to the light limit. I am now getting much stronger vibration but will keep going. My structural sensors are showing below the hull stress limit, and the speed monitor now reads 99.85 percent. Wow, we are so close and increasing. The speed is now at 99.99 and while the vibration is increasing to almost maximum, my speed is slowly closing the gap. The vibration is getting stronger, and I may have to break off. Come on, come on, and get there. We are really close."

The vibration started to shake *Odyssey III* more violently, and Alex's concern was beginning to overcome his excitement and he put his hand on the stick ready to pull back. "At least we have broken the record by a far margin and proved that the coil has merit. Maybe I should settle for this."

Then, suddenly the vibration stopped, which surprised Alex, and the feeling of motionless contrasted the previous vibration with an air of floating very softly. Alex looked at the speed meter, and it was reading 127 percent and was rising very quickly. Alex hit the display with his palm, but it kept rising. He then took a navigational check of three points in time against star positions, and the calculations confirmed the meter's reading. The meter was now past 335 percent and still rising, and again, Alex took a positional star reading, and the numbers again confirmed the speed. He was now well beyond three times the speed of light, and he had to take some time to absorb what the evidence was clearly showing. It was still hard to believe because his excited emotions took over his scientific logic and sense.

In theory, there was plenty of speed left, so he dared to push ahead ever so slightly, and the meter jumped to 150 times the speed of light. He could hardly believe the data! It was apparent that once the speed of light was passed, many laws of physics changed to mean other things as well as new ones introduced. He kept feeling himself to make sure that this was not a very vivid dream and that he was still very awake.

He then began to think, "This is really significant. Nothing in the galaxy is faster, and now we can really explore and try to find new life on other planets. Maybe another planet to colonize. But maybe the Green Government will disrupt other cultures, like in the many centuries of colonization on Earth. And maybe they will mismanage such a power, like the 20th century development of atomic energy for warring purposes. But what will the Government of Green really do with this? They will surely want to control this technology, and I cannot predict what they will do. I must maintain control because I cannot trust revealing this to others and the consequences that may unfold."

As the hologram went on, Tom really understood his grandfather's thinking and was very proud that he was connected to this fine and moral man. He felt the turmoil of the decisions to be made. Tom watched and listened very carefully while Alex tried a slow turn, and Odyssey III responded with a wide arc almost the radius of the entire solar system.

Alex now realized that he was so far into space that he may not be able to return, so he continued the circle toward Earth and carefully monitored his position so as not to zoom past his home destination in a nanosecond. *Odyssey III* performed with surprising agility, even at these speeds. The physics were different and the old traditional Newton's laws seemed not to apply.

As he approached back into the solar system, he began to pull back on the control and passed the timing of the slowdown to his navigational computer. *Odyssey III* was making more than 14 million miles for each second at this speed and required the nanosecond control of a computing device. *Odyssey III* started to slow—130, 98, 47, 17, 2, 1.7, 1.1—and suddenly *Odyssey III* began to shudder as it went back through the barrier then slowed to 75 percent of light speed. Alex was stunned because he realized that he was the first of any known creature to not only break the speed of light safely, but to also exceed it by a great margin and enter the world of very different physics.

Alex started for the landing pad on Earth, and he thought carefully what he was going to say without raising suspicions that this test went as it did. He wanted to hold back and think about the consequences of such a discovery. The report that he made was that this test was incredibly successful because he had broken the 75 percent barrier to an incredible 83 percent, and he recommended some possible modifications that just might make a further increase. All of his colleagues were elated, and in their jubilation did not question the results. That night, he went home to Maria and carefully motioned to her with his fingers that he had something very important to tell her. He suggested that tomorrow they would go down to a beach area on Amazon Bay so that they could talk with the confidence that no one would be listening. Alex stressed the importance of complete silence, and she seemed to understand without question.

Their son, John, was now 11 years old and quite knowledgeable regarding much technology, and he welcomed the adventure of going to the beach with his parents as a break from his learning. So Maria packed an old-fashioned lunch, and they all took the magnetic monorail to the beach area. It started as a cool day, but it was now warming to a level that would make playing in the water very pleasant. Alex spread the blanket out, and John ran off to hook up with some of the other children there.

Alex watched John run off and turned to Maria, and, in a very hushed but excited voice, exclaimed, "It worked! It worked far beyond our expectations, and I still cannot believe what happened. I wanted to wait to tell you first before announcing the results to the officials. There will be much commotion about this, and I am sure that we would lose control, and this might be used for some corrupt purpose. Our solution was so elegantly simple but not obvious. I wanted to wait to tell you where I could be sure that we were not being listened to."

Maria was caught with surprise; after all these years of disappointments, this did not seem real. Maria asked, "What happened? And how do you know for sure?" Alex explained the details of the whole event and what was beyond the speed of light. Maria, with a fogged surprise on her face, said, "I am glad that you kept this quiet. I have been very concerned that the Green Government might revoke our importance because we have made little progress in the last ten years. This might be good for our status."

Alex snapped, "No, we must not! I have been thinking beyond that and what is good for John. I don't want this life for him because he has become smart with a special mind, and I think that he will never be happy here. When he is older, he will have many of the same questions that bother us about our life here."

Maria was shocked, for Alex never talked like this before. She never had seen this rebellious side of her beloved Alex.

Alex went on, "I believe that we can take *Odyssey III* with John in hand and search for a better life, and we may find other life forms that are free. With this kind of speed, we can go anywhere in the galaxy. To explore the unknown and endless sky with all that it offers would be preferable to this controlled life we have here."

Maria was speechless as Alex went on, "We have the molecular reconstruction system that will provide food for our trips between planets, and John will continue to educate himself. I feel that there is so much out there, and this experience will be the best education for John." Maria was still silent with a blank look while Alex went on, "There just might be a better place, and I am so curious to find out. I don't think I could ever live here in peace again with the knowledge of this new power."

Then there were several moments of silence and Maria exclaimed, "This will be quite a leap of faith to leave everything that is familiar to us and venture into the uncertainty of the unknown. But we will never have to wake in the morning fearing that we may become unimportant. These thoughts have never passed my mind before, but I sense very strongly that this is the right thing to do." Maria then smiled, placed her hand on the cheek of Alex, and kissed him oh so gently. It was decided then, at that moment. Now all that was in the way was some detailed planning and keeping this from John's inquisitive mind.

Tom paused the holograph and sat back to admire this great example of intelligent courage in his roots. His heart was racing with pride and honor that he was part of such strong heritage. He especially enjoyed watching his father, John, as a child. Tom started the holograph again, and it continued with the preparations that were quite simple. But maintaining the secrecy was difficult, especially from young John.

Then, on the night of the highjack, Alex and Maria took John to the *Odyssey III* landing pad, and Alex told the only guard on duty that he and Maria were going to show John around *Odyssey III*. They would take only an hour or two, and this was going to be part of John's advancing education. The guard had no suspicions and thought that this was normal, especially for the leaders of the entire program.

195

Alex, Maria, and the now excited John walked the short ramp and into *Odyssey III*. Then Alex put the systems on, and the whole ship seemed to come to life. The most difficult part was the hour it took to spin up the inertial drives without raising suspicions from the guard. Alex started the drives up and, from the *Odyssey III* door, asked the guard to give him a hand with something. The guard entered and, being so close to the thieves, he had not the slightest clue what was going to happen. He helped Alex with a little made-up chore and went back to his post while the ruse went on right under his nose. Alex went through the start-up sequence, showing John all the steps so as to educate him.

Now the inertial masses were finally spun up to the required 500,000 rpms, and Alex looked at Maria with a smirk but cautious look. He then came to the door and waved at the guard, but before the guard could respond with a smile, Alex closed the door. He then sat in front of the console and told John to sit down for they were going for a ride. John jumped for joy and sat down as *Odyssey III* rose gently off the pad, and the surprised guard still did not realize what was *really* happening.

Alex continued, and now they were well beyond the reach of the officials. When they reached the Earth/Moon gravity midpoint, they maintained a steady position. Young John was grueling with excitement, and he still did not understand the real import of the situation. Alex looked at Maria and began to push the control slide forward, and the speed meter read 10 percent in a flash. The ship proceeded through 25 percent, 40 percent, 50 percent, and finally reached 75 percent of light speed. Alex then turned on the platinum Marlarium coil and pressed the slide higher. Maria watched as the meter read 85 percent, and *Odyssey III* began to shudder. As the meter reading increased, so did the shuddering. Maria looked cautiously toward Alex as he pressed more, and almost immediately, the shudder ceased, and *Odyssey III*'s meter went past 20, 35 and 85. Alex stopped the increase at a reading of 150 light speeds. Maria enjoyed her delight, and John still did not understand and just bathed in the excitement.

Maria was a navigational expert and went on to calculate where they were and where they were going and if there were any major obstacles in their path. At their speed, identifying an Earth-like planet would be very difficult, so they headed in a direction where a star was thought to have at least two very large planets in orbit. A star's wobble indicated the force of a large planet in orbit around the sun star. Maria calculated the distance and the speed required, and she knew when to begin the slowdown. John was now beginning to suspect that this was not just a joy ride and needed to be told the truth.

While Maria was doing her calculations and plots on the main navigational computer, Alex sat with John and explained, "We have discovered a great power that, in the wrong hands, would not be in the best interest of Earth. You know that we must get approval for everything we do, including your birth. Your life was approved by the government, and if they had not approved, you would not be here. So your mother and I decided that it was better to live free alone than to live in servitude with others. You may not understand this now, but we are sure that later you will feel better about this decision. We did not tell you because of the very secret nature of our leaving."

John had a startled expression on his face and with a tone of bewilderment replied, "But Dad, does that mean we are not going home? What about my friends and school? I won't have anybody of my age to be with. You and Mom had no right to include me without telling me. You talk of freedom. Well, what about my choices and my freedoms?"

Alex and Maria knew that John would react this way, and they felt that after some time, John would come around.

Maria had finished her calculations and course plotting, so Alex increased the *Odyssey III* speed to 200 light speeds, and there was no apparent change of acceleration. But the speed meter did read 200, and Maria made a navigational check just to make sure. Travel was very smooth, and they dubbed a unit of light speed as a Light Unit or LU.

It was three weeks later that they were close to their destination, so Alex began the slowdown procedure to a speed of just two LUs. They were now within the orbit of the planet farthest from the central star. Sensor readings, not surprisingly, showed that it was very cold and dead, but they were able to locate seven other planets, and one was a gas giant similar to Jupiter with a strong gravity field. It was the third planet from the center star, and it had a very fast orbit. It was very inhospitable, but what coined their interest was that one of the moons had an apparent atmosphere. They slowed to 1 percent of a LU, then progressed much slower, making sure that the inertial engines kept them safe from the very strong gravity pull of the gas giant.

Odyssey III went into a close and fast orbit around this very interesting moon. Spectrum sensors told them that the atmosphere was made up of 20 percent oxygen, 35 percent carbon dioxide, 15 percent nitrogen, and the remaining was hydrogen and helium. This appeared to be a very new atmosphere and was continuing to develop with much of the plant life. The mass and pressure were slightly less than Earth's, and Alex made the decision to land. John was elated after weeks of boring travel, and Maria was very cautious.

Alex slowed *Odyssey III* down to five times the speed of sound and entered the atmosphere. The titanium alloy oxide hull took to the heat very well with hull temperatures up to 1,000 degrees centigrade. As Alex got to 20,000 feet, he slowed *Odyssey III* down to a subsonic speed, and they all manned the sensors to find out more of this strange new place. John got totally involved and thoughts of Earth and his friends seemed farther away. He thought, "What kind of life may be here? Will there be people? Animals, or just plants?"

Adjusting for the density of the atmosphere, Maria searched the radio and microwave spectrum for any intelligent transmissions. There were none, but she found plenty of plant life.

Alex looked for a suitable landing site in an area that had thick plant life. It was very green, but the soil seemed to be frozen. There was considerable water in the form of ice with plants actually growing in the ice as well as in the exposed hard soil. It then occurred to Maria that there must be long times of darkness when the planet was on the far side of the gas giant during the course of its orbit. It was exposed to the warmth of the central star for only 70 percent of its orbit, unlike the normal 100 percent for a planet.

This intrigued John, and, making some basic calculations, he theorized that the gas giant, mother of this planet, could have been a star, but it did not have the required mass to start a fusion reaction. This was very similar to their own Jupiter but with a closer and faster orbit around its sun. It was made up primarily of liquid hydrogen, as was Jupiter.

But thoughts quickly turned to the landing and what they might find. John could not settle his excitement down. He had thoughts of finding an exotic pet, or there even might be primitive humans. *Odyssey III* slowly landed on a very flat and level section of plants and ice, and Alex determined that it was safe to open the door with only minimal oxygen masks to protect them from the high levels of carbon dioxide.

While the sun was warm, the air had a strong chill that was quite uncomfortable to their skin, which was so conditioned to controlled temperatures. John had never seen ice of this nature and quickly learned that it was slippery to walk on and that he could run and slide his way across the surface. That became his only interest while Alex and Maria took some serious readings and samples. Photosynthesis reared its familiar process as on Earth, and the prospects of animal life became very more likely, but they could not find even primitive one-celled species. They also discovered that under the surface of the ice, the temperature was considerably higher. What they found was made primarily of liquid water. Molecular structures were the same as on Earth in every way, and this confirmed, at least in this case, that the chemical structure of the galaxy may be universal without any strange molecules or unusual atomic structures. They gathered a considerable amount of plant life for recycling into the molecular food constructor in addition to water that was almost pure H_2O and without any animal matter and with only a few minerals.

Alex and Maria watched as John could not get enough of the sliding, but they called to him to return with them to *Odyssey III*. John's fingers and feet had become a little numb with the cold, so he welcomed the thought of a warm place and returned right away. They all entered *Odyssey III* and closed the door that sealed very tightly and showed no seams. *Odyssey III* slowly rose, and, when it was outside the atmosphere, Alex put *Odyssey III* about 1,000 miles away from the moon's surface while Maria started to look for far-off signs of another wobbling star that might have planets. She found one about 23 light years away that was close to the mass of their home sun and that promised to be a good candidate for planets. She set a course into the navigational computer, and Alex brought *Odyssey III* through the light barrier to 200 LUs.

John's fingers and feet were now back to their normal feelings, and he began to think of what might have been if there was intelligent life on their landing and how they would communicate with them. He asked his dad, "If we find life on other planets, how will we talk to them, and how will we understand them?"

Alex looked at Maria with a satisfied look that maybe John was starting to have a genuine interest in their adventure and replied, "Well, I don't know. Maybe we will wave with some kind of hand language. Maybe they won't have mouths or ears. They might even have a thousand hands to crush us with. Why don't you think about the problem and see if you can come up with any ideas." John laughed a little and seemed to go into some intellectual exercise with a fog on his face.

John was somewhat quiet for the next few days, and then he came to his dad with a plan to solve the language problem. He started out with, "Dad, we have to assume that intelligent life is very similar to ours since the molecular structures might be the same, and the plant DNA system is also very similar."

Alex listened intently without any interruptions, and John continued, "I think that if we make these assumptions and they are reasonably correct, we can construct a program that will sample sounds and reconstruct a language so that it could be translated into something we could understand. It may be possible that, if the plant DNA is similar, animal DNA would also be similar. Think that may work, Dad?" Alex was elated, and Maria smiled as she listened and looked on.

"Well, John, why don't you write a program that would do as you might think," replied Alex with an encouraging tone.

John said nothing and went to his resting place and started to work feverishly at his panel. The computer had the latest program paradigms and artificial intelligence, including voice input of complex mathematics and progressive generations of new concepts and thoughts. John could not seem to pull himself away from the problem for it was like a giant puzzle that challenged the core of his ego and interest. While Alex and Maria were a little concerned for their son's new passion and the possibility of failure, they were delighted that he was beginning to fit into this new life and that there was hope for his future happiness. They always humored John when he discussed some of his ideas, not wanting to discourage him, and he had some great system programming questions that sometimes went past their ability to answer. Alex expressed his concern that John may be way over his head and was in danger of losing his inquisitive nature with disappointment of a major failure at this young age.

John spent all his waking hours on his problem, and Maria had to take food to him to eat. This was the most intense that they had ever seen John, and they now began to worry that some type of space sickness may have overcome his sensibility.

Then one day John called his parents to come and see what he had done. They sat down with parental interest and low expectations, ready for disastrous results from their young son.

John started, "First, I had to create what I thought would be an alien language. That was the hard part, but I created a language with a vocabulary of 500 words and 60 grammar rules and then an algorithm to put them together; that was the easy part. Then I created a dialogue of questions and answers in their language so that I could answer and ask for debugging. That was the long part. So, let me take a question that an alien would ask. Then John entered a question and some dialogue.

Alex and Maria were quite interested, but they were both waiting for the usual disaster with a demo of this type.

This is what John entered in the alien language:

"Tihs is our pnelat and hmoe, and we are gald to meet you. You are wlcomee to saty wtih us. Our food is vrey good. We wlcomee you to eat smoe. Wrhee do you cmoe form, and how far is it to yuor hmoe? Why do you cmoe hree? Waht is the nmee of yuor sihp?"

And this was immediately translated to:

"This is our planet and home, and we are glad to meet you. You are welcome to stay here with us. Our food is very good. We welcome you to eat some. Where do you come from, and how far is it to your home? Why do you come here? What is the name of your ship?"

Alex and Maria's eyes widened, and then doubt set in that a little fraudulent prank was being thrust at their parental good sense. Alex thought that John's "space sickness" might be caused by loneliness.

John went on, "Well, I still have a lot of work to do in the grammar area, and then I need to work on trying to build an automatic vocabulary and grammar list based on a sampling of sounds. That way, we could create programs for new languages just by sampling some of the basic tones and construction."

On Odyssey IV, the hologram playback and the intelligence of Tom's dad as a young boy captivated Tom. He paused the hologram and took a little break for food, drink, and reflection, then came back to the images that fascinated him so. And he continued the hologram.

Alex skeptically asked, "May I try some, John?"

"Sure, Dad. Just input something in our language, and we will see what comes up!" said John proudly as he handed the input panel confidently to his dad.

Alex was taken aback with all this and was concerned that he might push John a little by breaking John's new system. Maria sensed this and gave Alex a "don't do it" look. Alex then gave the system this text:

"We are traveling the planets in order to find a new home and become free of tyrannical governments."

The system responded with:

"We are tvrelanig the pnelsat in oedrr to fnid a new hmoe and bmocee fere of xxxxxxxxxx gvemnentros ."

Which, again, was reconverted to:,

"We are traveling the planets in order to find a new home and become free of xxxxxxxxxx governments."

"Gee, it missed *tyrannical,*" came John's excuse. And the three of them played nouns, verbs, and sentences for another four hours without noticing the passage of time. There were many improvements that were identified, but Alex and Maria were ecstatic with their son's success at a very early age for such a complex project. John spent much more of his time making improvements, and Alex built some hardware to run the program in a portable fashion.

They were getting close to their next destination, and they prepared for the slowdown and search for traces of life in a limitless space. *Odyssey III* slowed to two LUs, then one, and finally down to 25 percent in order to make readings.

There were six planets of various masses in this system, but only one seemed to be in a position to have life of some type, so they slowed down and set an orbit around this very pale green planet. Maria's spectrum search showed abundant plant life and water, and, running through the transmission spectrum, she found many signals that caught everyone's immediate attention. She had made the appropriate adjustments for the atmosphere and found that the many signals across the spectrum were mainly in the FM range and some of the higher microwave ranges. And the signals were of intelligent life! Under the excitement, John was intrigued with the apparent dialog within the transmissions and recorded it for input into his translator. While Alex and Maria were searching the spectrum for any clues, John went to work with the data that he recorded for the translation process. This was to be his finest test, and he could hardly contain his excitement. It was decided not to make any contact until more was known and they were sure that it was safe or wise to do so. This would take much time and patience. This planet has very specific and intelligent life.

They spent two weeks in high orbit and, taking many readings, found that this was a planet very much like Earth with similar mass and atmosphere, making the potential of a contact with similar life more probable. John worked really hard with his language programs and the many recordings he made for input into his translator. He spent many hours rebuilding his intelligent algorithms with the new data, and he finally got to a point where he could identify a large vocabulary and grammar rule set resulting in 70 percent translation accuracy. This was much more than they had hoped for. Listening to the translations, the three were captivated with the information that was coming forth, and they were almost overtaken with the thought that this might be the first intelligent interplanetary communication.

They found out the following about their soon-to-be acquaintances:

The name of their planet was Argon with a population of about 350 million. Their industry was light but quite advanced with much technology similar to Earth's. Their main source of power was nuclear, but not in a reactor; they were able to derive energy directly from the radiation of refined dense materials. There were large, spread-out urban areas with very efficient transportation systems webbed within the cities and connecting to all parts of the planet. Between the cities were large agricultural areas. There were very limited aircraft that were slow and seemed to be restricted to the lower altitudes. Communication was restricted primarily to FM with some at the microwave band, and they seemed to carry mostly information with some cultural content. There was what seemed to be a government, but they could not find much in this area. Maria had isolated thousands of animal species from extremely small to some very large, and there were at least ten predominant species in large groups around most of the cities. The planet did not have seasons because there was no tilt of the planet's axis. There was no evidence of war anywhere. There was strong evidence of two genders, male and female, and many that were very young.

Now Alex and Maria were faced with the problem of how to make contact—or if they should—and John was jumping with excitement with the potential of meeting new people, especially of his own age. He just wanted to barge in and take their chances while his parents wanted to be very careful so as not to disrupt this society or endanger their own safety. To John's chagrin, Alex and Maria planned to wait for some additional time, to learn more about their society, and to plan a contact that they felt might be appropriate. They considered a message over the FM frequencies or a remote landing in some isolated place or just landing in a central location near a governmental area. These seemed to be the best of many plans, and John was strongly in favor of the third by being direct. While Alex and Maria were not influenced by their son's continuous promotion of a direct contact, they did decide for this method. It seemed that directness might be the best way with this apparent gentle and secure society, and an indirect way may cause unwarranted suspicions and hinder a trustful first contact. John was elated.

Maria had scanned most of the planet and found an area of about 200 square miles that appeared to be densely populated and had many large and small structures. This seemed to be a central location that might have some officials. Alex slowed *Odyssey III* down and out of orbit, then headed for a large clearing in the center of the city, approaching it at a slow 500 miles per hour. At 30,000 feet in altitude, they assumed that the residents would start to notice the large 100-yard oval hull shape of their vessel and would clear the area as *Odyssey III* came closer to the ground. At 5,000 feet, Alex slowed down to 100 miles per hour and gracefully headed for the open area that showed to be very clear of large vegetation and buildings. Then at 500 feet, he slowed *Odyssey III* to 20 feet per second and gently landed on the ground. There was complete silence, and the ship was filled with anticipation while Maria was scanning the area for life forms. There were many, all coming closer to the now still *Odyssey III*. Alex and Maria decided to wait for some time in order for the life forms to get used to this idea, and John was impatient beyond belief.

Alex then asked John to prepare a message to be transmitted over the FM range to announce their peaceful intentions, and John prepared the following for the translator:

"We come here in peace from far away and would like to make contact with you. We are very interested in your culture and wish to share ours with you. We are a gentle people with no aggressive intentions. Please believe that this is our reason to be here, and we will trust you by exposing ourselves to your world, and we ask you to trust us."

Alex and Maria approved this message without revision and instructed John to translate it and broadcast it over the FM frequencies programmed into the communicator. The message was translated and was sent as follows:

"We cmoe hree in pcaee form far aawy and wuold lkie to mkae ctnaoct wtih you. We are vrey itrenrested in yuor crutlue and wsih to sarhe ours wtih you. We are a glente popele wtih no asgrsisgeve itenionss. Paesle bielve taht tihs is our rsaoen to be hree, and we wlil tusrt you by epnosxig olesuvres to yuor wrlod, and we ask you to tsrut us."

The message was repeated many times over the next hour, and a response was not heard. Alex looked at Maria, suggesting, "Well, it is now or never. This is why we are here." Then he opened the hatch door.

The sun was very bright, and it took some adjusting to. There was a large crowd that watched very carefully as Alex, Maria, and John, with his portable translator strapped to his waist, walked out of the hatch door and down the ramp. At the bottom of the ramp, they paused and said nothing. Their hosts also did not say anything, and the quiet was anxious and blinding.

Then John moved forward, extended his hand, and, using the translator, said very innocently, "Hlelo, my nmae is Jhon, and I am paesled to meet you. I hpoe taht we can be fdirens." And with that he put a big smile on his face while Alex and Maria were absolutely taken back with their son's courageous action.

An older person from the front of the crowd came forward and took John's hand and with a soft voice replied, "I am Gala, and I am the spiritual leader of my people. We welcome you to our home and have many questions for you, as I believe you have for us. We assume that you come from a place far away among the stars in the sky, and we are anxious to hear of your travels to here and other places. While you are here, you will be our honored guests, and we hope that we can make your stay as comfortable as possible."

With that, all apprehensions that the visitors had melted away, and with great trust they came forward in friendship. There were many loving touches, and much of the talk the translator was able to convert on the fly. Alex turned and remotely closed the hatch door of *Odyssey III* showing no seams, and they all walked toward a large building.

Tom, as he watched the hologram, was becoming very emotional because it was on Argon that he was born. He especially enjoyed the role that his dad, John, played in the whole incident in the beginning.

They all entered a large building that was architecturally very pleasant with clean lines and openness to the outside that reflected an artistic integration of the building with its immediate surroundings.

The Argonians were very humanlike with only some very small differences such as smaller skeletal frames, a uniform light tan skin, and very light pastel brown eyes. They were slightly shorter than Alex and his family. There was a distinct difference between the males and females as in humans, and overall the Argonians were very beautiful people. Their gentle mannerisms added to their attractiveness.

They all sat down at a very low table with floor pads to sit on. John put the translator on the table, and, for the most part, it worked well after he made some adjustments. Soon after, some other Argonians came into the room with lots of food that was very appetizing. The table sat about twelve, and Alex, Maria, and John sat directly across from Gala and, with few words, began to eat. The hosts were very gracious and offered many of the treats in a very polite way as to strengthen the bond. The conversation went as follows:

Gala: "We are very impressed with your manner and the technology you have acquired. You are very much like us, and this confirms what many of our technology people have been theorizing. I am a spiritual leader and my colleagues, while skeptical over the course of our history, have accepted much of the physical evidence of life in the sky. Now your coming has given us a great gift of knowledge and we are delighted. And your ship vision is very graceful and impressive."

Alex: "We call our ship *Odyssey III,* and it has been our only home for some time. We are delighted also with finding you, which is the reason for us to leave our home. We could not be more pleased. We will talk of our world later and how we have managed to come here."

Maria: "We were hoping to find a new home in the heavens, and with some time and your gracious hospitality, we would like to consider Argon in such a way."

Gala: "Let us take some time to learn about each other and decide what is best. Until then, you are certainly welcome to be our guests, and we will do our best to accommodate your needs. I would suggest that you spend some time with one of our families as guests, and that will give us both the opportunity to learn more."

While all this was going on, John had his eye on a young Argonian girl who appeared to be of his age. She seemed very shy, and he finally got the nerve to ask her name, and she replied, "My name is Alla, and your name is John."

"How do you know that?" queried a surprised John.

Shyly she returned with a flirting smile, "I heard that from the older and larger female, and it appears that she likes you very much. Is she your mate?"

John laughed and said, "She is my mother, and that is my father." And they both giggled as children of that age would. Gala, smiling, pointed out that Alla was his daughter, and in some time she was going be of age. Alex and Maria thought it best not to comment regarding this subject in the context of their twelve-year-old son.

Tom paused his holograph to think about the wonderful visions of his culture that were before him and the heritage that blessed him so. And how his mother and father met.

Now, some time over the years had passed, and John was nineteen, and much had happened over the last eight years to John and his parents. They had been completely integrated into Argonian society and learned the language fluently. While they were careful not to pollute the Argonian's technology with what was on *Odyssey III,* they did help in some areas as teachers and consultants in the areas of physics and energy. John took a special interest with helping with much of the primitive but solid computing technology, and he developed many special friends, but most of all, Alla. They spent much of their time together with social and technology activities. Alla was a very talented mathematician whose skills blended well with Tom's programming talents and general knowledge of science. They were very complementary to one another, and Alex, Maria, and Gala were delighted with the prospects of a possible mating between the two.

Over this time, many additions and improvements were made to *Odyssey III* that included faster navigational programs, a revamp of the molecular constructor for better food, and a time body suspension chamber with a vibration recovery system that would allow a hibernation state for very long trips. The sleek hull was solid and required no modifications while the platinum Marlarium coil was upgraded to allow a smoother transition to light speed. This was all done with the limited tools and materials that they had available, and Alex and John would sometimes take *Odyssey III* a couple scores of light years to run tests. All the tests resulted in outstanding performance.

John was 21 years old when he and Alla became mated, and within a year, they had their first and only boy child. They named him Tomas Gala Crowley to the delight of all the grandparents, and they had all the dreams and expectations of a very close family. When Tom was seven years old, Alex and Maria, his grandparents, were both killed in a very rare nuclear accident, and the tragedy hit the family very hard as well as the many colleagues and friends they had come to love over the years. John was devastated because of the very special closeness they had developed over the years, and it took many months to recover his serenity from the deep pain of the loss. He had become very close to Gala over the previous years, and now this closeness seemed to grow to deeper lengths, and little Tom was not quite old enough to appreciate the impact of this death event.

Tom paused the holograph at this point and thought with great feelings for the grandparents he only had vague memories of, but he did feel the pain of the loss this many years later. He started up the hologram again and continued with the history and story.

John and Alla had become very prominent in the Argon community, and there was never any thought or talk that John was not of Argon and that Tom was a blend of the two cultures. In addition to her math interests and skills, Alla became very knowledgeable in the science of DNA. This was a new science on Argon, and she was able to determine that John's DNA, while almost identical to the Argonians, had a small defect that seemed to affect his emotions, and that flaw did not appear in the Argonian culture. While John was very secure in his attitude and emotional health regarding this subject, he did theorize that it was this defect likely in all humans that accounted for the Earth's violent history. Since this flaw did not exist in Argonians, this may account for the peaceful nature of the Argonian culture since the start of their recorded history.

Many years passed and the talents and knowledge of Alla and John were passed on to Tom, and, over the years, he developed into a very intelligent person. There was a tragedy though. The multiracial makeup of Tom resulted in his inability to fertilize females. He was sterile and would not be able to reproduce with a mate.

Tom's own memories took over at this point and he began to reminisce in his own thoughts without the need for the hologram. He especially remembered the day when he was 24, and he left Argon to find his own way.

John and Alla together with Gala had many thoughts for Tom, and they realized that he needed to find his own way, just as they had done. They had finished many of the advances and revisions on *Odyssey III*, and, while turning it over to Tom to find his way, they christened it *Odyssey IV*. Tom had intimate working knowledge of all the technology on *Odyssey IV* and now could travel in a very independent role.

Tom remembered the day when he left and the words of wisdom that his family had given him and the words still echoed in his heart.

Gala gave him his farewell with, "No matter what and who you find out there in your travels, remember to look for the good in whoever they may be. Trust in your deepest feelings and instincts for they will direct you to great things and protect you from those with impure intentions."

Alla followed with, "Hold yourself safe and true that you may find those who will return your love. Be tolerant of their thoughts no matter how different they may seem to be. Keep yourself open to new ideas and be willing to share of yourself. We will miss you so and will meditate for your safety. Hear us when we think of you, no matter where you are."

John was probably the most visibly emotional one and gave his son, Tom, a big hug and whispered in his ear, "We have given you much knowledge that may be beyond those who you will meet. Use it well and never forget that we love you so. I wish for your heart to find what is good and to have many happy moments."

Tom did not say a word with the strong feelings that he had in his throat, which choked his ability to say a word. He hugged his family, turned, and went through the *Odyssey IV* hatch and closed it.

Odyssey IV slowly and gently rose with a graceful sense, and John, Alla, and Gala watched with great emotion as Tom started his great explorations.

Santa's Motorcycle

A true story.

It was in the mid-1970s and there was a national group of young men who were part of a worldwide civic organization called the Jaycees, formally known as the Junior Chamber of Commerce. Their charter was to "Develop the young man through personal development programs and volunteer community projects." Their motto was "Young Men Can Change the World." After a bitter two-year political fight within the organization across the United States, the national bylaws were changed to accept women as full members and the motto then became "Young People Can Change the World." Local chapters large and small began the change over to full female membership, some chapters with great enthusiasm and some of the chapters having older members, with great reluctance.

A small local chapter just north of a large East Coast city played a key role in the long-fought political battle for the "Women's Option," and after many years of disappointingly low membership, they were starting to grow again. The new women members became active as full members and played leading roles in the many civic programs and personal development programs.

Peter, who was the president of this chapter during the "Local Option Battle," led the chapter in many new innovative programs. The most noted was a bowl-a-thon, which raised a record $1,800 in just his chapter during the first year of the program. The next year, this model program ran statewide and raised over $180,000. All the proceeds (100 percent) went to support a summer camp for special children, and with the publicity of these types of programs, the chapter grew to record levels of membership.

As was the custom of the Jaycee bylaws, Peter could serve as president for one year, and then at the end of his term, he was relegated to past president. This was so that new blood could take over and develop the chapter in their own way while learning themselves. This was a very important part of the self-development process and kept the chapters young. Being president was a tough and rewarding position for those who took it seriously, and it was considered the best job in the entire national organization. Peter wanted to keep the successful momentum going, and, close to the time of his stepping down, he wanted to encourage a new member, Jack, to run for the office of president.

Jack and his wife, Susan, joined eleven months earlier, and they became very active, quickly taking on the responsibility of two new projects. They were very spirited with a lot of enthusiasm, and their projects were very successful as well as fun.

Three months before the end of Peter's term, he approached Jack in private with the thoughts of Jack running as the new president, and to Peter's great surprise, Jack strongly refused. Peter still tried several times over the next weeks. He told Jack that he would make a great president because of his creative dedication and his way with people. Jack still refused.

One day, Peter received a phone call from Jack, and Jack opened up the conversation with, "Peter, I know that you want me to run for president, but I can't. I really can't do that, and I wish you would not ask me anymore."

"Why, Jack?" asked Peter.

"I just can't."

Peter went on, "Look, Jack, we have worked together for almost a year now, and you owe me at least a reason. We have become very good friends and need to trust each other."

Jack began to talk in a very insecure tone, unlike his usual high-spirited way. "Peter, I will tell you if you promise that you will NEVER let on to anyone under ANY circumstances."

"You can trust me, Jack."

Jack slowly and somberly went on. "I can't read or write; I am illiterate."

There was a deep moment of silence, and after some thought, Peter exclaimed with a curious question, "You have done some great work with us with planning and such. You are a very accomplished tool and die maker. How is this possible?"

Jack retorted, "I have learned over the years how to fake it, and I can read the numbers on blueprints. Susan helped me with the many project agendas, and I memorized them with her help."

Peter now had his composure back and strongly stated, "Well, that's OK, you have proven yourself beyond any question, and many of us really like you. You would be a shoe–in, and I would be behind the scenes helping you. You would have much quiet support, and I know you can do it."

After much discussion, Jack reluctantly agreed and later was elected president by a unanimous vote. His year as president was an outstanding one with the help of Peter and Susan. No one would have ever had guessed of Jack's condition. Jack led the chapter with many new programs, and the chapter grew in not only membership, but in spirit, and it was now considered one of the top chapters in the entire state.

As was the custom each year at the Jaycee State Convention, ten local presidents out of the 180 across the state were selected as "Outstanding Chapter President." Unknowingly, Peter had submitted Jack's name for this most coveted state award. The results, voted on by a very select group of state officers, were the most closely guarded secret until the final awards banquet at the convention. At the banquet, and after all the high-spirited speeches telling of the year's past events, the "Ten Top Chapter Presidents" program laced the conclusion of the convention as the highest and most anticipated of events. There was great silence as each of the top presidents were announced and asked to come forward to receive their coveted plaques in recognition of their successes and to say a few words. One of the key personal development programs of the Jaycees was "Speak up Jaycee," a program to develop public speaking and writing talents.

As "President Number Nine" was announced, Peter began to feel a great sense of disappointment for his friend Jack. No one knew that Peter had submitted Jack's name and that other members of the chapter did not share the same feelings of anticipation. Then the last name was called, and it was Jack's. An explosion of standup applause tore loose the dead silence. Jack, who was warned two weeks prior by Peter to be prepared for something special at the convention, broke down with emotion, and his fellow members hugged him and shook his hand. Many of the other chapter people from across the state who came to know and like Jack applauded, as this was the most popular selection by the office awards committee that "saved the best for last."

After what seemed to be five minutes of adulation, Jack composed himself and walked toward the podium to receive his plaque and deliver a very short speech of thank you for this great honor. He was handed the plaque and stepped up to the microphone. There was a dead silence broken by an occasional "Great job, Jack" from the audience.

He slowly pulled a three-by-five card from his pocket and proceeded to say the following openly in front of almost 1,500 people from across the state: "Two years ago, when I joined this great development organization, I could not read or write."

Jack paused with great emotion, and there was a dead silence of disbelief. Jack went on to say while holding the three-by-five card, "I have written this little speech for you, and now I will read it." With a shaky and uncertain voice filled with short spaces, he began:

"I was encouraged and given the opportunity to grow. I will always cherish the opportunity and will always have you all in my heart. Thank you so much for this great gift of personal development that has changed my life forever."

Jack left the podium with a great hush in the large conference hall. There was hardly a slow heart or dry eye in the place, and then again it exploded with applause. It continued and continued with the fear of not ever stopping. When Jack returned to his chapter table, Peter was waiting for him, and they clutched in the greatest hug of love that men could give each other. Everyone shared in this great goodness of the moment. This became one of the ultimate development programs of this organization.

One of the programs that Jack had innovated during his year was an old idea but new for the chapter. It was a "Toys for Tots" program at the Christmas season. The members would solicit toys and monies from the local merchants as sponsors for the pre-holiday party for some of the unfortunate children in the local community. After a spirited and social gift-wrapping party by several of the member couples and such, there were over forty colorfully wrapped donated presents of very high quality. It took an enclosed pickup truck, a van, and two station wagons to get the colorful presents to the Christmas party location at a local church hall. Each package had a specific child's name written on a large tag. The names taken from a list of the children attendees were supplied by the local school. The gifts for each child were randomly selected with only girl and boy distinctions (pink and blue, of course).

Refreshments were set up, and all the presents were carefully placed in back of a large chair reserved for Santa Claus who was to arrive later. Each present

with its large nametag was placed just behind Santa's great chair that was currently empty. It was very well organized. The children started arriving and diving into the cookies, cake, and juice with the usual uncontrolled running around. The few parents that stayed were treated with coffee, cake, and eggnog.

Then, the children were gathered around in a circle and heard "'Twas the Night Before Christmas" from a very large and well-illustrated book. Peter, the now past president, was selected to do the honors of reading, and he sat in the middle of the circle of children. Behind him was a Jaycee couple that normally played music at the local folk Sunday Masses, and they were playing their twelve-string guitars softly in the background. "Silent Night" and others complemented the moments during the reading, and some of the adults showed expressions of emotion while looking on. The children were delighted with the reading, and their wide eyes stayed still with interest in the story and the large illustrations. Many of them had never heard the entire story, and it was a good feeling of giving. Peter was having a difficult time maintaining his composure over the loveliness of the moment, but he continued to read. And the children listened.

After the story was finished, Santa arrived with the usual "Ho Ho Ho"s in a jolly style. Underneath Santa's red and white image was a slim young male member who worked very hard to look large and jolly with great amounts of padding. He strained to make his voice lower than his normal young and high voice. He was a happy sight, and he cherished the thoughts of playing Santa. This was his finest moment.

He sat in the big chair in front of all the presents, and he called to a few of the children, one at a time, to sit on his knee and do the traditional "What do you want for Christmas?" routine. They delighted in their many requests. Little William, at about seven years old, had been sitting in the front of the circle of children. He appeared to be very disgruntled and not too happy, and he had his legs crossed and his chin resting on his hands. Santa motioned to William to come sit on his knee and tell Santa what he wanted for Christmas.

William replied in a stark tone, "I want a red motorcycle, and you're not the real Santa! You would know that if you were the real Santa." There was a hush among all the Jaycees, and William's mother, a single lady of few means, flushed with embarrassment. Santa quickly put William down and went on with some of the other children. The room had become a little tense.

Then came time for the gift–giving, and Santa would hand out each colorful present to the child that corresponded to the previously written labels. There were all kinds of quality toys: Tonka trucks, fancy dolls, big games, etc. The labels of names were random and taken from the school-generated "Needy List." No one had planned to give a specific present to a specific child. Little William sat with his chin on his hands with the same uninterested and sad expression while the presents were being handed out, and the children started to play gaily with their newfound treasures. For William, this became just another disappointment in his life.

There was only one present left, and it was for William. When one of the Jaycees picked up the very large and clumsily wrapped package because of the unusual size and shape, a hush came upon the volunteers who so carefully planned this event. The hush was greater than the noise of the children, all playing with their new toys. Everybody seemed to focus on the package with great surprise. It was like slow motion with none of the noise penetrating their thoughts. Santa, with a very choked voice, called William's name, the last one to be called. Santa and the others knew what was in the very large package, and the hearts of all began to pound with great anticipation.

When William tore off the colorful paper, a brightly colored red three-wheeled motorcycle "Big Wheels" appeared. William's eyes exploded with excitement and screams of happiness. And he jumped on. Then he jumped off and ran to Santa, "You ARE the real Santa!" Shocked and crying, William's mother came to Jack with a big hug and exclaimed, "I did not know how to get that for

William. It just was too expensive for me to afford. Thank you so much. I will always remember you people."

The folk Christmas music continued to soften the noise of the children playing, and the "roar" of William's plastic wheels on the tile floor of the church hall seemed to punctuate the program. There were great feelings among the Jaycees that put this very special day together. They had reaped their reward for the effort.

Peter went up to his great friend, Jack, put his hand on Jack's shoulder, leaned close, and said, "See, there really is a Santa."

The Cognitive Farm

Like most people, the stress of modern-day life sometimes impales us into negative thinking that bogs us down into a path of unhappiness. That unhappiness then dictates how we might treat others in our daily lives, and many times they retaliate against our behavior, creating a deeper sense of unhappiness within ourselves. Financial, family, and social stresses need to be accepted, but we can stave off potential depression with positive thoughts.

I have learned to do this, and it has treated me to a new level of serenity. I try to practice constructive imagination when such negative thoughts break in and take over my serenity. All progress rests on constructive imagination, and we tend to be happier when working toward a specific goal such as we find in hobbies, books, and movies. Also, there are the pleasant thoughts of our pasts that can ward off and take the place of our fears and insecurities. I have learned that over the years things usually always work out, no matter how bad they seem at the time.

It is how we perceive things that may affect our emotions. I have learned that the clinical name for this process is "cognitive thinking."

So here is the story of my Cognitive Farm that gives me the childhood memories to replace my mental spaces of negativity.

I was born and raised in Cambridge, Massachusetts—just across the Charles River from Boston. We lived in one side of an old, large house that used to be a mansion and then was split into a two-family residence. We rented the second side from an old woman who inherited the house as an estate, ultimately to be given to Harvard College. We were fortunate to pay very little rent to live in this grand old house, which was at least 200 years old. It was located on Massachusetts

Avenue, the main avenue in North Cambridge that stretched from Arlington to Harvard Square at the center of the city. It was a very wide thoroughfare that was lined with real granite curbstones and old-fashioned brick sidewalks. Two-way trolley tracks split the avenue in half from the Arlington City line all the way to Harvard Square, about six miles.

I lived in the house from the age of two to fifteen and walked to school that was on the same block unlike the "three miles in the snow" story that so many adults talk about. The house was heated with coal, and the sounds of fall included the loud tin shuffle of coal speeding down a metal chute through the cellar window into a large coal bin. The smells of fall included the smoke from burning leaves throughout the neighborhood. We had a back porch with a screen door held closed with a spring, and the sound of slamming screen doors permeated the humid summer days throughout the neighborhoods.

The front of the house was guarded by a huge old elm tree of at least 200 years. Over the years the large roots of this magnificent "Poem of a Tree" distorted the brick sidewalk into gentle waves of red, giving character to the orderly array of bricks. Next to the tree was an iron hitching post from the horse-drawn past that was the source of much childhood play. It was in the 1950s and the hitching post had only memories of the past in this day of progress.

In the fall, winter, and spring, I played hard after school, having wartime battles, chasing down Butch Cavindish (it was his gang that ambushed the Lone Ranger) on horseback, and building roads with our toy trucks. In the winter, we built large snow forts out of the piles of snow pushed aside by the many snowplows that shaved the avenue clean on those blustery winter days. The noise of cars, trucks, and large wooden trolley cars are still memories of Avenue life. In those days, sonic booms from military planes were commonplace and a reminder that we were being protected from the growing nature of our enemies in the cold war.

My dad's sister Rose was the first to marry a Protestant in our totally Catholic French Canadian family. It was OK because Harold was a peach of a man that everyone liked and he had a great sense of humor that made him very pleasant to be around. He was an executive for Dupont, and they owned a twenty-acre farm in southeastern Pennsylvania close to Delaware, home of the Dupont Corporation. It was not a working farm as such, just a nice home with twenty acres.

I was very fortunate to have the opportunity to spend most of my summer school vacations on Starve Gut Farm, as it was called. Legend has it that many men went hungry building the quarter-mile road to the farmhouse from the main road.

For this young "Urban Cowboy," the visits became the most cherished time of my childhood that had great impact on me in my later life.

The farmhouse was unique because different sections of the house were built in different periods. The kitchen and large dining room were originally a log cabin with the original logs and mortar in place. Finished walls on the inside made this 18th-century section "modern." Old-fashioned square nails were predominant in the well-finished 200-year-old plank floors. The large living room was added later in the 19th century and was constructed of stone and had a huge stone fireplace as the centerpiece. The upstairs three bedrooms, sitting room, and finally a full inside bathroom were added in the early 20th century and built of the frame construction used today. There was a garage set aside of the house that was converted from a barn. The second floor of the garage was used as a chicken coop. On the side of the "barn" was a place where there were two recycle barrels—one for glass and one for metal. The garbage was composted for a large half-acre garden, and paper was burned and the ash was recycled into the compost pile. There was little that was wasted, and the farm was almost self-contained.

The farmhouse, sprawling elm tree-spotted lawns, barn, and Starve Gut Road consumed about five acres, and the remaining fifteen acres was leased for $1.00 per year to feed the cows of the adjoining milk farm. The 100-some odd milk cows took their nourishment from the pasture, replenished the soil with their manure, and gave us all the milk products; a give-and-take for all to benefit. The other side of the farm was a cow feed corn spread of about thirty acres, and the owners used refugees from the '50s Hungarian Revolution to do the planting and harvesting in exchange for little pay, room, and board, and, most of all, freedom.

As summer approached and the thoughts blossomed of spending my cherished school vacation with my Aunt Rose and Uncle Harold, my anticipation grew to the level of the night before Christmas when time seemed to stand still. I remember being taken to the train station, my suitcase being checked in, and a manila name tag securely fastened to my jacket. I was told that if I lost the clearly printed name tag that had addresses and telephone numbers of where I came from and where I was going, I would end up in Cuba, a fate worse than death for a nine-year-old. The train was powered by steam, and I can still remember the sounds of steam expelling and the smells of oil mixed in.

The train pulled out, and I was finally free of parental control and on my own at nine years of age. I did take great care not to lose my tag. I did not want to have to eat Cuban food (today, it is one of my favorites). I remember the train being very comfortable with big soft seats, and when it picked up speed, the soft rolling motion of the passenger car and the rhythm of the clickity-clack was soothing.

It still rings in my memory. I was looking out the window at the passing scenery when a voice rang out, "Ticket please, young man." I turned from the window to see the smiling black conductor looking at me and asking again, "May I have your ticket please, sir?" He called me sir, and at the age of nine, I had my short moment of adulthood. He was very well dressed in his dark blue uniform, and he maintained all the gentle firmness of being in control of the train. With great authority, he punched my ticket and said politely, "Thank you, sir."

I had my own money to buy lunch, and as the sandwich wagon squeezed down the aisle of the rolling car, I purchased a wrapped sandwich of my liking from the very neatly dressed black steward. His lily-white jacket stiff with starch contrasted his very dark skin. Living in a very white French Canadian neighborhood, I did not have the opportunity to develop any prejudices in this area, and I just enjoyed the adult treatment these fine men gave me.

Of course, I had to explore the whole train, going from car to car, fascinated by the connection between each of the cars and the motion and sound adventure. The clickity-clack would be sharper and louder when passing between the rolling cars, and when I closed the door behind me, the noise would soften to the pleasant rhythm again. The place that had the most interesting sounds was the bathroom. It seemed as though when the toilet was flushed, there was an open hole directly to the tracks and ties flashing by. The train's clickity-clack echoed out of the metal toilet bowl hole like a great rhythmic trumpet.

It was always wonderful getting picked up by my aunt and uncle. They had two cars and always used the 1950's Ford station wagon with real wooden sides to pick me up. The vision of riding down Starve Gut Road and coming up to the farmhouse remains strong in memory for me. This was the morning after Christmas Eve, and I had just opened my favorite present, only it was summertime, to be filled with all types of adventure presents of life.

After getting settled, I would immediately get into the routine of play with much creative imagination. Now this urban cowboy had a whole new world of plains, hills, and real cattle as a stage for creating scripts that would make Hollywood proud. Having spent time here last year, I knew all of the places to explore, and every year I would find more as my horizons would expand.

There were two dogs and a cat, like a farm should have. I don't remember the cat very much, but the dogs stayed in my permanent memory. Oscar (pronounced Oss-Carrrr as in German dialect) was an old grumpy dog that had a mean streak and did not want to play any of my cowboy and war games. On the other hand, Queenie was a young and spirited collie that could play all day long and always conformed to my creative scripts. We had a special game of hide-and-seek where I would get away from her, hide, and she would come looking for me. There were plenty of places to hide, and when she found me, we would both jump with joy and roll in the grass together. Queenie loved to run next to me on my "horse" in the fields with all the cattle (really milk cows). She was my Lassie, and we became very devoted to each other.

One of the nearby farms had an old-fashioned watering hole that would make Norman Rockwell proud. It was complete with a short pier for jumping and a classic rope swing over the edge of the pond hanging from a large old oak tree. The water was used for the cattle and was kept very clean. At nine years, I could not swim yet, so I was well supervised. Once, I put on a life jacket, the old-fashioned fabric orange type, and jumped gaily into the water. Unfortunately, the jacket was water logged and failed to keep me afloat, and all I remember is looking up at the surface, gasping in total panic. I was saved immediately by the scruff, choking and shaking on the pier. In all my years, that was the closest I had ever come to death.

There were many other memories of play and interest. I had made friends with the kids at the milk farm, and I got to see and smell the real stuff of a farm. There was a real silo filled with feed corn, manure all over the cement floor of the barn, and the smell of hay soaked with urine. Chickens ran free throughout the entire farm, and very often one or two would come up missing, so we never gave them names. Smells also included real fried chicken, apple pies, biscuits, and all sorts of other goodies.

One evening, I was invited to stay at the milk farm overnight. This was a great adventure for me because I really looked up to one of the older sons. He had a great knack for teasing the younger children with stories of ghosts and witches that lived in the nearby woods and of the great bull that guarded the north end of the fields. That is the night that I learned about the sport of "cow tipping."

The sun had gone down an hour before, and two of the older boys and three of us smaller kids ventured into one of the fields past the barbed wire fence. The field was slightly lit with a half moon, and when our eyes got used to the light, we could see the many profiles of cows relaxing and some sleeping on their feet. Watching out for newly dropped cow manure, we slowly approached one cow with the stealth of an Indian (as an urban cowboy, I was expert at this). We lined up on one side of the unsuspecting and sleeping cow and together were ready to give one unified push to down the cow from its unstable upright sleeping position. We were all excited at the prospects of this adventure and when we were in place, we were all to push hard at the count of three. At the count of two, the cow woke up, and while exerting a loud moo, kicked one of the older boys in the leg. And we all ran in panic. Not satisfied with our apparent failure, someone exclaimed loudly in an excited voice, "The bull is loose." We all ran in panic, not seeing but believing that we were in great peril, and we made it through the barbed wire fence. When we were on the safety of the lawn, we realized the bull was really not there. We delighted in this great adventure and talked about it into the late hours of what happened and what could have been.

Between the two farms near the road was an old dilapidated "hotel" all boarded up. One bright day, a gang of us decided to explore this great place, and taking a plank from one of the boarded-up windows, we got in. It was a two-story building used as a stage coach stop. Many of the walls had holes showing the lath slats and human or horsehair to bind the plaster. Upstairs were the many rooms, and the entire second floor had only two large bathrooms for all the residents to use. In later years, this former palace for travelers was torn down with only a foundation marking the spot, taking away our haunted playground.

In the later years, my parents would ship my beloved bicycle to the farm ahead of me. This gave me a new freedom to explore well beyond the farm, and I had to take care on the country roads because they were usually freshly tarred and graveled in the early summer. The summer heat would bubble the thick black tar where the gravel did not cover it. To step on this tar was to invite hours of cleaning with gasoline-soaked rags, and before we entered the house, a detailed shoe inspection always had to be done.

I was an expert "biker" and could ride fast with no hands. Queenie was always instructed to "stay," and she would sit at the edge of the farm road and wait patiently for me to return from my many missions. I loved to ride the roads and down to the railroad tracks about two miles from the farm. It was the source of all those nighttime steam whistles that sang the songs of ghosts in the midnight's quiet darkness. The tracks were fertilized with spent pieces of coal, and occasionally a steam train would come by with a smiling engineer hanging over the side widow of the locomotive cab. I would wave brightly and enjoy the noise, motion, and smell of this great dragon of transportation, and he would usually blow the great whistle as a loud voice of friendship.

On the road halfway between the tracks and the farm was a large house set back about 200 feet. It had a large, circular gravel driveway. Apparently some rich people lived there. Lining the road in front was a row of thick bushes where two chow dogs would lay in wait for cars and trucks to chase. I had to pass this place of monsters in fear of my very life, and it was the challenge that made my heart beat. So, I would get going as fast as I could and hope not to get my leg bitten. Usually they would not see me coming because I did not have the noise warning of a motor.

and I was past them before they realized that I had intruded on "their" section of the tar and gravel road. As I was passing, out of the corner of my eye, I could see their surprise and their instant reaction to my challenge. Darting out from under the bushes, both would run and growl with great violence and do their best to catch me. They never did, but once they got so close to my pants leg at the ankle that I could feel their teeth close to my ankle in my adrenaline-filled mind. Past a certain point they would stop chasing, knowing that they were getting out of their section of the road, and I could then slow down. With my heart beating with large amounts of adrenaline, I would catch my breath and cherish the adventurous victory I had just accomplished.

Across one of the other fields was a small sometimes working saw mill. The husband got very violent when he drank, which was most of the time, and his wife and three very beautiful daughters were always at risk. I was in love with the youngest of the three. She was about fifteen, the proper age for an eleven-year-old cowboy, and was very blond with what I remember was a great body. Their house was kind of a shack with an upstairs, and I liked going there to see the love of my life. Since they did not have inside plumbing, this was my only experience with a real outhouse. It stunk like heck, and it had an army of flies keeping guard over the very shaky structure. I had the privilege of using it once. It was an awful experience. For some reason, I did not mind the manure of the milk farm, but this was too much. The fear of falling into the hole was always at the forefront.

Then there was the one-acre garden of the farm. It was full of all kinds of fresh vegetables, and it was my job to collect beans, corn, tomatoes, lettuce, and all sorts of other vegetables for dinner. It was from my Uncle Harold that I learned to appreciate fresh white sweet corn. He would insist that the corn not be picked until the water was ready to boil on the stove. We would then pick the number of ears required, husk them, and run to the boiling pot, getting them into the water in less than five minutes. Salt and lots of butter crowned the rows of kernels to our delight. We, of course, had special corn plates so that the other foods did not mix with this great delicacy.

On the side of the farmhouse was a small grassy knoll with a great oak tree providing shade from the hot summer sun. A small stream passed close by on its way to the watering hole, and it provided well water for the house. Some days I would lie on the slight hill and look up at the cotton-puffed blue sky. I would sometimes fall asleep for 30 minutes or so with Queenie lying next to me. The breeze would rustle through the leaves of the great oak and would combine with the slight trickle of the small stream to create great "Songs of Life," which I still remember very clearly. This was nature's best, and I will always remember the quiet peacefulness of this great place.

Then the end of the summer would come and back on the train I would go to the hard smells and sounds of urban life. My manila identification tag would make sure that I would not end up in Canada, which was surely a better place than Cuba. At least in Canada they had brightly red-coated cowboys. My thoughts were rarely of the passing landscapes and telephone poles keeping time with the rhythmic clickity-clack of the wheels on the tracks. My thoughts were not of the porters and conductors. My thoughts were of Queenie, the cows, chickens, and roads of fresh bubbling tar. I would not appreciate the clean air until returning to Massachusetts Avenue with all the turmoil of urban life.

There are so many other Starve Gut Farm memories of sight, smell, and experience that have been chiseled into my permanent memory. When I was 13 years old, I was informed that my Uncle Harold had retired, sold the farm, and moved to Florida. I was devastated to learn that my farm summers would never be again. The thoughts of Queenie, my beloved Lassie, still embossed my thoughts. The next summer, there was no farm for me. Time had passed, and I grew older with a great emptiness in my heart for my past adventures.

Over the years I have recalled the many pleasant times and memories of Starve Gut Farm. I have learned the process of meditation and progressive relaxation in my adult life. Sometimes I would get some hypnotic therapy, and I became proficient with self-hypnosis using a tape supplied as part of the program. Most of these techniques would start out by getting you to go to a relaxing and wonderful place in nature before the deep breathing process would begin. I always returned to that small grassy knoll where the sounds of the great oak tree blended with melodies from the small stream in wonderful concert. The warm sun would always be there to gently warm my legs, arms, and body in a progressive fashion, leading to deep concentration to a far-off place. This was the place of my most memorable time and comfort.

My memories of the farm also gave me some balance in my adult life. Whenever I got stressed with some work of life issues, whether real or not, I could always daydream back to Starve Gut Farm. Those wonderful and positive memories managed to direct my thoughts to more positive visions. When our minds get into negative territory, it is wonderful to have creative memories to chase those stress thoughts away. These are the thoughts that affect our feelings and determine our level of happiness.

The great gift of "The Summer Farm" will always be with me as a "Cognitive Escape" from the turmoil of modern life and adulthood. It is a great gift that I will take with me when I leave this Earth.

The Green Belt

Curiosity of the current condition and status of the planet Earth overcame Tom Crowley's imagination to the point that he could not resist making a visit to the origin of his family, Earth. The "family album" hologram that he just viewed left his vision of the ice-aged Earth, and a visit to the once-blue planet captured his sense of mission. When his grandparents left Earth in such a hurry to get away from the tyranny of the Green Belt leaders, it left a very open question of what has happened in the last fifty years. He had no holographic record of such. So he decided to make the five-month light speed journey to Earth in order to satisfy his curiosity and put a sense of closure on his past.

Tom programmed the course to the solar system at the upper outer edge of the galaxy into his navigational computer and entered the suspension chamber in order to sleep away the months of travel time. He still had thoughts of the beautiful reptilian Elietians in his heart, and he missed their gentle nature. He looked forward to the time in which he would return to visit his "second family" on Eliet, but now he was eager to visit Earth.

He did not know what to expect and how the very controlled society on Earth had developed or even survived. His concern was great, for the holographic history showed a planet of violence that did not conform to the many peaceful societies he had encountered throughout the galaxy. He proceeded with great care and planned to approach the planet from far off until he could determine if it was safe to approach. He slowly succumbed to the suspension chamber's sleep program.

225

The trip took almost five months at the *Odyssey IV* full speed of 250 (250 LUs) times the speed of light. Close to coming out of light speed, the suspension chamber woke Tom automatically, and he immediately entered the vibration chamber for 20 minutes to recover from the long sleep. While getting some food from the molecular constructor, Tom went back to the holographic record of his grandparents' escape from the planet Earth under the siege of a full ice age and the Green Belt's violent politics. He mulled over the many pictures of Earth of that time. Tom had not seen a planet during an actual ice age. The pictures showed the bright greenish-blue ring around the equatorial circumference, and the terrain going north and south gradually turned to brown and finally, to the bright white of the extended polar caps.

He was still several billion miles away from Earth when the auto-navigation started the slowdown, and Tom became anxious about what he would find. Since it had only been fifty years since his grandparents left, his expectations were that not much change had taken place. When *Odyssey IV* crossed the orbital path of Neptune, he slowed *Odyssey IV* down to five LUs and charted a course to just cross the path of Mars and stop to make some sensor readings and observe any transmissions that might give him some sense of what might be ahead. Arriving at that point, he turned his sensors and radio receivers on to begin cursory probing of the planet.

His long-range high-resolution visual camera captured an amazing view of Earth. The planet's poles were solid white and extended 30 percent of the way in each hemisphere. The Green Belt around the equator was still intact, and between the ice and the Green Belt was a band of reddish-brown like that of Mars, implying no life. This was a sight that reinforced the power of nature and the fragility of life. After making adjustments for the atmosphere, he began to pick up some transmissions that were about twelve minutes old based on the distance. There was lots of chatter, music, and much video transmissions. This is what he had expected.

It was not long after that the alarms went off in his sensors. They had picked up four ships heading directly his way at about 75 percent of the speed of light. Tom decided to depart, and just as he set *Odyssey IV* to turn and go to light speed, his sensors showed some very powerful laser energies emanating from the four ships. They were firing at *Odyssey IV* without even knowing who this might be! It would take about two minutes for the laser energies to reach Tom. He immediately set *Odyssey IV* into light speed, and within thirty seconds, his ship was well on its way to safety. From the four Earth ships, *Odyssey IV* just seemed to disappear because the light from *Odyssey IV* moving away at 5 LUs would never reach the positions of the attackers. The light physics just followed along behind *Odyssey IV*.

Tom was taken back by this aggressive action. He had not experienced this violence anywhere in the galaxy, and his naive thoughts almost got him into trouble. He was now prepared to be very cautious of these dangerous people. The only defense for *Odyssey IV* was its speed for it had no weapons or protection. There was never a need.

Tom sat for awhile well away from the solar system with his sensors on full penetration and the alarms set to sensitive. He was well beyond the range of his attackers. He then started to imagine a plan to try to get close to Earth and decided to swing way out to the top edge of the galaxy and enter from the northern pole. He also calculated that if he came out of light speed at just the right time and came to a full stop just over the pole, he could get close and remain undetected. This was a very exact calculation so as not to crash to a pulverized state at the pole. He was confident that he could do this within a safe margin, and when he was at that point, he would descend to 100 feet off the ice surface so as not to be detected by the equator sensors of the Green Belt residents.

Tom carefully entered the course into *Odyssey IV*'s computer and ran a few simulations just to make sure that he was precise enough. He also created a little emergency course program: if *Odyssey IV*'s sensors identified any ships or weapons being fired, the computer would immediately take *Odyssey IV* to safety in less than a second. It would appear to his attackers that he just disappeared, for the light would never reach them. All was set, and Tom gave the command.

Odyssey IV quickly took position about two billion miles from the top of the solar system. It was poised to come in at the most northern part of Earth and stop 100 feet above the actual pole; it was an exact maneuver. Tom gave the command and found himself at the pole position 100 feet above the surface in a short period of time. His sensors showed nothing in the area. The bandwidths of the Earth satellites could not pick him up because of the speed in which he came in. Now he was too close to the ground to be detected, and he could slowly creep south at 100 feet off the surface, blending into the rough contours of the ice. His sensors were ready to give the signal to *Odyssey IV*'s inertial drives in case of another attack, and he would be gone in an instant.

Tom charted a due southerly course that would take him to the Amazon Bay area, and he would carefully monitor for any sensors that might detect him. He set the speed to just under that of the sound barrier. He wanted to go as fast as possible without creating a sonic boom that might be detected.

227

The ice was at least two miles thick and riddled with canyons carved by the rushing flow of enormous amounts of water from the now melting ice. *Odyssey IV*'s contour guidance system made for perfect flight through the maze of canyons, which decreased the possibility of being detected. It was a smooth and acrobatic ride, and when he was about 20 percent of the distance to the equator, the ice seemed to start thinning dramatically. There were torrents of fresh melted water sculpting the ice into massive canyons some five miles wide and one to two miles deep. There was a blue glistening tone reflecting the sun off the very clean and bright ice.

At the fortieth parallel, Tom began to see some of the exposed earth banking much of the melting torrents. The water seemed to get wider and deeper very quickly, and Tom was being treated to the birth of huge canyons that would live for millenniums. The erosion was swift and massive, exposing multicolored layers of earth, and the once clear water was now of a bright red. Tom followed one of the largest canyons, and the ice soon succumbed to the multicolored layered erosions with a floor rushing of redness. It was like Earth was bleeding profusely while being born again.

It was not long until plant life began, turning the browns into greens, which became darker as *Odyssey IV* traveled south. The eroded canyons were now crowned at the top with flat mesas that started to become rich with plant life. Tom was watching Earth get re-sculptured as it had been in prehistoric times. The massive movement of large amounts of water and soil overwhelmed Tom's memories of any other geological sights that he had seen in the galaxy with the exception of the static nature of the huge canyons on Mars.

The foliage became thicker, and the scant brush turned to scattered trees, then turned into large fresh forests. Tom came to a large flat valley surrounded by sharp mile high hills with large lakes and rivers. It was a beautiful sight, and Tom slowed *Odyssey IV* to about 100 miles per hour in order to enjoy the sights. Tom decided to land and selected a field encircled by a lush forest split by a small river. And *Odyssey IV* gracefully set down onto the soft, rich, grass-covered soil.

Tom carefully scanned the area for life and motion, and detected only small masses, some in the forest and some in the air; life was everywhere. He did detect some life that conformed to the profile of humans. After scanning thoroughly, Tom decided to open the hatch and get a first-hand look. He had swallowed a small remote device that would allow *Odyssey IV* to be able to track and find him wherever he was, even from far off. And he could issue commands to *Odyssey IV* from afar. Leaving his escape program of light speed when detected on, he slowly walked down the ramp. If detected, *Odyssey IV* would fly off and wait for instructions.

The valley was laced with wildflowers, and the air was prolific with birds and butterflies. The air was the purest he had ever experienced. As he was looking at the edge of the forest, he noticed some movement and concentrated on that spot. The motion got stronger, and soon four human figures appeared very slowly. They seemed to be as interested in Tom as he with them. For some reason their mutual curiosity overcame their fear, and the four slowly walked toward Tom standing at the ramp; Tom did not move. As the four came closer, one was a male and the other three female. While their clothing was very primitive and of animal skins, they were expertly assembled and quite neat.

The four slowly came closer, and when they were about twenty feet from Tom, they stopped. They all looked at each other for a period, and Tom remembered the courage his father had when they first greeted the Argonians. Tom broke the silence with, "Hello, my name is Tom, and I am pleased to meet you. I have come here in peace and hope that you will trust me as I do you." And he extended his hand.

One of the women, a very attractive blond, smiled brightly, extended her hand, and replied, "I am Carol, and we are pleased to meet you. You are not of the Green Belt, so from where do you come?"

Without too much detail, Tom smiled and returned with, "My ancestors are from the Green Belt, and many years ago they escaped and settled on a planet called Argon where I was born. They were very afraid of the growing tyranny in the Green Belt."

The male was of a dark complexion with black hair and dark brown eyes. The two other females were of a lighter complexion, dark brown eyes, and black hair. They seemed to be very interested in the combination of Tom's light hair and pastel brown eyes. They had never seen such a combination.

The male asked, "Are there many planets with life on them? How long does it take to get there? What are they like?"

Carol shushed him with, "There will be plenty of time for those questions." Then she turned to Tom and asked, "Why are you here, and what are your plans?"

Tom told her that he was back to visit his roots but was very apprehensive regarding the Green Belt society. Then he asked if he could stay and if there was a safe place to hide his *Odyssey IV*. They offered to host Tom and told of a place where a very large cave had been carved out on the side of a cliff by the river. Carol offered to show Tom, and he took her aboard *Odyssey IV* to find the cave. Slowly, *Odyssey IV* rose softly, and with Carol's guidance, Tom found the cave and parked *Odyssey IV* under the huge overhanging rock that hid it from observation from the sky. Tom left the escape program on, just in case. Carol was overcome with the nature of *Odyssey IV* and had many questions that her gracious patience held for a later time.

They left *Odyssey IV* buttoned up, and Carol led Tom through the woods to a clearing where there was a small settlement. A slow-moving river, a branch from the main river, split the area. There were many dwellings made of wood, mud, and hay for the roofs. Smoke permeated the air, and the smell of cooking meat beckoned to those of the hungry. There was a very large garden with a variety of vegetables, from potatoes to corn, tomatoes to carrots, etc. Along the far bank of the river were many fruit trees of apples and pears. It was a self-sufficient community, as basic as it was. Tom had seen these items only in pictures and welcomed the reality of their presence.

When Tom and Carol appeared from the forest, most of the residents came to meet them as they had expected his coming from the others that initially met him. These were a happy and peaceful people and seemed to have all that they needed. There were many running children whose voices could be heard constantly, reminding everybody of the happy life that the community enjoyed. The children's voices mingled with the soft rustle of the trees. There were many hand-made tools of iron and some steel, but no modern weapons were visible, to Tom's relief. Only those primitive weapons required providing food. While simple, their tools were of high quality.

That night, there was a great gathering of all the people with much meat and plants to celebrate Tom's coming. And lots of questions and answers were exchanged. Tom told of his heritage and the fleeing of his grandparents from the Green Belt and of his birth on Argon. He also shared the many places he had visited throughout the galaxy and the nature of those cultures. It was like that of a great storyteller sharing stories, complete with a warm and glowing fire that seasoned the air with the romance of the moment. And they loved the stories.

Time passed, and many excused themselves and returned to their dwellings for the evening, leaving Carol and Tom alone. There was considerable chemistry between the two, and Carol was not committed to a mate. They talked for a long time, and Carol shared her knowledge of the Green Belt.

She went on, "It is told that our ancestors of ten generations ago were expelled from the Green Belt and exiled to the ice. There were several attempts to return, but many were lost at the hands of the Green Belt armies. The society of the ice had to make do and develop the foundations of their survival. Most had died, and only a few survived. Today, we are an independent people with a good life. Many of the sciences of our ancestors were saved, and we understand much, but our ability to make tools is very limited. We have the knowledge but not the manufacturing means. We have strengthened our agriculture and animal flocking, and we have learned to make and use good steel implements and ceramics. We spin and weave fabrics but are limited due to the unavailability of suitable materials. We make paper and pen, and educate our children with that of the memories of our ancestors and carefully document everything for future generations. We know of no other settlements and believe that we are the only survivors, and we live in four large areas that we call towns as ancient history tells us. There are about 4,000 of us and we believe that at one time, there were as few as 500."

Tom was fascinated because now he had a small view of what happened outside the Green Belt, so he asked, "And what of the Green Belt and those who live there?"

Carol went on, "We have never seen the Green Belt, and those who were sent to find out about it never returned. On occasion, we get visitors we believe are from there who fly overhead as if to check on us. We thought that you may be one, but when you landed and we saw you, we realized that you were from another place. They do leave us alone, and we do not go near them. There are many stories of the old days when the ice first came and many perished."

There were a lot of feelings generated between Tom and Carol, and their attraction grew strong. Tom asked Carol to tell something of herself and she went on, "I have never taken a partner because I am a little different and have found no one that I am attracted to. I would rather live alone than live a life of compromise. It is lonely though, and sometimes I just want to let go to one of the men who are pursuing me in order to quell the loneliness. Most of them have given up, and now I have a more peaceful life. So I work hard to contribute to our people and find that being busy helps me to cope with the loneliness. And what of you?"

Carol's openness and situation brought his feelings closer to her, and his heart began to make a place for her. She was quite lovely, and her body attracted Tom. He answered her with, "Well, most of my time is alone, travelling between the many planets and visiting the many cultures that are out there. I have made many good and deep friends that I cherish but have never taken a permanent partner. I have had some encounters with great romantic feelings, but never to the level as a partner would be. I, too, am lonely for a continuous partner but have not found the right one."

There was common ground in their desires and feelings. As the fire began to die, coolness filled the air, and Carol moved close to Tom. He put his arm firmly around her, and she felt very good to him. She liked the attention and cuddled a little against his body as they sat. And they mutually liked the feeling of togetherness.

It was late, both were tired, and Carol suggested that they turn in. Tom was not sure what that meant, and Carol had not planned for a guest. Her modest lodge was clean and comfortable but not used to a male guest, and it was not until they decided to turn in that she realized that the only place she had for Tom was her bed. After a moment, she started to relish the thought of physical male company that she was very attracted to and offered, "Tom, I only have one place for you to sleep and that is in my bed. It is warm and comfortable, and you are welcome to be with me."

A chill went up Tom's back and he, in a not-too-eager voice said, "I would like that if it is not too much trouble."

Tom took his clothes off while Carol was off doing something, and he got under the covers, which were made of some very soft fur, making the floor bed very comfortable and luxurious in a primitive way. Carol returned, and with her back toward Tom, slowly took her clothes off in the dim light. Her body was athletic and toned, and the curves of her hips reinforced the look of a beautiful woman as the moon shadows accented her shape. She turned and was more beautiful with very sculptured lines. Her breasts were firm and did not need support clothing to enhance her beauty. Her blonde hair went over the front of her shoulders and halfway down her chest.

She slowly slipped into bed and cuddled right up to Tom, who welcomed her with his arms. And they held each other close with their bare bodies and started to kiss softly and sensually. It did not take long for the kisses to get stronger and more passionate, and Tom touched and kissed her all over while she caressed the back of his head, shoulders, and other parts of his body. They were both ready and came together very naturally and slowly. They fit together very softly and completely. After, they both slept well, close to each other. There was never a question that this was unnatural.

Tom was surprised when he was awakened to the call through the forests, of a large rooster at the early start of daylight. Tom had never heard the call of a rooster before, and its loudness really caught his attention. He could not imagine what type of large animal this might be, and when he saw one, he was truly surprised at the smallness of such a loud animal. Carol was already up and dressed, and, noticing Tom's awakening state, she bent down with a bright smile and compassionately kissed him with her hand on his check. They kissed a little, and Carol offered Tom some morning food that was being served at a common area. Tom dressed, and they headed off together to eat.

There were lots of people for Tom to interact with, and this was one of his favorite things. He was learning more about these very special people. One of the things that caught his interest and attention was when young men became of age, they were sent to one of the other towns so that inter-mating was spread out, reducing the risks of birth defects. The women stayed in their respective homes.

It was a beautiful morning, the sky was bright blue, and a rare, soft breeze rustled through the trees. Just then, a sky ship flew over the area. It was very similar in shape to *Odyssey IV* but much smaller. None of the residents were concerned for this was a common event and represented no danger. Carol remarked, "Those are people from the Green Belt checking up on us. They never bother us and have never landed. We have never seen one."

Just as she was finished, the ship did land in the field where *Odyssey IV* had landed the day before, surprising everyone. Soon after, four armed and uniformed men came out of the woods toward the center of the village where many of the residents had come to cook and eat in a community fashion. They sternly looked around with an air of authority, and the apparent leader asked a few of the people if they had seen anything strange in the sky the day before. Everybody lied beautifully as if they had rehearsed a script. While he was talking, the other three walked around looking for anything strange or out of the ordinary. One stopped and closely looked at Tom's blond hair and pastel brown eyes and remarked, "You are not of this town. Where do you come from, and why are you so different? I have not seen eyes such as yours." And he called the apparent leader of the four over to look at Tom.

Tom had much experience thinking on his feet in conversations with the many encounters with aliens all over the galaxy. He responded in a stuttering and awkward manner as though mentally defected, "I don't know. I think that I came from over there," pointing as a child would. Carol picked up on his ruse and came to Tom's side stating, "He is but a child, and his mind is not as quick as ours. He was born of parents from the same town and has been immature from a young age." Tom looked away and up toward the sky as a child would when trying to be obscure. He cocked his head toward his shoulder, which he shrugged and looked back at the questioner with his head turned slightly away. He was careful not to overdo it.

233

Carol went on, "He is one of our examples of us breeding too close to each other. His mother was of my color, and his father, who is dead, was of the dark color. He is very strong but is slow to learn, if at all."

The ruse was convincing, and the interrogators moved on. They slowly walked around observing others in the area, and then stopped at a small girl of about six years. The apparent leader bent down and with a smile asked, "You sure are a very beautiful little girl. I have a little girl like you, and she is very pretty, too." She smiled shyly with her mother aside of her with great apprehension.

He went on, "Did you see any new people come from the sky to your town yesterday?" With a shy voice, she responded and pointed to Tom. And the interrogator smiled and returned to Tom, and with a sarcastic and firm tone, "You come with us." They brought Tom off to their ship, closed the door, and took off. Carol and the others were shocked. It happened so fast.

It took about two hours to get to the Green Belt, and upon landing on a pad next to a large official-looking building, they disembarked to a large group waiting for them. Without a word, Tom was escorted down a maze of corridors to a stark room that appeared to be an interrogation place. There were only two steel chairs and a small table in a very bright white room. They sat Tom down in one of the chairs and left Tom, locking the door behind them. He was now very alone and afraid of what might happen. Time went by—it seemed maybe three hours. During that time he thought of the many adventures he had with the many very gracious and lovely people and the love he had shared with them. He was sad to think that he may never see them again, and he missed the safety of *Odyssey IV*.

Tom called out several times, but there was no answer. He tried to maintain his childish style just in case they were recording him. This was like nothing else that he had experienced, and he was very fearful of his potential destiny. The stark loneliness of the room was beginning to work on Tom's fears, as was probably planned by his captors.

After some time, the complete silence was abruptly broken by the sound of the door latch being operated, and its loud echo after so much silence added greatly to Tom's discomfort. In walked an official-looking man dressed in an off-gray outfit that only slightly contrasted with the bright whiteness of the room. He walked toward Tom with a very friendly smile and introduced himself, "I am William, and I was assigned to you as your host. I am very sorry that we have had to detain you, but we have to do what we have to do. If there is anything at all that I can get for you, just call, and I can assure you that I will do my best to help you. Do you understand me?"

Tom said nothing as he just looked up. William left, and Tom was alone again. Much time had passed, and Tom lay down on the hard floor to try to sleep. Just as he dozed off, a very loud, high-pitched horn blasted the room, startling Tom awake. This cycle went on for eight more hours. On occasion, Tom called for William to bring water, but he never did. Tom was now exhausted, becoming weak, and almost ready to say anything. The cycles of almost sleep and wake-up noise went on for another ten hours, and Tom was way out of control of his senses. He cried many times. Only his Argonian part stayed alert and kept him from a total breakdown.

The door latch broke the white silence of the room, and it was William again. William queried, "Why haven't you called for me? You do not have to do this to yourself. Let me help you." Tom was totally dejected and confused. He was actually beginning to believe that he was responsible for his situation. His captors have succeeded in creating a paradox in Tom's mind. Subliminal messages had been piped into the room, further deepening Tom's thoughts. As William was leaving, he had indicated to Tom that a friend would very soon visit, and all would become right.

The time passed for another ten hours of attempted sleep and wakeup when the door latch again broke the painful silence of the room. A tall, gentle man walked in and introduced himself as Mister Tobbs. Tobbs told the very weak Tom that he was now going to help Tom, but he had to ask just a few questions first and this ordeal would end with some food, drink and a nice comfortable sleep. Tom did not respond. This is the transcript of the questions:

Tobbs: "We have deducted from your DNA profile that you are a descendant from Alex and Maria Crowley. These people are criminals of our society and stole some very valuable technology. What do you say to this?"

Tom: "I know not of these people."

Tobbs: "Yes, you do. You are not from this world, and we are very interested how you got here. We did track your ship for some time, and you cannot deny these facts. What do you say of this?"

Tom: "I don't know what you are talking about. I come from a small town and do not know of this ship you ask about."

Tobbs: "Our sensors are telling us that you are lying. So, I will give you some more time to think of your answers."

235

And Tobbs left with the loud echo click of the door latch. Tom was becoming emotionally and physically exhausted and on the verge of a major breakdown. And the time of sleep deprivation continued for ten more hours. Someone had placed some water for Tom from time to time.

Tobbs came again and asked Tom if he had remembered his past and that of the Crowleys. Shaking, Tom replied, "Yes, they were my grandparents. My father was their son, John. And I am John's son."

Tobbs: "Good, now! We have made much progress. So you are not of a town, you are from a far-off place. Is this true?"

Tom: "Yes, this is true."

Tobbs: "We found some strange DNA in your being. Well, then, tell me where you are from and how you got here."

The Argonian part in Tom had given him some inner strength and the ability to think a little clearly aside from the great pain he was in.

Tom: "I am from Argon, which is about 31 million light years from here. My father, John, had married an Argonian, and I am their child. Since I am of mixed heritage, the Argonians were concerned that I might spoil their DNA structures and ultimately destroy the pureness of their race. They do not believe in killing their own, so they exiled me to this place. They brought me here and left yesterday, I think."

The lie sensor was not able to detect Tom's untruths because he was talking from the Argonian side. As such, Tobbs was taking in the story.

Tobbs: "How did these Argonians get here from such a distance, and how did your parents get to Argon?"

Tom was now on a roll, and his story was unfolding in his imagination.

Tom: "The Argonians have very powerful technology of space travel and weapons. They have the ability to travel large distances instantly, and it only took us three weeks to get here from Argon. They are a peaceful people and mean no harm."

Tom was able to trip the lie sensor with his "peaceful" statement, and Tobbs was taken back. The inference taken from the lie was that the Argonians were powerful and violent people. More of the story was unfolding in Tom's mind, and Tobbs was taking more in.

Tom: "Since I am half of one of them, they cannot kill me, and they are required to protect my interests."

The lie meter was silent while Tom continued to tell his story.

Tom: "So, they knew of Earth from my parents and grandparents and decided to exile me to this place after years of observation of your ways. They monitored your transmissions for some time, and they decided that I would be safer outside the Green Belt. It is their intent to check on me from time to time."

The lie meter was still silent.

Tobbs: "How did your grandparents get to Argon?"

Tom: "I am not sure, but I am told that when my grandparents and father escaped from here, they were picked up at the edge of the solar system by the Argonians and brought to their home planet. My father married an Argonian, my mother, and when they found out I was sterile as a result of the bonding, they decided for my exile."

The real truth is that Tom's grandparents found the planet of Argon and were welcomed to stay and live their lives in peace, including Tom who was born many years later. They loved Tom as their own and were a very peaceful people with no inclination of violence. He also hid the fact that it was his grandparents that broke the light barrier, but gave the credit to the Argonians to further emphasize the strength of their technology.

Tobbs was taking in the whole story and excused himself from the interrogation room. Moments later, a small girl brought in some needed food and drink. Shortly thereafter, Tom was taken to a resting-place for some severely needed sleep.

It was twenty hours later when Tom woke up. He was immediately visited by William, his first contact who promised to take care of him but really did not. He opened up with, "Well, Tom, how are you feeling?"

"I don't really know," replied Tom. "I seemed to have slept for a long time."

"We have had much discussion among ourselves, and we are not sure what to do with you," William carefully nodded.

Tom had done a great job creating the vision that the Argonians were very powerful and that they cared for Tom's well being. William and his superiors were afraid at this point to make any decision regarding Tom's disposition, so they decided to be cordial to Tom in the meantime. They were afraid of what the Argonians might do if they harmed Tom. They were going to let Tom roam around this one central area in the Green Belt with two guards to follow, of course. They felt that it was better to gain Tom's confidence if they were to find out more of these Argonians, a certain and real threat to the Green Belt society.

William had made arrangements with the local visitor-boarding place for Tom to stay under the observation of his two guards, and he was free to go where he wished. After walking around for two hours about the various areas, Tom went back to his boarding place and, in what was a lobby, entered a very appetizing eating place. He ordered some food, ate, and retired for some sleep. His freedom about the galaxy was on his mind and the welfare of *Odyssey IV* concerned him, but he knew that *Odyssey IV* would be ok with the escape program he had set up. Even worse, he thought that there might be a good chance that he would be imprisoned and not get back to his safety. He never felt so helpless and in real danger.

The next morning, Tom was awaken by William and two other officials, and they invited Tom to breakfast as an opportunity to query him further in a non-intimidating way. While they were sitting waiting for the food they had ordered, William opened up the conversation with, "Well, Tom, what do you think we should do with you?"

Tom hesitated and responded with, "Well, I certainly don't wish to go back to those people and their dirt huts and smelly food. I would like to find something here in the Green Belt." So far the lie meter had registered the truth, and Tom was able to keep his Argonian wit about him. To this point, he had succeeded in diverting their perceptions, and now he was setting them up for further possible deceptions. As they were eating, an extremely attractive woman entered the eating area and walked directly to Tom, William, and the other two seated at the table. William introduced her to Tom and invited her to sit down, which she did very seductively. Her name was Melody, and, of course, Tom was very attracted to her.

William then explained, "Well, Tom, we have assigned Melody to you as sort of a guide while you are here. She is specially trained and will serve all of your needs." Melody smiled at Tom, and the only thing he could say was, "Very nice!" And she deepened her smile at Tom with a grin that caught Tom's sexual appetite.

Shortly afterward, William and his colleagues left, and Tom was left alone with Melody. Nothing was said between the two for a few moments, and she broke the ice with, "Well, what would you like to do today? Name it, anything that you would like."

She was wearing an almost sheer peach-colored dress that contoured her very shapely body. Her eyes were turquoise, and her hair was light auburn and extended a little past her shoulders with loose curls at the ends. She was very unlike the other women that he observed in the Green Belt who were very reserved and carried a stern professional look.

Tom, with sort of a inquiring tone, said, "I watched some old holograms many years ago showing my grandparents on a picnic at a place called Amazon Bay. Is it still here?"

"Yes, I know it well, and I go there often to relax and meditate. I know of some very lovely and secluded places there where we could enjoy the scenery in our own privacy," was her answer. She continued, "We could pack some food and wine and take the magnetic monorail there. It does not take long, and we could possibly stay overnight. I know of some special places."

Tom's desires at this time were high but not higher than his caution. He was not that naïve but wanted to take advantage of the situation and look for an opportunity to escape back to the safety of *Odyssey IV*.

The high-speed magnetic monorail ride to Amazon Bay was fast, smooth, and very comfortable. Melody had packed some lunch, and as they sat watching the sights speed by, she became very touchy with Tom. He was very comfortable and enjoyed the feelings with guarded reservations. He looked forward to seeing the place of his grandparents' hologram. Melody was becoming more affectionate as the time went by, and when they arrived at the Amazon Bay Station, Tom was quite excited. And Melody was quite confident with her abilities.

At the station, they acquired and drove a small electric wagon to a secluded place that had a quaint cottage on stilts that overlooked the bay. There was a large number of local wildlife including many small primates rustling in the trees and a large variety of very colorful birds screeching the songs of their day's activities. The cottage was of quality materials, including a well-stocked food area, and the wraparound balcony gave a full 360-degree view of the area. It was a romantic place. Some of the areas on the way in reminded Tom of the familiar scenery in the family hologram.

As Tom was on the balcony leaning against the railing looking around the bay, Melody poured drinks for both of them and joined Tom. After handing Tom his drink, she began to cuddle up to him, pressing her soft and shapely body against his. He turned and held her close in his arms while planting a very sensual kiss on her lips, and he proceeded to kiss her neck and shoulders. Melody responded very passionately, enjoying Tom's advances.

It did not take long for them end up on the very luxurious bed, and they made love several times during the next hours. It was obvious to Tom that Melody had strong feelings for him, and that made their togetherness that much more enjoyable. The next morning, they lounged around for awhile eating some breakfast, and then Tom became very interested in Melody's background, asking her, "What is your history, and what do you do here in the Green Belt?"

Melody went on, "I was born of non-useful parents outside the Green Belt and when I was eighteen, the officials invited me to take residence in the Green Belt. They provided me with a very luxurious home and gave me all the things that I needed and wanted. All I had to do was to keep a selected few company from time to time and satisfy their physical wants and needs. I have been doing this for eight years, and I have few complaints. They seem to really like me in comparison to their mates, who tend to be very unemotional or unloving. I fulfill a very large emptiness in their lives."

Tom listened intently, and when he thought she was finished, he inquired, "And you are happy doing this?"

She put her hand on the side of his cheek and with a very low voice and concerned expression replied, "It is what I have to do to survive, but I look for a more loving life. One that I believe that I could have with you."

Tom felt a level of sorrow for Melody, and he gave her a warm, comforting hug, holding her for some time. He really liked her and was trying to think of some way to help her with her paradox.

Melody went on, "I have dreamed of the day when I could spend all of my time making just one man happy and becoming close as one. But that is not in the future for me. And what of you, Tom?"

Tom carefully unfolded his story of his grandparents, their "capture" by the Argonians, and his birth on Argon, including his early youth. He was sure the officials were observing them and wanted to reinforce the tale he had left with them. He also told her of his fear of the very powerful Argonians and how lucky he was that he was not destroyed. They accepted his father as an alien and his mother as an Argonian, but it was unacceptable to them for Tom to be a hybrid. It was their prejudice and fear that motivated them to exile Tom to the roots of his origin.

Tom continued, "The last thing that I want is to be exiled outside the Green Belt with those primitive and dirty people who live in dirt homes. I am not used to such a meager living. I know that the Argonians will be back to check on me from time to time, and in spite of their violent nature, they have chosen not to destroy me because I am partially Argonian. I do not know what they will do if they do not find me. They are very good at tracking those who they wish to find. Their space and weapon technology is far beyond anything else in this part of the galaxy."

Tom was sure that he was creating great concern in the minds of the Green Belt officials. Melody was spellbound with Tom's plight, and she considered each of them to be in the same situation, which tightened her bond with Tom.

They spent another two days in the cottage by the bay and then returned back to the urban area. They were met at the monorail station by William and the two others. This reinforced Tom's perception that he had been spied upon because the officials knew when to meet them without being given a schedule.

Tom and Melody were taken back to the white room where Tom was first taken for interrogation. As they entered the room, William looked sharply at Melody, and she left without a word or look for Tom. He tried to look surprised but knew that this had to be and that she was given to him to get information. It was a fun time with her, and he was further saddened by her position.

William started the conversation with, "We have had much discussion regarding your disposition and have decided that it would be in your best interest to return you to the outside. But before we do that, we would like to host you for some more time."

Tom objected with, "I do not want to go back out there. I am comfortable here and urge you to reconsider this decision." Tom really wanted to get back outside the Green Belt from where he was taken but wanted to reinforce this position so that they would likely send him out as punishment. They were also afraid of what the Argonians may do to them if they could not find Tom, and they certainly did not want Tom running around outside the Green Belt as a potential threat. So their paradox continued. And Tom's inner concern to get back to *Odyssey IV* grew deeper. He kept trying to think of an opportunity that could get *Odyssey IV* to come and get him.

They returned Tom to the place of boarding as before, and soon Melody showed up to continue her assignment. They were very glad to see each other, and Melody expressed a deeper desire to stay with Tom. They spent the next two days seeing the sights and spending time together with lots of sexual activity, which they both thoroughly enjoyed. On the third morning, Melody suggested that they visit the great coliseum that hosted many of the special events, including major sporting events. Tom agreed that this might be interesting, and after cleaning up, off they went.

It took about an hour on the high-speed magnetic monorail to get to the coliseum, and after they departed from the train, Tom was impressed with the colossal nature of the structure. It was one of the biggest he had even seen. They wandered around the many access areas lined with entertainment and food vendors that were mostly closed because there was no event, and the coliseum was empty of the usual crowds. It seemed that Melody and Tom had the whole place to themselves, and their attendance was greatly dwarfed by the sheer magnitude of the structure's mass.

After meandering through the many coliseum areas, Melody took Tom to the playing field, and, standing in the center of the field, Tom again, with a 360-degree view of the entire structure, was overcome with its sheer size. The field alone was at least 300 yards long by 100 yards wide. It quickly occurred to Tom that this might be a good place for *Odyssey IV* to land if called. Tom carefully structured his thoughts and needed some time to plan whatever might work for his escape. So he took Melody firmly in his arms and started to kiss her passionately, which quickly led to some aggressive sexual lovemaking in the center of the field. It was exciting for both, and Tom was able to maintain his composure to unfold his plan. When finished, Tom rolled over on his side away from Melody and regurgitated the *Odyssey IV* control module that he swallowed earlier and began to issue some commands. He figured that the signals would not be picked up because he was broadcasting outside the spectrum of the Green Belt frequencies.

He first gave the command for *Odyssey IV* to engage the escape program and then to come back to Tom's location in the coliseum with the same maneuver he used to enter Earth at the North Pole. Without Melody noticing, he executed the command. Back at the cave where *Odyssey IV* was parked under the cover of the cave's overhang, *Odyssey IV* slowly and gracefully began to slowly plot its way out into the clear. In a few moments it was outside Earth's atmosphere and out to the orbital path of Mars, which only took three minutes at three LUs. If detected, *Odyssey IV* would be visible for only a split second then disappear because its light would follow out into space.

Odyssey IV's navigational computer then executed the entry program into the center of the coliseum where Tom and Melody were still holding each other. The maneuver would happen so fast that *Odyssey IV* would not be detected and would simply appear 100 feet off the coliseum field. The apparition of *Odyssey IV* in the coliseum happened in an instant, and it surprised Melody. But before she could react, *Odyssey IV* lowered to the ground, opening its hatch. Tom jumped up and ran toward the ramp, and Melody, thinking quickly, followed close behind and made it through the hatch before it closed.

Without missing a beat, Tom hit the escape program, and *Odyssey IV* was off, but he now had to deal with the presence of Melody, something that had never happened before. Tom slowed *Odyssey IV* to a stop when they passed the orbital path of Neptune, and he kept Saturn between their position and Earth in order to stay hidden from the Green Belt sensors. Melody had little inkling of what had really happened, but she knew that they were someplace far away from Earth. She stayed close to Tom as he was dealing with *Odyssey IV*'s controls.

When the chaos of the escape was over, Tom began to realize the real impact of Melody's presence. Melody sensed this, and began to cuddle close to Tom and use their closeness to strengthen her position, whatever that may be. Tom thought that he could not return Melody to Earth, either inside or outside the Green Belt. The knowledge of what she had just seen could not be provided to the Green Belt officials, and he knew that they would quickly extract that knowledge from her. He also felt that she would likely be killed, and his feelings for her were too strong to consider that situation. Tom never had a passenger on *Odyssey IV* like this, and while it interfered with his independent nature, he felt that he was responsible for her well being.

Melody felt this situation, and in her fear and insecurity, cuddled a little closer and whispered to Tom, "I want to go with you. I cannot go back for fear of what they might do to me. Please take me with you. I won't interfere with what you are doing."

Tom had very strong feelings for her, and in his mind he decided to take her to the safety and care of Argon, his birthplace. As a human much like his father, Tom felt that she would be welcomed. And besides, the thought of having such a sexual person as company delighted Tom over the usual loneliness of the trip.

Tom put his arms around Melody, looked into her eyes, and softly said close to her ear, "I would be delighted to take you with me. I care for you very much, would not like to see you hurt, and I welcome your loving company." And he hugged her closer with very comforting strength. She hugged back, crying a little and kissing Tom's neck very sensually. Tom plotted a course for Argon and set *Odyssey IV* at 250 LUs, and, taking Melody's hand, took her to one of the very comfortable resting places with a very luxurious bed. There, Tom held her very close, comforting her, and his strong chest feelings assured him that he was doing the right thing for the both. After some time of comforting hugs, caresses, and closeness, they came together in some very close and sensual lovemaking.

Tom and Melody spent two days together, enjoying each other's company and the many molecular reconstruction recipes Tom had collected from around the galaxy over his travels. While Tom's sexual appetite for Melody and hers for him made for some great physical closeness, their feelings for each other's souls grew very strong. At one point, Tom turned off the gravity matrix in order to experience the feel of weightlessness in space, and while floating softly in *Odyssey IV*'s main cabin, he made love to Melody. They could experience just their own physical and sexual feelings as they held each other without needing to touch any other surface. This took Melody's breath away, and she was overtaken with pleasure.

Their conversations just flowed with mutual understanding, complementary ideas, and emotional dreams. They were coming together intellectually and in heart, as much as their physical connection. It was becoming a total package and both enjoyed the ease and softness of their togetherness.

On the third day, Tom took Melody to the suspension chamber to spend the next five months of travel asleep. Tom set the chamber's clock to wake them about a week before getting to Argon so they could spend more time together and get ready for their arrival at Argon. The time went by, and then they awoke a week before their arrival. After five months in the suspension chamber, Melody was very weak and spent about twenty minutes in the vibration chamber with Tom. After some time, they both got out, and Melody was still weak and had to lie down.

After those five months in the suspension chamber, she had become very weak, and Tom had never seen this reaction before, which made him very concerned about her welfare. After carrying her to one of the resting areas, he sat on the bed beside her, trying to comfort her with his care and touching. He did make some warm Argonian broth and slowly fed it to her, trying to help her get her strength back. But after three hours she seemed to get worse, and Tom became quite concerned because his strong feelings for her clashed with his thoughts that she may actually not make it.

Then, she became very limp with the feeling of death. And unlike Tom, he cried. He had never felt quite this way before in all his travels and experiences with the opposite sex. Without realizing it, he had fallen deeply in love with her, and his feelings did not become obvious until the time of her departure. He cried for some time.

When *Odyssey IV* reached Argon and landed on its pad, Tom emerged with Melody in his arms to the surprise of his good friend, Gala, who helped Tom with Melody's body. Tom did not have to say anything for Gala to realize that Tom was in great hurt. They took Melody to the local hospital, and Tom asked his doctor friend to try to find out why she had died. Tom just could not believe that it was the suspension chamber; and it was not. It turned out that the Green Belt officials some time ago placed a small module inside Melody that administered a poison to her if she had strayed from the Green Belt. Tom became very angry that the evil in these people was strong enough to resort to vengeance, even when no threat was evident. Death, forsaken of death. The doctor also indicated that, as was with the human side of Tom, Melody had a major DNA flaw.

Tom had not experienced this level of anger at any time in his life. The gentle Argonian side of Tom was in great conflict with the anger and vengeance of his human side. He began to think of ways to revenge the death of the woman he had come to love. These were unusual thoughts for Tom.

Tom spent some time and comfort with his great friend Gala and began to prepare for his next journey, with a heavy heart and great sadness for the woman that became his first real love.

Nails to Rails

Margaret was a very capable businesswoman running the tobacco and tea trading company that her late husband had built up in the 1820s. The state of Virginia had become a center of trade, and in spite of her gender, she was very well respected as a valued member of the all-male business community. Her independence and quick business mind gave her the reputation of someone who was keen and profitable to do business with, disguising the common belief of the time that business was no place for a woman.

Her only child and daughter, Caroline, came to inherit many of the traits and confidences of her mother and at twenty-one had not married yet. She was beginning to become the target of many in the community of being different for not having married and come under the guidance of a man. Caroline liked most of all to help her mother with the business, and she gained a sharp eye for finances. She also helped her mother on many occasions make many of the appropriate financial decisions that greatly enhanced the profitability of the business.

It was on one fine summer Sunday at the annual state fair and picnic that Caroline met William, a recent Irish immigrant who was of fair complexion and was a large, well-built man. He was the son of an Irish ironworker, and William had apprenticed in iron foundry processes in his home just outside of Dublin. It was 1845, and, as many Irish immigrants did to escape the great famine in Ireland, William came to America to build a new life with the prosperity that this young land promised. He was able to avoid the traditional Irish movement to the labor force in New York by his focus on Virginia and the more rural nature of the trading center.

He had started a small foundry that produced construction nails, a very valuable commodity in the immature but growing nation. He was becoming very successful in just two years and became a major supplier of nails for framing construction as well as floors and walls. Not many craftsmen could match the quality of William's work of the highly valuable commodity.

There was instant chemistry between William and Caroline. As a second-generation Scottish immigrant, she loved the thick Irish brogue that dawned William's personality, and his natural brightness lit her face with smiles of attraction. After courting for six months, they were married to the delight of Margaret and, of course, the local community. Caroline could now be accepted as normal in the community under the wing of a man.

Within a year they had their first child, a boy that they named Toby, and two years later, they were blessed with twin girls. Caroline was now very busy with the traditional job of full-time mother and home teacher. She believed that as immigrants, education in the ways of their new homeland would be critical for their happiness and success as contributors to the community, and she wanted to teach her children in the ways of this new land.

William worked twelve hours a day trying to keep up with the extremely high demand for nails. At night he would research more efficient ways to raise the production of nails produced. He also found that by adding a small amount of coal dust to the molten iron, the resulting nails were much harder. This increased the demand to the point where William could not keep up. He decided to hire some help and was able to acquire the help of two Irish brothers. They learned the nail-making process very well and were able to increase production from two barrels a week to eight. William could now concentrate on managing the business and marketing to other areas. As time went by, the nail business grew to very lucrative levels, and within three years, they became one of the more wealthy families in Virginia.

Pierre, a French Canadian escaping social persecution in Nova Scotia, came into their lives as additional help in the foundry. Pierre was a hard worker and was blessed with a natural sense of humor. He enjoyed playing little tricks on the two Irishmen during the normally boring but hard workday. They all developed closeness that none of them would admit, but they continually challenged each other with pranks of humor. While Pierre brought a sense of lightness to the foundry, production went up to eleven barrels a week. William paid his three workers well and made sure to stay in touch with their needs. He provided lodging as part of their employment while many of the other businesses used some black slaves but mostly indentured white workers from Europe.

One September day, William decided to make the long trip to South Carolina to market his nail products into a new area. He arrived five days later in his one-horse buggy and turned into the local inn. They recommended a stable to board his now tired and hungry horse and store his buggy. He cleaned up and went to the local eatery for some fine southern food, and it was there that William noticed a pamphlet tacked to the wall of the eatery entry that loudly publicized in large simple letters an estate sale that included a bevy of slaves to be sold. The event was going to take place the next day at the old farm to the east of town. This interested William, who had a great curiosity as to the nature of a real southern slave auction, and he decided to go.

The next morning after a large breakfast, he went to the stable, got directions to the farm having the estate sale from the attendant, and took off in a bright trot. It took an hour to get to the farm, and when William arrived, there were about twenty well-dressed locals milling around waiting for the auction to begin. There were all types of items on the block including furniture, horses, plows, and, of course, nine slaves. William casually looked over the many material items with remote interest and then went over to where the slaves were sitting. There were five men and four women but no children. William looked over the waiting slaves with a cautious and interested smile. One caught his attention. He was a large man of about his early twenties and dawning bright smile on his face. William stopped and faced the smiling man directly. They were both of the same build and height and seemed to match up like similar bookends of the same shape but made of different materials. Without a word, they stared at each other for a good time, and many thoughts seemed to transpire between them.

William broke the silence with, "What do they call you?"

"I have taken the name of Washington. I did not know my parents, so I took my own name at the age of eleven years." replied the slave with a big smile. William took an immediate and strong liking to the man, as Washington did to him.

The auction started, and there were many successful bids on many of the items, most of which were sold. Then came the time for the slave auction, and for some reason, William became very anxious. Washington was the last of the slaves to be auctioned, and the auctioneer opened the bidding at $75.

"100" announced a bidder. "150" announced another. The bidding became more aggressive, going from $150 to $400. Then, in a stroke, William raised his hand and shouted, "450." There was a moment of silence. A bigger smile could be seen on Washington's face.

"Going once, going tw…" The auctioneer was interrupted by a nicely dressed gentleman with a loud, "500."

This struck William, and he immediately responded with a loud and sharp, "600." He did not know why, but this seemed to be very important. There was a long breath of silence, and then the auctioneer exclaimed "600, going once, twice, and three times. Sold to the Virginian."

Now, William had no idea what he would do with a slave. It just seemed like the right thing to do at the time. Six hundred dollars represented two weeks of nail production, and he was very worried what his frugal Caroline might say when he returned.

The local sheriff that presided over the auction came to William with Washington in tow and handed the now-shackled black man over to William with the warning, "Be careful of this one. He is strong as an ox and real smart, so make sure you keep him tied up." He then handed William the shackle key.

William thanked the sheriff and took Washington, who was carrying a medium-sized bag made of rough burlap, to his small black buggy. Washington sat in the back on the buggy deck while William ordered his horse to move out with a sharp tone and a snap of the reins. About a mile from the farm, William stopped and told Washington to get off the carriage. William then took the shackles off with the key and threw them off and away from the road into a field.

"You are a free man now!" exclaimed William. "You can go where you want and do what you want."

Washington took a very strange look on his face as he thought on this new quandary. Washington, at twenty-four years old, had never considered that freedom would come in this manner. It was beyond his current expectations, and he did not know how to deal with this new position. He responded to William, "Master, where should I go and what should I do? I don't have no home to go to now that I am away from the farm, the place of my birth."

William did not expect this reaction and began to think that he should have stayed out of this business. Washington's thinking and talk were way out of the normal thoughts of William's traditional thinking and conflicted with what he was expecting to hear.

"Well you can come to Virginia with me. We will give you a place to stay and you can help us around the foundry with sweeping up floors and stocking coal and iron ore," was William's solution.

Washington could only agree for he had no other place to go. William motioned to Washington to get aboard on the front seat of the buggy. William climbed aboard also and sat next to Washington. William then handed the reins to Washington and softly ordered with a smile, "Here, you drive." Washington was shocked and with a surprised look and expression, told William that he never drove a buggy and did not know how. William took the reins back and assured Washington that he would know how before they got to town. And he did with William's caring patience.

The two drove into town with Washington at the reins. Many of the townspeople stopped to look at such a strange sight. William sensed that this might draw trouble from some of the town's wise guys and took the reins back, relieving Washington of his discomfort and potential trouble for both. William stopped at the local store and purchased some provisions for the long trip back to Virginia. They left as soon as they were set, and about a mile out of town, William handed the reins back to Washington with, "Here, you drive."

Washington, with a delightful smile replied, "Yes, sir, most certainly."

The trip back to Virginia took four days instead of the usual five, with the two driving. William had to buy a new horse halfway through the trip. He was able to determine that Washington had a very bright mind, and he was beginning to find a real place in mind for Washington in his nail foundry and develop a strong story for Caroline to accept his "new acquisition."

It was not long after they had left the town that William realized that Washington had some reading and learning. William's perception of a slave based on the words of others was that they were of ignorance and illiteracy. William had never been this close with a man of African descent kept in the fields of bondage. William finally took up the courage to get personal with Washington and asked him how he had to come to have some education, and what of his parents.

Washington began with a trusting tone, "I am told that I was separated from my parents at a very early age and that they were sold to another, and I was kept at this plantation. I do remember when I was able to begin working in the fields at the age of eight and had the label of field slave at this early age. During my years, a house slave lady would pass me books to read from the master's library and with some help from one of the young plantation daughters, I learned to read and write some. Reading became the freedom of my mind and soul. And I also have been keeping these here pages as I had writ them." Reaching into his burlap bag, he pulled out several wrinkled pages of his writings.

There were over a hundred pages wrapped in some fine cloth and tied with cotton twine. "Them's my words and thoughts for the last twelve years," Washington said as he handed the wrapped pages to William. William was astonished with the depth of writing contained in the pages as he reveled through them. Many of the words were crossed out and corrected by Washington's own hand. In many places the grammar was poor but the meanings came through in solid style and with great feeling.

William shared many stories with Washington along the way, especially the history of Washington's namesake, the father of our country. He told Washington that in the early part of the revolution, General Washington recruited many blacks for the Continental Army. They were paid, and if they stayed for a year, they were given freedom from bondage for them and their families. Over 30 percent of the Continental Army was made up of black men soon to be free. His "brothers" made a large contribution to the freedom of America. Washington loved the stories, and his eyes grew intent and wide with each word.

William told his new "employee" that President Washington was also a great maker of valued nails in Virginia and that many were found on the Virginia estate, Mount Vernon, when it was restored for history's sake. It was beginning to look like William had made a good decision.

Washington, on the other hand, did not know what was in store for him. William spent the rest of the trip telling many stories of America's history, and Washington could not get enough. He had never heard such words, and he listened intently while driving the carriage. He took everything in, sometimes asking a question that William would answer with a very little creative story. Sometimes Washington would ask deeper questions of the history, and some William could not answer. The two of similar build could be heard along the way, by the trees of the forest with William's strong Irish brogue and Washington's southern plantation accent. They shared much together and became closer.

William was very glad to be home finally and greeted Caroline with a huge hug and kiss. Toby and the twins were also so glad to see their dad again. They all stared at Washington, who was still sitting in the buggy. Caroline, with a big smile, asked, "What in the world did you bring home this time?"

William with all kinds of planned foreknowledge exclaimed, "This is our new worker. He is an educated man, and I thought that he would do well keeping the foundry picked up. I found him in South Carolina." He did not share that he had to pay $600 to free Washington from his slave fate. William took Washington into the foundry and showed him around and introduced him to Pierre and the two

Irishmen as "our" new employee. Pierre's reaction in his French Canadian accent was, "Ah, he is a big one, but yes. He will be good help for us, no?" Then he took Washington to the rear of the plant and showed him the very nice worker quarters where he would be staying and told Washington that he would get him some better clothes tomorrow.

You could see it in Pierre's eyes that he could not wait to play his usual pranks on this new team member. The thought of race differences and of the "lower nature" of the slave position never crossed Pierre's and the Irish boys' minds. They just accepted Washington as their own, which brought them together in spirit and friendship with a common cause.

Four months proved that having Washington as part of the "family" was very pleasant as well as productive. Washington was quick to learn the foundry of nails and added much real productivity to the operation. He was paid as the others and saved much of his earnings, for he was not used to spending money. This was new to Washington, and it gave him a great feeling of self-worth and pride to see his account grow. Caroline took a special liking to him, and on occasion, she advised him of personal financial affairs. The money he did spend was on clothes, paper to write on, and fine pens to shape his words.

Toby was now becoming very active in the business and looked forward to the daily work after his studies. He began to develop a very sensitive relationship with Washington, and with a little pushing, he began to expand Washington's grammar skills and some basic math. Toby borrowed four books from his dad's small library for Washington to practice his reading: *The Bible, The Merchant of Venice* by Shakespeare, a booklet copy of the U.S. Constitution, and *Common Sense* by Thomas Paine. With the addition of Washington and Toby now helping in the foundry, the production went up to 23 barrels a week. And they still could not keep up with the orders.

Washington and Toby teamed up to pull off some of the best pranks on Pierre in retaliation for the many Pierre jokes; things were going well and the whole "family" enjoyed their happiness. They even raised prices 30 percent, and the orders still kept coming, and their wealth grew beyond their wildest dreams. William, Caroline, and the children moved into a larger house and gave their first house to the foundry workers to live in. And Washington kept writing in his journal every day.

It was a year after Washington came to the foundry that William became very ill with pneumonia. The doctors could not break the fever, and William grew sicker. A great sadness came over the group when William succumbed to the illness and passed on. Caroline was especially affected, not only because of her love for William but also for the memory of the early loss of her father. Another man in her life had left this earth and had left her alone. Washington was devastated with the emptiness he now had for the only man that treated him as an equal and freed his body. He did find some comfort in the few passages in the Bible that he now had partial knowledge of. He cried many a night with this great loss and expressed his feelings among the latest of his written pages.

It took several weeks for the foundry to get back into full production in spite of the great sadness and emptiness without their beloved William. Caroline continually prompted everybody to move on, and she continued the dream of the departed William. She held the group together with her strength and commitment, and the foundry prospered in William's spirit and memory and under the leadership talents of Caroline. Washington's knowledge of the foundry had grown from apprentice to expert, and, combined with Toby, he made many enhancements to their products.

In 1859, the talk of war for State's Rights grew, and the fever of potential violence became very real. The Union Army had come to Caroline to begin producing bullets for the potential upcoming conflicts. The entire production was forced to output just the large 50-caliber shot. This brought the reality of violence to the group, and this made everybody very somber. With the passing of William and the prospects of a hell war, there was little happiness in the days that followed.

Caroline and her mother, Margaret, were of great conflict with the current political events. While they were totally against the maintenance of slavery preferred by the South, they were very strongly opposed to the federal government's export taxes now being levied and the continual federal control over the states commerce. Great emotional and financial pressure came upon both Caroline's efforts as well as the export/import business that Margaret had so carefully maintained over the years.

It was a cool and clear late winter night that Margaret went to visit her daughter and grandchildren. Toby was in the foundry with Washington, experimenting with some new mixtures of carbon and iron and the various ways to temper the resulting hot metal into quality steel. The twins were reading in their room. Caroline made some tea, and together with Margaret, they sat in two wicker chairs on the front porch. The sun has just gone down, and dusk was moving forward to total darkness with the stars starting to brightly prickle the black velvet moonless sky and seemed to come closer than usual. Margaret expressed her displeasure with the local political climate and suggested that a move west to California may be appropriate. Caroline admitted to her mother that she was starting to have the same thoughts over the past months and expressed her fears over the potential of war and all the violence that it would bring. They talked for a while on this subject and decided to not make a decision until they talked with the rest of the family and workers the next day. In spite of their desire to wait for a family approval, they had already made the decision firmly in their hearts to leave and go west.

The next day Margaret came back to the house and, with Caroline, assembled the whole group together. The girls were fidgety, Toby and Washington were attentive, the Irishmen were still yawning from the previous late hour's play, and Pierre portrayed his usual smile over his crossed arms. Caroline pointed out to everybody the uncertain nature of the local politics and felt that it might be very dangerous to stay in the area. Business was becoming very difficult, and the risk of disaster was high. She then pointed out the opportunities that California offered and suggested that they go west to find a better life. There was shock laced with fear of the unknown among everyone, and nobody said a word.

Caroline then outlined a basic plan. She wanted everybody to stay together, convert all of their belongings to gold, and take much of the foundry equipment with them. They were going to start over in a new land, and she asked everybody to think on the prospects and to ask any questions over the next two days.

The next day, Pierre was the first to express to Caroline what he wanted to do. Over the years he had saved considerable money and wanted to go south to Louisiana where many French Canadians were settling from the Western European oppression in the far Northeast. He felt that he could begin a new life there and find himself a woman of his own decent, which he longed for.*

The two Irishmen came to Caroline with a proposal to keep much of the existing foundry going and offered to buy the business out. They felt very strongly about staying in Virginia, and Caroline agreed to a token amount for the foundry but also made it clear what equipment would be going west, and everybody agreed.

* *The Northeast persecution of the French Canadians caused many to immigrate to Louisiana, and this provided the basis for the Cajun culture. The persecution by the Anglos was based on the French heritage, and mostly because these people mated with Native Americans, the "lowest" form of life, lower than slaves and women.*

Washington was very afraid to approach the subject with his insecurity of the future. Caroline sensed this and went to Washington with a bright, "Well, Mister Washington, what do you want to do?"

"I don't know, Miss Caroline. I have a good portion of money, but I don't know what to do. My whole life is here with you and young Toby."

Caroline, smiling lovingly, looked up at Washington and, with her hand on his cheek, offered, "Well, we will need lots of strong help on the trip. Why don't you come with us if you wish? You certainly have become part of our family."

Washington's eyes grew wide with white and moisture, and his big white teeth sparkled beyond his lips. "Oh, Miss Caroline. I would love to hep you and the children." This was in spite of his fear of the unknown. Caroline told Washington that they would be honored to have such a fine man to "hep."

So, over the next four weeks, plans were made. The foundry equipment going was shipped to St. Louis, Missouri, and stored for pick up later. The large house was sold, and all the cash from the proceeds and bank accounts in dollars were converted to gold. This turned out to be a strikingly good decision.

The Irishmen continued to make bullet shot for the Army, and Pierre left for Louisiana. Caroline and Margaret purchased three very high-quality wagons of fine oak and fifteen horses of great strength (four for each wagon and three for spares). The wagons were loaded with most of their prized possessions including Washington's now accumulated books and the others from William's small library. He had also purchased a fine leather brief to hold his papers, writing paraphernalia, and many blank sheets of fine vellum for his inner thoughts to become visible.

The gold was spread out into three parts and hidden in each of the wagon floors. Some was left as a decoy for possible robbers on the trail, an event that did not happen.

When everything was in place, the three wagons pointed west with a full load of family and possessions. Their destination was St. Louis, gateway to the West. Caroline with the two girls drove the first wagon; Margaret with Toby, the second, and Washington took up the rear. It was a fine spectacle with little remorse or concern of what they were leaving. They never looked back. Only the thoughts and excitements of the "Promised Land" occupied their minds. They just did what needed to be done without reservation, and they were all together with the hopes of good fortune and safety.

It was very early spring when they started, and they managed to travel 25-30 miles per day. It took seven weeks to get to St. Louis from Virginia. They set up camp on the outskirts of the town. The next day, Caroline, Margaret, and the girls went into town to inquire about joining a wagon train west to California while Washington and Toby stayed with the camp.

Riding three of the large wagon horses bareback into town was a sight. Caroline had the first horse, the two girls rode together on the second, and Margaret rode the third. The weeks on the trail had taught them much about horsemanship. In this case, "horsewomanship."

As they rode down the main dry and dusty street, they marveled at the many unfamiliar sights and busy activities of this new place, which was in stark contrast to the desolate past weeks on the trail. They stopped in front of what appeared to be an official-looking building, and they all clumsily dismounted their very large steeds. The twins were excited about being off the trail and went to the local store with Margaret. Caroline went into the building to make her inquiries. She learned that a new wagon train and the last of the season was forming to make the trip to California and was scheduled to leave in six days. She was told to go to the west side of town and contact George or Jacob Donner. They were brothers, the wagon train masters, and they were responsible for assembling the parties and leading the train westward.

Caroline became excited that progress was being made and that her expectations were being met. It was a long, tiring trip from Virginia. Thanking the very pleasant gentleman who helped her with the information, she went to the store and told her mother and the girls that a group was assembling at the far end of town. When they returned to the horses, they realized that there was no way to remount the very large horses. Washington helped them on at the camp. Caroline was able to hoist the girls onto their horse and managed with great effort to help Margaret up and on. Standing at her own, she was approached by a fine looking man of good and strong stature who had witnessed this spectacle.

"Need a heppin hand, Ma'am?" was his offer as he bowed somewhat.

Blushing, Caroline replied, "Thank you, sir. If you don't mind."

Up and on in one motion, Caroline thanked the gentleman with a grateful but strong tone and a very independent smile.

"What brings you ladies and your fine horses to St. Louis?" asked the stranger, looking up at the now-mounted Caroline.

"We are going to California with our men to start a new life. We are now looking for the Donner brothers. Do you know them?" queried Caroline.

"Well, that's nice. You are half-a-way there. My name is George Donner, the one and only. And I am at your humble service," He replied with his hat removed and a deep bow and big smile. "Follow me, and I'll bring you to the assembly camp."

Things were now really coming together in Caroline's mind, and her apprehensions were beginning to greatly diminish. It took only fifteen minutes to reach the assembly area where there were already at least fifty wagons of all types assembled in neat rows. George Donner, with his brother Jacob, explained to Caroline that the charge to join the train was $150 plus fifty cents a day for each horse to feed and water. Caroline agreed, signed a paper, and handed Jacob $500 in gold coins to seal the deal. George also indicated that she would be responsible for her own food and said that they were assembling a small herd of cattle for meat along the trip. She could have meat on a daily basis from the herd for twenty-five cents a day, and Caroline agreed and gave Jacob an additional $50 in gold coins.

George relished the thought of having such an attractive and smart woman on his train, but kept his flirting down because of the respect for the men she may be traveling with.*

With help from George remounting the horses, Caroline, Margaret, and the girls returned to their own camp on the other side of town. When they arrived, Caroline told Toby and Washington that everything was set and that they would clean up camp in the morning and join the assembly area. While in town, Margaret had managed to acquire a couple of chickens and two dozen eggs. That night she cooked a fine Virginia meal of fried chicken, pan biscuits with honey, and pan-fried potatoes. The dream of eggs on biscuits and Virginia ham in the morning for breakfast was in everybody's mind after their celebration dinner.

They arrived to the camp at high noon on the next day. Now, George was impressed with the spectacle of horses and wagons that showed up with this stately group, and he now knew that they were people of means, especially while having a "slave." George showed them to their position in the camp and questioned Caroline if her husband was going to join them soon.

Caroline, with her hands on her hips and elbows pointing back, announced sharply to George, "I am a widow and in full charge of this family, and if you have any further inquiries or concerns, please direct them to me, SIR!"

George was taken back by her response but favored in the thoughts that this very fine woman might actually be available.

Five days later, just before full dawn, the train was assembled in a line with over 250 wagons and over 1,500 people. George, leading the group, signaled for the start, and off they went westerly toward the land of opportunity. Each day, George would take special time to check on Caroline's three wagons, just as an excuse to see and talk with Caroline. She sensed and enjoyed his interest in her, but that also made her a little uncomfortable. He was a fine looking man, and she did not want to take the chance of derailing the California objective with a romance of such.

* The history of facts regarding the Donner party were changed for this fictional story line. The Donner party left from Independence, Missouri, and the tragedy took place in November of the winter 1846-47. George Donner was married and had his family with him as well as his brother Jacob and his family. The actual trail followed the most northern part of Colorado and connected up with the Oregon Trail.

It was one week into the trip one early evening as dinner was being cooked that George came to the camp of the Caroline group. It was a great warm evening painted with a panoramic pastel sunset seasoned with a light cool breeze. Approaching the camp, George respectfully removed his hat and approached Caroline. He saluted and, with a respectful voice, said, "Good evening, Ma'am. How did you come of this fine example of a slave?" He didn't know how else to start a conversation. Caroline smiled and looked at George remarking, "That's no slave. That's my younger brother." George was taken aback, thought a minute, and slammed back with some humor, "Well, then, who is his mother?"

"I am, mista," shouted Margaret with her hand on her hip. "And he is a free and educated man."

They all laughed and talked some of the trip and what was to come— especially the challenge of crossing the Sierra Mountain passes into California. They had to make time before the winter snows set in, and Caroline offered George to stay for dinner, which he did. After dinner, George invited Caroline to take a walk around the large perimeter of the circled camp, and she accepted.

After a few minutes of walking, George broke the silence with, "You know, Miss Caroline, you are a fine lookin' woman that any man would be proud to be with. This is going to be my last train west, and I have a fine ranch in the Northern Colorado Territory that is just waiting for a woman of your quality. I would be honored if you would settle with me as my wife. I would be very good to you and treat you with all the respect that you deserve."

Caroline was taken back and the only words that came to her were, "Well, Mister Donner, is that a proposal?"

"Yes, Ma'am, it sure is," he answered with anticipation in his voice.

"Mister Donner, I am sure that you would make a fine and proper husband that any woman would love to be with. I, however, am not of the marrying type and must continue on with my family and business plans. This is my import for life."

Disappointed, George made a few more suggestive attempts without being too aggressive. He just knew in his heart by the time they got to California, she would agree. He was satisfied that he had made his intentions clear.

It was thirty-five days from the start of the trip that camp was made in the central part of what would be the state of Colorado in about fifteen years. Margaret had not been feeling very well for the last week and tried to hide her discomfort from the rest of the family so as not to become a burden. That night, she felt too bad o hide anymore and disclosed her anguish to her daughter. Caroline became very concerned and began to pamper her mother to try to make her more comfortable. That night, Margaret's condition worsened and Caroline sat up and stayed with her. It was just before dawn that Margaret began to cough violently and spit up a small amount of blood that trickled down the side of her mouth. There was no doctor on the train, and they were at the mercy of nature's fate. Margaret died shortly thereafter, and there was great sadness of the loss.

It was of her intelligence and independence that passed on to her daughter and grandchildren that gave them strength. Washington was especially affected, and the last time he cried was when William succumbed to his illness. The sorrow was broad and deep for all.

The next morning, Caroline went to George and shared with him the events of the night. George tried to console her, but the thought of getting through the mountain passes before the snows set in was in the forefront of his mind. They just could not delay even for a morning. It was with that that Caroline proposed to the rest of the family that they settle right where they were and not continue on to California. Caroline felt that this was a sign from her God to settle here, and she talked this over with the now solemn group, and they tearfully agreed. Caroline went to George Donner and informed him that they would not continue on. George assured Caroline that he would return in the spring after his responsibility of the train was over. The train left northward, and George caught up with it in an hour after his stay with Caroline. He would never return.

There was a small town of about 2,500 people three miles back east of the peak of a tall mountain range. They stayed in camp that night without the usual joy of meal and socialization, and they made plans to go back to this town in the morning. It was a solemn evening with a great sense of loss.

The next morning on the way east to the town, they were surrounded by eroded hills of bright red and orange that was layered with white sandstone that they had not noticed earlier. This made a strong impression on Washington, even through his sadness, for he had never seen such rock and soil before. For some reason, this attracted Washington's imagination and wonderment; he felt a special connection to these colorfully layered hills.

The three wagons stopped at the edge of the small town, and Caroline, Toby, and the girls walked into town leaving Washington to guard the wagons. They went straight to a large store that carried all types of items from hardware to clothing, from pans to tools, and all types of canned and bulk foods including dried meats and cheese hanging from the ceiling beams. This seemed to be the center of activity, and there were several people outside the store as well as inside.

Caroline asked the tall, lean proprietor where a good place to camp might be while picking out some basic bulk foods and a slab of bacon. Sam, the owner took an immediate liking to Caroline and her family. He had indicated that ten miles west there was some land by a river that might suit their needs. It just so happened that Sam owned the land in that area, and there was plenty of water fed by the many springs in the area. She also asked if there was an appropriate location to place a grave, and Sam gave her directions to the small cemetery at the north end of town.

While this was going on, Sam's thirteen-year-old daughter, Maggy, working behind the counter, was mesmerized by Toby's vision. Her thoughts were of love forever, and Toby slightly glanced at her as the child she was.

Four weeks passed after setting up camp by the small river, and Caroline was beginning to become eager to start their new life. She had found a large house that came up for sale and bought it outright with gold coins. They all moved in and started to settle down and think of future plans. One day, Toby and Washington took one of the wagons and two of the four barrels of nails they had brought with them into town. They stopped in front of Sam's market and brought the two barrels into the store, hoping that Sam might want to sell the nails for a percentage of the sale price. As they entered Sam's store, little Maggy screamed under her breath with her newfound infatuation with the older Toby.

When asked about selling the nails, Sam replied in an excited voice, "You have what?"

"Nails, large and small!" was Toby's reply. "We have lots of nails and can make lots more. That's what we do, make nails!"

Sam's eyes widened and his voice rose to an excited pace, "Well, heck, we burn houses down around here just to recover the nails. I'll sell all you have. In fact, there is a lot of buildin' going on 100 miles narth of here, and I am shura they will buy all yous can make."

It took two weeks for Toby and Washington to set up the foundry in an old barn that Sam owned and that they rented for use as a birthplace for the coveted nails. They had made a deal with a local to provide the freight shipping using the wagons that Caroline brought with them. All was set except the most important thing: iron ore to smelt and founder the nails. In Virginia, ore was acquired from Pennsylvania and delivered to the foundry.

One day while Caroline was in town buying some fabric and food supplies, she had mentioned the plight of the lack of iron ore. One of the patrons, an older man of white hair and beard, approached Caroline, and with a gruff but assured voice, said, "I hear you need some of that there iron ore."

"Yes, we do!" Caroline responded surprisingly and curiously.

"Well, I have been prospecting these hills for twenty years, and that's all there is out there. Nuthin' but lousy iron oxide. It's all that red stuff in the hills," continued the old man. "Just look out that window at them red hills. That's all worthless iron ore. There's no silver or gold. Just all that worthless crap gittin' in the way."

Caroline's heart jumped, and she asked the old man if he knew how to get the ore out of the hills. "Sure 'nuf. Got plenty of it. Nuttin' but pure rust."

Caroline offered to buy with gold all the red stuff he could deliver. He thought that she was a crazy woman, but the thought of "taking her" for some gold put him in an agreeable frame of mind. Caroline offered the use of one of the wagons. Everything was set.

It took two months to get the foundry up to a production of three barrels a week. Sam was more than delighted, and word quickly spread around the territory of the availability of the coveted nails. Again, they just could not keep up with the demand, even at twice the Virginia price. They hired and apprenticed four local men and paid them well, and the production went up to twenty barrels a week. The growth-crazy area gobbled them all up while buildings were being put up all over the Colorado territory.

One day while Caroline was in the store, Sam asked her if she had heard what had happened to the Donner party. Surprised, she said that she hadn't, and Sam went on to explain that crossing the mountain pass, they all got snowed in. "There is talk that they even ate the dead in order to survive," remarked Sam. This stunned Caroline, and in her disbelief, she thought of her friend George and thought of what would have happened if she had continued on. She thought of the ranch patiently waiting for George's return and the proposal that he had made to her. She could not get the vision of the Donner horror out of her mind and could not believe that something like this could happen to someone she knew and liked.

The foundry went on for another year, and Caroline now had ten employees. Washington, having a love affair with all that red stuff, began to experiment again with Toby, trying to get harder nails. Over the next two months, not only did they get excellent results, they figured out how to make smooth round nails instead of the rough square ones. The now shiny steel nails were much sharper, and the smooth round shape made them much easier to drive. Within six months, all demand for the square nails was replaced with even larger orders for the new steel round ones.

Washington's reading also progressed, and he especially liked the book *Common Sense,* which talked of the equality of the common man and the tyranny of a monarch-driven society. He related to the proposition that even the common man was able to take part in the government, and he dreamed that this could be a possibility for him someday. He was able to make the connection between the "Common Concepts" and the "All men are created equal" part of the Constitution. In fact, he was delighted when he found out that it was Thomas Paine (the author of *Common Sense*) who wrote the Preamble to the U.S. Constitution. As his reading ability grew, he began to enjoy many of the other books in the small library. His writing skills also improved. When he was not working in the foundry, he could be found under a tree or by an oil lamp with his face buried between the many soon-to-be-full pages containing the words of his thoughts. Occasionally he would ask Toby or Caroline what a certain word meant. Without realizing it, he was becoming a finely educated man, and even his math skills were maturing. He was able, on occasion, to help with the foundry books.

Five years went by, and the foundry grew to fifty people and had an output of 100 barrels a week. They now had three sizes of nails for the many different uses. The town a hundred miles north was now known as Denver, and it was growing fast. It was becoming the social center of the territory, with much wealth coming from the silver mines in the area. The foundry had now grown to be a factory, complete with an office for Caroline and a clean place for the workers to wash and to eat the lunch that the foundry supplied.

Sam's daughter, Maggy, was now nineteen and a fine vision of a woman with a soft and lovely face on top of a shapely body. Toby had noticed this since she was sixteen but was afraid to approach her. Her infatuation with Toby grew to a sincere love. One morning as Toby and one of the foundry workers were delivering three barrels of nails to Sam's store, a great moment of fate came to Maggy and Toby. While carrying one of the barrels into the store, Toby dropped the heavy load onto his foot. Even though he was not seriously hurt, Maggy ran to Toby's fallen figure, worried and trying to comfort him. This finally broke the ice between the two, and a year later they were married to the delight of Sam and Caroline.

It was about a year later when a well-dressed stranger showed up at the foundry office door. It was obvious from the dust all over his dark blue suit that he had come far, but he looked very business-like and official. He opened the office door with the tingling sound of the little bell on the door, and Toby turned in his chair to greet the stranger.

Toby, with a big smile, immediately welcomed him with a bright and curious, "Howdy, stranger. May I help you?"

The stranger took off his dusty derby and replied, "I understand that you make high-quality nails of all types."

"We sure do," replied Toby with great pride. "We make the best in the territory and lots of 'em."

"Well, I need a bunch of some very special nails," said the stranger as he pulled a big black railroad spike from his carpetbag and dropped it on the counter. "I need all you can make of these. I represent the railroad, and we are laying lots of track north of here. These are used to nail the tracks down to the wooden ties, and their quality is crucial."

Toby picked up the spike and called for Washington to come into the office. "Yes, Toby?" said Washington with a big smile as he walked through the office door from the foundry. Washington's face was full of foundry sweat.

"Can we make these?" Toby queried with a wink while handing the spike to Washington.

The suited railroad man looked in disbelief at Washington's stature and asked Toby why he had a slave so far west.

"He is a free and educated man, my good brother, and he runs this foundry just fine," replied Toby.

Washington took a bite on the spike and with an authoritative and knowing tone exclaimed, "This sure is soft steel and probably does not have the right amount of carbon and isn't tempered correctly. I don't think it would hold much after a time, and it might evin break under a hamma."

The railroad man smiled, knowing that Washington was very correct, and he asked Washington if he could do better.

Washington looked up to the ceiling and said, "We might have to do some testing, but I think we could manage."

Toby thought for a minute and offered to make a barrel as a sample over the next week and offered to ship them north to the railroad center.

In five days, Washington and Toby took the small carriage north and delivered the barrel of nails. The railroad man was delighted, and before they could return to the foundry, the railroad ordered an additional hundred barrels. Well, this put Toby and the others in a real pickle, but they were able to fulfill the order with the help of Caroline, Maggy, and the twins. Orders started coming in from the southern part of the state where a new narrow gauge lumber railroad was being built out of Silverton. The railroads continued to place orders, and the foundry grew to almost 400 people and four large buildings, and they were now the economic center of the mid-southern Colorado territory.

After two years of making spikes, the railroad negotiated for the foundry to make actual rails of hardened steel. Ten years later, the Colorado Red Steel Company* was the largest employer in the west with the exception of the now cross-country railroads of the Union Pacific, Southern Pacific, and the Rio Grand railroad.

The twins had married men from the Denver area and left the family to start their own lives up north.

Washington had become very active in the affairs of the local politics. Caroline encouraged him to get his journals published as a book, and, after much discussion, he did. The book was called *Washington's Freedom*, by William Washington. He took on a first name to add to the "Washington." He chose William in honor of the man who gave him the opportunity of his life. He was now known to everyone as Mister William Washington, and he was so proud of what he had accomplished. His cheery style always made him a pleasure to be around.

The territory had now become a state [of Colorado] and the local Springs area was to become the second largest city in the new state. This presented much confusion and controversy among the leaders of the community. There were several town meetings to discuss how to approach and organize the new government, and they made little progress in their confusion. When William W. found out about the meetings and the trouble they were having, his curiosity got the better of him, and he started to attend on each week that the meetings were held.

With his presence, neat attire, knowledge of the country's laws and history, William became very visible with his command of the English language and knowledge of the Constitution that he loved so much. While he did not want to take a position on the government's roles, he became a well-respected and distinguished member of the community. Now he was always asked to attend the monthly town meetings, and on occasion, he was able to clarify confusing issues,

* *Fictional name*

making an invaluable contribution to his neighbors' efforts. He was finally free of the slavery in his heart and soul and was secure in his own self-respect.

During one of the meetings when a great impasse was stalling any progress or solutions, one of the new community leaders turned to William and asked, "Well, Mister Washington, what do you think?"

William stood up very humbly but proud and began, "It is up to many of the people here to make the decision on this matter. Each of us has an equal share in the direction we take this small but important government. No matter what our social position is, how much land we own, or how we sweep the floors, we all have an equal share. Our great nation is built on the equality of all of us, and with our own *sense of the common good*, we shall all be equal and free to direct the course of our future. So, we as a new city under the state, which is under the Constitution, should all take a vote on this issue and move forward." And William sat down.

It was thirty years after Caroline and the rest settled in the small Colorado town, and in those years they had built a successful life, providing the area with the basic materials of growth. Toby was now in full charge of the large steel company. Caroline spent much of her time helping the needy and being a well-liked and respected socialite. Most of all, she enjoyed her grandchildren, and sometimes would take the stage to Denver to visit with her girls and their families. She hosted many parties and even financed the building of a great new hotel that was the finest in the state of Colorado, and put the new city of Colorado Springs above the status of just a small town.

William Washington became sort of a local philosopher and, as a well-educated man, he helped many of the locals with his gentle advice. He especially enjoyed ordering clothing of fine gentleman quality from the eastern catalogues. He had become a very well-liked and active member of the community, and he was now a truly educated man, and none looked at him as a "lower slave". It took time to overcome his black image and some of the prejudices many people thought and treated toward him. In most cases, Washington's strength and self-confidence wore away most of the normal prejudices from many people. With his care and understanding, most people respected him as a fine man. He just loved to give of himself, and each night he relished his happiness. His book sold over 100,000 copies in ten years.

The area was beautiful with layered and colorful terrain, the westerly horizon of tall saw-toothed mountains and the growing skyline of the small city made for a delightful setting for a home. One late fall afternoon, William made a visit to Caroline's house. As they had done so often, they socialized and reminisced over the years. This day, they sat together on the large porch surrounding half of the stately house. Caroline made some tea that William cherished, partially because of the taste and mostly because of the opportunity that it offered to socialize. Caroline and William did this many times, and both were very devoted to the hearts of each other. It was as if they were brother and sister from the same mother.

The sun had just hidden itself behind the tall peaks, and the light was now soft and gentle over the Spring's area, casting the usual long shadows of the mountains over the valley. The sky was beginning to turn pastel pink over a light blue canvas, and there was a lovely sense of quietness as they sat drinking tea together.

Caroline broke the silence with, "Well, my fine friend William, we sure have done much and had a wonderful life."

"I sure wish that our beloved Mista William could see this," replied Washington. "He was a fine and good man. He gave me my life and freedom. You, Miss Caroline, gave me the rest. I will always be in your gratitude."

"That was not me, Mister William Washington," Caroline softly spoke. "It was you that freed your own heart and mind. You freed your own self from the chains of bondage that live in the hearts of those who hang on to their old thinking. You have even written a book that has been published. I have never heard you complain or refuse to help someone. You always took the time to read and ask questions. We learned much from you, and it was your giving nature that freed your soul. It is you that I have to thank for your help and kindness. You are a very good and fine man, just as our William was, and we could have never done this without you. You gracefully took the place of my William in my life and soul."

Washington bent his head, and it was obvious by the tears rolling off his cheeks that he was very touched. In a shaky voice he began, "I guess the good Lord has smiled at us. I feel that we have done His will by hepin people to grow themselves. He has given us the reward of happiness and peace. I sure hope Heaven is this good."

"I don't know about that, but I feel that when we leave this Earth, we will take these feelings with us and have them forever in our souls," replied Caroline in a very satisfied voice.

Washington touched the top of Caroline's hand, and with a quiet whisper, he said, "I guess this is what real love brings to us. This is good."